The Life and Breath of a Nation's Birth—

VALLEY FORGE

FICTION BY MAC KINLAY KANTOR

The Children Sing (1973) • *Beauty Beast* (1968)
Story Teller (1967)
If the South Had Won the Civil War (1961)
Spirit Lake (1961)
The Work of Saint Francis (1958)
Andersonville (1955) [*Pulitzer Prize Novel, 1956*]
God and My Country (1954)
The Daughter of Bugle Ann (1953)
Warwhoop (1952) • *Don't Touch Me* (1951)
Signal Thirty-two (1950) • *One Wild Oat* (1950)
The Good Family (1949) • *Wicked Water* (1949)
Midnight Lace (1948) • *Glory For Me* (1945)
[*On which the motion picture*
The Best Years of Our Lives was based]
Author's Choice (1944) • *Happy Land* (1943)
Gentle Annie (1942) • *Cuba Libre* (1940)
Valedictory (1939) • *Here Lies Holly Springs* (1938)
The Noise of Their Wings (1938)
The Romance of Rosy Ridge (1937)
Arouse and Beware (1936)
The Voice of Bugle Ann (1935)
Long Remember (1934) • *The Jaybird* (1932)
El Goes South (1930) • *Diversey* (1928)

VALLEY FORGE

A Novel

MacKinlay Kantor

BALLANTINE BOOKS • NEW YORK

TO MY GRANDCHILDREN

Michael, Tommy and Suzanne
Jeffrey, Lydia and Melissa

VALLEY FORGE

1

I remember, I remember, 'tis a joy to recall.

'Twas a placid day and the weather be warm. It seems like no truth now, seems like a mere dallying, but the hours were sunny, and when we marched we marched lazing, trailing our arms.

We'd been well-fed. We'd had coffee. We loved it so: 'twas grated coarse and made from grain, but we termed it coffee, and some still bore a speck of sugar to put in. So marching somewhat laggardly as we went, we rounded a turn and heard laughing shouts ahead.

A passel of little boys, already tired of staring at soldiers, had turned to giddier enterprise: a stream itself, and they were clamoring there, skipping flat small stones acrost the water. Oh, some said *skip* and some said *jerk;* some might have said *whisk;* but I reckon *jerk* was common.

I seen this myself.

A big horse was pulled in and a tall man swung down from the saddle and 'twas Zexcellency himself.

The boys stopped with their stones in utter awe at witnessing this bold soldier dismount to stand amongst 'em.

Now boys, says he, I will show you how to jerk a stone.

So he did. Took a small flat rock from one and showed 'em as they crowded near at his behest, showed 'em how to curve the finger round the edge.

'Tis best this way, he said. He cast his first stone,

and the thing curved in the air immediate before it struck the water and dove deep.

He may have been disgruntled but he made no unhappy face. Zexcellency was like that: always calm. You couldn't see his face change in warfare or out.

He took up another stone and cast it, and it went skate-rise-skate-rise-skate-rise, it seemed a dozen times, and the boys let out their breath together in a yip, admiring.

See how? the tall man told 'em. I found ill-luck on my first venture but this is more to the manner!

Again he cast a stone, and it went skipping upon the very surface like it was a maid lifting up her petticoats and dancing in springtime.

Once more, oh sir, please do one more! the boys were crying as he mounted.

But he said with gravity, Ah no, we have a war to fight, and he went riding off, and so we all took up our grounded arms and marched in his fine track as well.

2

SLIME was white to begin with but nobody could mark its beginning, always people had gone before, slipping and sliding as they pushed themselves, always someone else had trod the ice and left marks of mud in which the red was showing. It was difficult to walk (you could not call it march, call it draggle), it was arduous to push against that bitter breeze, and once in a while a flurry of snow came stinging, and when had they eaten last and what had they eaten last; but still there was blurred jest which ran among them, wagged back and forth from mouth to ears and then through the bleak brains and out the mouths again, and people cried, No bread, no soldier. Others sneered and made it beef and others named feathered delicacies and said, No goose, no soldier.

I ain't got the strength to goose or be goosed.

It dunt matter to me.

Take my family—all good children of the Romans, though I hain't been to mass since Hec was sucking. But you can say for me—and this is Friday—No fish, no soldier.

Aw, fuck you Catholics!

Fuck you right back!

Wind increased and took malicious words away and spread them out and frosted them and still the men were inching in their frieze.

Malachi took shuddering stock of his own position and clothing and accoutrement and body and soul; and Winny did the same and also a man called Axle and also a boy known as Caffrey and also a sergeant named Peach and a fresh recruit named Hurtz. They took stock and noted and then were too thinned and iced to note again.

They beheld the hats on their heads; caps of wild animal skin and round ragged hats where some had attempted to pin them up as tricorns, and some were still decked with scraps of evergreen which they had worn handsomely when they were younger and abler and not such starvelings and not so thinned and not so scrawny. Here was Fritz in a fine hood which had been given him by a lady who saw him striding or trying to stride and quivering as he passed her door, and she grabbed the hood and rushed out and slapped it over his frosted ears and so he wore it, grinning back at her and winking a squinted eye as he went. There were scarves covering some of the frosted ears, and some had no scarves at all, and here was a man with an old undershirt knotted over his head and dark feverish eyes burning out at all and at no one. Even some groups stepped in cadence or tried to and what was that sound up ahead? Was it a fife attempting to be blown? Ah no: a winter bird in the wind, and what was he doing there, and how could he discover berries in bushes, or nuts or grain upon the ground, or any kind of provender? So he must perish, and lie trying to secrete himself beneath his wings until the treading feet came mashing him and he let out his pitiful bit of blood with their jauntier richer human type upon the adamant earth.

Many still wore their leather hunting shirts and that was good except when they were wet. The hide drew and tensed against their bodies, but their bodies were beaten things to begin with, and how might there be any spirits dwelling within, how might spirit and intent persist? Oh look at lucky ones with mittens! But many had no mittens, even mismatched and mismated ones, and they would try to march with their firearms trailing, muskets seeming to sag and bend as they carried them with muzzles down. And what of powder? Powder in all its wet, and would the good flints spark when they needed to spark? And hey a new wild breeze came racing, it had fangs in it and the breeze's teeth were sharp.

And here was a staunch old Scot named Currie, and in dream he was back on his native moorland and marching to earlier battle at Culloden. And did he hear the guns assailing?

Get down below the shirts and jerkins, and see what was around their maleness and their rears above their nudity.

'Twould freeze the balls off a bear.

Hell, you wouldn't know a bear if he come and bit you.

'Twould freeze the prick off a hell-screamer.

What in hell's a hell-screamer?

Kind of like a painter.

Ain't no painters here. Too cold.

I'd eat one if he come.

They're kind of cat. Can't eat no cat.

I seen fellers from the Seventh that et a cat.

Come now.

Sure as hell they did. Great big fat one, she was full of kittens. She come out and run in front of 'em and one of 'em heaved a rock and he got her with that rock. Next minute they had a fire going and they stripped off all that fur and she looked just like a rabbit. And the little kittens was inside her and looked to me like they was wiggling around, only they wasn't yet born and couldn't squeak or nothing like that. And they boiled her in a pot and et the meat and it was stout but feasible.

What you spose it tasted like? Like ground squirrel?

I never et any.

Like coon? You've et coon.

Well, maybe.

You oafs make me want to puke.

You wouldn't want to puke if you seen that cooking pot before you now and all them stewed morsels and—

You keep blethering and I'll puke in your face.

Try it!

Laughter ruled briefly over sneer and contention.

Rigid imagination had reached the point at last of examining the soldiers' loins and seeing them for what they were: balls blunted and dwindled, the pricks seeming puny and worthwhile only to poke and spear but never to achieve the pulse and delight of youth and power again. The balls—snow-balls in truth. So you got down to the lower limbs and there they were, all scratched and bludgeoned and chilblained, some hairy, some hard, all seeming frozen, and—below them—the feet. Some had boots and some had moccasins, some had socks or stockings wound round and tied with cord or scraps and some had nothing at all. You couldn't tell which was toe and which was heel. They were clubs at the end of limbs, anointing snow and ice as they pushed across each rude encumbrance, and with so many treading and staggering there seemed an actual puddling among cakes and blocks and ponds.

One dream was of a chimneyside and fire leaping, pothooks in their place, pots suspended, and ah, the odor spearing aloft, and here was a beaker of pewter. 'Twas a funny-looking object. It had kind of a long handle so you could hold it over the heat. But what was brimming? Milk and homemade toast, and oh so good. The toast was of grandmother's bread, all hot as it came from the baking, and she'd cut off the ends: two slices that you liked with crust all over them. You toasted them upon a fork (or maybe she had toasted them for you if you were ill or were a very little boy at the time, too young even to toast, but not too young to eat and fancy the fine fare). So she had put in salt—'twas something of a rarity but it flavored the milk—and then she added a mite of treacle or honey for sweetening and here was the butter she had churned, and she slabbed it on, great wads with a knife, and then put this heavenly toast to soak in heavenly milk. She said, Eat up, Honey, and she called you Honey too, even when she had put the honey in the milk, and so you went seeking with your fingers and the toast fell apart under their pressure. You could kind of grab and wad it up and stuff it in your mouth. And oh, the warmth and richness of the old cow's milk, richness of the bees that sweetened it, and sometimes there was even a bit of wax which had come along from the hollow tree or the hive, and you could chew it and feel it kind of gumming up . . . beeswax in your mouth.

This was all a dream.

Like home-boiled eggs and home-fried eggs with slabs of pork to go along.

Oh, the notion of green corn, fresh broke from the summery stalk. Your mother was Mistress Felton. She had the huge pot heating and once again there was salt here too and fresh-churned butter standing by. And she'd say, Now you go and pluck it. Hasten, cause the longer 'tis free of the stalk the duller it becomes. So you'd run with whoop and joy—out you'd go, down the rows, seeking, watching for the fattest ones and even so early in your life there were worms that got in ears sometimes and when you parted the tough brown silk at the end you had to look and see if there was a worm, but usually there wasn't any. And thus you'd gather them up, put them in your arms, take out your shirt and make a bag of it and carry the bag and sit upon the steps to peel the green shucks loose, break off the bit of damp white top which clung at the end, and you'd feel like a squirrel or critter of some kind a-eating corn . . . let us laugh about it. You'd feel like you were your own cow a-munching. But you weren't munching yet. You had to clean the ears and then take them quick and pop them into the kettle whilst Mistress Felton watched you and said, That ain't enough. Your father and your uncle eat so hearty, you go and fetch more. And out you'd scoot and feel the green warm smell around you as you snapped the ears. . . . Once again you were all at the board and eating. In your house you held good fortune. 'Cause so many children had to stand and pace and worry and fidget whilst their elders ate. But here there were only three elders: Mistress Felton and Master Felton and Master James Felton, who was usually called Master James alone, to distinguish him from his brother; and then you and your two sisters. There was room for all to set upon the benches and how that corncob felt with pale kernels a-pressing gainst your fingers.

No corn, no soldier.

No salt, no soldier.

No fresh-churned butter, no soldier.

There'd be the taste of other foods, so many, they'd come a-palpitating. You'd see them round about: slabs of meat, the greenery fresh-plucked, the apple tart, the pumpkin pudding, the flapjacks and the gingerbread.

Memory became a winsome and dangerous thing. Abolish it.

You trod the hard and sour-frozen path, and there was a knot of men hovering ahead. Someone had tumbled, no, yes, he had fainted. Boys lifted him to one side and they were bending over him and one bold comrade ripped off a kind of cloak to put around his body and cover thick the fallen man. You caught a glimpse of his face as you went past: the very nostrils pinched and dried, the very icicles formed around below that nose, the snot and other wetness mixed therein.

On they plodded, one said that the Schuylkill River lay ahead. Would there spread ice or no? Would their target lie on the far side or the nigh; if the far side, would they cross dry of foot?

Ho, blundered feet which were unfeeling clods a-pounding trodden ground!

Or would they build a bridge of boats?

Whence might the boats appear?

Close up your file! A wan young captain pushed his skeletal steed along, but few dared lift their sodden heads to look.

Close up your file!

They reeled in drear disorder. Some gossip filtered down. . . . They were to encamp at Valley Forge.

But 'tain't a forge. 'Tis little like.

If they got a forge, I'll guarantee to blow upon it.

This smith, perchance he'll take his red-hot iron and bend it round your hoofs.

Couldn't come too hot for me.

Oh harken to who's talking now!

Fuck you!

They trudged in pain akin to devilment. Few there were who munched upon a dream, but some there must have been. In every Jewish army there must have strode one petty David; in every Roman horde, one tired plodder must have played the Caesar; while some Irishmen were singing at the Boyne.

Woods lay dim and dowdy, but at least one pair of eyes beheld a sparkle coming from them. And then it vanished and the air was drab again.

3

WHEN General Washington thought of the Congressmen of these United States, he had to use an almost physical effort to assemble them as being human, subject to natural frailties. He tried to think of them as being courageous. He knew that many were capable of demonstrating courage individually. He thought of people like the Adamses and John Hancock, who would be practically useless in the active military field and yet brilliant in a bartering of political and organizational tactics. On the other hand, he knew of individuals who were fairly slobbering with venality, and had taken their inclination toward corruption along with them in their saddlebags when they went to York.

Consideration of Congress as a whole bore penalty.

One intimate shivering memory would not be put down. He remembered . . . long before . . . there was a time nigh onto forty years earlier when young rowdies had come a-visiting, and he ran with them along the banks of a creek which shivered its way down to the Rappahannock. They came to a pool which in his notion he always called *The Pool* because it was where he had first learned to duck, dive, splash, mudcrawl, and finally to swim dog-fashion. That must have been when he was three or four. He was a trifle older now, and wished strongly to appear as a brave character before these haughty and somewhat elder children.

They said, It looks cold in there, I'll wager 'tis cold.

9

See how the ice freezes on the surface! The elderly bent-shouldered Negro whose misfortunate fate made it necessary for him to stumble along with this tribe of monied white changelings—Sam tried to be heard, with his musty Black tones badgering against the outcry of the youths. Sam said, You bet you las' shilling it's cold in there. 'Twould freeze the balls off a brass monkey!

The visitors burst into gleeful howls about this. Apparently it was the first time they had ever heard the ancient expression, and they squeaked with glee at the idea. Firstly, that there could be such a critter as a brass monkey. Secondly, that its balls would be frozen.

About that time the young heir of this masterly plantation dove headlong from the bank to show his contempt for icy water, cringing, expostulation, elderly hazard as to difficulties involved, and the rest of it. He went in clothes and all, and with grim glee came up quaking out of the water to listen to outcries of the rest, the shouting admonition of old Sam, and to feel a selfish dignity even though he knew that he would soon be chastised for his foolishness. To himself, it was not foolishness at all. 'Twas an essential demonstration.

It was roundabout. He could never consider affirming or trying to explain this impression to wife, mistress, aide, secretary, or whom-not. To tie up momentary consideration of Congress with a comparison with that cold smash and dip in Virginia many decades before. Yet each time, even for the scantiest passage of a partial second, he nerved himself, caught that quick deep breath, felt the tremble of his fingertips.

Ordinarily he saw the Congress flanked into a single room (doubtless 'twas a church) and seated in long rows. He knew that there must be slim or brawny persons among them, yet in that initial instant they all had the bodies of white pigs or maybe geese, or even fabled swans a-puffing. They had long curved necks or else no necks at all. They bent toward the speaker. Who was the speaker? 'Twas himself sometimes; and he was pleading honestly, directly, firmly, telling them the truth; and were they harkening?

Aye, harkening, but ending up only by taking his ideas under advisement, never acknowledging the urgency which prevailed.

GENERAL ORDERS

*Headquarters at the Gulph   December 17, 1777
Parole Warwick. Countersigns Woodbridge, Winchester*

THE COMMANDER IN CHIEF, *with the highest satisfaction, expresses his thanks to the Officers and Soldiers for the fortitude and patience with which they have sustained the fatigues of the Campaign. Although in some instances we unfortunately failed, yet upon the whole Heaven hath smiled upon our arms and crowned them with signal success; and we may now upon the best Grounds conclude that by a Spirited continuance of the Measures necessary for our defense we shall finally obtain the end of our Warfare, Independence, Liberty, and Peace. These are blessings worth contending for at every hazard. But we hazard nothing. The power of America alone, duly exerted, would have nothing to dread from the forces of Britain. Yet we stand not wholly upon our own Ground. France yields us every aid we ask, there are reasons to believe the Period is not very far distant, when she shall take a more active part, by declaring War against the British Crown. Every motive therefore irresistibly urges us, nay commands us, to a firm and manly perseverance in Opposition to our cruel oppressors, to slight Difficulties, endure Hardships, and contemn every Danger. . . .*

He might not address them in physical presence and by word of mouth. His place was with the Army, his soul belonged to the Army, his soul was a portion of the Army. As a substance it walked a road among them.

Can you see your soul stalking there?

Yet his imagination led him so often away to address those contemptible rows of staring faces. Now seldom did he see them as minikins. They puffed up increasingly as porkers arrayed in wigs and clothing, and sometimes strangely they had their women sitting with them.

This is my country? The puffy men, the women with their furbelows and false fronts, their fancy bonnets, their fairly gilded petticoats—are they the natural substance of our nation? his heart was crying.

Yet if you sent the substance of a new nation into conclave, there would be demonstrated stupidity and bickering as fatal to the nation's vigor as was this ruling body, this fancied plague of plumpness and apathy.

Housewives who whispered scandals in the churchyard or on their way home from Meeting could never prove themselves as legislators fit to substantiate a course. Neither could their men. The men would be more at home with reaping hook in hand, or working with a stone to turn the infinite edge of an axe, or to run the bear to ground in his dangerous cavern as Old Put was alleged to have done. The Commander had loved to twit the salty farmer about that. He himself had ducked and dodged. Instantly, instantly! That scant morsel of a second when the Indian's powder had flashed in the pan and he heard the bullet plunk into a tree behind him instead of plunking into himself.

Or in the city . . . to tend shop, to deliver the burden. In the village . . . to feed the horse, and drive it with its cart. To feel and exert a husbandry. To cry, Maria, we're fresh up from plowing! Binny and I can eat a ton, I'll wager you that!

It constituted a puzzle he did not wish to solve, although he would have been glad to solve it, but he knew that he had not the impulse or—let alone impulse—the power to do so.

I consider it not much of a rarity, he thought in a torn and lonely moment of the night, to find a man who is equally adept at the forge or in the field or laden with his weapon at the firing; but seldom can he preach capably also from the pulpit, and at the same time have recognition of a Plato or a Demosthenes. Seldom can he tell you also how many hundredweight of indigo were borne by the vessels last year. Seldom can he tell you any pith in what he'd said before the Privy Council eleven scant months agone. Seldom is he able also to chase butterfly, to catch it for a child, and name the tiny critter as it flew.

His Excellency knew that he must banish this chimera of bland stupidity and cultured (save the mark) oafishness before he should be able to deal effectively with the Congress. He must seek out and recognize that there were some men of strength and purpose who sat there. There were pounds of valor in the purses of the few, if but farthings in the pockets of the many.

He wished suddenly almost youthfully that he might subjugate these trials of his reckoning, by wiping them out with sport of the body. At least for the time he spent so engaged, the infernal challenge might be forgotten. But Martha dared not come as yet and there was no other handy receptacle for his fervor.

He examined the sky in the east . . . the far southeast now, because it was that time of year and the shortest days were dawning. Was there a pinkness? Was there a lightening? Was there new snow? And was it light enough for him to ring his bell for Billy Lee to saddle up a horse, that he might ride and take once more the grimmest joy in his inspection of the stagnant icy thousands around him scattered?

His surveyor's mind saw no bright target, with hands waving a-thwarted to beckon his attention.

He thought, Mine instrument is keen but it must have humankind to support it.

Oh, immortal Jehovah, I hanker for the full advocacy of humankind! I have it here among these waifs and wisps who are truly as tough within their battered hides as hickory saplings, and have so shown themselves to be.

He slumped back, turned over. He did not even sigh, for he was too tense. He buried his face against his arm and lay there alone.

4

THE day had been raw and rainy, but cleared as the sun hung low. There came a silent smartness in the paling air.

Axle, said Master Sessler, addressing me by my nickname, which pleased me.

He was dainty in manner of speech; but when others began to call me Axle instead of my true name of Carlton, he had abhorred the informality. It became a persuasion, however, and other people addressed me thus, and Master Sessler, with whatever reluctance, fell into the pattern. Governor Hutchinson, yclept Tommy Skin-and-Bones, went driving in a coach with some royal personage all a-glitter, and I was dared to ride also upon that coach as I'd claimed to companions that I was fain to do. They scoffed, and wagered a penny apiece that I dared not do this thing, and I ventured to match the bet. 'Twas simple as it came about. I waited merely for a few shreds of darkness and in a drizzle at that. Then, after the coachman had mounted to his seat and taken up his reins and whip, I leapt in flaunting fashion to the axle and rode the journey. The prentice boys saw me going and saw me coming back.

I was splashed and muddied a bit, but able to spring off with yell of derision. We all fled away while coach-man and passengers were gaping.

Axle, said Master Sessler again.

I came to him. What would you, sir?

I must to Mistress Hobbings'. She's poorly again and I need see that she has proper care this evening and night.

Mistress Hobbings was his sister and a cross-grained crone if I ever glimpsed the like. But I was mincing in manners, and pretended to be much concerned about this harridan.

I do pray that she keeps better, sir.

He stared a moment, and then a grin came upon his seamed face, a leer that I didn't like. Such smirks of his were apt to betoken blows or short commons. The blows I could accept with calm, as any husky prentice might; but the short commons were a bruising notion, for his tables were spread thinly at best.

He said, Rapscallion that you are, I've glimpsed you by the window a dozen times when it was more fitting that you be seaming bolts. What of that? Hey?

Sir, I only worried about the weather. For I knew that soon you would be a-going out.

Oh my soul and body! he exclaimed. I should give you the flat of my hand a dozen times for that! Would you be joining with those hooligans?

Oh no, sir. Not I.

The sneaks? The rats? The fly-by-nights? The wharf-mongers?

He'd struck my rebellion on the head. He only crooked his finger and pointed. My chain hung in the corner.

That was simple. I knew the chaining was due to follow, but it was necessary to make protest about it.

Oh please, sir, I cried in lamentation. Do not chain me up again!

He crowed, Whatever may be the tides of opposi-tion, I shall remain a decent Colonist, and loyal to our good King. No prentice boy of Thomas Sessler's need go a-helling.

I wailed and faked for another minute, but not too much e'er he might grow suspicious. Then I made solemn show of meekly accepting the restraint. 'Twas the warded lock which he prepared—the same he'd used before. We'd employed warded locks commonly in furniture. The one he fetched was of the padlock type, great and heavy. He wrapped the chain around the hasp three times and then sank it home and turned his key.

There, that'll fix you. Pray have no further notion of becoming a Yankee dock-rat.

I pleaded as if I were a simpleton. What of my supper, sir? Though I asked with dignity and not too plaintively.

Bread and cheese. Good enough for anyone.

He went to the pantry and came back with a more generous helping than I had expected. All too frequent he regarded modest fare as good discipline.

There, lad, he said. You can reach it, you've got free play enough on that chain. If you would sleep before I return, your pallet's under the table.

He owned a fine quilted greatcoat. Now he drew it on, and gazed in a small mirror, settled his cocked hat with fussy adjustment.

It's three long years agone, he said. Nearer four. But I remember what happened in King Street. I was standing nigh . . . you hadn't come to me as yet. Oh, I witnessed them lying dead and wounded. I care not to observe such doom for any prentice boy of mine.

He went out, I heard him clomping down the stairs. Quickly from the window I watched his sparse figure treading precisely until he turned off, headed for his sister's.

Give a few minutes. Though I was reluctant to invest the time before I freed myself and went my way.

He'd found a broadside which I had saved, and that won me another scalping. It happened something over a fortnight since.

Friends! Brethren! Countrymen! Thus read the address at the top.

> *The worst of Plagues, the detested tea shipped for this port by the East India Company, is now arrived in the Harbour; the hour of destruction, or manly opposition to the machinations of Tyranny, stares you in the Face; every Friend to his country, to Himself, and to Posterity, is now called upon to meet at Faneuil Hall at nine o'clock in the morning this day, at which time the bells will ring to make united and successful resistance to this last, worst, and most destructive measure of Administration.*
>
> Boston
> Nov. 29, 1773

Truly I wondered at my master's lack of vision. How could he think to put a prentice to work with all those wards and gimcracks, and not consider that he'd employ a bit of tallow, fill a crevice or two, and construct himself a key to fit? To be altogether certain, I'd scraped out some extras, and had them hid with skill in other spots if he might change the area of my chain.

I'd made a pocket for one key inside my coarse shirt. I fetched it out now, and with little difficulty the warded lock opened and the hasp swung free.

Air was growing nippy with all that clearing outside, and when I swung the window open a hubbub from the docks came up to greet me. Perhaps he had not locked the door? I ran to see. But it was buckled staunch, and any captive might have died outlandish death if fire came. But I was prisoner no longer, nor had I been on other occasions.

I waited at the window until two men passed by beneath, and then scooted down across the tiles . . . put my hands upon a cornice . . . dropped easily to the street. There was grass where I landed but it was frosty hard. Nevertheless I was prepared for the shock of hitting. I gathered myself up and ran down the course, twisting my tippet around me and hunting for the small wool cap I'd put inside my shirt. I felt sprightly, eager, delighted with freedom, anticipating fierce things to come.

What first? To Griffin's Wharf? That was where the *Beaver* and *Eleanor* and *Dartmouth* were moored.

Or should I hasten to the Old South Church? Assembly had been called for there.

Streets were jambed further on and I heard talk bombarding. Indeed throngs still assembled in Old South so thither I was running.

Outside the place and in that nervous dusk the people teemed and talked, and it seemed I had a dozen ears.

You should have heard young Quincy speak.

Aye, that I did. I was compelled to leave, but now I'm back again and can't get in.

Too many folks.

They're waiting to hear from Rotch. He owns the *Dartmouth*.

Did he go up to Milton?

Aye. To speak to Tommy Skin-and-Bones.

Our rat of a Royal Governor!

Aye, true.

He should be flung from Griffin's Wharf and take a ducking.

Some would shout treason at that.

Many would.

Blood was steaming inside me as I heard and as I wished so many things at once. Wished that I were able to be with that guard upon the wharf . . . twenty-five men in deed and word, and they were most determined. They'd been guarding now for weeks . . . also I hankered to have stood on King Street when the soldiers fired. I didn't crave to lie among the dead or wounded, but prayed that I had had a weapon in my hands myself. I would have fired back! Or maybe would have fired first, before that ignoble Preston shouted out his vile command. Wished that I had been able to throw more than snowballs at the lobsterbacks.

I had hurled snowballs verily. We boys owned a sweet way of icing them. We'd make the balls hard and wee and fair to handle and hurl. Then we'd freeze them and such a wicked weaponry had they become. We hid at night in ambuscades to pelt the foe, and there were stories about how such scamps had been caught and beaten here or there. Some said they'd seen a younker bayoneted, but others said it wasn't true. Nevertheless the lobsterbacks were fearful of us just the same, and one could never blame them honestly.

Rotch is returned.

He just went in with two more.

I concluded that if Rotch could go into Old South, I could also, and was sly and quick and small enough to do it.

In my bumbling forward, I could witness the voice of Mr. Rotch from the chancel but could not determine exactly what he said. I heard the cramped bystanders interpret as I inched my way.

He says that he cannot send back the ships.

Governor Hutchinson will not give him a pass!

Samuel Adams was a-standing and I could hear what he said. He recited as if he had learned the line already . . . as if he had recited it often before a glass (as I did sometimes on those rare occasions when I was idle, and had chance to practice mimicry of mine own).

This meeting can do nothing more to save the country.

The rout went boiling up, as if this vast unseemly congregation were entranced and surpassingly it was. Yells issued from the galleries above, which were dark enough and unlit by the few candles which had been set forth.

Voices were caroling, *Oh-Ah-Oh-Ah-Oh-Ah-Oh-Ah-Oh-Ah*. Which caused the skin to prickle, for that was the war whoop of the Indians. Well I knew, along with the rest; I'd played Indian from the time I could crawl. Veterans of frontier encounters insisted that that was the whooping commonly used when braves went forth with scalping knives and bows and arrows and old muskets they had traded from the French.

The moderator was a-crying, Order, gentlemen! Order! Order!

Our crowd seemed to heed and the yelling died down. One young man called out suddenly—also from the gallery—and his voice was easily heard.

Did anybody ever think, he cried, how tea would mix with salt water?

Again the cheering, the war whoops, and again the tall figure of Samuel Adams rising as if to beckon us on.

This meeting can do nothing more to save the country.

Oh-Ah-Oh-Ah-Oh-Ah-Oh-Ah!

Sound of feet overhead and about was like a hammering of winter thunder. I was kicked and pummeled by the unheeding who were all a-rush for the door. I yielded, felt myself swept along with them.

Outside I slammed into two friends, the Manchester boys, Jabez and Tolman. They said something about lampblack.

Where'll we get it?

Or chimney soot. We'll smear it on.

They ran for a roper's shop and I hustled with them. We were all in palpitation. The blood and bones and heart and circulation of rebellion were surging over us and made us warm within, heated and dangerous without.

The boys' uncle owned the roper's shop and we went pounding in as he sat calmly before his fire, a-reading of a pamphlet.

We were all a-cry. Master Buffington, sir—Uncle Melly—Have you any soot?

He looked calmly at us over his specs as if he'd been anticipating this adventure all along. Other chimney, he said. Fire's out and chimney's cold. You want a mite of tallow to go with it?

Tallow and lampblack together, and we smeared and smeared.

There's that duster over there, he said. Your auntie employs it now and again, but it's falling apart.

We needed no further instruction, but started hacking away with a pair of the roper's shears. We smudged tallow in our hair and the sundered feathers stuck to it.

Ain't got any red paint, the old man told us. Reckon you don't look like Indians anyway. Look more like something come from the nether regions.

Oh-Ah-Oh-Ah-Oh-Ah, we cried in fierceness and in thanks.

We went tearing toward the wharves where other youths were joining us. I possessed only one regret as we flew, and that was about my tippet. Already it was tarnished with the stuff and I would have a pretty time trying to wash it out if in truth ever I managed to do so.

We possessed no hatchets and about us scores of bedaubed rapscallions were brandishing them.

Then a kindly voice spoke in my ear, or above it. I looked up to see Mr. Wendell Smith, who was rich and of power accordingly. He had brought his grandfather's clock, servants sagging under the weight of it, to my master to have the lock and hinges fixed; and he had come back a time or two to observe how it was going, and if the weights were hanging true, and if the little bird that peeked from a tiny balcony was able to make his manners when time demanded it.

Why, Axe, he said. You lads are chipper enough, but you'll have a crotchety time clawing those tea chests open with your fingers. Here, now.

He had a cluster of small axes with him and doled them out, adjuring us to caution.

Hear now. When you come back upon the wharf you're to take these to the ironmonger's across the way, and he pointed out the sign. It's Mr. Lee. He's a loyal enough Bostonian to give us the lend. Mind now, and don't forget.

We promised faithfully and it was good to have weapons to brandish in our hands, for we felt more and more like the heathen we faked to be. We yielded ourselves in glamour to Mr. Smith's direction, became a portion of his private gang of fiends, and muted our voices when he instructed us to do so.

I looked back at the waterfront and up and down. It appeared that all Boston and indeed all of the Old Bay Colony had moved to watch us and more were herding closer with every tick of the watch if I had owned one and it was a-ticking.

Out opposite were the British, riding at anchor. They seemed but a hundred rods away. Quickly I wondered, as indeed many others must have guessed, as to whether the cannoneers were standing nigh their stations, with matches ready to apply to petholes of their cannon. Lobsterbacks had fired upon unarmed citizens, mainly a mob of boys at that, not too many moons before (as my master reminded me). Would these royal guns now sweep the waterfront? Such notion brought a lump to my throat; suddenly I thought I couldn't breathe; and all in the same instant I felt dedication to a task which I had never felt before.

I held up my smeared head and features with seemly pride.

Master Smith was marshaling us. We headed for the nearest brig—the *Dartmouth* she was called. Men and boys were crushing on ahead and smearing the bulwarks as they crept aboard. Then the bulwarks were under our own hands, and we too were scrambling, and then standing on the very deck with the bold Smith ahead of us.

A man stood before him, bareheaded even in this chill, and with his hair tied in a queue. I remember that he had it wound with a ribband of blue which could be seen fairly as he held up his lanthorn. I thought he must be the captain of the brig but my companions told me later, Nay, he was but the mate.

At any rate we felt more secure and potent. For if the warships were to fire now, they'd only be raking their own English vessel with canister and maybe sinking it to boot.

We could hear the voice of Smith a-speaking flat and sharply but with assurance.

If you please, sir, may we have the keys? And lights, in order to see our way below?

The seaman looked at him with calm, and spoke no word in reply. We might see his face clearly in the small light that he held aloft . . . the face was hearty and old. He'd fought the French and fought the Spanish, you could tell that in his attitude . . . or least-ways he'd sailed amongst them, if indeed he had not fought . . . but he had been exposed to danger e'er we came aboard this craft.

He turned and gestured. A cabin boy far smaller than ourselves stepped forward, gaping and fright-ened but bound to obey.

Fetch up some lanthorns, the mate was ordering of the child.

He turned back and took from the pocket of his jacket a bundle of keys and these with coolness he gave to Master Smith's keeping.

I surveyed the landward side again and not only town and Colony seemed present but the whole mess of modern humanity—solid and substantial, a vast commingling of faces and bodies and weird lights pok-ing out. One sensed that more would be appearing. Where in fact they came from nobody might know. In wondrous silence they stood and watched. You had a feeling that if indeed they did speak, it would only be with a groan of awe. We were treading where we dared not tread, yet responding to summons that speared us on. The marvel of it pierced me—we were all seemly portion of a proud assemblage who dared to carve our way in spite of Crown and Parliament and old King George himself.

I didn't go below, nor did the other lads. Thus I have no knowledge of what the interior was like. They required stronger backs and mightier bodies than ours to lift those heavy chests and lug them up on deck.

The first few were more or less fought over by eager hoodlums grabbing forth; but more and more appeared, and suddenly there was scarce a sound except some brief direction here and there. The chests were fairly piled amongst us.

Well do I recollect the first blows I struck. . . . I'd possessed no idea chests could be so thick and heavy. I'd seen only the middling chests of tea before, and never one as mighty as these. My hatchet might not assault successfully without harder blows than I'd used at first. And finally the lid was cracked . . . then sundered. . . . I chopped again, again. The hole was large enough and gaping, and my hatchet went down into the stuff, and perfume was all around. Then hoist and lift to the gunwale, let it totter there, and pour out the tea and hear the rustle as down it went and hear cold water splashing to receive it, and then when the chest was empty, push it over, and all those splashes were resounding. Occasionally there wafted a laugh, a challenge, someone did cut himself, I remember blood a-running. The wounded man thus had to go ashore with red paint mixed amid his lampblack.

There was talk about the chests themselves. Some saying we should hurl them overboard; others decried the idea. They tried heaping them upon the deck, but people were tripping over the lot and thus there rose fresh laughter and curses and outcries.

Remorseful was a word I'd learned newly in my reading by candle scraps when I could manage to do so; and *remorseless* was another. I felt them both at this wild time. I felt *remorseful* because I was in truth so *remorseless*. So were we all.

We had come into this thing in the manner of playing a prank but soon the hours became dreariness. Many participating did not give a hoot about the tea or its status, for those were complications beyond our ken. We had turned out as boys will forever turn out for big doings . . . our primary endeavor was frantic, but pointless as at a Guy Fawkes revel. It was sheer fun to play the part of a destructive lunatic.

Still none of us had realized that so much work was waiting, and that we were involved and responsible, each in his own measure, for the task being carried out according to the way our leader set.

Argument kept ensuing about disposition of the chests. Some said, Hurl them into the harbour. Others said, We are not seeking the chests, we are seeking tea. I heard one tall Indian say to another, Leave us toss the chests back below deck once they are emptied, and then other voices broke in a-wrangling.

The skin of my hands was grated and oozing. My arms held no feeling. My legs were sodden, worse than when I had been drubbed by the cruel but hardy lockmaker. When first light of dawn was showing (and people guessed that it was appearing before actually the transformation came about), we could only gaze with apathy and be glad that night and task were both coming to an end.

They said that there were three hundred and forty-two chests of tea aboard those craft and every one of these we emptied. More tea, more tea, some bolder ones were shouting, but at last there were no more filled chests to be dragged aloft. Mr. Smith himself went below to make certain that all the cargo had been discharged. Through the night I reckon he was up and down that ladder a dozen times, or perhaps scores.

Vaguely we'd heard of what had happened to cargoes in other Colonial ports . . . how it was landed in Carolina but merchants refused to handle it, and it was stored in darkness and ooze and soon became unfit for any consumption. We'd heard of Philadelphia: crowds turned out, and the ship owners retreated back to the Mother Country, and also did the same in New York Town.

I attempted to go below in fawning loyally after our mentor. But there loomed the stern face of the mate, and he jerked his thumb toward the upper deck, and back I returned in haste.

Our rabble was already striving across the bulwarks and creeping toward the wharf.

Firm big hands were on our shoulders. Do not delay, lads, the voice of Smith was saying. Take those hatchets back immediate, and then we'll march in triumph.

This we did. Weak-limbed or no, we hastened to join the other savages and form a column, though it was bound to be disorderly. From somewhere had appeared some fifers and drummers too, and they marched at the head, breaking out in that elderly "The Gobby O." I found later that men did call it "Paul Revere's Ride," and there were other titles, and even afterward, when war swept us all away, there were some who called it "Jefferson and Liberty." 'Twas an engaging march. Exhausted though we were, we hustled along, crying *Ugh-Ugh* and giving our version of war whoops in between.

There came slight commotion up ahead. The procession halted beneath a window and there was the British admiral, framed as in a portrait, watching out.

He spoke with sarcasm, and we could hear him well, for the crowd fell silent when he appeared.

He hurled at us the greatest scorn imaginable.

You've had a splendid night for your naughty behavior. But he who dances must pay the piper!

A voice shouted back, urging him to come outside. Someone addressed him as squire and there scrambled rowdy laughter.

One man called back to the admiral. His voice rose strongly above cheers and hooting and gobble of war cries.

If you will but descend, we'll settle up the bill with you, and make it most immediate!

The angry face fell away and disappeared. You could hear the admiral's hands a-fastening the window.

We marched in final triumph. The fifers were a-playing "The Picnic" now and small drums and the single larger one rolled thunderous.

Oh, hasten to the village green.
Fling cark and care aside....

Somewhere along the route while that pleasant tune was still ascending and while both crowds and paraders made their noise, we'd reached my own neighborhood. I fell out and slipped away.

My great fear, above tiredness and strain my body'd been subjected to, was that I would be scourged. I felt that I'd collapse if the beating were proffered, and lie limply upon the floor and let Master Sessler pound me.

He was long come home. If he'd lain down awhile he'd risen when our parading lunacy approached. He was watching from the window, like Admiral Montague himself.

When Sessler saw me, he made but a single gesture, motioning me to ascend the staircase. The door was standing open when I got there. From across the room he ordered me, still by gesture, to shoot the bolt home.

I should have known you'd be among 'em. How did you get loose?

I could only shake and stare. I dropped my gaze and could but think, Oh please, don't scalp me. Oh, I am an Indian and quite deserving of it.

But nerve and boldness which the caper had instilled came boiling up and I said a thing that would shock any master.

If you beat me now, so help me God, once I am loose and shed of my apprenticeship, and grown taller and stronger as I mean to grow, I'll return. If only for the purpose of beating you as well. I swear it solemnly. I'll beat you silly.

He looked me in the face, as much of it as he could see beneath the grime and lampblack and shreds of blood from off my hands. He perceived that I was meaning what I said.

He ordered, Go clean yourself if so you can. It's daylight now and we have no holidays hereabouts for miscreants. Go clean yourself, do you hear?

So I heard, and went to try and do the trick with water and soft soap, and how that soap was stinging on the raw abrasions of my body.

But how my soul felt strengthened by my own words and by my grim intent.

5

THEY were ordered to rear their cabins in special position. There was no profit in raving against the surveyor who laid them out. They held that surveyor to be Zexcellency, and Zexcellency had been a surveyor before most of these soldiers were dreamed of, even by their mothers.

Other engineers did the rest of the planning perhaps, and passed word down to company commanders, and then the sergeants and corporals took over. Huts were to come in three lines in this area, each line of huts four deep, and five yards (as the stipulation went) asunder. Regular cabins, sixteen by fourteen feet in dimension, six feet high at the eaves and higher than that if the roof were peaked. A chimney was to be built on the east end, the door was stipulated to open on the south.

There existed difficulty in parceling out axes, for the burden trains had not come up . . . engineers were slipping and sliding far back on icy ways. The group mustered a fair corps of hewers; the city personnel who were not axe-wise or axe-conscious had the best of instruction. Also they could drag logs, dig out rocks, make themselves generally useful. Very few were useless. There was weighty incentive: cabins spelled shelter and fireplaces would soon be hot, and so would the men who pushed round them.

Except for one wide glade, trees stretched from road to creek and up to the foot of a miniature mountain and back to the Schuylkill again, and west to the village and tattered houses nearby. Most of the forest was of tulipwood, black birch, maple, chestnut, elm. Wiser and more experienced choppers advanced to the task of getting out the tulips, even when most were too large to be used in the actual construction. They had to come down, space must be allotted. Many of these huts would squat within the earth first, but there followed head-shaking over this.

You'll be full of water soon as it melts. Come up with 'em high and dry!

But there's warmth in the ground—

Pile warmth upon your roof!

But—

Sound arose with axes gnawing as if some scores of beaver were at work. The trees were a-tremble, quivering, saying weakly, How come these folks to be here? Why are they ripping us apart? Will they soon leave us be?

Squirrels curled in winter sleep, and they were flattened or stunned and in some cases set free and frightened, as the forest came down. The men ran after them with whoops and captured most which had survived the tumble.

Even that first day the rough façade began to appear torn and shredded. Birds—the few woodpeckers and nuthatches—jostled out of the way. They got themselves wisely loose before men could catch them and make soup (though most of the birds were small).

No firearms were to be discharged: too many soldiers in the brush. A man who discharged his piece might get fifty stripes across his bare back.

Wrangle and hubbub ruled in their fashion, but somehow soldiers still acted in response to orders. The brush fires glowed and roared. Smaller shrubbery and

tiniest branches must be cleared—you couldn't oper-
ate amidst them.

This is the Valley for certain. But where in hell is
that Forge?

Other people were saying the same words or voicing
identical thoughts in some other manner; and the very
management of axes, the felling of trees, the burning
of minor branches brought stimulation. The Army
whistled, picked up its lean starved self and shook its
shoulders, rubbed nervous hands across its face,
blinked its eyes, felt that somehow things were better,
even though as yet there was no food.

By His Excellency
George Washington, Esquire,
General and Commander-in-Chief of the Forces
of the United States of America.

By Virtue of the Power and Direction to me
especially given, I hereby enjoin and require all
Persons residing within seventy miles of my Head
Quarters to thresh one Half of their Grain by the
1st Day of February, and the other Half by the
1st day of March next ensuing, on Pain, in Case
of Failure of having all that shall remain in
Sheaves after the Period above mentioned, seized
by the Commissaries and Quarter-Masters of the
Army, and paid for as Straw.

Given under my Hand at Head Quarters, near
the Valley Forge, in Philadelphia County, this
20th Day of December, 1777.

G. Washington
By His Excellency's Command,
Robert H. Harrison, Sec'y

The group arose from their slumping among fires
before sunrise. They had among them but four axes
which were singled out to those reckoned to be the
most efficient in the handling; they were willing to
demonstrate by the sweep and depth of their kerfs.

A corporal and two privates went in search of horses . . . other people had seized or impressed some . . . there was troubled neighing and panting here and there amid the loosening forest.

But in our case 'twill be Shank's Mare and Shank's Draught.

I'm happy to be Shank's anything if'n I get my oats.

Wouldn't winter-killed corn do?

You find it, I'll eat it!

Some made the sound of horse-approval by blowing through loose lips.

The corporal called the roll. All responded except a private named Mum Foyne and no one knew what had become of him.

Seen him when darkness fell. He was dragging brush long-side me.

I member him too 'bout that time.

Maybe he's laying sick somewheres?

They looked about vaguely, none with much attention.

Corporal Winsted said, I won't report him to the provost, not yet. He mought creep out of the brush fore long. Wolcott and Hurtz, come drive stakes to mark out our site.

He had it that a notice had been published abroad: Zexcellency was offering a prize of twelve dollars *to that squad of twelve men in each regiment who shall conclude the construction of their cabin in the most rapid yet seemly manner.*

I swear. Let's get it for the best one in the Sixth!

What'll we buy?

Rum! most of them yelled.

They were become beasts of burden and with something like jocularity they harnessed themselves as such. Miscellaneous ropes hung across shrunken chests and chafed down into what flesh and muscle still remained. Even so they dragged and drew. No sinks had been hacked out as yet, at least none in their area. Two went into thicker as yet untarnished woods to answer the sharp rumblings of gas and petty discharge of nature, and they found a dead horse freezing but with its mended harness still unclaimed. They returned triumphantly swathed in a welter of tugs and reins, and soon the rest of the squad were harnessed and dragging logs. It was a task, raising them one atop another, and then came the roof slanting from a center rod resting on deep-sunk end poles. Shorter logs were used to build the bunks, three in each corner so there might be twelve in all. Every man present except two had participated in house-raisings theretofore and the novelty of this procedure did not puzzle or offend.

Amidst their tussling, a cart came driving up and a keg was pulled from it and set upon the ground.

Pickled pork, pickled pork! the men were roaring in no time at all.

What have you there, soldier?

A bit of pickled pork, sir. Will you have a bite?

No pork, no soldier!

Pickled pork, you have a soldier.

They gobbled greedily and in minutes. Theirs was the last case to be delivered, the shipment had run thin. They saw people in squads beyond gazing with wistfulness but, if any individual had desire to share, it would have been quelled speedily by watching the attitude of comrades. A lieutenant drifted past and they knew him though he was not of their company. (At least some knew him because they came from the same region.) They passed out a few trifles with the lieutenant at first refusing; then with his refusal quelled by gestures, he snatched the bits and ate them down.

Lord be with you all, he said sanctimoniously and went his way.

Those who knew him found out later that the lieutenant was bound for his commanding officer's headquarters to resign and go home. He could resign, they could not; but he might find his way to the small house where his wife and children squatted and—oh, to discover them thriving and not wholly emaciated!

When's the next sowbelly coming?

God knows. I could eat a barrel full!

You do it and you'll pollute the hull damn woods!

They returned to their building with a relief they had not known in days. Some even talked learnedly of being certain that the vaunted twelve dollars was now within their grasp. Some could already taste the rum in their throats or so they claimed. There were sloughs of melted earth round where the fires had been, and several went to scooping this out with whittled spades and fetching it to smear between gaps in the logs. Others worked from the outside: you'd have soldiers with lengths of flat wood shaved off by the chopping, and they'd be stuffing these in crannies and others would be applying mud and going back for more when the stuff they were carrying grew stiff and frozen.

Supper is ready.

What you got for supper, lads?

Oak chips and tulip branches, sir!

If God had stood upon Mount Joy (doubtless there were those who thought He tarried there), it might have taxed His wisdom to understand.

How high these walls got to be?

Six feet.

Nay. Zexcellency ordered six-and-a-half.

Who told you?

Corporal Winsted.

Ah, tell him to fuck his own behind! Six feet is tall enough.

Yeh, you preach that 'cause you're shrimp-sized.

I'm big enough to twist your eye out any time. I got good claws.

With a dozen allotted to each hut, this led to considerable wrangling. Though in common cases, as is the way with soldiers, they had fallen into coteries of three or four. There was amiable demand, even in such privation, to get the groups together. A wise sergeant could have prevailed and minimized ordinary human hostility. There were few wise sergeants. Some of the men were wiser than the officers.

Meanwhile in York, twenty-two miles to the west, a Congressman sat himself down to his meal. Congress had been in session in York since September and it was a fair place to get through the winter. Though there was dullness to be contemplated in the coming of the Christmas season, and this Congressman especially wished that he were home in Philadelphia. He held dreadful fears about the British who had taken his house there.

But still it was a good thing to sit in Mistress Dessner's lodgings and begin his supper.

May I compliment you, Madam, upon your chicken broth with these—ah—

Oh, chicken bread broth, sir! My ma, she learnt to make it when she was a girl in Switzerland. You have to have the bread just right—a special kind of dough. And then the bread is old bread, with flavorings and bits of chicken picked out, and then of course the broth from a stewed chicken with mayhap some onions and—

Delicious fare, Ma'am. Ah. Here we have these splendid chops again! You do broil them well.

'Tain't broiled a-tall. Those are fricasseed. Here, sir, I offer some nice fresh mashed potato, and the gravy to go with it. And will you have some of these pickled beets with home-boiled eggs? My grandmother, she taught me how.

And will you have some more gravy?

Chicken balls. Pudding. Cold roast meat in slices. Will you have some beans. And oh, the cake to come. The pumpkin pie! The sauces and the mince. And oh, the beer and brandy to go with 'em!

No chicken broth, no soldier.

No pickled eggs and beets, no soldier.

No pumpkin pie, no soldier!

No homemade cheese—

At Valley Forge, Washington had not moved into his new quarters as yet. Madam Washington would come to join him when the present owner, Mrs. Hewes, had been properly put up in another place with her personal possessions.

Washington thought of a member of Congress in York, that same gobbling one perhaps. He thought of another who would be inert until it was reported to him that some waggons had broken down in a nearby road, and would he come to see? He went to see what was happening in the nearby road, and yes, the waggons were broken down, and yes, the teams had broken down as well. Waggoners poured out things to lighten their loads; and so fish oil had been mixed into the flour, and it was all uneatable, and the pork was frozen and then thrown out because it was too weighty. That was the way the waggoners managed their burdens and they were not supposed to be there anyway. They were supposed to deliver that food to the Army, and in proper condition, but it didn't happen too often that they came boldly to the Army. There was the ruling fear of British raiders in between. So they preferred to go to York and say to Congress, What shall we do with these shortened loads?

Washington thought of another member of Congress who this night would lodge in bed with his mistress and who meanwhile in private was entertaining his pretty young mistress at supper, and so what do we have, landlady?

Oh, sir, it's duck with stuffing.

Aha, aha. I hope you haven't cooked the duck too brown!

Oh no, sir. My boy Ebby, he went and shot these ducks this very day and I have saved out one for you and one for the young lady and they're just done now, and should you like some creamed potatoes with 'em?

Why, that wouldn't be bad a-tall.

And what about some garden peas, sir? Fresh from my second crop before the wintry weather, and I put them down in a keg, and they're still good because of the cold.

Peas with duck? Aha, aha! What say you, Tabby?
The girl would coo and make a happy sound.

And then there's apple tart. 'Tis fresh-baked, sir.
And spiced with mine own spices!

Aha, aha!

Your Congressman again!

Suddenly deep in his heart His Excellency hated
the Congress but he could not hate what it represented. He could retain venom for the carelessness,
squeamishness, of weak mankind.

Oh, Heavenly Father, are not some of these men
bold? Are not some true and honest and vibrant with
energy? Cannot I depend on some?

He indited his freshest letter to the Congress, one of
many.

> *Unless some great and capital change takes*
> *place . . . this Army must inevitably be reduced*
> *to one or another of these three things: starve,*
> *dissolve, or disperse in order to obtain subsistence*
> *in the best manner they can.*

In the end their hut was built mainly of tulip tree
logs. Some recalled how when children they were puzzled by the tulip tree designation. Each shafted up in
a narrow dignified black column, so very black was
the bark, and speckled blossoms fell down in spring.
What of garden tulips? There was talk of bulbs
brought over on ships from the Low Countries,
brought from Holland itself. Something about people
eating tulip bulbs when otherwise they would have
starved to death; but how could garden tulips grow
into trees?

Three bunks, one above the other, in each corner.
The chimney was scrabbled on the east side, and men
dug out a large stone from nearby and with appalling
expenditure of energy they dragged it to serve as
hearthstone. Most other people were not so wise or
knowledgeable about the properties of a fireplace, and
used only the earth itself; but these knew that this

stone would hold heat after it was scorched hot and black, and would issue forth that same warmth for a time after the fire was burnt down.

Apathy affected men because of energy that poured out far in excess of any natural strength properly nourished and disciplined. They poked and drooped in labors with tired faces seeming to sag. One spoke to another and they looked at each other, and the one man tried to remember what he had said and the other stood doggedly trying to recall what he had heard the other say.

A ration of potatoes came round and the men put them into stewpots, wizened as they were, and some were fortunate enough to have a few turnips to go along. Later there might come pork. Aye . . . here 'twas, not as much as they'd had the day before, but it went well into the froth.

There existed another group from their regiment, two cabins away, and those toilers won the twelve-dollar prize. They were called Them Philadelphia Folk, but actually only two of the squad hailed from Philadelphia. Even the excitement of proffered bounty from His Excellency had lost much of its charm, and faint hurrahs of the Philadelphia recipients went mainly unheeded. Bonfires still burned, out in front of the fresh ranks of newly contrived shelters, and many of the soldiers lay close among beds of coals because their cabins were not chinked as yet. The corporal told off four men to proceed with chinking for an hour and then designated four more to succeed them. They were able to occupy their shelter by the time the third night came stalking.

What's gone with that blame Mum?

He's flinked, that's all.

Just flinked, plain and simple.

Maybe he's laying dead in the brush somewheres.

No, everybody's been in and out through that brush, hundreds of soldiers. They would of found him if he was laying there.

But where would he flink *to*? Ain't no place near-by.

Well, he hain't about.

If you find him, tell him his bed is ready and waiting.

Worst one in the house!

Nope. Mine is worse. I'm getting all that smoke.

Whyn't you move and take Mum's bed?

Nope. His is full of smoke too.

The corporal said, If he ain't back by roll call I'll turn him in. Then he'll get scalped if he comes back.

Git the gauntlet!

Serve him proper!

That it will!

They spoke thus nastily of their vanished comrade, but most felt a slight sense of loneliness and deprivation. They had been fond of Mum as in proximity most of them had grown fond of one another. They felt for him more embarrassment than hatred. The soldier's primary task was to keep living himself, and to cause other human beings to die, and it was a grievous thing to recognize that Mum now seemed failing somehow in these requisites.

6

WHEN Malachi Lennan was especially disheartened (he did not know that he was starving, but he was disgruntled, drained to pallor by the unsucculent fare on which he'd tried to feed), he thought of his mother.

She served as guide and goddess.

She became the serene witch unto whom he might appeal in extremity.

So he prayed to her now, saw her beyond the borders of consciousness and realm of life itself; because she was gone from him permanently.

He thought of her birth as being reminiscent of that of the Christ child. He imagined the Christ child as a woman, a moody female instead of a male, but possessed of those sundry rare virtues.

His mother's name had been Telitha; his father and other intimates called her Telly. She was a remarkable mixture—sometimes silvery, sometimes grim—but rising into blitheness repeatedly: a mingling of Pennsylvania-German and Scottish bloods, with splashes of Irish and Welsh thrown in along the way.

Malachi envisioned her as when they went into comparative wilderness which yielded eventually to pleasantness in a new place beyond. He had attained to seven years by that time, and walked staunchly and alertly as he could manage beside the horse which carried his mother. She rode on a pillion with numerous bundles and cooking pots and jars fastened around her, all containing provender and necessities for the new life ahead, and with Malachi's baby sister hanging in a sling fastened around the mother's arm and neck.

Morbid she might be at times but she did not encumber children or husband with any voiced doubts. She merely suffered in silence until brightness claimed her again. When it came it had all the spreading glory of stars . . . the best promise of the wilderness, forest, and pleasant farming country. She was a bird chirping happily, an animal running and blithe. She was a noble doe poking her head out of a thicket with fawns crowded behind her (but never a deer to be shot at).

Malachi enjoyed the draping of her loose linsey-woolsey gown and—he might not realize it at the time —but he had seen her spinning that same fabric and then weaving it into cloth. There was a loom in their home because the home was a large one, owned by his grandfather, or partly owned—owned actually by creditors who pushed them out when Grandsire died.

That was the reason why they were hitching a little to the west.

You are so sober, son, she said. So very sober.

He responded, Huh? (That was a word that came from far away, a bare admission to being drawn into the toils of conversation again.)

You are so sober, little boy. You scairt?

He said that he wasn't scairt.

You scairt about Indians?

There ain't no Indians.

These were woods, and faraway ones; and Indians lived in faraway woods. He had heard old Mr. Musgrave tell about the Indians. Mr. Musgrave had been a fur trader and had ranged the woods most of his long life. Just a month before Grandsire died, Mr. Musgrave had been sitting by their fire as he often did at night and they thought that Malachi was in bed, and the other children in between him and little sister were dead so no one had to be persnickety about them. But Malachi wasn't asleep. He was lying under the wide bed built into a corner of the room. He was hidden in shadows and all too aware and palpitating while Mr. Musgrave talked.

Well. They took this Iroquois. They told him 'bout what the Iroquois had done to them. They was Montagnais, and they give that Iroquois quite a talk. They said the Iroquois people had been mean to them— right mean—and now he was going to get a dose of the same thing.

Well. They lighted a fire. When it had caught on pretty well, they each drew out a firebrand and started sinking it gainst the fellow's skin. Then they'd back off a little and stick him again, somewhere else.

Heavens and earth! Malachi's mother was exclaiming. Heavens and earth!

Then they'd douse him with some water so's they could go on and do it again.

Lord, said Malachi's father.

That was just the start of it.

What was you doing all this time?

Nothing I could do. Just stand and watch. They was friendly to me and they kept offering me firebrands too, telling me to join in. I said I wouldn't have nothing to do with it.

I should think not! cried Telly. But I don't see how you could stand there, standing it!

I couldn't hardly. But there was nowhere else to go. So they got tired of burning him in general. Then they pulled out his fingernails and burnt the ends of his fingers where they'd pulled 'em out.

Lord! Poor devil! What was he doing all this time?

He did cry out, but I don't think as much as they thought he would. Then they burnt him—I hate to say this, Mrs. Telly—but they burnt the end, the end of his thing. His tool—his thing that made him a man. They burnt the end of it off.

Then they took a knife and scalped him.

Then they took some cherry gum off a cherry tree and heated it up in a little pot till it was steaming hot. Then they poured that over his head where they'd scalped him. Where all the blood was running down.

Telly said, I just don't think I can stand to hear any more, Mr. Musgrave.

I asked him, said Malachi's father. I asked him to tell us 'bout the Indians. You better give heed.

Well. Then they cut him down near the wrists and they pulled out some of the sinews. Just jerking hard as they could jerk. They made little kind of pinchers with sticks, and fastened 'em on to the ends of the sinews, and pulled and pulled. They couldn't get 'em all loose that way, so then they cut 'em off.

All the time they was asking me, Didn't I want to help, on that there Iroquois?

I said I didn't want to help. If they wanted him put out of his misery I'd take my rifle and do the same. They said, Oh never, never. Indian words to that effect. They said if you kilt him he wouldn't feel any pain. I said nevertheless I couldn't stand what they was doing, and I was going to scat before they started in on me the same way. They said, Oh no, I was their friend. I wasn't no enemy like that Iroquois, and I hadn't been mean to 'em or anything. But I said I was going away anyway—I couldn't stand this. They finally give me leave to go ahead and shoot, and I pulled up my rifle, and it was one of the happiest shots I ever fired in my life. Least he couldn't feel anything else after that. I was made happy that he couldn't.

Relief at the notion that the Indian would suffer no more caused Malachi to burst with sobs which sheer horror had prevented him from uttering before. He was dragged out, shaken and endeared and packed away in the bed. He went to sleep holding his hands alternately over his ears so that he couldn't hear any more in case Mr. Musgrave got to talking again, and over his eyes, squeezing hands hot and hard against the teary blobs, snuffling a little, and so pent that he felt veins knocking in his head and all through his body.

Still he strove cheerfully enough into comparative wilderness when the time came for them to leave, principally because his mother loomed dashing and able.

His father Gideon appeared every bit as able as his mother, but the child was grown closer to her. His father had been enamored of the three elder brothers—Timothy, Titus, and Philemon—who perished within the same month when stricken with the pip. It was a disease appearing to center in throat and tongue. The tongue swelled in the patient's mouth and cut off his breath. Fully a quarter of the children in their farming community had died of that disease and in the same season. Malachi was too young to remember the savagery of the onslaught and his younger sister was not yet born when it happened. He heard tell however. He heard his mother talk with friends also bereaved, and he witnessed the women weeping when they sat apart from the rest.

Telly did not haunt the graves of her lost children, though some people did. Especially Malachi's father, when he had been working hard all day. After he was fed in the evening, he'd often say that he was going to take a little walk. Malachi wondered where he went on those walks and finally followed, he followed several times. It was always the same. His father went to the little graves, each with a stone above it on which the child's name was scratched out painfully. Timothy, Titus, Philemon. Their progenitor stood weeping above. Watching, the surviving brother wept as well. He could not resist the onslaught of sorrow, although these hidden skeletons were merely names on rocks to him.

The women held seemingly endless wakes.

It was truly a black death.

Oh no, Mistress Feenson. 'Twasn't that. The Black Death was long ago, back across the water.

I've hearn tell.

Some call it the choking disease.

Some call it by other names.

Yes, Mary, I'm aware. I've even heard it called separation of the tongue.

Strikes different children different ways.

Take my Esna. She suffered paralysis, could scarcely move. My other child died of it too, but didn't have no paralysis.

Robert couldn't see to read, and he truly was a persistent reader. It paralyzed him in the eyes. He was inclined to read the Scriptures. Attempt to spell them out. He gasped and said the printed words were fair swimming in front of him.

When I think what a woman our Esna might have grown up to be! Oh, I'm not prone to complain about my sole miseries. Other people have got miseries too in different ways.

Certain. Not all the miseries of mankind or womankind are contained in that sickly pip.

But I swear she would have grown to be a comely wench! So agile and spry she was, always, as a girl. Might have been wedded by the time she was fourteen.

Well, 'twas the Lord's will.

Yes. Will of God.

Malachi's mother said abruptly and with feeling, I don't believe 'twas the will of the Lord. Not any way.

Dear Telly, how you talk! 'Tain't righteous for us to—

I don't believe 'twas the will of the Lord. I think 'twas the will of the Devil prevailing. In time to come perhaps, the Lord will display to Man the error of his ways and maybe show us an error in the treatment.

Maybe there'll be some manner to overcome it.

Maybe.

But leave us mourn no longer. We're powerless to control.

Gideon said to his Malachi, We might see some of the big trees. I been among 'em.

We had big trees to home.

Not like these trees. These are the real big ones. The true forest.

I still think, the boy insisted, that we had big trees.

What would you say to one that was a perch and maybe a third more, straight through the trunk as you sit beside it?

Malachi didn't know what a perch was.

Well then. Say a peck.

I don't know that either. I know what a rod is.

'Tis all the same. How big's a rod?

Malachi had managed to spell out a rod and then had written it painstakingly and painfully in his copybook. Sixteen and a half feet.

Then say the big tree—and I've seen 'em—I 'member this one was a plane that measured twenty-two feet right through the trunk. Must've been nigh onto fifty feet around it.

That's big, whispered the boy, awed.

Whole forests of 'em. Big trees like that. Only way to get among 'em was by Indian trail.

Malachi thought of the Indian being tortured as

related by their neighbor the eyewitness; and a constriction entered his throat and he felt chilly.

What's the matter?

Will—will we see any Indians?

Oh, you're still wherreted 'bout *that*, his father muttered contemptuously. Naw. I don't expect we'll see none. They ain't at war hereabouts.

In their tiny family caravan marched a second horse, nameless as yet and commonly called the colt, loaded heavily so Gideon could not bestride him. Also three cows plodded unrestrained; and four sows which had been attended by a boar shortly before the family departed. The sows were fastened together so they might not stray loose, and it was part of Malachi's job to herd them along with the rest of the party. Their feet grew sore and they liked to squat and chew their feet. Malachi had to be forever running back with a stick and a shout. There had been a family dog named Bijah but he was killed by another larger dog shortly after their departure when straying on romantic errand. By disposition Bijah had been rather surly so he was not deeply mourned. Malachi's chief practical wonder was whether he would be able to knit on his own galluses at night when they were camped down. He had the common chore of knitting suspenders, and he needed new ones badly. There was no disgrace about knitting: all boys he knew knit their own suspenders. But he felt that this night between the rigors of the journey and the fear of Indians which still beset him, he would be too tired to handle needles.

Given to dreams and imaginings despite weariness, he saw his dead brothers grown tall in fancy, trooping along with the party. Actually there had come close to being a First and Second Timothy, but the First Timothy was expired when Telly gave birth to him; so the Timothy who existed for some years was really Second Timothy. Malachi saw in fancy all three of The Vanished as resembling his father. They were rangy, round-shouldered, cryptic. They were possessed of inexhaustible skills with axe and rifle or shotgun.

His father won or placed high in shooting matches held occasionally by farmers and hunters of their countryside.

If Timothy, Titus, and Philemon were present, they would have had a much larger caravan, although— Halt now and consider. One or two of them might have been married by this time.

Malachi thought it more convenient to consider them unmarried.

At the last logrolling and house-raising which they attended Malachi had seen his father participate in a tree-felling contest after the main work of the day was done. Cider circulated . . . even Malachi and other boys had their sips when the old constable who presided over the jugs seemed looking the other way and especially after he went to sleep. Malachi had seen Gideon drive a small stake into the ground and point out that he would vanish that stake into the earth by felling a tree against it. He was a good axeman—all the farmers were good axemen, they had to be—but he was better than the average. He chopped down a six-inch oak in what seemed like seconds, stood close to the hacked trunk, struck the last two or three dangerous blows whilst the tree was tottering. Down it went and put the peg into the ground out of sight. There spouted hilarious shouting. Gideon won three shillings in bets.

A miniature painter ventured their way but they could not afford to have any miniatures painted, even the cheapest. The Squire ordered one done of himself and one of his wife. Two or three other neighbors ventured thus to add to their personal treasure.

However, the Lennans did possess Aunt Hasty Storr. They took her in during one mighty winter when her own little house burned to ashes. She was both elegant and eloquent with ink and a fine steel pen which she said had been cut in the German States. She made drawings of the elder members of the tribe on paper which came also from the Old Country. The bones stood out in all their faces. (Not quite so much in

Telly's because she was of a different blood.) But Gideon's bones were there to see and to be approved (or looked upon with distaste, perhaps) by all beholders. They loomed in the cranial conformation of his three elder sons. The pseudo-aunt (more comfort and hardiness to the family than most real aunts might be, which was perhaps the common characteristic of adopted relatives) said that there was no use in drawing a tiny child like Malachi—he was just a baby still —his face would emerge only as a blob. To mollify the mother, she did make a trivial sketch which was more caricature than portrait.

Their brief experience on the trail in this season had brought Malachi and his father closer together in pattern than they had been before, despite perpetual weariness which assailed the small boy. Gideon said that in the fabled South, they called every man who could work a *hand,* and boys were half-hands, or each boy was half-a-hand. At the vast age of seven, he readily admitted Malachi to be half-a-hand and even more. Malachi had already learned to swill the hogs; and could do any amount of fetching, although the buckets and baskets he used were smaller than those lugged by adults. He took cows to the woods, their own cows and several of the neighbors'. He went after them when the sun was low and they needed to come home and the milch cows needed to be milked. They had bells on the cows, and during a march such as this, the bells were stuffed with leaves or moss so that they would not jangle all the while. But at home, in native thickets and pastures, the reassuring clank of their equipment told where they might have strayed while grazing. They went willingly and came back dutifully. When they reached their own dooryards they turned, in contented fashion, at the gates of their domains. Horses would go farther afield and needed to be hobbled while they grazed. Hogs were an almighty problem for a variety of reasons. The cattle alone offered a serenity which was penetrating and all-ruling, almost like a faith in Jehovah.

Malachi knew his Scriptural quotations with the best of them. He surveyed his father now and thought, The sword of the Lord and of Gideon, except that his father had no sword.

Wondering aloud. Why does it say the sword of the Lord and of Gideon? You hain't got no sword.

'Tis symbolic.

I don't know what that is.

Well, why do we bow our heads when we pray? And why do most folks close their eyes? Because they are communing with the Almighty, and would not want to be blinded by His wrath in beholding Him. True, you can't really see Him, but 'tis a symbol of His power. Take our neighbor, that infidel, Jim Howyer. He doesn't bow his head when people pray. He just stands there staring. Righteous men believe he's marked for Destruction.

When will the Destruction come?

At the Lord's decision.

Gideon and Telly had been wedded when he was sixteen and she fifteen. She was a bereft young mother in another year and then mother-mother-mother again. They were aging now, they were up in their thirties, but aging amid vigor. Malachi looked at his father and considered Gid Lennan to be handsome. He would not be at home at a levee or in a ballroom, he was not like the Squire, but coarse strong dignity stood out. His hair had been yellow-gray from the time his son could first remember him and would be gray-yellow until true old age struck him down or until he perished earlier of—

Ah, why should he perish?

Dear God, please do not permit him to perish!

What would we do then?

The notion of his father's vanishment, with mother and baby bereaved on Malachi's puny hands, was unendurable. He banished it from his mind.

Gideon seemed to have more bones beneath the skin of his countenance than most people owned. His eyes were gray-green, wide apart, deep-set but still seeming to protrude boldly from the cavities in which they lived. His hands were vast, gnarled and seamed and scarred from labor, still seeming capable of tenderness.

He is a bold and stout person, said the boy in his thoughts. I must not let him put me away from him because of these gravestones which we have now left behind.

When there was opportunity, he said to his father, That tree you chopped—

What tree, lad? Oh *that*. They wanted to make it impossible for me. Wind was from the west so if they'd set the stake directly west 'twould have been simple. But they placed it to the southwest, so I started cutting from the east. You might have observed that I made the first cut on the east side. Then I cut a butt-kerf on the other side. Cut it more than halfway through the tree. Then 'twas time to watch the wind. If you'd been close enough you would have heard the tree crack. Had to change hands, of course. Some there be who can't do it when they're chopping, but I can. I carved in on the south side, but the weight of the tree went round to where it wasn't cut through. When she fell, she fell to the southwest just as I'd planned. Did it in a little over two minutes, 'cording to the Squire's watch. I'm a fair axeman and proud to be.

Telly had been listening. Now, Gid. Don't you puff with pride.

I ain't puffing. He asked me to tell how I done it, and I told him how.

Telly said, You are a good axeman. You're a good man, Gideon.

In such pleasantry as they seemed to be exchanging, there dwelt an intimate affection which must have existed all the while. Yet their surviving son had never sensed it until now.

7

ONE had departed, since the dance of flames suggested bonfires he recalled from earliest youth: bright leaves busheled together.

As if his mother said, Clear the yard. Sometimes she was still citified enough to term it lawn. Then out they'd all rush in revelry to the task, and heap the rich painted harvest in barren spots so as not to mar the grass. There extended patches where vegetables had lifted their stalks in warmer season. (The mother and father spoke commonly of the kitchen garden: how might it be a garden if a kitchen were not entailed?) Soon bulky heaps crinkled and bunched in gay pinks and tans and yellows; but as darkness descended the colors could be identified but feebly as they waited the leaping sprites of flame.

The boy's name was Ebenezer Mumford Foyne. Commonly he was called Mum.

Littler ones pleaded and squealed as if driven lunatic by the prospect in store, and by incense of the millions of leaves letting out their perfume even before they were charred.

Oh Mum! Please Mum, do fetch a coal!

Grinning eerily, as if he were a prentice devil ready to make rage, he walked in stripling humor to a fireplace inside and lifted up a glowing lump of oak with ready tongs. He strode out, dropped on knees beside a pile. He puffed but twice, and then the blaze went shredding ardently. The children danced and squealed, they whirled their arms on high and flapped their little hands. . . . They worshipped fire, never shrank be-

50

fore it (though they'd known tragedies with flame or they'd hearn tell; but being still so small they all forget).

They wanted to be imps.

Then a forkful lifted over . . . another pile was bursting . . . now another.

Mind there, Sissy, stand you back. Your gown came close!

The children whirled and jogged, spoke broken words of worship, gave out frail small howls which were not even words.

Neighbors came to witness, to caution further.

Ellen, don't you git too close!

Some kind minds among the neighbors remembered the lure of elder bonfires when they were young and bouncing too.

Mum had tallied nigh two years of soldiering and if one couldn't glide past sentries after that, he deserved any bullet which might come his way. The wealth of fires close at hand made it easier in inner regions. He'd been tapped for a patrol the day before and he'd lurched where hills and roadways lay and where creeks and rivers ran, not too precisely, but still they were creeks and rivers in general.

He'd not head back east for a certainty, nor to the south. British riders owned the hills and ditches. He'd heard much of Tarleton's wild people on their pounding horses, and had even caught a glimpse of Tarleton himself, or so he fancied . . . when Mum lay flat behind a log ('twas after Paoli and well beyond Chadd's Ford). In retreat he'd faded loose and lay concealed; then there befell all that push and flash of cavalry going by, so brightly uniformed and be-sabered and be-pistoled. There was dash and caper about them which the Continentals never owned; yet the Continentals could offer violent account of themselves in an even fight. They christened Tarleton a beast. He loved to ride down one lone man, or two, and leave them pulped, beaten, not able longer to see their own blood oozing. Obviously he thought it comical to observe his steeds going over them as his troopers yelled.

Mum would decamp in a westerly direction. Avoid the inns. Avoid open roads where waggon trains were meant to toil (but scarce any went toiling).

Mum wore a haversack containing his few personal belongings and they were few indeed, and he had his stand of arms complete as he had been required to furnish. He had a good rifle, a cartridge pouch, a bullet screw, twelve flints—he carried actually seventeen by now—a strong pouch or bag that would hold four pounds of ball—he had only two—and as the regulations said, Such other accoutrement as might be proper for a rifleman. He didn't know what accoutrement meant. There was a tricky sound to the word which he had heard quoted rarely by officers and never by common soldiers. Still he could have passed inspection and even a rigid one. He was better equipped as to clothing than most. He had a stout pair of moccasins only middling worn and taken from a dead man three weeks before. Oh, everyone robbed the dead, and robbed not only the dead, but frequently enough the wounded or sick and still living, unless they had friends around to prevent it. Action of the soldiery in such cases was uncertain and could not be prophesied with veracity. It depended upon circumstances and on the mood of the men themselves. Sometimes the same man would steal from others, sometimes he would endow them with attention, even clothing to keep them warm, and with such scraps of food as he might have saved for himself and now offered in charity. Some men thieved aggressively, for often it happened that thieves were set upon by others who were sick and tired of their ways and themselves were beaten and thieved. There came no rhyme or reason through the hardship and starvation. It was not a case of brightly bedizened young soldiers marching off to battle with their heads high and nostrils flaring and a steady gaze. Zexcellency was experienced enough and saddened enough and wise enough to know that a series of battles and campaigning could not long continue in this fashion. He knew that there would be little army in the end, and though Mum had thin idea of what Zexcellency knew or believed, he felt the disillusion in his young bones just as many an older man had felt it. Officers resigned by the scores (it came to be by the hundreds). An officer worried about what was going into the pot back home . . . were his wife and children starving? The haunt was prevailing, it occupied his dreams, got in the way of his soldierly duties. Soon the soldierly duties shrank in significance and proportion . . . there lived only the other dread. What of Clara? What of Lemuel? What of James, Tommy? Druscilla? Ruthie, Gram, Antonia? Indeed some came to their commanders with tears barely held back from frozen faces (faces frozen in habit of emotion or sometimes in actuality). Some were dissuaded from their intent and went back to serve and lose their blood and die somewhere along the line of the future. Many others merely dissolved, disappeared.

These reflections could be identified barely in a boy's thoughts. Yet they haunted, were puzzled and challenged and were forced to be yielded to. The word *deserter* carried an awful connotation and you thought of men picked up and striped thirty-nine or fifty strokes or even more. One man was abusive and belligerent when they caught up with him. They dragged him back. He tried lamely but rigorously to assault the guards who pulled him. He got a hundred stripes and then had salt water poured over his back and lay there, an object of contempt, and so he died. More survived, were drummed out of camp, ran the gauntlet, the savage privates croaked in Indian fashion as they beat them while they ran. Some ran too fast, were brought back surrounded by bayonets, made to run again.

One general told a surgeon while they breakfasted, Sir, this is not an Army. It is a mob.

His words were speared around, quoted and misquoted far and wide.

Mum had various small adventures as he went. He saw a bulk ahead of him as warily he moved in the open road. The bulk was a waggon abandoned. One ox was dead near it. Maybe it had been one of the team drawing the waggon, maybe not. Mum examined the waggon. It was full of barrels of pork which had rotted when the liquid was poured off in order to lighten the load. If you craved rancid pork, and many had craved it, it was your dish. Mum broke off an icicle of the stuff and carried it with him and melted it with his mouth as well as he could and sucked from time to time until at last he gagged and threw the wad from him. There were a few dead and frozen horses. They lay scrawny throughout Valley Forge as well.

He began to puzzle about the designation. He had mused on it before, they all had mused. Where was that forge indeed? Under ice. In the crick, the men said. The lobsterbacks tore it all apart and dumped it, weeks or months agone.

But why, but why?

Didn't want us to use it, I reckon.

Thought maybe they was forging out stuff for the soldiery.

For us?

Could of been.

Mum began to suffer the illusion and delusion that he bore upon his back and shoulders a monstrous weight. 'Twas an old man of the sea, an old man of the hilltops. He knew not where it came from but still it perched. He could feel its claws grinding through his shabby deerskin hunting shirt and crunching talonwise upon flesh and bone. Why ride upon me? came his gaunt protest. He even turned his head to see if he could find it squatting, but no, but no—there lumbered on him only burden of night and cold . . . ah, lie down somewhere.

Suddenly the smoky realm from which he had deserted seemed to lure and beckon. Mum even turned and tottered a few paces, cutting back along the route he'd come.

A rabid wind declared, Hold yourself upon the ground.

And die.

He coughed out some muddled words . . . didn't recognize and could not translate anything he said. A-prowl upon that misery of road and path he swung, heading to the west again. Horses had marred the solid litter of the way, their dreary turds lay piled. He passed a toppled cart, one wheel still attached, the other gone to Lord-knew-where.

Mum stiffened, saw a light, a window's brightness, a house his reft mind recognized. A house with warmth and safety—

Never safety.

If they were of American persuasion, with stark rebellion in their hearts, they'd call the soldiery.

Then he'd be striped.

The gauntlet. *Oh-ah-oh-ah-oh-ah-oh-ah.*

If they were still king's folk, they might assault him while he lay inert, might smother him with goose-stuffed mattresses. He'd heard gossip of matters like that. All had heard. So many soldiers . . . been smothered—

Still he went lurching toward the light.

He halted, stood slumped, and worshiped this beam.

He'd heard Roman Catholic boys and men a-talking, something about religious candles—maybe these wan beams were such.

He forced his feet to go a-prowling on. A structure other than the house loomed in front and to one side. A wide-spaced door seemed open to the south but low, so low. Mum's feet were a-stumble tripping over straw, so much strewn straw and thin but solid too.

There permeated a smell. *Yell to the hogs and let them know I've come.* His taut drawn lips tried to shape the cry with which men greeted swine since there was first a piggery. *Oh, sooey, sooey, sooooey.* . . . The few soft syllables pressed out, but it was scarce a summons; and no big bodies lifted lumbering, in grunt came.

Mum had dropped into the empty hog house and went blindly forward on his hands and knees. His rifle struck against the door and faltered him. He swung the weapon to one side and blundered on. The hogs smelled strong but seeming warm as well.

Good shelter—here—away—

And solid walls around.

The ugly wind can find me not.

At first he heard the labor of his own hurt breathing, then he was deeply in collapse. . . . Perchance, I think, perchance I die. . . . It seemed that he was screwing at his eyes, or someone was, to force them open.

A wan brown light approached. He saw it coming, watched a mingled patch of shadows and the shafts of gleam, yet he could not manage up the strength to discipline his weakness, to go beating for his weapon. . . . Didn't know . . . where was his rifle laying?

There lies no powder in the pan.

Can't fire it.

I'm just too tuckered.

So watch the lanthorn heading forward.

And lilting down, that beggar's light.

A-halting at the door.

A girl's pale voice spoke out. Don't you dare to move. I got a pistol here.

Drearily he felt his breath go from him. He must have said some words as he was sighing, but he couldn't count them.

What say? The girl came closer, or she held the wan brown light much nearer, he didn't know.

He said it once again, this time he managed. I don't care what you got.

You be a soldier?

Yup.

King's or ourn?

Ourn, he said. You be king's people here?

He was surprised . . . in vagueness. . . . He heard her laugh come tittering.

You ask that of my pa and he would thrash you black and blue. But he ain't here. I got to mind the place myself, for Ma ain't fit. That's why I carry out this pistol.

What ails your ma?

She's just plain tired all the time. Granny Stern come round to see her and she called it weariness of the heart. She just lays and sleeps, like I said, and then cries herself to sleep again. She's acted so ever since my brother Paul was slain.

Where did . . . Paul get killed?

At Paoli. In the Massacre.

I was there.

Paoli?

Yup.

He heard her breathing heavily (like unto quiet tears). Then ran her voice again.

I want to hold this light a trifle closer.

Why?

To see what kind of face you got. Hold tight.

Mum lay huddled, motionless, the light drifted nigher, nigher, he could feel its heat.

She drew it back on a sudden.

Why, she said, you're but a boy.

I ain't no boy.

How old be you?

Sixteen. I ain't no boy.

You look to be.

Don't matter how I look to be. I'm an old soldier.

That was what Paul always said he was, truly. Eighteen years of age.

That's only a couple more than what I got.

But somehow there was now the implanted notion that flesh related to her flesh had been valiant or at least engaged. He wondered dully where Paul had stood when the bullet smacked him, if indeed it was a bullet and not that sharp pierce of steel.

You bend closer and hold that there light so's I can see your face. I shown you mine. Now you got to show me yours.

The girl said, I'm sixteen too. Studying to be an old maid.

You hain't got a man?

Not now.

She had put down her pistol, and she held the tan lanthorn in both hands and her face crept out into the reflection: entire head and part of the neck and shoulders. No matter what warfare he had witnessed he was still too inexperienced in measurement of humankind to dissect her face according to previous knowledge gained, and say, She betokens this or that in character. All he knew was that he had not been prepared for such charm. Her hair seemed brown and chopped briefly after the fashion of these perilous times when there could be spared little opportunity among girls, be they of country or city, to go plaiting, braiding, curling. Her hair was cut short but there was wildness in it and her forehead was high underneath. He thought the eyes were pale. (He found out later they were blue.) The lips looked like a pulp of fruit. He'd seen an older neighbor girl like that before he trotted off to be a soldier. Her reputation was bad. Her brothers tried to avenge it by throttling and dragdowns and fisticuffs, but still other men sneaked out in the dark and met her: and there were some yowling small fry at home, no matter how the relatives resented community understanding of their problem.

This new girl's lips might be a joyous pulp but Mum foretold that she was pure.

He mumbled, I can't understand why you're not wedded.

I tolt you I wasn't spoke for. Not no longer.

Were you spoke for, before?

We sort of believed. That was all she told him.

Was this feller shot down too?

He got took prisoner, and put upon an English ship and then they fetched word that he had died. I guess they starved him quite to death. They've starved an awful lot.

Mum said with some excitement, while he had not actually applied the designation to himself before, I'm starving now.

You do look peaked. Want I should fetch you something?

He bantered her question back and forth in his brain. He wanted to shout, *No water, no soldier! No rock, no soldier!* but had not the strength, and realized that anyway she wouldn't understand. The fact that she owned power and resource to bring him food was hard to grasp by any legs or feathers as it flew.

Whatever she might offer (a notion still assailable and full of doubt. You could not just say casually in this empty-stomached and empty-throated world, I'll fetch you food to eat. It was not to be believed)—

I can't just keep calling you You. What's your name, Missy?

Candace.

He managed a laugh. Can I call you Candy?

They all do, mostly. Even the preacher; he calls me Little Sister Candy. What you want to eat? Tell me your name.

Mum, he said.

Are you a-telling me not to speak?

No. It's Mumford, but folks call me Mum.

Then— Very well. What can you eat?

The first course was a pudding of Indian meal, molasses and butter; then came a course of veal and bacon, neck of mutton and vegetables.

This friendly heady notion replete with all sensation came storming from past and future, flooding for all time and for all the hungry, a blissful polyglot.

This plain Friend, with his plain but pretty wife with her thees and thous, had provided us a costly entertainment; ducks, hams, chickens, beef, pig, tarts,

*creams, custards, jellies, fools, trifles, floating islands,
beer, porter, punch, wine, and . . .*

Was such fare eaten twenty years before, or even
one hundred, or would it be waiting in flame for someone to cook it in the future?

Mum said, Anything you got, Candy.

There ensued a fitful fainting silence in which he
must have been living and breathing but he held no
recollection of so doing. He knew only that he subsisted in hog-shed darkness, fearing because she was
gone, waiting her return.

Mum, I don't think you ought to eat no more.

But it's so good.

'Tain't all that good. Just oatmeal mush.

Got cream on it.

Yes. But I don't think you ought to eat no more of
that headcheese neither.

It's so wonderful.

It ain't all that much good, she said. I helped Ma
pick out the meat. She got the makings from an old
Pennsylvania Dutch woman use to live nigh us.

It's right good.

But you just been swilling it.

With last scraps melting in his mouth, he considered. It was no use going into the fact that he had
plenty of excuse for swilling anything, but he felt unsteady, and there was a hurtful place in the core of
him.

Candy—

What?

You know what you done?

I don't know what you mean.

Know what you done? When you went away to
fetch this food and—and everything—you left your
pistol laying right here on this kind of curb, right on
the clean straw. You must've put in this fresh straw
after the hogs was butchered.

I guess I did, count of the smell. It kind of helped,
but—Why, here's my pistol!

Yep. I kind of slept a while and then I wakened, and you hadn't come, and I was thinking 'bout you and how you was fetching me things to eat and how kind you was and—and I put out my hand and it flopped right on the pistol. Candy, you couldn't shoot nobody with that. 'Tain't loaded. You got a flint in that lock, but no priming. You let me snap it now, I'll show you. 'Twouldn't shoot. I'll bet you hain't even got a ball in the barrel.

Well, she said, I couldn't load it. I didn't know how. Father didn't know any thing 'bout guns till he went a-soldiering. We never had any here to home, 'cept Brother used to go out and shoot with a borrowed shotgun. He got birds.

Lady Candy.

Why you call me that?

Cause you are a lady. You got that light. Let me see your face once more, fore I go to sleep.

Again there was that sound of a sigh which was more a lamentation than a mere drawing in of breath. She lifted her wan light and held it close, and there was such nobility in her manner that the boy longed to scream, Put it away! Put it down!

Even before she did lower the light away from her countenance—

Candy, I'm—I'm kind of weak. I don't want to throw up, right here in front of you. But I just might. One of the elder men, he had some nature of doctoring experience. And he said that 'count of very little food we've had to eat, our stomachs had shrunk down. If you put a lot of food in 'em, as I just done—well—

Politely she said, I'll go now. Go in to Mother, and let you sleep. I would—She seemed considering even as she spoke—I would invite you into our house, and put you in a regular bed. But there's Ma. She might start weeping again.

Oh I'm right happy here. Just let me sleep.

She went away and let him sleep and there were torrents flowing in his ears, his head felt light as any thistle seed a-blowing, and then felt pressured again with the blood a-pounding. He wondered about his middle; he cleared his throat, thought of throwing up deliberately to ease that ache inside.

'Twasn't necessary. The ache diminished and he thought again with more excitement of more food to come, and so at last he slept, and so at last the armies strode and wrestled far beyond him. He heard, as all soldiers must hear from time to time, the snap or roar of firing, heard howls that went with it, the shrill yelling of certain wilderness riflemen with a long howl of the lobsters coming on. War was panic and trickery— his half-identified meditations told him that, and yet far, far beyond, off there in multiple struggling distances, there boomed that notion of a cannon's note. From somewhere Zexcellency came riding, and the men cried out to honor him with all the breath they could draw into their lungs and force out again through their throats.

Candy said that her mother, one Purity Garrett, was read out of Meeting when she wedded Candace's father, one Lewellyn Pembroke. He had toyed with Quakerhood but considered the Society of Friends too restricted in code and antic for his taste. The girl described him as a seeming mild and restrictive person with a stony core of inflexibility. She did not employ these words (could not have done so, nor could Mum have understood them aptly) but she managed to convey the notion, and he was open to receive it.

As a youth and now again nearing forty her parent was honest and bold.

Father went to the fighting as well as my brother did. Got himself a precious bad wownd at the Brandywine Crick. So now he's home for good, 'cept being gone on this errant.

Your family's a fighting one.

When were you birthed, Mum?

Tenth of February. When were you?

Sixth of October.

So I'm the elder, Candy.

True. Want I should fetch you another munch?

He giggled briefly and explained that his innards were still protesting the generosity of provender she had fed him twice before.

Like there was a little man somewhere inside me, and he's plumb scandalized.

But we got to succor him, Mum. Next time I go houseward I'll fetch you back some hard-cooked oatcake. You might nibble that, a bit at a time. And course I milked Dimity last eventide. Bring you a gourd of her best.

You're so kind to me, Candy. So very kind.

She nodded her fair brown head in acceptance. It's like I was doing it for my brother. And for—for—

What was this other feller's name?

Constance. Constance Pettywell.

But you wasn't never Cried?

Not Cried in Meeting. Not yet. We hadn't been. Not—

I take it he was a Friend. Like your mother?

She shook her head. The Pettywells are all Congregationalists. True and staunch.

Then after lengthy pause she said, We would a-been pledged. If the Army hadn't broke out.

And after an even lengthier time. Mum—

What say?

You hain't tolt me why you're here. What you're doing. Why—first I thought you was kind of scout. But how could a scout be laying in a pigsty? Scouting out nothing but straw and old smells? Then—I keep hazarding on it—

He confessed to this girl, he would have been able to confess anything to this girl. He muttered, I run away.

The admission of guilt amounted to publishing it as if upon a broadside done in printer's ink. But his words were so weak and wounded that the girl bent toward him to hear more aptly. He uttered his confession again in louder pitch, and it became a shout resounding from a belfry.

I run away!

He progressed through an entire session of court in instantaneous process: he was the accused, prosecutor, defender, jury, judge, and baliffs, all ground into one miserable personage. He wished to scream *guilty*, but could achieve only a growling sound.

Candy slapped her hands over her eyes and began to cry. You're a deserter! God pity you!

No, I hain't no deserter! I just run away, I tell you! I just run! To be a deserter you got to—why, you got to *desert*. You got to desert! Real and truly!

The girl kept blubbering. Heaven have mercy! Heaven have m-m-m-m-ercy! Her lips mangled the words.

You don't understand! If I was an officer, I could resign. You want to know how many officers resigned since Paoli? Just scores of 'em. Some say hundreds. They get scared 'bout what's going on at home, or they get wretched with something or other, or maybe they don't like what their commanders tell 'em, but anyway, they can *go*. All they got to do is *resign*. 'Tain't the same with us privates. Some of us privates have seen a lot more war than the officers. But we can't resign, much as some might want to do it. We got to stay. We got to *serve*. When an officer resigns and won't be balked, Zexcellency has got to accept his resigning. He just *has* to, 'cording to the law of the land. I mean law of the Army. Oh, I was sposed to leave my weapon, too. This here gun and the accoutrements to go with it—my pouch, bullets and corkscrew and stuff, and flints. 'Cording to directive, I was sposed to leave 'em all, but I didn't. So am I a robber, Candy? I guess that makes me one. They got a hard time acquiring arms and munitions and that's why we're sposed to leave 'em. But these was my own, I tell you. They was the property of my cousin Ralph, and he left 'em to me when he died of consumption. He was a great hunter fore he got so sick, and he called me in and took my hand. Little Mum, he always called me. Little Mum, he says, you go fetch my gunnery, and by that he meant his rifle and all, and I brung 'em to him and he fair put 'em into my hand, or tried to, then he grabbed my hand and his own was so thin and kind of weak—I 'member how the blood vessels stood out on it like they was about to burst and he says, These are yours. I ain't got anything else to leave, but I want you to have 'em.

So I won't let the Army take 'em back!

Now he was crying also. The two sixteen-year-olds sat together and wailed not in concert but somewhat in rivalry.

I didn't have no bayonet for my rifle, but I got one forged. You take a look. You'll see how it slides right down on the barrel and it can be fastened there with one turn of the screw. All in all, you take my rifle and with the bayonet and ramrods and warm farming wire, and the brush on the farming wire, and the catteridge box and the rounds of catteridges already rolled up in paper, and the flints and all that—why it's worth—the whole thing—I'll bet you—five pounds if it's worth a farthing! What'll five pounds buy, anyway? Pay a man, and a good one, for two weeks' work. Or it might buy fifty bushels of coal. Or fifteen cords of wood. I know I'm disobeying orders from Zexcellency, but I can't help it. He'd published an order that no soldier was to carry off any arms if they was fit for use. They'd be bought, and hard money paid for 'em. They'd be valued and then paid for. But I couldn't help it. Zexcellency didn't know how Ralph lay there and faded, fore Heaven gathered him in; and he put 'em in my hand. Actually. So to speak. We ain't got as many catteridges as them lobsterbacks. Ain't allowed to carry 'em. Paper and powder are too hard to come by. But they can sew destruction, Candy. I done it myself. I killed lobsters just the way Zexcellency said. He tolt us that he recommended a load for our first fire with one musket ball, four or six or maybe even eight buckshot, 'cording to the size and strength of our pieces. He said if the enemy was received with such fire and not more than twenty or thirty yards distant, he had no doubt that they'd be repulsed. Well, you heard. This ain't no child's play and I ain't no child. I'm a man and I carry a gun and I know how to make use of it. All sorts of these fellers are silly. There was one who forgot to stop up the end of his powder horn and when the powder flashed off in the pan of his gun, the powder horn exploded and a whole gang of soldiers got burned. People have died from being kicked in the breast by heavy loaded guns. There was one feller only a year or so ago, 'bout the time I first joined the Army, he loaded his gun double, didn't realize that he had, and then when he fired it that shot went through a double partition of inch boards, right through one board of a bed or what you want to call it: bunk or berth. It went right through the breast of the man who was sleeping there and he never knowed what hit him; and then that load struck a stone chimney on the other side and you could see the place where it struck. These are powerful things and it's righteous I should have mine own, 'count of it was given to me. 'Twas deeded fair and square, right on the edge of eternity, with death's breath blowing gainst my cousin. These things are *mine*. I aim to keep 'em!

She snarled, and he orated in contention, as no animals housed in this shack had ever done. In his last splintery instant of existence before he left this world, Mum would remember how Candace looked as she faced him. It was full daylight now. The sun was shining brokenly. He saw her with the old quilted comforter coat swaddled around her, her hands clenched inside her mittens, the quilted bonnet on the back of her head, her burnished hair seeming to blow wild in front of it, her eyes puffed pale, and seeming to be extended little windows through which you might peer to see the soul blazing within.

For pity sakes! You know so much about your rifle, you go and use it! You hear? Go back where you belong!

All right, God damn it, I will!

She gasped her low-pitched female sobs and hurled them at him and at the entire realm of existence as women have always done, will always do. The voice, broken . . . *oh-ho-ho-oh-ho-ho* and she went storming out of the place.

There would need to be vibrant response somewhere or other and already he heard it, a plaintive wavering voice crying in the background beyond Candy's lamentation. Voice saying, Candace, Candace, and all bubbly and frail and yet coming through to his ears.

It was the mother. She'd heard their yells, even inside that house and lying on her mourning bed from which she did not desire to rise in ordinary spells; but there was nothing ordinary about this circumstance; so she had risen, come to the door with a blanket round her, like a snowbird perched sadly upon the steps of her own house.

Their voices sounded: one of them so thin, so far away, yet the boy could hear what they said.

Candy. What ails you? Why you hollering?

The girl snorted and bubbled, and doubtless was wiping her face as she strove to recover. It's just that —Ma—I got to feeling bad. I got to—thinking 'bout —them being gone and fallen. I got to thinking 'bout them being dead.

I know, Daughter. I know. Weak little words of understanding were like a junco's peeping about the winter itself. Then the door closed.

Mum readied himself for the long striding back to Valley Forge. The consideration of his penalty was not even active in his brain. Away off there somewhere was the notion of a scourging gauntlet, cold shirt ripped from his back, the lash resounding perhaps amid his own cries, perhaps he could restrain himself, say nothing, feel only the bucket of salty water splashed against his back when the castigation was over. Or would it be the gauntlet, or would he be tied up to freeze against a tree, or— He barely cared. That was all blank and miles ahead of him. He knew only that he must return as he had told this damsel that he would do. He was confident, or at least hopeful that she might fetch him some article of food to sustain him on the journey. Oatcake. She'd talked about that before. . . .

He readied himself as well he might, looked to his arms, examined his moccasins, tried to arrange rags of wrapping left to him. All the time he was thinking, Candace, please come so I may start.

It was gratifying to hear her steps in the coldness. When finally she appeared she bore a leathern pot in one hand and a wove-wrapped parcel in the other.

First off, she said, Dimity offers her best. You down it now, to give you power to journey.

He drank the milk steadily without removing the hoop-bound pottle from his mouth. He was entertaining filmy notion of some way in which he offered a toast to the unseen cow.

Candy gathered the pot back into her hand and looked in to make sure he had drained it.

She offered then the chunk she had wound up in her scarf. 'Tis oatcake and cheese to ration you.

No oatcake and cheese, no soldier!

What say, Mum?

Army talk. Don't pother to pay heed.

But you are going back—

All the way, Missy.

And you swear you won't take to straying again?

Pledge it. No matter what waits.

Pledge it again, she whispered. Swear in the memory of them that's gone before.

Pledge. But I daren't take this. This shawl or whatever—

'Tis a tippet of mine own. I got another, and part of another is half-knit already. The wool came from off our own sheep and I helped my pa to shear it and I carded it too, and then I spun the yarn. I want it should help to warm you in parlous times.

Mum hesitated for a moment, then bowed his head and gathered the gift and held it against his chest.

Candy, I crave—

You crave—?

Candy, may I come back again? I'll not be fleeing, I'll be as good a soldier as I can—

Course you will, came the low steady voice. Course you will. I'll greet you with pride, if'n—when you come.

Candy. Might I kiss you good-bye?

Their mouths met. They kissed good-bye.

8

AFTER I'd left Medford Town, I heard a horse a-coming up behind me pretty fast. The horseman had caused houses to spring to life behind me, but of course I didn't know that. Spatter of hoofs come closer and closer, and I concluded I'd better get out of the way, and did get out of the way. Pressed off into some bushes until that intent rider passed me by, and course he didn't observe me, and I didn't see him 'cept for the bulk and rush.

I went striding on, and the first farmhouse was only a little way ahead. Candles had been lit, as I could witness through the windy. A man was standing there, examining some kind of gun. Looked like a fowling piece but I couldn't be sure: he was weighing it in his hand, up and down. I journeyed on.

Soon I come to another dwelling, and lights too, and people hastening in their nightclothes.

Beyond that all the places along the road was lighted, and in some I'd hear doors opening and shutting, and hear people talking, too—kind of calling back and forth. I couldn't make out what they said.

Next place, a horse was fetched out the stable, and a young girl led him round to the front. Feller 'bout my size and build—he rushed from the house, carrying a gun and what seemed to be a powder horn and shotpouch; and just before I got there he mounted and galloped off, ahead.

I couldn't figure what was in the wind.

I'd been fishing, and then voyaged in a sloop all the way to Jamaica, and helped unload our ketch. Junk fish they was, but the Jamaicans fancied 'em.

That's where I long to be now, 'stead of in this soldiery. I'd list aboard a vessel and serve as a fighting sailorman, if there was any ships to journey on, but none there be.

Been at sea since I was small . . . I was a cut-tail. You don't know what that is. Well, every fish I'd ketch with a line—like cod, say—I'd hack out a triangle from the tail, and that would show that the fish was mine, to be distributed accordingly. Practically all the schooners had cut-tails aboard. But my salt water days was past, though I didn't know it then.

In gaunt desire I reckon others dream of meats when they are hungriest. Think of racks of ribs, haunches of venison, beef cutlets. Think of spits groaning under the weight of turkeys heftier than sheep, and the Pennsylvanians dream of scrapple fried gently in a big hot spider. Or sausages with stuffing popping out whilst they're a-cooking.

I think of things that swim the waters, so thick sometimes in streams that a horse could never step there thout killing 'em in multitude; and a harvest in some other currents where they could be ladled out in baskets thout even risking bait. But mainly I smell the brine and panic for a-voyaging, as much as I yearn for cod.

I'd consider not a sturgeon three or four yards in length, but sprightly fellers weighing maybe a dozen

pounds, and being hawked for twopence or three-
pence at the most. Salmon I've commonly hungered
for as well, and do not scorn the notion of shad when
many people do. There's legend of a family who considered it bad taste to display their shad, though all
were fond of it, when neighbors termed the shad as
hog feed, fit fare only for hogs a-roaming in the streets.
But this family truly fancied shad, and wished to dine
on it; they had their platters handy and were just
a-serving up the stuff, when someone approached their
outer door, and banged on it; and those weaklings
dared not open up their house until the luscious shad
had been hid away! That certainly was to their shame.

I've thought of our voyages to the Black Islands,
as some of us termed Jamaica. How we'd journey
loaded with trash fish which sold so briskly in those
tropics. Other cargo would be aboard as well: timber
in the way of planks, a ready sale. We'd be carrying
sometimes the Negroes who had misbehaved as slaves
and were hawked for sale in that distant place. Although they'd yell and croon about it and take enormous oaths about being honest characters henceforth
if they was allowed to remain back home in our Colonies.

Then down at the Island, once we'd unloaded, our
return cargo was dragged aboard . . . rum and sugar,
wine or spirits (some they manufactured from the
cane, like rum; some kinds were made from fruits).
And coffee, coffee, coffee, to substitute for tea which
was already beginning to be frowned upon, 'count of
the tax we had to pay. And chocolate too.

We'd fetch it all back.

In the very notion of this extravagance, I smell the
salt again, and wonder where the pirates are.

'Twas the same way all along, with people rising
and alert. Men and boys exploded from behind me
and when they loped past I could see that they was all
armed.

Begun to get a little light, fore I reached Lexington.

There they were, lined up—doubtless the same ones who'd passed me a-riding and many more. 'Twas bright enough to see faces by the time I got to the Common.

I witnessed my old schoolmaster. Master Twelf, he was; and I observed many more people that I knowed. All they said to me was, Welcome, Winny Winsted. Go get your gun.

Couldn't conclude what was afoot.

They said that the redcoats was coming, though I hadn't seen none. But they said, Don't stick around here thout any gun. They're coming. If you listen careful, you can hear 'em marching. So I took their word and put my ear nigh the ground. Sure enough, even the ground was going rub-a-dub. The lobsterbacks was marching up along the road.

There'll be firing hereabouts. 'Tain't wise for you to be unarmed.

I lit out for home, fast as I could speed.

Our house was luminated up a bit, and I saw my mother walk past the windy before I got to the door. I whooped out, and she recognized me, and rushed a-hastening. She was customed to my coming in at odd hours and times, 'cause one never knew when those boats would make harbor. She hadn't seen me in a long while.

She give me her kindly greeting.

I'll go and get your father's musket.

I looked round the kitchen and you never see such a mess. There was a couple of kegs turned on their sides, and turnips all over the floor.

Ma, what on earth?

She says, Oh, that's just count of some black pease I had put away for the Committee.

Black pease?

I didn't know what she meant.

She says, 'Twas gunpowder. We had it secreted here and there. The Committee fetched it to me, and I been concealing it. Had I known you was on the way, I would have rolled some cartridges for you.

I told her that the lobsterbacks was approaching and I'd heard the very batter of their feet.

Yes, she says. Still, I don't think 'twill be much of a battle. I doubt if anybody will be shot. Sounds to me like it's all a bungle. But you better take the gun and pouch and your fraction of powder here in this horn, and go.

So I gathered 'em up and went to the door. I complained that I was right hungry, but she said there wasn't no time to eat now.

You got to take your place. The Committee 'spects you, I know they do. If your father was alive, he'd be there already.

She hugged me good-bye, and I went out the door and stood momentarily a-listening.

Behind me she repeated, I don't think 'twill be much of a battle. If a single shot is fired, I reckon 'twon't be heard past the Corners.

Precisely at that moment there come the first shot, long e'er I could hasten to take my place in the ranks. It snapped out, and then you could hear it echoing and echoing.

'Twouldn't be heard past the Corners?

It went *dong* and the resounding started in.

Away from the Common and out the village and off, that shot went whirling. Echo, echo, echo. Redeeming itself again, and wafting across meadows, past the ditches and cool springtime fields, and over woodland and away away away. Just one single shot, but it was going all around the world, and people were a-sensing it, whether they listened consciously or no. They would be hearing it for all time, and on through history, until no longer there was any man to listen.

Iᴛ was upwards of twenty years since George Washington had observed Braddock alive or dead—he saw him dead the last time, he helped in the lifting of the wounded man who was filling up with blood, remembered the mass of his officers left to puff and swell in wilderness with first the Indians around them and then the flies and finally the animals to tug at corpses. But when he saw Braddock in recollection it was not in final ignominy of the man's defeat and death. Instead he saw General Braddock as being absurd, no matter how many years he had in the service and those were already more than forty. He saw the martinet, sitting erect and haughty in the chariot he had purchased from Governor Sharpe of Maryland. It was a handsome vehicle—blue, red, with gold on the wheels—and Braddock's driver sent it dashing on cranky traces which were the only ones available. The thing bounded, bumped, tore, and it would seem that the puffy major-general might be jolted to a pudding. But he kept on for a time with his entire staff flying behind him on their horses, and musicians of the Grenadier Guards beating out their traditional march as the crazy caravan rumbled.

Such panoply might have had some military effect on wide-eyed peasants of France or the Lowlands. It did not impress the Indians hereabouts for there was none to witness. The Indians were far ahead, hived in brush beyond high hills.

Washington heard the tale told of Braddock's sister who was a gambler pure and simple, and wagered all her worth away at the tables of Bath in England, till there was not a farthing left and the boards still gave her back nothing. The woman put an appropriate noose about her neck and, swinging high, let herself die accordingly. She awarded cogitation to a horrified public in a note she left behind.

To die is landing on some silent shore.

Poor Fanny, Braddock was alleged to have commented when they fetched the news to him. I always thought she would play till she would be forced to tuck herself up.

Such comment might have been germane summary of the general's entire attitude toward war and life itself. He did have a little sense jounced into him during the banging rambles in the chariot. He bounded up to Fort Cumberland in the racked vehicle and received his appropriate salute of seventeen guns; but the chariot had vied with too many rocks, logs, and chuckholes, and was become a quaking wreck. It was dragged into an appropriate thicket where nature might complete the ruin which man had begun.

When Washington visioned it, even after all this time, he saw it going down as a hulk to shelter squirrels, mice and other critters—the birds above all—to be wallowed with snow and the long season of winter, and then to rot further in each warm season until naught remained but a few shreds of metal which in further time would vanish under leaf mold.

In like manner he saw the hastier vanishment of one young officer representing all who would succumb.

You strive to the Army, Angie? Or the law?

If 'tis all the same to you, Worthy Parent, I would prefer the Army.

Ah yes, ah yes. So did my brother.

Take Franklin, thought His Excellency. In time, great men would try to sum him up for what he was. In time the world would try to reckon his accomplishments, discover and catalogue the treasures he stored within his remarkable self, and then gave back unto the world with cheer and harmony.

What is the lightning? What is this fierce snap and quiver in the air?

And so the kite, and so the string, the key, and fire coming down.

He set the type for the Philadelphia Assembly . . . as keenly apt as when he set type in galleys long ago: a printer's devil and then a printer.

He was urgent in our American spirit, reckoning and contriving.

This had not been done before? Why should we not perform it now?

Braddock needs waggons (it is 1755). Why do we not give him waggons? The Assembly does not even build the road this general declares for, and two dozen waggons are all that they can find.

So he needs waggons.

Franklin will find him waggons.

So he needs packhorses by the hundreds? Franklin will provide.

They'll all be lost when the Indians send them a-scurry, or strip them of hides when soldiers have died or are still a-dying.

Was Franklin squeamish and betrayed? Often he felt squeamish and betrayed; so he needed to assemble his strength again, as a fighter gathers in his muscles and learns to expend them more wisely when he buffets in the future.

The boy officer lies sightless but still staring, flat in summer woods among brothers and underlings and overlings, his round skull stripped and anointed with the red treacle of one-time vigor. Even in noxious weather the small bugs find him and the eyes puff up, until finally they too are nibbled out as well.

What an ending for the packs of good things! *Six pounds of loaf sugar. Six pounds of muscovado sugar.* The Shawnee would like the sugar. They like sweet things, they howl and say their word for them.

Two pounds of tea. One of green, one of bohea. The Indians sniff suspiciously at these, and so at the six pounds of ground coffee and the six pounds of chocolate which were in the pack as well.

Eyes vanished, the very orb of head seeming thrown back in rigid denial, as if to decline to accept the face it is compelled to wear.

Might we not have been of kin? Call the name Wessyngton, Wassington, Washington as you choose. Call the native region the East Riding of Yorkshire, call it Northants, call it Kent.

What a long way from his little town of Chilham!— and everyone knew the castle on the wide hill. Every able child in the village had climbed the steps of the Digges family, or run upon their wall or herded on their grass. 'Twas home and seat of the Diggeses, but seemed better to belong to the babies of Chilham. And so too, strangely, did the pub and the valley below, the shop where groceries might be bought if one had cash and desire.

Six pounds of rice, six pounds of raisins, one Gloucester cheese.

You strive to the Army, Angie?

What else among those groceries, oh prime red hen with blood now turned to black, and dried with beetles still sticking in it?

Why, one keg containing twenty pounds of the best butter, 'lieve you me.

To be purchased in a shop?

Assuredly, if one has not the facilities one might possess in his home.

Ah yes, I understand. Then you enjoy butter?

Aye, that we do.

So do vagabond Indians as well.

Let us not forget the final items in the load. *Two dozen bottles of old Madeira wine.* Hail again! And finally, *Two gallons of Jamaica spirit.*

And I ask, Do Indians and French know what to do with wine and spirits from those far islands?

Aye, that they do and did!

The news comes to Franklin. Much bad news had come to him at other times in his life. Much bad news will follow, but there will still be brave good tidings so many times as well.

Just now he is occupied with thought of those waggons and the horses to go with them and the drivers. Pray for the mistaken commander who went that way in boldness and shared the redcoat disaster.

Oh my, says Benjamin, and he goes to walk, but now is followed even in the streets by men who cry out and try to tag the skirts of his coat and seek to impell him to say how much restitution shall be awarded (to folk in York County and Lancaster County who supplied those turnouts for the expedition) and just when it will be paid. Franklin feels that the indebtedness must be handled promptly and says that it shall be.

But grief and blessing to you, man! Do you ask that I set the day and hour in this very moment?

Waggons again. The busy press which in his mind is turning out its leaflets. Waggons! From here to New York and on to Boston. Along with Philadelphia, these cities shall be the crux of our new-fledged Americanism. Good roads shall be built, and the wheels must turn.

There are horse blocks scattered throughout our cities now, and some few along the way. Why not a horse block every mile? Now, how do you measure a mile? Why, I shall measure it nicely. I shall measure the circumference of a wheel upon my waggon. I shall invent a machine to coordinate the information supplied by the wheel, and that machine shall inform me when we have journeyed a mile; and I shall stop, mark the point, and the horse block shall be put there. Every mile marked by a stone! The stones are solid. They'll be capably distributed when I have done this task. The men shall come with larger stronger conveyances for stones, and they'll be put out and set up properly, and marked.

The mind that dwells in me is sportive, alert, always inquiring. As a boy I went to England, did not drink as the other printers drank, so they laughed and called me the Water American. Now in sagacious years I am in France, and here I find honor and gallantry to be offered out by the Court of Louis, and indeed all of France. They recognize how honorably we strive!

But, General Washington considered, My recollection has risen rapidly as I might gauge my speed in a fox chase over my own acres or those of the gallant bespectacled Fairfax who races alongside. It is 1755 again, and the Indians and the few practical French pick off the wretches of Braddock's pack with persisting skill. I am still ill of health, and have jolted disheartening leagues to become but a fellow rag in this torn pattern of madcap retreat and butchery.

Franklin again, Franklin forever! Raise it like a bragging shout of the Loyalists, and take note of the adjuration which he addressed to General Braddock.

> *The only danger I apprehend of obstruction to your march, is from the ambuscade of the Indians, who, by constant practice, are dexterous in laying and executing them; and the slender line, nearly four miles long, which your Army must make, may expose it to be attacked by surprise on its flanks, and to be cut like thread into several pieces, which, from their distance, cannot come up in time to support one another.*

And what said Walpole? His wit was sly and bitter as ever. He spoke of *the slowness of General Braddock, who does not march as if he was at all impatient to be scalped*. Walpole could sit in London with his quill dipped into a pot of vitriolic ink and never even guess the reply which was offered to Franklin.

> *These savages may indeed be a formidable enemy to raw American militia, but upon the King's regular and disciplined troops, sir, it is impossible that they should make an impression.*

What wrote I indeed to my brother, when speaking about my first affair-at-arms, when I was in the wilderness, at but twenty-two. I fortunately escaped without any wound; for the right wing, where I stood, was exposed to, and received all the enemy's fire; and it was the part where the man was killed and the rest wounded. *I heard the bullets whistle, and believe me, there is something charming in the sound.*

Oh I was young, was young, and the bullets seemed young too in recollected spasm. They still drone in my ears across a long generation of time, after Walpole had caught my words from whatever source and let them reach the ears of *Georgius Secundus*.

The British king jeered at my statement about the bullets, nor can I blame him now.

He would not say so, if he had been used to hear many.

Years later I was asked if I had ever made such utterance. All I could tell them was, quietly, If I said so, it was when I was young.

Now I lie in my tent. They call it a marquee, save the name, but I would stretch shelterless upon the ground as I have lain so often before, were it not for the crying need of a commander. My faithful Billy Lee has found me a bearskin robe. Whence he got it I know not, nor would ask, and thereon my blankets are spread, and I am stretched among them.

In this desolate region which I aided in selecting, my army crouches round about. The sick and the hale as well, though mercy alone knows why there should be any hale. But such there are bound to be. We had them in the far-gone wilderness, and so often, so young at the time, I was among the hale, but sometimes listed as ailing.

Ailing even then. I was jolted long distances in the bed of a waggon when we went to that rendezvous beyond the Monongahela, and I was barely up and scarcely about on that fatal July the Ninth when the yapping and the well-aimed shots tore from the woodland. I remember the Frenchman who led them on, we

knew him by his garb. He was an officer and a bold
one at that, but hastily he dumped himself upon the
ground when our riflemen put him there.

I recollect how my first horse went down under me.
He was sinking, going forward. He tried to blow out a
whinny—What was this? Had he balked at a jump?—
and then his legs were gone and I was pitched forward,
losing my boots in the stirrups as even he quaked in
sudden death. Someone was mounted and coming past,
I knew not who he was, but snatched at the bridle rein
and motioned and he came down and I went aloft into the saddle.

There were hundreds of them, we heard later six
hundred. We knew not at the time, but there were
enough to keep the storm persistent. A hundred were
sending out their sporadic fire; another hundred were
ramming loads; another hundred were lifting their
arms a-sighting. Every tree, every log had its denizen,
each thicket held its throng.

Hitching and driving, I got myself close to General
Braddock and saw his countenance. There was that in
his expression which seemed to cry, Why don't they
come out and fight like men? This is not the way it
was in Holland! This is not the way it was in the rising
of the Forty-five . . . not Culloden.

I desired to scream in extenuation, Ah no! 'Twas not,
my dear General. This is in the woodland of the new
world and peopled by woodland creatures of a fashion
unknown to you or to any other English, or by the
Scots at Culloden. One of your crested ones was there
as well, but in the other ranks: one Mercer to be sure.
He stood and rallied with those who spat out their bullets in the cause of the Young Pretender, and now he's
on your very own staff. Wars have thus their way of
disporting the enforcements.

The very cannoneers were streaking away from
their guns and was it for this that the cannon had been
boosted and dragged across a hundred streams of one
size or another, all those green and luscious and threatening miles? My God, give them canister, sweep the

woods, I heard one a-crying, and his yells turned out
to be mine own and then my second horse went down.
I was lucky. He threw me loose, though bullets pasted
through my very clothing. I sought to be a cannoneer,
rallied some to support me, I touched the piece off and
the charge went into the woods with lust. If those bat-
teries had stayed and fought we might have harried
that stretch of coverts. No Indian will stand and fight
or crouch and slay when helled by cannon fire: we'd
proven that before. I knew it now, but little profit in
the recollection.

All of General Braddock's military family had gone
down, spattered with blood: his aides Orme and Mor-
ris, and Shirley his secretary. Dehorsed, dehorsed
again and again, he was up in the saddle once more,
trying to rally and resist. 'Twas not like this in any
campaign and so he seemed to know.

He may have welcomed the bullet which claimed
him at last. It went through his right arm and into the
chest, deep in the lungs we reckoned later. Captain
Stewart and another Virginian were close at hand and
dragged Braddock to a cart and so they sought to take
him away. The dead and wounded lay waiting the
knives which would quickly flash above them or be
sheathed between their ribs when there was still life and
the Indians knew it.

Wipe the rout from memory. There is no profit in
contemplating further. The hundreds stretched upon
the ground, the very waggoners cutting loose horses
from their teams and fleeing on to Dunbar's camp,
where I was myself sent when the general ordered me.
He could still try to cry and command at the time, but
Heaven knew this was no longer any parade of
Guards.

So I was sent off to Dunbar's camp and was not nigh
to the general when he talked that night. One told me
later he did not attempt to speak at length. He spoke
aloud only once, as if in great surprise. Who would
have thought it? he said, and remained stony for hours
afterward.

He did not die till four days after the battle, and died in the night, there at the Great Meadows where I myself suffered pitifully the year before.

They came to me and said that he was gone. I went to find him lying white and seeming already shrunken within his bulk. Who would have thought it, indeed? I tried to seek out the chaplain but he lay groaning somewhere among the wounded. They put the Book of Common Prayer into my hand, once they had dug the grave and they said, Sir, will you read?

Please then, a torch.

They fetched a pine knot and I turned to the burial service for a soldier who had yielded up his life whether foolishly or no. But die he did, and thus was accounted brave in his dying.

Forasmuch as it hath pleased Almighty God of his great mercy to take unto himself the soul of our dear brother here departed. . . .

10

THE complainer went by the name of Eustace Ballantine, so commonly he was called Yoosty, and he strove to visit General Wayne since he had heard that General Wayne was a native Pennsylvanian, as were the members of Yoosty's own household, and might thus recognize the peril involved and also the aggravation and also rupture of responsibility (though of course Yoosty could not have termed it thus). Furthermore and finally: a shattering of every ancient code which began in caves or with Adam and Eve, no doubt: that

This Is Mine, Not Yours; and You May Not Take Mine.

General Wayne sat humped, a-writing, but looked up at last when he kept hearing Yoosty's grunt and sigh and swallow in nervousness and terror.

Who in hell are you?

Yoosty Ballantine, please you.

How came you here?

I walked in, sir.

Past my sentinel, devil take him!

Please sir, I waited till his back was turnt.

Why come you here to bother me?

Yoosty opened his mouth and made as if to speak but consternation claimed his breath. His jaw flapped, wide and speechless.

What age have you, you truant guy?

Eleven, please you.

You please me not! No justice in your gaping there and heckling me. Get out! I'll need to have my sentry thrashed for this—

Please—'tis of our cow—

What of your cow?

A soldier comes each morning and he milks her dry.

Then bid him not to!

Oh, that I did, sir. He laughed at me. But we do need her milk. What might I do, Your Honor, 'bout the soldier?

Shoot him!

What—what say—

Shoot him! Now wherret me no longer!

And when Mad Anthony Wayne had turned his back, Yoosty attempted to make manners by stamping and scraping, and then went speeding out. The sentry hollered at him but on he ran to the small house beyond the ringing guards about the camp. There, at home, breathing fast, he loaded up the heavy gun with buck and ball, and hid it fast away, and waited in such fashion for the thieving soldier.

The soldier came in dawn, he carried once again

the wooden bucket sacred to his pilferage. And Yoosty waited till the soldier walked apart a distance from the cow, so she would not be hit; and laid his gun across the fence rail, and fired as he'd fired often at a wood-chuck.

He'd loaded up the musket far too heavy and the shooting knocked him flat.

His older brother Noah heard the shot (Indeed. Who could not hear it? Thunderblast!) and came a-dangling mid his crutches.

What have you done, you limb?

I shot the s-s-soldier, and tears were spouting forth.

Shot him! Jehoshaphat! So you have! But why?

General Wayne, he tolt me to!

Noah looked long at the mess. The cow mooed out. She was affrighted, but still waiting to be milked.

Noah sighed deeply. He had the cragged face that cripples often have with eyes intensely bright and round. He seemed mysteriously aware of things that happen other places as well as here. He said, Well, stir you, Yoosty boy, we needs must bury him. You fetch the pick and spade.

So Yoosty fetched. They hacked out the hard mean earth and stones, they carved for hours, cutting deep the grave. They buried deep the soldier, 'twas a hearty task at best and worst, they buried him, he lay all vanished, with the thaw to be corrupt, his comrades knew not where he'd gone, they hazarded a guess that he had flinked away, he lay inept, in time serene, his people up in York State thought him slain in battle, and such blank honor they awarded him.

He lay there long, lay long. So many years would pass before the shovels dented at his bones when some mild husband-man was digging out a posthole.

The bones were lifted, they were spread, and neighbors came to see. . . .

And who? . . . And who . . . ?

11

THIS individual's first memory of horseflesh was actually of ponyflesh. He was carried along to visit at a house in Shropshire but he could not remember coach or journey. Only he knew the woven cart in which he was borne about the place, along with nurse and groom, behind a small plump steed which blew noisy bubbles from its nose, and farted at near-to-regular intervals when made to trot. At some later moment in the visit, the child Banastre took the traditional French leave from companion cousins and went to find the pony, one Pudge. He discovered it in a grazing pasture of limited dimensions, apart from the horses which considered this miniature beast insufferable, and would have ruined the creature with kicks and toothy choppings if they'd achieved the chance. Pudge was up against the fence by the time the lad reached him, and stared with wide welcoming eyes (freedom might be achieved, even by office of a bantam attendant). Banastre crept up over the rails—not exactly swarming, but climbing with sure purpose—and dropped down upon the chunky back. Actually he was a chunky little boy himself and perhaps they were well suited to be together but Pudge was disinclined to believe this. If the pony permitted a rider astride before this time, the invading boy had no idea; but the back was there and it seemed to this venturing infant that the beast needed to be ridden. He fastened his hands tightly in the mane and bade Pudge to do his best or worst. Best and worst consisted of a spirited lope, and bucking which sent the venturesome child into a bog.

His howling fetched nurse and attendants who meted out various shakings and cuffings. He was dragged away a-blubbering, but still that fatal taste for a horse rollicked within him. A toy wooden horse with a red leather saddle was purchased, and stabled in the nursery at home in Liverpool. A stylish portrait painter was entertained by the family at this time, and he had some idea of painting a mounted Banastre, keeping cavalry guard on other relatives. By this time, relatives had identified a psychological and physical spasm peculiar to Banastre as a temper-fit. The temper-fit in this instance took the form of young Banastre Tarleton's hurling a Venetian glass decanter in the general direction of the artist, and his upsetting the hated wooden steed and attempting to force the toy into a fireplace. Accordingly, Dapple Grey was banished (awarded to a gardener's child) and later in London, Banastre achieved the immediate ambition of his life which was to be escorted to ride on Rotten Row. Very nearly it took a royal decree to banish him from the Row by the time he was seven in 1761. It was rumored that various riding grooms were driven into alcoholic retreat: it was either that, or explode their tempers and give young Banastre Tarleton the hiding he deserved, which, though undoubtedly well-merited, would have put him into physician's care.

This youth had a suspicion of books and tutors quite well-founded, since in such fashion knowledge was supposedly drilled into one. Banastre Tarleton was more or less certain that he had achieved a mastery of all necessary knowledges in some miraculous manner, already in his life. Essential facts and skills had to be hammered into him. It was found that this could be achieved by stopping his allowance, which was in fact one far too munificent for a boy of his years and inclinations. He was taught to multiply and divide; showed a surprising interest in certain historical scenes; picked up enough adeptness in French to make him socially desirable, it was hoped. At what was politely known as the military arts he was in truth sublime. His weight was still on the side of the somewhat corpulent, but it was corpulent muscle reposing beneath the darkening and soon whiskering exterior. Banastre grew vitally interested in the activities of the Royal Pistol Association, which he was invited somewhat reluctantly by the committee to join. The Royal Pistol Association soon declined, failed, went into ineptitude and obscurity, as it became obvious that Banastre Tarleton possessed a skill with the sacred weapon which few might equal, and even fewer might exceed. Most people of his ilk were members of a hunt but this young gentleman joined two, the Venge Brook Hunt and the Billingsfield Hunt, as soon as he was of a size that made it necessary to tolerate him. Dogs did not interest him particularly, so he was no Master of the Hounds, but he was in at the kill, mud-stained or not. It came to be a habit to refer to the fox as first in at the kill, then Banastre Tarleton, with the Master of the Hunt and the Master of the Hounds a poor third and fourth.

His romantic life was studded (if such a word might be used in this sense) with common exploits among plump and amiable servant girls, and included shortly the visiting young aunt of a neighbor, and quickly thereafter the profligate mother of one of his common riding companions.

In such process he fought his first duel at a tender age. He was a trifle tardy in raising his piece, and his adversary's pistol ball slammed rudely against the edge of young Tarleton's shoulder. His first notion was that this primary duelist who stood before him had been guilty of unethical conduct and had struck him with the blunt side of an axe. In that same partial second he realized what had actually occurred, and saw that this was occasion for mercy and dramatics.

I yield, sir, he said, smiling quaintly as the man opposite him stood as a fair target with pistol now empty. Banastre Tarleton fired easily into the air. His opponent stood open-mouthed but mightily relieved; and then, when they went forward to clasp hands, spoke blunderingly. He quavered, in effect, I am in your debt, sir! He became a rabid if unpopular sycophant of Tarleton's on the instant. When Banastre was posted to the Dragoons, this worshipper followed him into His Majesty's service, to be killed later in attempting a jump which no one in his right mind should have attempted except perhaps Tarleton himself.

He participated in two more duels after that, achieving one dead and one wounded. Soon with a Dutch-born mistress of his own, he set up on Curzon Street. He was respected by all the unrespected and by a sprinkling of the respected as well.

In his early twenties he had advanced to the status of brigade major and in rumor was reputed to have had several horses shot dead under him. This may or may not have been gospel. Detractors growled that Tarleton deemed it a savage triumph to ride a horse to death. Admirers pictured him as practically bundling ailing steeds into bed with him . . . at least he slept in their stalls and coddled them with whiskey and sugar. (Military legends attend the grim as well as the angelic.)

He organized his dragoons into a flying squadron, trained with glee to prevail against rebellious Yankees in a manner he may have termed gallant but which his antagonists regarded as repulsive.

It was not alone that the Yankees smarted under the loss of Philadelphia, their largest and still most winsome of cities; but to see it turned into a capital of revelry under the administration of that arch-reveler, General Howe, was become an irritant flavored with gunpowder and perfume. Soldiers went trooping out to Germantown and the Brandywine, crying their slogans against autumnal stars and clouds. This rebellion must be put down and obviously was, to date; yet with impudence the surviving Continentals established themselves at Whitemarsh, to dare the British again even so close at hand.

One of Howe's military family was quartered in the home of Mistress Lydia Darragh, the meekest Friend to be observed in or out of Meeting. Given not to fripperies like his less staid commander, this man held a meeting of stalwart principals in his own domain, after bidding the Darragh family to retire early to expedite his conference.

Tomorrow night, said the plan of campaign as read aloud to the intent, General Howe's army will march from the city and take the rebels by surprise.

Mrs. Darragh had indeed retired early, as bid by authority. She had also arisen early, as bid, she later declared, by an even higher Authority. In her stocking feet she proceeded to the staff officer's room where at that very moment she was kneeling with receptive ear against the staff officer's door. Later he went to Mrs. Darragh's own bedroom to rouse his hostess, that she might set the downstairs bolts after the last officers had departed. He had fairly to pound on the panel to rouse her. How soundly that woman sleeps! was his natural comment.

Next morning she tied on her sober bonnet and announced that the flour supply was exhausted. (It was indeed. She had put the last of it into the fire an hour before.)

Then, said her kindly husband, if thee must go to the mill, thee must take a servant with thee to bear the flour home.

Lydia went, left both flour and servant in some never-detected limbo, and carried news of the impending attack to Washington's headquarters amid the cold fields at Whitemarsh. In later darkness British forces tramped out to take the rebels by disastrous surprise. After minor exchange of musket fire, they came tramping back to Philadelphia again. The Americans had been drawn up in formidable line of battle, their cannon ready to sweep the fields.

A puzzled staff officer questioned the staid Mistress Darragh and got nowhere.

Were all other members of her household a-bed when the conference took place?

All of them, she said serenely. I instructed them to turn in as thee bid me to do.

I know you were a-bed, commented the hapless officer, I had to knock violently to waken you.

Tarleton and a group of devilish youths who might for want of better designation be called his staff, were quartered in a prim-looking house belonging to one Mrs. Sarah Weeking, Widow. Their hostess was plump as to body, coy as to spirit, not especially beautiful, and as heavy as one of her own polished tables. She had no voluptuous experience since her parting with the late William Weeking, a banker of minor note, and actually not a devotee of the voluptuous life in any way (if one could judge from his grim-looking portrait which hung in the library). Quite naturally Banastre Tarleton took the woman to bed with him on the second night of his presence in her house; and certainly he had a portion of power in shaping the beautiful smile which formed itself on the widow's lips and which she carried contentedly to her very grave. Tarleton may have giggled about this dalliance to his friends, but always he bowed and scraped before the widow in public, and taught her artful tricks of the flesh in private. There were prettier and younger females to be had in town, and on occasion he pleasured himself in such fashion, with Widow Weeking confident that he was gone chasing Colonials.

In the more grim and determined conduct of his career, Tarleton busied himself in shaping up a kind of flying squadron of cavalry with whom he might harry, burn, and wreck; and whose exploits brought utter terror to the nearby portion of Pennsylvania populace. In this season the troop adopted the traditional coonskin cap of the frontier as their common badge, and seemed to ride all the more flaunting and eager. These dauntless souls were armed with a brace of pistols apiece and some of them had four pistols—two at their belts and two adjoining their saddles. If they could have bestrode horses of a common color, they would have been even more spirited. Tarleton imagined them all on whites and he had a favorite white gelding in his own stud, but all horses were at a premium just then, so the roans and chestnuts must necessarily troop alongside the sorrels and bays. The commander developed among his men a particularly loathsome but effective trick wherein mounted troops were deployed against infantry and especially scattered infantry following a pattern common among militiamen from the open spaces. In demonstration of this tactic, the mounted man accepted the fire of the groundling, preferably at a considerable distance if he could tempt the Continental soldier into firing. Then, if he survived the blast, he rode upon the militiaman or whatever, at frantic gallop. The enchanting notion was to ride the man down, and the horse would be especially trained in such maneuver. It would race up to the man, be pulled in short, and at the same time lift its forequarters into the air in the split second of the halt, and then come down with hoofs extended. It was a fearsome maneuver and fearsome were those dragoons who employed it, and of these one Group Major Tarleton was the most desperately effective of all. With fire and sword and fire and pistol, he ravaged much of the nearer countryside. Those who despised him declared that he ravaged with unnecessary brutality, and that every house he burned was inhabited by some docile granny. Those who admired him swore with equal sincerity that he had routed out legions of spies, traitors, and thieving roustabouts, in a holy crusade. Since the entire purpose of warfare, however, is but to kill, burn, and generally destroy, it may be recorded that Banastre Tarleton was one of the most effective soldiers who supported the Crown. Any discerning American should have wished that he was on their side instead of the king's.

He spoke with easy courage and genial tongue when he was so moved. One night he led his wolf pack in a surprise sortie against a remote farmhouse, tenanted at that time by a scant group of Continentals commanded by a slender sandy-haired captain who in the future might take pride in the sobriquet of Light-Horse Harry Lee. Balked by a barricaded door, Major Tarleton essayed entry through a window, which manner of approach necessitated his spreading himself out over the windowframe. Inside, a harried Continental soldier lifted his musket, took deadly aim at Tarleton's head, and pressed the trigger. The result was a misfire, as occurred so often if the pan were empty of powder.

Tarleton saluted the foe with a gentle wave of his iron hand.

Most unfortunate, old chap. Do try again. Better luck next time!

12

HIS name sounded like a good fruit. He had been christened Salem and his family was called Peach. He was a fifer from the bare beginning. He used to chuckle about that when employing such phrase. He said, Bare beginning? Yup, 'tis right. I even recall when I couldn't fife, so I must of stood there naked at the start and blowed my gob-stick to signal when I sought my dinner.

He knew not whence the word *gob* sprang in such usage (perchance from a naval whistle blown by a bosun in the Royal Fleet?) nor did he care. Also one's mouth was termed a *gob* in vulgar fashion.

A primary melody in his fervent store was called "The Gobby O": a rolling march, six-eight time. Long years afterward when Boston Town had gone to warring, and was burnt and starving and unfleeted and unfed, he heard the tune come pacing out afresh from some throng of new musicians, and they termed it "Paul Revere's Ride." Paul Revere's Ride indeed! 'Twas elderly before Paul Revere e'er saw the light of day, let alone any lanthorns in the steeple of the Old North Church!

Now Salem Peach was on duty with the Army as principal musician. A fife major; a sergeant, no less. He signaled with his gob-stick, cried six-eight, and the notes went wafting. So be it! exclaimed the children who composed his corps. We're playing "Jefferson and Liberty"!

Plague take you all, Salem Peach was grumbling when they'd rolled up to the piercing high octave of the final chorus. 'Twas elderly before the great good young Thomas Jefferson was whelped.

Oh when did liberty begin?

I reckon this tune was an airy whimsy when the light of day first shone on drums and fifes.

His natal home lay far up beyond the Old Bay State. The original Peaches grubbed for their living amongst lobsterpots, but Salem had conducted a score of other businesses in a score of other places, and was on the Boston docks the night those black-faced Indians swarmed to dump the tea. He it was who rallied a band to head the march, when all the rascals went posting up the street at dawn. Some tried to sing the wording when "The Picnic" shrilled and rub-a-dubbed. They didn't own the righteous words, they sang them anyway.

> *Oh, summer flow'rs are fair,*
> *And summer has begun—*

Pester them anyhow, but have a laugh along the way.

'Twas black December on that famous Twenty-third and so we played *Oh, hasten to the village green,* and the wild young rabble cried of picnics one might venture on.

And blossoms fill the very air
As blossoms seek the sun.

He would lead his fifers in their cooing offering a hundred times to come. Lord alone knew. Mayhap a thousand times? Salem Peach might only close his eyes the scarcest second, and he'd always see those fierce smeared vagabonds of Boston Town a-helling in their stride.

Here at Valley Forge his underlings were crying havoc. . . . Too cold, they wailed (it was a constant grief), too icy, and the wind forever blows so keenly, 'tis torment if you try to purse your mouth above the fife's blowing hole, the breezes take your melody away before you've ever puffed a note, no mortal could blow *do* or *re*. Salem knew their trouble; it was true; so he pondered on a mouthpiece.

There was a tinner nigh to hand, a-shaping bits and buckles for the horses' harnesses. Salem wasn't deft at drawing but he managed to sketch out a plan. 'Twould clamp on, he explained. Just like a tiny hollow cannon, kind of, with no wheels upon it.

The first one didn't work: too wide a hole . . . the second was immensely better.

That there's the ticket, Salem said. Now please to make some more according to such pattern. Soon they had mouthpieces to clamp above the blowholes of their gob-sticks and they could fife in any windy weather.

He'd stood and listened to the lobsterbacks long before they were commonly so called. He heard them blowing out their plaint with snap and snarl. He'd heard them on their native heath and near their native heather. He'd subsisted as a bagman in both forms: first, as beggar outright; and later in the role of peddler a-selling. He'd worked his way across the ocean time after time; and had wandered afoot from Maryland to Georgia. A slight wiry man, there was something of the red squirrel in his nature and attitude.

(He liked to climb and there was a sauciness about him.)

Some talk of Alexander,
And some of Hercules,
Of Hector and Lysander
And such great men as these.

But of all the world's brave heroes
There's none that can compare,
With a tow-row-row and a tow-row-row,
To the British Grenadier!

Salem Peach was haunted by a certain melody. 'Twas a memory of something else, a toying rune that might abide with him while he slept and be alive and luring in the middle of the night when he wakened. Then he couldn't sleep more. The tune came aping through his brain and he heard it fifed in a kind of reverse fashion.

What was the last line? Grenadier. After all those tow-row-rows. He heard it clearly. A bickering imitation in some ways, but still a captivating one.

The same notes. 'Twas "The Squirrel Hunters."

. . . Your final decision of the single word *Grenadier* stating itself within your mind if not your heart and soul. Pompous and implacable. Three syllables, forsooth, *Gren-a-dier* with no twist to the final utterance.

Here stand I. Here march I. My buckles and belt plates are polished to a gloss. I am a musician of the Grenadiers, hence I wear their high bright hats and accoutrements. There is no king but George and he is mine. I adhere to him nobly. Devil take Mister Pitt. A day may come when he will stagger to his stairway, threatening you feebly if impetuously, but that day has not yet appeared. He speaks contrary to thought of king and therefore to thought of Parliament. Devil take him again and let me be a Gren-a-dier. Leave us carry no parcels of patience with any oafs who might offer contest to the bursting of hand grenades or any other weapons of the king.

But—harken! Be that a lilt within the breeze? It takes our very notes, though slow and casual-like, and makes bold to echo them. Might notes of music still be innocent or do they put a thumb to their very nose and wave their fingers? There rises some awful conflict here, but truly too a heartiness. It is slanting and lounging. Somehow it bears a pattern of a Pennsylvania and thus also a Virginia rifle carried at the slope. The ball is small, 'tis true, but it can bore from far away and if 'tis aimed at you, you're dead before you know it. The drums which support the notes are stained and bashed, but the heads look fresh and tightly drawn and cornered down. They build a boom and not a spiteful tapping. They come rolling from a wild land of new-split fence rails, red-headed woodpeckers, hogs roving thinly at first but thickly later, and wild Indians prowling to the door to beg or to scalp you if they took the notion. The very children wear dirty linsey shirts or gowns, but their eyes are bright as those of wild mice, and they drink down sugar water in season. Whoever heard of sugar water in a village in the Midlands? No one. No one.

Ah-too-rah. Ah-too-rah. There is something coarse-woven and especially honest here, but still with a naughtiness about it. The very thickets bear coarse and unusual blooms or fruit. Pussy willow buds at one season, gray and dainty as the fur of a wildcat's kittens. Chokecherries and Juneberries in another time.

Then come the butternuts. What know your king or Parliament or Grenadiers of butternuts? They've never wettened their cold clean fingers with the yellow juice. They've never held the nut lengthwise, tapped its rich, fresh-dried peak upon the tip, and struck it one sharp blow, and seen the long slivers of the hull go flying and the rich yellow meat inside, to be a sweet fatness a-clinging to your fingers when you snatch it up.

Even in frost of a later time (it hurts to say it now) it echoes like an ancient hymnal.

An American goes picking up limbs of cottonwood, by golly damn, and tromping amid abandoned stalks of ragweed and sunflowers and goldenrod as he does it. His very boots go smashing through a pond of ice, and the turgid redhorse a-lurking underneath may go a-flying to warn the catfish in their own dark haunts.

Step with caution, though the hardihood of bucks is long since vanished and the wild Virginia deer drop their fawns in thickets as the spring comes in.

What lies beyond those blooming mountains to the west?

Whisper it. *The buffalo.*

There hasn't been a buffalo of any sort in Wilts or Berks or Suffolk since the last squat bog-dwellers shook their stony spears at them.

Where you bound, Grandpa?

Figgered to head west. Reckon we'll try a flatboat on the Cumberland.

What? Cumberland—in England?

Nope. Say we'll try the Tennessee.

Oh try them all, says Salem Peach. Oh, try them all.

Sometimes the fife tunes are brittle. Sometimes they betoken danger. Sometimes they're only the merriment of happy peasants dancing, then stepping in some manner of an old country circle.

But when we make with "The Jaybird," one of the briskest two-fours ever whittled out, it isn't any English jay we hear a-shrilling. Nay, it's an American bluejay, complete with his perky blue and white and black, and with the sauciness of sumacs in him. He's just chased a warbler into a poplar thicket, and he's kind of hanging by his toes and looking arrogant and calling murder when he sees an old raccoon a-wandering.

"Wrecker's Daughter": there's a dainty one for you. And "Flying Indian." And what of "Oh Tell My Mother When I Go Home"? It has wild persimmons roosting all the way along. "Go To the Devil and Shake Yourself." 'Tis madcap as the jaunty sycamores and has the wild red haunts, the Tuscarora and Onandaga, a-threading through their native windbreaks all the way.

Got scairt by a dream the other night, the way men do when they're pinched and hurting because they hain't got enough to eat or because they're bad situated; or the way men do sometimes even when they're strong and happy and comfortable and well-fed. Ain't no rhyme nor reason about this so I shan't pursue it.

But I was standing erect and kind of mildewing by the fire, and the great question was put to me by winter and loneliness and the bare puzzle of existence here. Spose there weren't no more Valley Forge, my notion says . . . or any way to die pinched and forlorn if one's heart and soul demanded it?

Would we be better if we was softer?

Would we be easier and freer and more kindly anointed if we let the demons grab us, 'stead of resisting them? 'Twas a puzzle, and I hain't got all the answer yet and maybe never will have. And maybe 'tis all like a plaster your mother lays on with mustard seed when you are threatened. It kind of burns the skin but helps to cure the disaffection underneath.

I thought, maybe I'll die here. Maybe not. I know a lot of folks will die here. So they'll be buried, and in time will be palavered over, and maybe in a future age whole congregations of individuals will come to pay a kind of national respect to their bones. Don't know, of course . . . 'tis all wild as the catbirds. Just a guess, but the king and his petty counselors (and the major ones too) will be dead and gone. So will American patriots residing here and tormented now.

But somehow in our graves shall we hear the mem-

ory of drum thuds, and fifes a-speaking eerily and
high? Will we still go pushing to farthest streams and
valleys, and see the burnish of a new sun a-coming,
and think it's good?

I pray we will. I pray we will.

13

HE was lengthy on guard duty and his elbows ached
from holding his piece, then his feet began to ache,
then his shoulders. He was accustomed to this. Primarily his shoulders were iced first although you
couldn't feel weariness and droop, then they began to
sag away from the cold, then they hurt. He discovered
that his shirt had drifted down around his waist and
he pulled it up and bunched it so that he would be
warmer. It was odd the way you were comparatively
warm if your shoulders were warm. He had seen
drawings of Britishers who wore heavy knitted scarves
around their necks, and no coats at all. Maybe that
was the reason. It was not actually snowing. Frost
drifted off trees and seemed blowing down from
Mount Joy and got in the way of your eyesight and
you had to blink and ponder with your eyes if your
eyes could be said to ponder, to discern and estimate
motion or approach. He saw people leave a distant
cabin, go away, and saw another man come back to
another cabin but no critter moved, all else seemed
inanimate. He heard horses' hoofs tromping a few
times and did hear some horses talking and saying
that they didn't like this situation at all. One of their
cronies was dead now. He had fallen and drooped, lay
close to the ground just before daylight ended, the eve-

ning before, and several men who were wise in the keeping and management of horses came and examined him and then there was a conference and an officer came and there was another conference, and later a single shot rapped out, hard and echoing, and the horse seemed to sink lower in his posture. No doubt a detail had been described for the purpose of dragging his carcass away but the detail did not come and so now here close to sunrise (if there had existed sun behind this drifting chill), the horse lay as if in prayer, praying for himself and his brothers and all other horses to come and suffer in the future. There he lay.

At first approaching hoofs and shoes seemed phantom hoofs and shoes, but truly this new beast was well-shod and the clinking rang sharp and true. When its shoes struck a stone it went *pink*. Conger put his rifle into position and a figure bloomed icily moving, and was on a whitish horse, and tall.

Conger rattled out the formula. Halt Who Goes There.

Friend.

Advance, Friend, and be recognized.

(Except naturally he said *reckernized*.)

The man on the horse said, Shem and Ham.

Conger said Ham and Pease. Then he shivered. With faltering voice he said weakly, Your Excellency.

In truth it was Zexcellency and he looked so calm and all-knowledgeable. Washington sat there on his horse and the horse blew half-frozen moisture from its nose. Washington's hand automatically came up on the rein and then lay back again.

Conger said, Your Excellency, I was with you. When we tried for Fort Duquesne.

Zexcellency said, You seem overyoung for that, my boy. What is your unit?

Now Sixteenth Pennsylvania Reserves from York County. I was a waggoner.

Your name, my boy?

Conger told him. I was a waggoner when we went to the Monongahela.

At what age?

I was all of fourteen.

And proud to be above thirteen in age, no doubt.

Yessir, Your Excellency.

Zexcellency said, I seem now to recall that General Braddock wrote in one of his reports—nay, 'twas in a letter. He wrote, *In every instance, but in my contract for the Pennsylvania Waggons, I have been deceived, and met with nothing but lies and villainy.* 'Twas well said. That is high praise for a younger.

Yes, Your Excellency.

Again Zexcellency spoke to him and yet the soldier could not have told anyone what he said or mentioned any word he himself had spoken in reply. He was so taken by the study of this commander, so admiring and enthralled, he'd seen him pass, he remembered seeing him ride, he had not seen him shoot, he had heard the fire, and all he could think now consciously was Praise, Your Excellency! A Man, a Man! He peered up into that face, he thought it snowbound. The eyes looked out under the large brows as any eyes of a well-established commanding officer must gaze, eyes that said, As your commander, I hold your life in my hands. I will not dispense it needlessly, but there will be some mistakes. The military leader who does not learn at the onset that others have made mistakes and he himself will be guilty of them, does not deserve the title of commander. Nevertheless I will conduct my portion of this war as seemly as I may, but I expect those subordinate to me to do the same. You are suffering as a single facet. Oh, suffering! I will endure agony in many as well as in mine own event.

He had the notion that Zexcellency's expression was not grim in an intent of conducting warfare against his own people and nation. It was grim in contemplation of the disappointments and pains which must come to his people. If a leader be not dedicated to the mastery and welfare of his own tribe, then he was no true leader in any sense. Conger thought suddenly that this man had been appointed by God as well as self to command. The nose on his countenance was large and long and strong. The mouth was wide and strong. The teeth within it were not strong at all. A fellow waggoner had told him a story during the retreating disorganized end of the Braddock campaign in Pennsylvania: how he had seen Washington's face swollen by toothache, then relaxed and diminished later when he was spitting out blood and pus, then shrunken down to the point where Zexcellency (not then His Excellency) could put his big tough fingers around the tooth and draw it out merely by engaging the muscles of hand and arm. He had seen Washington do this. It made Conger's stomach turn over, and also his heart exult with admiration of one who might do this thing. He wanted now to say to the commander, Do you have false teeth implanted, Your Excellency? and nothing would have been more ludicrous than to mention that. The false teeth were coming but they were not here. They would not be here for another seven or eight years at least.

That—that—that is a beautiful horse, Your Excellency.

His name is Blueskin.

Howdy, Blueskin, said the sentry, and Blueskin blew out through his nose in reply.

I must away on my rounds, Sentry, and dawdle no more.

God bless you, Your Excellency.

Washington went away without another word and the sentry watched him go until he could not estimate disturbance in the blowing mist any longer and until even the pricking clang of Blueskin's motion had vanished too. He started thinking impressive thoughts about commanders, subordinates, and all the pageant of their lives, and the majesty of his own contemplation overwhelmed him and he felt ready to cry, and did cry a little, though the tears were frosted between his eyelids and he had to blink his eyes rapidly in order to see.

14

I authorize and empower and command you forthwith to take, carry off, and secure all such horses as are suitable for cavalry or for draft, and all cattle and sheep fit for slaughter, together with every kind of forage for use of the army, that may be found in the possession of any of the inhabitants, causing certificates to be given to each person for the number, value, and quantity of the horses, sheep, cattle, and provisions so taken.

When Wayne pressed forth it was in a manner which suggested that soon he would fly rather than ride—that his brawny horse was about to sprout wings once it had gathered sufficient force in the journey.

A lone sentinel had strayed some distance from his established post in order to intercept the officer as he came scooting past. He flung up his rifle in attempt at salute.

He shrilled, General Wayne, sir, but was so baffled by the onslaught of Wayne's journey that he uttered the words weakly. Yet somehow they pierced in at the ears, lodged in the brain, and the rider swung about and came rocking back.

Did you address me, Sentry?

Yes sir, I did, sir.

What's ado? Be quick with it. Are you of my command?

Yes, sir.

With what?

Sir?

Name your unit. Quick, now!

Sixteenth Reserves, sir.

God damn militia, said Wayne.

Yes sir. I was at Paoli, sir.

Wayne snapped his eyes shut, thought quickly, made a face. How now? Sixteenth Reserves weren't there.

No, sir. I been bandied about. I was there with the Twenty-second.

More like it. What want you of me?

Sir, it's about your cavalry.

Nonsense! I've no cavalry!

The horses, sir. To—to cross the river. I guess you're going to. That's what folks say.

So the most secret plans are gossiped by troops! You're living proof, Sentry, damn it. What's your name?

Malachi Lennan told him his name as if he were pronouncing his own death sentence. I've got a horse, sir.

Stuff! Here, in the camp?

No sir. But I heard you was needing mounts, and people to ride 'em.

What manner of guff are you spouting, child? You say you have a horse but he's not here in camp. What precious good can come of that?

Sir, he's not far away. He's at Tibbie's Mill.

Then if you left him at Tibbie's Mill, the British have had him long since, I wot!

No sir, I—I left him with some people. He's fine.

Fine, is he? How do you know?

I've been to see him, said Malachi weakly. Been twice.

How the devil did you get there?

I walked, sir. By night. I—I wanted to see that he was all right.

By night? With no pass?

No sir, I didn't have no pass.

Then how in the name of all that's holy did you do it?

I snuck, sir.

Anthony Wayne seemed to forget that he was in such haste and he slapped his saddle and brayed as if he were a mule instead of an officer on a horse. Damn our pickets! That shows how much good they are! I swear, those Highlanders could march into Valley Forge with their bagpipes playing, and our worthless sentinels wouldn't see or hear them!

His name is John, said Malachi Lennan weakly.

John? Rattle-pack name for a mount. Why John?

We had him from a colt, and I was 'lowed to name him, and he liked honey from bee trees, and I give him some. Third Chapter of Matthew, sir. When John was in the wilderness. He ate honey and locusts. But I didn't have no locusts.

Wayne was still laughing, he regarded these details with increasing whim.

You're right! I do need mounts, and if you wish to come with me, by God, I'll detail you for it. Here, take this.

He pulled out an orderly book and scribbled for a moment with one of those newfangled English pencils.

There, that'll get you past our people, if they're alert enough to see you. God knows about the British! Take care, child, don't go to doom if you can help it. We need both you and the horse. Where's your hut?

The jubilant Malachi pointed. Over there, sir. Second ring. Number Seven.

The general told him, Show my scribble to your corporal or sergeant or whoever's in command of your detachment. Show it when you come back—*if* you come back—and then report to my grass-guard down by the river. Nigh the bridge to the left.

He burst into a brief short roar. John indeed! Honey but no locusts! Well, we have crying need for mounts. Take care, soldier.

He went flouncing down the slope, riding as if utterly annoyed that he had been so delayed. Yet one last spasm of merriment sounded in the light breeze and Malachi Lennan heard it as Wayne rode.

Both times when the youth had gone to visit his horse he had gone by night, there had been no other way to manage it. He preferred to go by night now. At dusk he presented his pass from General Wayne at the sentry post where two men were on duty. It seemed that one could not read and he gave the sheet to his mate. Malachi was warned to look out for pickets. These were forever on patrol and it was rumored that commonly they would shoot first and ask questions later. It was a long stint, but he had done it before, and twice, and without benefit of a pass or permission, and had come back with a whole skin. He was not fearful now, but kept his ears open for the approach of hoofs. He heard them coming twice, saw them pass from the thickets in which he hid himself each time, knowing not whether they were Continental or British, for both batches were roving continually. He reached the house of Farmer Spicer earlier than on any previous occasion, for the excitement of his errand gave him speed. He knew he would be weary unto death by dawn but felt older and wiser than he had felt before. It was as if he stood aloof and admired himself for having had the gumption to confess his story to General Wayne and win Wayne's courtesy.

On the Spicer door he pounded out the series of raps agreed upon—three loud knocks, then two, then three, then two again—and the old man and woman came beaming to welcome him. They had both sons and grandsons in the Army (but none now stationed at Valley Forge), and it was as if they regarded Malachi as a substitute relative, especially since he was able to pay in gold for the horse's keep.

John Horse was in good condition, they said, and waiting in the stable. They would be sorry to lose him.

Quickly they doused the lanthorn's gleam and Farmer Spicer pulled some embers together in the fireplace while Mrs. Spicer hung up a pot which had not yet grown cold.

'Tis good stew, they told the boy with pride. Onion and bird, and such a bird you'd never guess!

They sat as they had sat on other occasions with ears attuned to the possible approach of hoofs. But they always come by day, the old man said. I feel we've naught to fear at night. Three parties of foragers had stopped by since Malachi was last there; two of lobsterbacks, one Hessian. Nay, they had not considered taking John. One cow had been led off weeks before, the other was hidden in the brush. But she was sore put, Farmer Spicer said, sore put indeed. He'd cobbled together a shelter for her, a kind of stable made of tag ends of brush and branches pulled together. But oh, poor critter, she was still hard put.

Malachi paid over a last fragment of gold. His tiny purse was growing thin nowadays what with this drain upon it, although he owned property to the west now held in trust for him by a kindly neighbor. But there was no way in which he might claim the income, if any were available, with conditions as they were. So he fetched out his horse and John was glad to see him, and said so again and again amiably, although the boy tried to hush him up.

Best to lead him, Malachi Lennan was told. If you're mounted you couldn't hear others coming so well.

I know. I'll walk and lead him. Best to ye both, and my good thanks for the provender.

So you set store by it, the old man mumbled. Bird and onions, eh? Now what was that bird? What would you declare it to be?

I don't know, said Lennan truthfully. 'Tweren't chicken.

Crow, said the old man, and tasty, weren't it? He got pulled down by the cold and was right easy to ketch.

Malachi led John all the distance back to Valley Forge from Tibbie's Mill. It would have been a weary stretch but his heart was live and dancing and his spirit soared accordingly. No parties of ranging horsemen interfered. Once he sensed an approach, and led John quickly into concealment, and put his hand on his muzzle to still him if he should snort. Were those feet of horses he heard? They turned off in some other direction. Young Lennan went on without further incident, and the challenge was welcome. He'd feared the sentries might shoot first as had occurred. The sentries were a new pair now, and both could read, and the pass from General Wayne worked its magic. They laughed about the advent of John, teased his owner a bit. But now the owner could ride and be mistaken for an officer on horseback on his way to where the grass-guard was quartered on the bank of the Schuylkill. The corporal there was ornery and ill-disposed to awaken. He wore a hood and cloak and (praise him for luck) had blankets as well, and a tiny fire beamed. He roused reluctantly, awarded not a glance to the precious John when the animal was put in with others. There came a certain amount of snorting and fussing. Most of the stud were wintered cozily in their straw. Almost Malachi Lennan felt inclined to sleep there with John, but the attitude of the rest precluded this winsome endeavor. He said good-bye, and carried John's saddle and bridle away with him. At Hut Seven Malachi found that this adventure had robbed him of his own berth. He needs must take the bottom, close to the chimney where the smoke fell thick and sullen. 'Twould be dawn soon and probably he would be routed out, but General Wayne's note was his pass to freedom and ecstasy and now the rest might envy him. He lay tense and hard awake for a time. He should have felt beaten, he did not feel so. His hands were tingling, his feet and legs were bundles of ache. He thought, I'm stout. I'll weather it one way or nother. Weariness claimed him at last and he was drugged and heavy when hut-mates were rising. But the sergeant recognized Malachi Lennan's new status and let him sleep, and he slept still, even while cooks were at work with their fodder and scrawny tags of beef, or was it beef? Some sort of meat. *You could see the butcher's breeches buttons through it,* went the time-honored taunt. Malachi had a fit of coughing from the smoke but aside from that he lay serene and conceited in the fact that he was permitted to lie there.

Know what I had in the night, when I was gone to Tibbie's Mill?

No call for you to go storying.

I hain't storying. I went to get my horse, count of this new duty.

Oh, what did you have at Tibbie's Mill?

Stewed crow and onions.

There was silence for a minute, then came the inevitable question. How was it?

Right tasty.

We hain't got no crow and onions but there's a scrap of meat left for you. Your share's here in this pot.

Leave it be. I'll eat it when I get back. Now I've got to go see about my horse, he said with vanity.

John raised his head and complained loudly about the lack of oats when Malachi came to him. He had first however to run a gauntlet of sorts composed of men of the grass-guard who twitted him about John and asked if the horse were a veteran of the French War. 'Pears to be, they said in railery.

Some of the herd had nosebags, some did not. By dint of corruption in the employment of some silver coins of which he had a small store, Malachi obtained both nosebag and oats, and had the satisfaction of seeing his steed munching with the best of them.

A cry went up for all personnel to report to a captain stationed at some distance. Mounted men were to be told off into four parties, one commanded by Wayne himself, and the boy hoped that he would be assigned to Wayne's contingent, but was disappointed. The corps of looters, plunderers (they knew not quite how to term themselves), would be divided into four sections, two commanded by captains, one by Wayne, and the fourth by a foreign colonel named Roedvig who boasted but one arm. His right arm had been amputated. He appeared well mounted, and on occasion held the bridle reins in his teeth. Lennan was told off into his section. One detachment would hold to the left, in the general direction of Perth. The next would aim toward the Morristown region. The next toward Bisbee. Wayne himself would proceed in advance with mounted pickets to guard against surprise by roving British raiders who might be beyond them. It was rumored that lobsters had already combed much of the nearer region adjacent to Valley Forge, but it was not known how far to the north they had proceeded. A few waggoners, starting with no cargo whatsoever but expecting to be heavily laden on their return, were held to the rear behind each mounted detachment. Couriers would speed back and forth to fetch tidings and bear orders for specific procedures. This procedure held aspect of a general invasion rather than a mere foraging party. All personnel quivered excitedly at the prospect, and became more especially aroused when they were ordered to leave their rifles and muskets behind and be armed instead with dragoon pistols. These pistols had been captured from the king's forces, taken off a ship stopped at sea. Several men crowed that they were familiar with the weapon already, had used it before. 'Twas known as the Queen Anne pistol. Two of the weapons were issued to each individual with a comparable supply of powder, balls and flints. Actual departure was delayed. Men would report at sunset and rest adjacent until an order came to advance across the Schuylkill in later darkness. Malachi felt sublime. He returned to Hut Seven to deposit his rifle, to exhibit his pistols and counsel the rest against snapping the flints idly, as he indeed had been counseled himself. He picked his duds and prepared for the onslaught to come. By this time every man in the group envied him mightily. None of them had seen John, but the virtues of that steed lost nothing in Malachi's enthusiastic account of the horse's charm.

The old fife major sergeant named Salem Peach summoned him aside and presented him with a haversack—as a loan, he said.

Only one thing, sir. (Most of them called him *sir* on account of his age and experience.)

We mought run afoul of lobsters. Could be I wouldn't be coming back.

The fife major smiled serenely and patted the boy's shoulders. Life is chance, was all he said.

———————— 15 ————————

IN the nipping air, Mum heard cavalry approaching, a scatter of seconds before he could see them, but there was time for him to dive for shelter behind a clump of stark bushes. They came springing, a herd, perhaps there were twenty or thirty in this delegation and most of them wore fur caps, and they rode in a manner of riot or else in fashion to suggest that they were putting down some riot which had whistled or roared. These were no Green Hessians by any means, these were British, but madcap and devilish as they hurtled.

Now they were past, leaving spice of frost dust settling behind them, and had whirled off beyond the next twist of the road. But in their course they frightened him because he saw some looking back, pointing in the direction where Candy dwelt. 'Twas as if to say, We missed that before, we'll burn it now.

Then the youth felt disgusted at his own worriment. There were a dozen other things they might have been indicating.

Mum came out of concealment and skulked ahead again, going warily and surveying in caution before he rounded the next bend. He had expected to find slaughtered countrymen in the road. He found instead only a newly dead dog. Indeed he thought he'd heard a yelp when the troops strove pressing ahead, and here was the beast, they'd ridden him down. The poor corpse was hacked nearly to pieces by metal hoofs which had minced him. A few days before, Mum or his mates might have seized upon that bloody thing and borne it to the cooking pot. They had not eaten dog in his hut, but they'd heard of others who ate them and he knew of two half-grown puppies belonging to officers, which had vanished mysteriously. Rumor had it that those who fed upon the pups had eaten well. But now he himself had eaten well, served by the generous Candace, and he had no notion of lugging that diced-up relic along with him.

He rounded the bend, then halted, appearing to be suddenly ignited in his tracks as something ahead of him had now been ignited. A house, he'd passed it with caution before. It was ablaze, dark smoke bubbling and rifting thickly with reflected color of flames beneath.

House-burners. He'd heard of them as he and all the Army had heard of Tarleton. If crows flew over the countryside, Tarleton was rumored to have said, they should necessarily carry their own provisions! Hayricks, strawstacks, the stored oats, the hidden corn. All were reduced to ashes as the wild raccoons hooted in sport.

Were they coming back?

The boy's breath turned to gum in his throat at the notion. Hadn't he witnessed them pointing previously, indicating the Candy house, the Candy stable, the very Candy pigpen; so they'd be next. And what befell the women in such case?

Mum felt that he must now represent the entire Army which he had deliberately shunned and fled from. Such torment would be his logical penalty and he must pay it to the core. He'd drawn the charge from his rifle earlier, but rammed it back again before he left the Candy place. Powder in the pan—ah, so. He lifted up the weapon, picked the lock loose to see that it wasn't broken. His right hand went round to the inscribed powder horn on his left side. He drew out the stopper, dusted powder.

There. Enough was in the pan and no breeze to blow it loose.

He stoppered the horn and let it fall against his rags.

Now then. Almost he spoke the words aloud. Come ye.

> *Done In The Year 1776,*
> MY HORN.
> *Here-in is flame to put to flight*
> *A hero or a coward wight.*
> *'Twas paid for in the honest coin*
> *Of Ebenezer Mumford Foyne.*
> *I pray that I may never flee*
> *But stand stout as the soldiery.*

He entertained no notion that if he shot down one, the rest would retire. But now he was the Continental Army, a sole representative perhaps, but nevertheless a force to stand with power in his ambling trace and clip one of the invaders when they'd rocked nigh enough, as they were rocking now. He had wild notion that he was a king or president in this momentary pageant. He became no portion of an American monarchy—there was none such, but he was an embattled democracy—captain, general, Congressman and all, and all, beleaguered in taut and experienced young muscle. He sought no shelter, occupied no ambush. Indeed he could have lingered in none, there was neither tree nor bush to be had. Merely the frost, the rigid snow weeds sticking up through it, and now dragoons were yelling as they came.

Mum heard the spatter of some ill-aimed firing—never could you aim a pistol effectively while galloping like that—and the balls went *crease-crease* in air near at hand before he even heard the bang of gasses ejecting them. He brought the sight of his rifle up a little, then down again, hard upon the bouncing target which was a big horseman out ahead.

Suppose I were to shoot down Tarleton himself! Oh, what a ballad would I be!

His sight was solid momentarily upon the target and he pressed his trigger and the little flash rewarded him before the gun was firing and then he heard it fire, heard the explosions, yielded to the thud. He felt a grin cracking across his face and the barest identity of this smirk in imagining crossed his mind . . . something he had read in earlier boyhood in a story about gnomes, and someone grinned like a gnome and he thought he was grinning like one, though he was still not certain what a gnome might be.

In that tossing force of horseflesh and human flesh there fell a momentary gap. He saw a hand wave high, heard some sort of yell, saw a green-jacketed large figure spreading itself backward as the rest came on to fill the gap which it had left.

Directly over him towered horses and riders. He heard the beginning of a snarl of one animal—but only the beginning—and then the beast was reined in over him.

He did not even feel it hit. He felt himself flung wide and loose, saw hoofs arching overhead. That was all he knew and all he saw.

I pray that I may never flee,
But stand stout as the soldiery.

16

HE was named Hellen Striver. His father was in-debted deeply to a man named Hellen, and had sworn he would name his first offspring after this sublime benefactor be the newcomer girl or boy. As a child he was known as Hell among the rabble with whom he sported. This cognomen they plastered against him even after Hell entered the militia and later, along with the rest of his unit, was sworn into Continental array.

He was a sober individual, and patient. Seldom would he voice complaint, but now the stricken aware-ness of private responsibility to weaker ones obsessed his reckoning.

He had been pursuing a dream turned at last stag-nant, bleak, unproductive of benefit.

He was on a vessel of some sort (actually he had never journeyed on any vessel except a tiny boat in a river) and they passed a tropic headland, an island dressed in sumptuous greenery.

He was on deck.

He was aware increasingly that the fabled shore on which he'd hoped to pace in reverence was but a fancy which plagued the hopeful and left them yearning but still victims of fraud.

He was one of many millions who cherished the same fierce hallucination of Liberty, Independence, Freedom—call them what you might.

Merely he was another dreamer fondling that iden-tical illusion of time and space.

His island faded into a wafting of clouds, no matter

how he blinked his eyes. It grew less certain of texture, more sunken into purple sea and hint of twilight.

In awe-filled imagination he conceived himself as standing before Washington.

Your Excellency.

Verily, Captain . . . verily what?

I take my pen in hand—

Instead you should draw out your blade from its scabbard!

Your Excellency, I did attempt to do so.

Captain, where were you, with us?

Long Island, may it please Your Excellency. Jersey. The Maryland shore. Back to the Delaware, sir. The Brandywine. Now—here.

A sight of soldiering has been your honor and your privilege, Captain.

I take my pen in hand—

Pray do not take it. It has been my custom not to plead with any subordinate who acted within the limit of military discretion. You possess such license, Captain. Pray do not exercise it.

I take my pen—

Because we have lost so many! One day it is fifty-seven by actual count and reckoning. Next day, twenty-three more. Next day, seven additional. Next day, perhaps thirty-one. That many officers, Captain, have resigned their commissions. Do you now compel your commander in chief to subscribe to the brutal opinion of General Wayne? *This is not an Army, sir. It is a mob!*

With all respect, Your Excellency, may I call your attention to the existing conditions in this armed force which permit an officer to resign his commission, although an ordinary soldier cannot resign from his enlistment. Were I a private, sir, I would not be able to confront you as I do. But as an officer, I have this rectitude. May I most respectfully inquire as to what course you might take, were you in a captain's condition, younger by far than you are now and with no fortune to attend you? What if Mistress Washington and some small children of your own were held to be in want and—

Captain, would you be so considerate as to withdraw now, and address my adjutant?

I take my pen—

Morally, Captain, I hold to the belief that in a time of stress, such as we now endure, resignation is tantamount to desertion, let the regulations say what they will! Pray be gone. I have an order to write for perusal by my subordinates.

Oh most sainted Commander, please to hear my petition, my plea, my prayer! You should have seen my little Rachel, as last she was when I looked upon her —so toddling, so sunny and a-beaming. The pucker of dimples deepening into her round cheeks when she smiled upon anyone! And now I have it that she is ailing, wan and drawn. The last I was informed, our sturdy son Ronald had lost his spirit and was gone into apathy. The new baby Madge herself was said to be fitful and staring into space, and the baby's cheeks were sunken as well. And what of my precious Mistress Rebecca, the wife of my heart? The wife who enchanted my heart and spirit, and ordained the power of her loins and my own? The once blooming damsel whom I used to chase amid wild fruit trees when we were out a-berrying? I behold her sober-hearted, wan of face, leaving the small ones at home with meager fire. At least, God save Your Excellency, we military have our fire here and plenty of it. But I think of pinched fingers and runny noses, and winter creeping in through cracks. 'Tis a pretty piece to the house of my own father and mother, but dear Rebecca, she goes even there. There are eggs to be had—not many—but she takes her few and buries them amid the corn shucks of her basket, that they be not broken when she returns. My people would give her milk as well, but the cow was long since herded off by looters. Am I still to play the soldier or the captain, if you will, when I must be cozened by such images? Images be damned! I hear and taste as well! And worse than that, I explore with my own hands. I press my tired fingers upon the pulses of the little ones at home. Do I feel palpitation, the rapid trotting of the life within? Or does the quiver lamely die, and do I hold a tiny corpse plastered in my arms? The very puppies of our dog are wilting because their mother has so little juice to feed them, and they whine, small bodies and large heads, when they come tugging at her limpness. Fire, fever, Satan himself! I see such perils to be descending down upon my dears, and turning them to cracklings like the burnt-up corn that once had filled our granary but now is gone. Once we had a king, sir, but he acted out the role of idiot; and so we rose up strong to force him to desist, and to claim that we were bold Americans and would have no more of him or of his Parliament or Crown. Now, sir, I'd rather dwell in political serfdom and barely look the other way when the king's messengers and hirelings went posting by, and ignore them, and be a Colonist, even when figuratively spat upon. So long as my children were able and rollicking, so long as there were vegetables in the pit, apples in the barrel, meat upon the hearth, and the dog ran a-rollicking to sport among her pups, and the hens did squawk and flee from that old rooster! So long, sir, as I plowed my furrow, wrote my line in script, counted up pennies behind the counter, or peddled whatever wares I might possess. I was a subject of the Crown, a tethered bird to be batted back and forth by any whim of Parliament or of His Majesty himself. Now I am a free man, no hireling, as so declared by members of that same Congress who prevail in York while we are frozen here, and while my people freeze within their empty home. I risked the whim of bullets as the others risked, and some might never risk again. So many, oh so many! And like you I stood and rode among their stained red offering. The punch of musketry I'd gladly risk again, so often as you let us, sir, or ordered us to go, or placed us out on guard, or sent us into yonder powder smoke and said in essence, Go into yonder powder smoke, and so we went. That I can swallow as

I'd swallow down the burnt powder smoke after I'd licked it from my fingers. *No powder smoke to lick,* the men might cry, *No soldier!* But I cannot accept the whimper of my own wan young. I hear it piercing through my brain no matter how much sleep I need or long for. If any man can take that, he's a nobler patriot than Hellen Striver. Forgive us, noble partisan and staunch Commander, but off we go! I care not if one hundred and fifty-seven wrote their resignations heretofore or if a dozen do within the next lean hours, or if a hundred more will do so in the month to come. Musket bullets I'll accept, or whining of the grape or even solid plowing of the cannonball itself, and so I too am ravaged by its force, and all my flesh and ribs go flying off in all directions. I'll accept and dare death, as any soldier in any army in any time has had to do and will, I fear, do in the future. I go to find my folk and succor them as well as I can do! Plague take the raiders on the way, plague take the Hessians and the Highland Scots, and shanty Irish with their wild and bleary eyes! Plague take the lot, and let me be a victim of the Crown!

Please to remember this: I go because I am forced to go, and not because I wish to go, God damn it!

Let me sign my name and, spurting tears, I'll throw the pen away.

17

WHAT of the road nigh the river?

I'd say there mought be two score waggons frosted in the ruts.

Be they any animals?

Two or three dead ones alongside. But the waggoners have up and taken their teams, and gone.

What made them depart?

Wrangle with the quartermaster. They had to appeal to someone yonder, and no permission came.

What permission sought they?

The right to haggle and get whatever price they pleased.

What be the supplies in the waggons?

Well, there's a sight of shad. The waggoners lightened the barrels by pouring off the broth in which it was packed; then come a thaw, and then freezing again. When it warms, you can ladle out the shad, but it's all together, no fish will come singly.

Be there odor?

Aye, that there is, when the sun comes up, or when the sun comes out. But I 'et of that shad and 'twas good. Filled me up even though eaten raw. Seemed like I never set my jaws around such welcome fish.

Be there pork?

Aye. But once again the waggoners poured off the juice to lighten the load. It's in poor supply. As for beef, the men laugh aloud and say that they can see the butcher's breeches buttons through it.

Now here's two sledges here. We can soon build two more if we set ourselves briskly to the task. Then with four sledges and good men a-hauling, we could pack the whole load.

I fear not all. But we could haul in a goodly share. Let's to it.

> *Oh mother did you ever see*
> *Such harmony in infamy,*
> *Such able toad to play the frog,*
> *And squat within my pint of grog.*

What's ado here?

Seem to be onions. A smithering of potatoes alongside, but they're sorely wizened.

They'll come to life in stew. I do wish that we could bide with salt.

They've salt in Hut Seven, I hear tell.

> *None for you, none for you!*
> *Soldier I can tell you true,*
> *None for you!*

Then let us all lay to with a will, and drag this to camp.

May heaven damn them fleeing waggoners! I'd like to drag *them* to camp!

Let's ketch one! Haul him all the way! Drag him in the snow like a sledge. Make a rare 'zample of him!

Aye, that we shall!

This was in a lull which found fulfillment seldom, yet it had happened a time or two. Here they caught an appalled tongue-tied youth, a relative of one of the waggoners, who returned to the stranded caravan to pick up some tool or other he'd left concealed when he fled. He was handled badly, for all his tears and chatter-voiced expostulations. He was mauled back across the line (where sentinels should have been patroling, but were absent for food, shelter, or on some excuse of being sickly).

The men said they'd make him run through the gauntlet. He struggled and ripped while vicious hands shredded the shirt off his back. But then some officers came to intervene, and let the lad flounder free; so he ran and hid behind a brush pile and peeped out at his persecutors warily as an animal might do.

On the second occasion there ensued better fortune. This might have been termed Action By The Committee On Punishments And Various Deviltries Played Against The Continental Armies. The man was a large-framed lout and hefty accordingly, and able to lay low the first ranks who sought against him. But they kept coming in, he was torn down by the weight of numbers, his wrists were tied behind him, and it was pointed out that his coin purse was tied around his neck. He yelled that they could have everything in there. Yea, and there was silver too, a good bit! Let them but loosen him and he'd go home and fetch more money, he swore he would! He'd buried it neath his scratch-fire pile!

But the Army hooted its derision: such promises were fitful, cowardly, and not to be believed. They formed a gauntlet of sorts, 'twas more like a loose mob, and held belts, straps, thongs, whatever switches might be wielded readily. They wrested the victim's elbows and brought him spinning among them. This was no exemplary team or a display of honest punishment or decree by honest judge or jury. They closed round closely to thrash and buck, the giddy and malevolent did the worst (as so often they do manage). Soon the waggoner was howling, No more, no more, oh gentlemen, oh soldiers, oh patriots all, I see the error of my ways—ways—ways—*ways!* But after that his voice could make but a mumble, the whinny of a starving colt. Barren trees looked down to pity him and silently declaim, You're done.

Salt was little in supply, as commonly occurred; some coarse stuff was found in the cargo of another waggon, filthy and knobbed, good only for animals to lick as they craved. Some wads of this residue were dumped into a wooden bucket of icy water. Those in fancied momentary authority cried out, Give way! Give way! and the tormentors spread apart, and the flushing cargo was heaved upon the gashed raw back and chest and belly of the waggoner.

They left him a-groveling and groaning. Men waited at a distance to see him later climbing to his feet, seeking to stand and walk, tumbling flat once more, then summoning nerve to try to walk again. He pitched and wallowed, going on and on, heading for whatever hive he dwelt in, perhaps along the Schuylkill past ranges of the camp. They watched him tremble on. One called out derisively, and soon a dozen more (sentries and the like, some officers among them). They crowed, Oh, waggoner, waggoner, pray fetch to us our boon as you contracted for to do!

Dirty jeers were mottled, mingled all together.

Waggoner, waggoner! *Waaaggoner!* A doleful shout, repeated to haunt him till he'd fallen again. He finally vanished staggering around the furthest bend and thus was watched no more. But scant trees and dried reeds and ivies echoed it, 'twas a quaint persistence after all the jaws and lips and lungs a-making it were gone or fallen still. *Waggoner. Waggoner. Waaaggoner....*

18

JAN. the 1. A happy New Year 1778. Behold the man, three score and ten upon a Dying Bed. He'z run his race and got no Grace an awful sight I sed. Nothing very remarkable this one day of Jan. Anno Domini.

Jan. the 2. This is wuss than Whyte Marsh. There we had no tents but we have got none here neither but are now in huts, praise be, and we wurked so hard to make them. At Whyte Marsh we use to com-playne, but little did we know. We thot it was bad, Ho Ho. We had nothin to cook our food in and that was prity poor for the beef was very leen and no salt nor any way to cook it but to throw it on the Coles and brile it; and the warter we had to Drink, and to mix our Flower with, was out of a brook that run along by the camps, and so many a-dippin and washin in it which maid it very dirty and muddy. Ho Ho agin. Look at us hear. Had we like the same rashuns we had before, we would think livin on the fat of the land. Hear we got today only corn flower to mix with water and make cakes, and put it on the fire or in frunt and hard to cook on chips of wood. What you got, soldier? Why I got corn cayke thin as a cobb-webb. *No corn cake, no soldier.*

Jan. the 3. Nothing much happent today cept we pulled guard. Nothin much happent cept nearby there was hollerin and shots was fired. We didn't know what happent and don't yet.

Jan. the 4. This is Sunday and we turnt out for sarvis. The Reverent Mr. Ganoe preached. He had a good tex. He preached on several tex from Izaia but the one we like best or leastway I did was Chapter 9, verse two, the people that walked in darkness have seen a grate light. They that dwell in the land of the shadow of death, upon them hath the light shine. We thot that good, and believe the light was shinin on us. Our hutmate Fife-Major-Sarjint Peach turnt out with his fifers and drummers and oh, how they played before they piled up their drums for the sarvis; and after they played too. Twas good and we was proud.

Jan. the 5. Nothing remarkable this day onely I was chose cook for our hut consisting of 12 men, and a hard game too.

Jan. the 6. One feller comes up with a paper. He would not say where he got it, but oh gracious goodness, it was a rashun proclaim by Congress way back in June of 75. Hear is what they got. One pound of bread. Half a pound of beef and half a pound of pork; and if pork could not be had, one pound and a karter of beef; and one day in seven they shall have one pound and one karter of salt fish. Hear ye now! One pint of milk, or if that cannot be had, one gill of rice. One quart good sproos or malt beer. One gill of peas or beans. Oh my. Six ounces good butter per week. One pound good common soap for six men per week. Half pint of vinigar per week per man. If it can be had, it says. They must of been quite fat with all that. Oh to be a sojer that long while ago.

Jan. the 7. This day they dump down a keg of soft fish for us. Guess it was spoilt. All messed in together but we thot it a wonder.

Jan. the 8. I felt sickly and out of sorts and was let to stay in my bed but oh, what smoak.

Jan. the 9. Roomers has it that a bad woman come to a hut of General Learneds men hard by us on the right and was found and sentens to be drummed out of camp but we heard no drummin and do not know the truth.

Jan. the 10. Feel much better now. And was able to stand guard, but oh the cold. One man alone somewhere was said to be found froze to death and still standin with his musket. I know not but as always they say, they say. Zexcellency has sent out a new order agin foraging but people sneak out just the same. There was said to be a sheep stole last night and many folk had mutton, but we did not share but we got some vinigir and cider and it was a good tot.

Jan. the 11. Sunday agin, abide with me. Account of bein sick last week I was not made to go to sarviss but several did go despite the cold and they come back and said no preacher, no sarviss. One man has a Bible and he lent it and I read a bit. I spelt out a chapter in Psalms number 93 and felt much better and almost holy. The Lord on high is mitier than many warters and we might add to that if aloud to, mitier than much ice, which we have so much of now.

Jan. the 12. Some folk were a-foragin. I won't say who. An fetched back a mess of ground corn. Twas real meal and we made caykes and oh so hot and good.

13 Jan. All are laughin over a screed said to have been written by a surgeon in this place and copies maid and going round. It gives reezons for the Army winterin here at Valley Forge and what reezons they be. First, he says, there is plenty of wood and warter. Secondly, he says there are but few families for the soldiery to steel from—tho far be it from a soldier to steel. Thirdly, feeling close to God is of value to all. 4 ly, there are warm sides of hills to ereck huts on. 5 ly, they will be heavenly minded like Jonah when in the belly of the great fish. 6 ly, they will not be-

come home sick as is sometimes the case when men
live in the open world—since the reflexions which rise
from their present abode will lead them to more noble
thot of employin leezure hours in fillin their knapsacks
with all materials as may be necessary on the journey
to another Home. What, another bad blot. Oh you
nasty Sloven! How your Book Looks!

Jan. 14. A Wednesday, which is for me sometimes
my lucky day. Snag for guard duty again.

Jan. 15. My friend Eben also hutmate says he can
prophesy weather and this mildness must vanish soon
and we will have it rarin cold agin. He says everything
that aint froze now will be froze. We will see.

16 Jan. A big tomcat got loose from somewheres
and run around like he was crazy with folks trying to
ketch him. He ack lost and just wild and was in good
shape, almost fat. Soldiers yelled Don't eat him, he
belongs to one of the generals. Some say Wayne,
but we knew this not to be true. Some said General
Poole, some said Greene, but nobody knew for sartin.
He kep loose and when last seen was streakin for the
Gulph Road. What a time, and funny too.

17 Jan. It has turnt right cold agin as predict by
Eben. He and I had no reglar duty and struck away.
He said ack like we was goin on important business,
and so we did, carryin our guns briskly and nobody
said a word. We went clean around to the crick and
down it looking for that blame forge. We went clean
past Mount Joy and on and on. He tolt me it were not
a forge like for shoeing horses but a place where they
made iron of all kinds. One time he had relations in
wrot iron business. There was ruins of a wheel, great
big, and what he called a bloomery where they melted
iron and all. But it was rooint by the Lobsters and
what a mess, up and down the crick with ice and all.
We got so cold we would of been glad had they fired
up the forge agin, and got back to our hut more froze
than alive. Even thick smoak seemed good after that,
like I am havin trouble now trying to see as I inscribe.

Jan. the 18. Holy Sabbath agin. We clubbed our

clothes count of the bad weather and half went to meetin and half stayed home. The half that went to meetin come back and said there was no preacher but we were tolt one come later. I read my Scriptures agin. This time Second Kings, 6th Chapter. There was a great famine and an asses head was solt for four score pieces of silver, and the fourth part of a cab of dove's dung for five pieces of silver and what on earth is a cab? And the woman said to the King that she would give him her son to eat and it said, So we boiled my son, and did eat him. No more Second Kings for me. Until a preacher tells it right.

Jan. the 19. We have still got some small amount of beef left in our hut, but everybody laughs and says that it is so thin you can see the butcher's breeches buttons through the meat. We had a few days supply but we just bout run out. They say there are waggons and carts stalled all along the roads.

Jan. the 20. Beef all gone now and we are down to cookin corn cayke agin and mighty thin at that.

Jan. the 21. A Wednesday agin. My lucky day. Oh luck, where have you gone? We would go out and wade through snow to get some of that stuff in the carts and waggons but they won't let us go, though some people sneak. But I gess what they get is froze solid. They say General Mifflin is sposed to give us food, but where is he? No place about. We call him General Shittflin and were he hear now, I venture twould go hard with him.

Jan. the 22. They give some cider today to go with our shovel cayke. More was stole by some of our men. I will not say who, nor tell a word, but some grew somewhat tipsy and oh my head and my hand is strayin as I try to write.

23 of Jan. Soldiers talk of desertin and goin home, or somewhere, but it is awful talk, and I try to close my ears cause I would rather die and starve here than be called a coward to myself.

Jan. the 24. Ho ho. We have beef fetched in and it is good fresh beef jest slottered. We eat all we could and some et too much and got sick but not the undersined. I got one small piece stoled away in my shirt and will eat it if I wake up hungry. Oh what a fine piece of cattle. Moo cow, moo, moo.

Jan. the 25. The Lord's Day agin and a preacher we had never seen before preached and it was from Samuel. I fear some was ill-behaved. He said how they brought beds and bastons and vessels and then they had wheat and barley and flour and parched corn and beans and lentiles and parched pulse. What was parched pulse we did not know, but those misbehavin would make noise when he said these things and should of been run out of meeting. He said honey and butter and sheep, and cheese of kine for David and all the people that was with him to eat. He said the people is hungry and weary and thirsty in the wilderness, and those ill-behavin yelled that they was. It was Second Samuel just before the part where Absolom gets caught up in the oak tree and hanged and died of it. I keep wondering what was parched pulse that they ate.

Jan. the 26. There was three men whipped today quite bad. This we did not see but we could hear them yell and they was said to be tryin to desert for they did run away and got caught. I would not of looked at it had they made us to stand aroun. I would of shut my eyes.

Jan. the 27. Twas on this day one year ago they told us that my own father was kilt. He was with a foragin party and they run into some Lobsters and there was an exchange of fire. Only two Americans was kilt, but my father was one of those. Solemn thots on this most solemn day. I pray he may look down from Heaven and aid me on my course.

Jan. the 28. We got potatoes and onions and grain and other good things. Everybody feels so much better and fairly spoiling for a fray. One surgeon was heart to say that he bet we would storm Tophet if we was ordered.

Jan. the 29th. There is talk that we might march

and surprise the Lobsters in Philadelphia who would not be expectin us count the weather. A great notion and we are ready.

Jan. the 30. I give serious thot to the notion of stoppin this record. It is too great a chore and I make blots and all. Had thot to keep it up for one year, but devil take the hindmost and I will be the hindmost.

Jan. the 31. Tophet, hear we would come if aloud to. Thus endeth my little record, blots and all. I mite burn it in our fire, but why? Will keep it for my children, case I ever have any.

19

THIS young man called his horse Opale because the animal seemed opal-colored when first he saw him. He bestrode Opale in battle, away back in that muggish September, and it appeared that the battle consisted mostly of riding up and down ridges at this point. Seemingly conflicting orders had been issued, and many of the troops knew not where to turn or how most capably to present their front against the enemy.

The young man said to his blowing horse, Since I name you as Opale, you in turn should call me Uncertain because I cannot seem to make up my mind!

They went plunging off, trying to rally troops again. A musket ball hunted a home and found it in the left foot of this young man. The impact nearly knocked him out of his saddle. Even in early shock and numbness, he remembered brilliantly something which he had been told by seniors, he didn't know how many times. He had been told when a bullet struck you, it did not feel as you supposed a bullet striking you would feel. It felt instead like someone had hit you with a shovel or club. You felt the doughty blow but you did not feel the bullet piercing in. That knowledge came later, after the first shock had passed off, and when the blood was flowing and beginning to feel warm.

The young man made an effort to go on with his self-appointed task of concentrating and directing the disordered troops who had become so confused by a variety of orders—some of them shouted by a bothersome expatriate who, like himself, had hastened to America to take part in this war, although for a different set of reasons than those which impelled the young man.

The young man spoke, and found that his lips were blurring as he tried to talk. He said, *Attendez, Opale!* We'd better get out of this!

So he turned the horse's head, he remembered lifting his hand in a mock salute or wave to some of the soldiers, and then he kept pressing Opale's head around, because in this moment Opale was truly reluctant to leave the fighting. They went down into a marsh, crossed a small stream which he didn't know they were crossing until he heard the plashing of the horse's feet and legs, and then they were on more solid ground beyond and nobody much was around, or even near, and the wounded foot felt heavier and heavier and the boot itself was so filled with blood that it kept running over the top of the boot and crawling down the leather. He wanted to say aloud, This is bad, but he could not think of the correct word in English, and it seemed ordained that he should speak in English because the proper orders for the movement of troops should have been given in English instead of in French, and he could not think of the word for *bad* when he wanted to say, This is bad, so he heard himself saying firmly, and still in that miraculous English, This is *ungood*, and then he reined his horse and hauled his blood-soaked boot out of the stirrup. He didn't remember getting off the horse, certainly he couldn't lift his left leg over the saddle, so he must have gone down on the left side after he had twisted his right leg across. Then he remembered standing on the ground, breathing heavily, and his breath sounded very far removed from him. Someone else was doing the breathing.

It seemed to be in syllables. Remote and yet identified, the breathing seemed to say *Ha-hush,* so many times that he found himself trying to imitate his own pattern of breathing by saying *Ha-hush, Ha-hush.* He didn't know whether it was in English or in French, and then he was down on the ground. He thought he was still clinging to Opale's rein, he could not be sure, but it felt like it, and he had heard someone calling in the distance and saying something about, Over *there,* and something about himself. He was not confident what was said.

Came immense wrenching pain as his boot was removed and he was not sure whether it was cut off, whether the leather was actually split, or whether the boot was merely dragged loose, but there was that pain for a moment, and very bright lights, bonfires and fireworks. In a tennis court, he thought, and he could see the little balls flying back and forth and he himself was playing, but should he play tennis with his foot and leg feeling as they did? He wanted to ask someone, but he was in a dingy mist and it seemed easier not to ask. He heard someone say something about a tourniquet, and that was a word he knew, and he tried to explain to them that he knew it, but all he'd feel was the tight band going around his leg and then he opened his eyes to see better, but could only see that he was at some distance from Opale. The steed was standing with docility and perhaps quivering a little because he had been ridden so hard that day, and who was doing this to him? And why? And it was good for them to put on the tourniquet, because the bleeding would be stopped, or at least held in check, and there was so much blackness in between various portions of his life.

He thought, Retreat? Retreat into blackness? I shall not! I shall not conform!

Then he thought, Conformity is for the old, not for the young, and I am still very young. Some say I am too young, and award me jealousy in proportion. And then he thought, How old am I? I became twenty years of age last week. I have a wife and child. I have a small son and there will be another infant soon. I have a baby son, but he is far from here, and he is with my wife Adrienne, and there are such quantities of ocean lying in between.

That bullet has not killed me. *Très bon*. My own father was killed at Minden before I was two.

And then he thought of Doctor Franklin, he thought of spirited encounters with Doctor Franklin, and then Doctor Franklin went away from him and the band around his leg was tight, and people were lifting him up and carrying him. He tried to contend foolishly that perhaps he could walk, they need not hoist him so, but next thing which happened was that they deposited him in the bed of some sort of cart, and away the cart went, away and far, and he found peace in lying and listening to its going.

Someone must take care of my horse!

He considered instructing people about what should be done with the horse, and then it seemed too much a summoning of effort, so he need not tell them after all. He wondered only what His Excellency would think, and would he be angry with him for becoming wounded?

In France, when he was tiny, playing with other children, they had superstitions about the moon, but he could not remember now just what they were.

So amiable, he said. So kindly to all.

We played a game, but I cannot remember the nature of the game. It had something to do with running and being prisoners of wee girls in their gentle frocks, oh so slight and soft they were, a-dancing in the moon and running to and fro.

Dans le jardin d'mon père
Les lilacs sont fleuris. . . . .
Auprès de ma blonde
Qu'il fait bon, fait bon, fait bon. . . . .

We were prisoners of the girls, and they put us in a pen among the flowers and I fear we trampled many in our sport. An old servant rushed out and she was highly indignant because much of her work was in that same garden, and she attended those beds with care, and now we were exulting among them. Leave off, she cried. Go away! I shall report you to your parents and you will all be flogged! See what you have done to my flowers! And then we went skimming off, laughing at her when we had reached a safe distance, and we looked up again, saw that hearty kindly-natured moon as if it were applauding us and saying, You are children. You can do no wrong.

La lune, he said.

A voice told him, Yes.

Clair de lune, he said. I love (though he would have pronounced it *luff*) moonlight.

Ah yes, 'tis very bright tonight, but you must not talk now. You must rest.

Why must I rest?

You are very tired.

Where am I now?

At the Plough and Harrow.

What be that?

The Plough and Harrow? It is an inn. You are here now resting. You must sleep.

He slept, and when he awakened again he felt stronger. He looked about him and there was a woman sitting near.

Dear lady, who be you?

She smiled and said that her name was Mary Gorman. I do a sight of nursing, she said practically. I put a new tourniquet around your leg and cleaned you up a bit. She did not explain that the British musket ball had carried leather from his boot clean into the wound, into the leg itself, and bits of this had to be pulled out with tweezers.

Again he rode in a cart. He could be braced up with cushions and look out at the world. He wanted to know the destination. Where was he being conveyed. To Bethlehem, he was told.

Bethlehem? He thought of the infant Jesus. He thought of Mary and Joseph and wondered what had become of Opale, who was now his favorite horse among the mounts available, but no one could tell him. When someone finally did venture a reply, it was merely to say, Opale is fine. He must be retired to the stable until you have recovered. So he hoped that this was true. No one other than himself should be taking Opale into battle if another battle loomed imminent.

He felt that his recently acquired American status was become garment and decoration. He held no tolerance for the acrimony which fellow French officers, called *fellows* only because of their nationality, awarded each other. And even gave unto himself with a prissy and snarling vigor. He had offered to serve in any capacity he might, and assured His Excellency that he would be waggoner, scout, pantryman, sentinel, would willingly collect firewood or try to shoe the horses. He would do anything, to serve without rank or emolument. Washington himself deplored *the driving of our own officers out of the service and throwing not only our Army, but our military counsels, entirely into the hands of Foreigners.*

An equally honest man in turn, his scion wrote bitterly to his wife while he still languished in the Bethlehem hospital, *All the other foreigners now employed here are discontented and complaining; they are filled with hatred toward others, and they are hated themselves.*

But he had enough native passion to enable him to rise above such backbitings and look ardently upon his own recovery. He had a crutch, two crutches at first, and he hobbled about on those and kept swinging his wounded limb back and forth until the decorous nurses cautioned him afresh. I must garner strength, he told them decisively. I must return to my command, although still unsure of exactly what his command might be. He graduated from crutches to a single crutch, then to a cane, and declared finally that the end of such hospitalization had come. He must go to the Army as speedily as possible. At first he asked for a cart. None was available. Then he connived and bribed, the latter was the easiest way. He owned a fortune and could spend money even in bribery without risk or evil. Word was brought one bright morning that a groom, two guards and a retinue of horses were all in attendance. He hobbled to the door and gazed out. Opale! he cried, and turned to sign an order releasing himself from the hospital and signed it with a flourish.

When at last the Army encamped at Valley Forge, he was still receiving treatment for his wound, though now he could get about with power and pride. He went to the house of a surgeon named Stevens to have the old wound examined. He ascended to the second floor of the house and probably was watched with a certain amount of awe and felicitation as he did so. He was so handsome, so sprightly, his bright eyes danced! There might be a felicitation in the very manner in which he looked at you, but the daughter of the surgeon was ill-equipped to take stock of his charms after this new patient had lurched to the second floor. He heard a slight scuffle and looked around. One of the French officers was struggling with little Betty Stevens, determined to embrace and kiss her.

I have, the witness thought to himself on the instant, one good foot left to kick with!

The snarling malcontent felt a grasp upon his collar, his pawing hands fell away from the girl as she trembled loose, and he saw the same glint in the pale eyes which had shown at the Brandywine before and after the bullet found its mark. The senior officer spoke not a word, but his hand was cemented on the young ruffian's collar as he dragged him to the stair-

way, and there the good foot was drawn back and he
kicked with it, hard and savagely. The fellow went
sprawling and floundering, all the way to the foot of
the stairs, and staggered achingly away.

Oh sir, cried Betty aloft, and fumbling with her disordered gown. I thank you, sir! I do, I do! But please,
sir, I wish to know your name!

He bowed his courtly bow and said, In the name of
France, such contemptible behavior shall not occur
again.

But sir, please to tell!

I am the Marquis de Lafayette, and he took her
hand and bowed above it.

20

MAYHAP she might have no fire a-burning?

Mayhap there might be no candle gleam?

Mayhap she might be suffering from that ill peculiar to womenkind, and announce through the bolted
door that she wished him well, but he should come
some other time?

Mayhap—

But when he reached the squared log which served
as footbridge across the icy creek, he could discern
twinkle and wink, as if the light saluted and said,
Come ye forward.

He proceeded cautiously for the footing was uncertain; and then rounding the next slight bend in the
path which served as walking-way alongside the frozen
morass which the road had become, he recognized that
both glow and candle gleam were undeniably there.

His heart and energy rushed warmly to greet them and to be enfolded in turn.

He took off the ruined wad which was his right-hand mitten and rapped with hard thin knuckles against the panel. He rapped three times and repeated this sequence, and then waited, and finally could hear the rustle with which she approached.

Who's there? she asked.

Baddeley, he said. Might I be allowed to enter?

Very well, came her soft whisper, and he felt that there might be breath of anticipation therein. Came the grating as metal bolts withdrew in their sockets. She hauled the door aside, wide enough for him to enter, and then closed it quickly and shot the bolts home.

She was, as always when she met him, muffled up in a quilted robe and with her face buried far back in the hood that went with it. She was shy beyond the point of winsomeness about her scarred face but little did he mind, little did he mind.

What fetches you here? she asked.

The same fever that always frets me when I think of you, and when duty does not determine otherwise.

He heard her breath go in. You speak jestingly of duty—

Not I. But two more left today. This very day two more are gone from my own regiment.

Who be they?

I doubt you know them. Or maybe you do? Mayhap they be friends of yours too? Siffert and Gwynn?

The bonnet was shaking slowly. I know them not. Pray, may I offer coffee?

'Twill be a warmth. What be the coffee? Grain?

She laughed and said, Nay. 'Tis raspberry coffee from my own dried berries. And I have a speck of sugar to go with it.

Baddeley removed his short deerskin cloak and shook it in front of the fire. 'Twill be warming and welcome, I am sure, but I know of a warmer welcome.

He sipped the drink when she offered it. 'Twould be waggish, Mistress Gracie, if you were to term it tea instead of coffee. 'Tis right sweet tea. And very welcome.

Responding to luxury of the drink, he was able to survey the room now, study it, observe what changes had been effected since last he was there.

You have up your quilting frames. Also in the room beyond.

Yes, Mistress Deborah Hewes hath ordered them. But now I am out of yarn and need time to spin it.

Mistress Hewes? Is she not the lady who let her house to His Excellency?

The same. They say that Mrs. Washington will arrive shortly and there be'n't enough comforters. These I am to make.

Ah, Mistress Gracie, said Baddeley. Please to be kinder to yourself.

She shook her head. I fear you have flinked out. Not I.

Then have you leave?

Oh, in a way, he told her carelessly. My commander knows that I'm abroad somewhere or other. So long as I'm back by dawn—we have hours.

After they were undressed and burrowed deep among feather beds, she engaged in that usual delayed anguish he had grown to expect. He knew that she did not wish to remove her hood, desired to have her poor face buried in the depth of it. He murmured again that he held no hatred for her pockmarks. He thought them noble indeed; regarded them as a portion of her; made bold to kiss the scars.

She wept afresh. It was so dreadful, she wailed. It claimed his life, and he was such a good man.

I have no doubt, the young officer told her. You offer the manner of elegance and courtesy. And, he added boldly, I fear one might not demonstrate those, did she not truly own the same virtues in turn.

I'm an unseemly sight! Oh I am, I am!

Untrue, he said. You're a love, my dove.

Pray don't make sport—

Oh lud, he said. I'm not making sport. Let me hold you closer.

Her sobs began to soften as he let eager hands run over her gentle body.

Ordinarily he held by early nature and through experience to the manner of a modest but affectionate man.

Jem Baddeley was but twenty-one years of age, many officers were younger by far. The fabled Markee himself, doted upon by Zexcellency and worshipped by most of the Army as well, was younger still. He paced in legendary style, but Jem did not nor might he crave to. He was the product of kindly parents who held not much of the world's goods. They found their pleasure in simple matters close to hand and reared up their children in this wise. Jem had two slightly younger brothers who pressed him for physical attention in various infant strivings from the time they were all grown large enough to be rowdy. He had to lay them on their backs then as well as later. In the time when they had entered their teens, the wrestlings, sometimes anointed with fisticuffs as well, caused them all to be ordered out of doors. Actually one of the youngers was bulkier than he, but Jem managed to maintain not only the dignity of elder years but the resolute power of muscle and bone over muscle and bone (when ordered wisely). Thus he gained energy in a community where physical force was desirable still. He was about to be married at sixteen when the summer complaint took the life of the young lady affianced to him. He mourned her steadily in his heart, still forcing himself to go about workly duties with serene appearance. People who dared not do this he might have termed as *Mollies* and would have been mainly correct. Life was a risk at best and most family burying plots had their short and slim graves among the older stones of elders. Along about the same time Jem was introduced to storied and active romance through the kindly offices of one Miss Kätchen, a cousin come a-visiting the Hermels family next door. 'Twas early autumn: she made a squeal over hazelnuts. She came from the city, she knew many nuts but not the hazel. Jem led her on appropriate expedition into the great park of brush behind their two places. Few trees stood there except for a moderation of hickories and slender oaks: generally the area was bushy. You could stand or fall or squat amidst this shrubbery and not be seen a pole's length away. Such woodsy intimacy might readily enhance itself into a vivid and more romantic one. Miss Kätchen had achieved considerable experience in this natural art, and was bountiful in example and instruction. Thenceforth Jem's honest eyes seemed to grow wider apart and more tolerant and whimsical when turned in the direction of females than had been their wont before. He learned an important—and to some a devastating—truth as he now preyed leisurely among available females of their community. He found that a weighty percentage of the primmest-appearing and tightest-mannered masked thus a leering tavern-maid's desire for rowdy antics with the male.

Another young man, huskier than Jem by far and with lowering gaze, was named to be lieutenant of their newly recruited troop when military activity commenced. This gentleman was the son of a veteran, pompous and tight-mouthed, whose skills existed apparently more in the manner of attribution than true accomplishment. The son, one David (dubbed Goliath behind his back), ran hoarsely about at the very first encounter with the enemy, waving a sword, firing a frightened pistol somewhat indiscriminately. Definitely he led in the retreat if not the attack. The company rebelled, sent David-Goliath a-flouncing, and elected Jem to be their lieutenant on the spot. They profited from the calm of his command. There was nothing pell-mell about him. His colonel observed a man, who, when ordered to hold, would hold to the best of his and his soldiers' ability; and when told to retreat, would maintain an able and preventive fire toward the rear. Jem was made captain after the Brandywine.

No one of these military janglings or heroics he carried into bed with him to delight the widow's ear. She was sensible, tolerant in her reaction to the war as it affected her hurtfully, as it affected all. Nor had she dreamed of ever gaining such passionate surcease for her other wounds.

These two, Gracie and Baddeley, were excited each by the other; they held respect rapidly increasing into fondness. He was far removed from the state of self-conscious bletherings and she became so too, once she had sobbed away her self-conscious wailings concerning the scars which she regarded as deepest infirmity.

He said, Small eyes, and his tongue found hers. She held him close, tightly, while his tongue touched each eye hidden under its lids in turn. She switched her head to one side and he said, Small ear, and found it, and then she turned her head again so that he might find the other. He said, Small nose, and gave it an awarding lick. Then he said, Small mouth, and turned and put his own open mouth against hers, which was gaping enough for her to gasp right into the breath of him. *Oh, my Lord! Your tongue inside—please, please,* which all became a mere mumble, for he knew what to do, and did it, and they strained united wetly thus. Her body from the neck down was shapely as that of any fancied nymph. A procurer for some general or member of the lorded gentry would recognize what glory lay beneath the quilted wrappings with which she constantly bedecked herself. She might have won a house in Soho, or at least in a Philadelphia now ruled again by the king.

When finally he took his face away from hers, he planted his widespread hands on either side of her body, and felt her legs curved up and her feet clasping him behind. He made entry in one lengthy moist delicate plunge and she pleaded for his mercy and ardor, and also whatever ardor and mercy might be offered by a heavenly being. She tried to gasp, Oh

my God, but it came out with the words bumbled . . .
sounded like she said, *Oh my gourd* . . . and then
she came, violently, with repeated delicate quiverings
against his happy immersion. She was now an officer
in the rapt league of her sisterhood: all those dainty
women who can come and come, again, again, wild
quaking shots building up to a volleying in kind.

Oh my love, she wailed in weakening frenzy.

Oh my dear, said he.

Later she offered more raspberry tea, but he shook
his head and smiled, and she said, I know your need.
'Tis of something more substantial, and then she
heated up a pot beside the fire which he pulled together, and soon the pot was sighing. Before too long
the steam came up and tilted the lid and made the lid
sing against the rim.

What is this? he cried when he managed to sip from
the great iron spoon she brought. Oh, it tasteth. Truly!

Now is it indeed so?

Heavenly fare, he said. Awarded by an angel. Oh
damn it all. He was looking up at her now. You put
that accursed hood back on again.

I needs must, she said softly. Then in even lower
tone, I'm pleased that you find the fare to be accept-
able.

I told you that it came from Heaven. But it's not
beef.

Nay.

Or lamb.

Go on.

Or mutton, or— I know it may not be pork.

'Tis hare, she said. I learned it from a German
neighbor. Mrs. Barnitz.

Then 'tis proven that the rabbits do gambol there.

What say, dear captain?

The hares are in Heaven, he said, with angel fingers
to do the proper bidding. And he kissed hers and she
laughed lightly and drew them away.

When he was finished, she offered more. He shook his head . . . the first pot had been so generous.

No more. In fact, we're doing rather better now in camp.

I trust. But you must not come here at least for a week.

I doubt that I could appear. But why?

She gestured toward the frames. We must to the quilting she said, with all hands we can gather. We shall be working long into the nights, depending on weather. Some women may be biding here.

Then I'll not risk myself among them.

She whispered, Nor should I permit you to. I'm bit by jealousy.

They pressed in last embrace.

Once he was removed, once beyond the pressure of small light from her doorway, he turned at a handy spot and waved to her, and kissed his fingers. He knew that she must be watching to see him do this.

He was young, untraveled, untutored except by warfare. He had not read too many books and yet his people spoke gently and had a fruitful decency about them.

His notions were vague and ill-formed. Yet he thought of many other men in other climes in other times, all going away from the women with whom they had made adoring and adorning interval. He thought of them walking thus, going mostly in solitude, and mostly in darkness. Some might face a misery, but more he hoped had held their heads on high as he was holding his.

21

CORPORAL Winsted said, Well enough. We got permission which amounts to orders. I name Wolcott, Axle, Caffrey, and Eben Armstrong. You others stay with me here and we'll keep chinking.

There came protest from the discarded.

Now I'm a-giving the orders. You others can go on the next round.

A chatter of dismay rose from those selected. We hain't got nothing to carry things in!

Then get it from folks wherever you go. Get something. Baskets, canisters, anything.

Will the sentries let us pass?

The corporal waved in demonstration. There's other parties going out already. See 'em? Zexcellency's instructions have been published abroad, and you won't need no pass.

The nearest batch of sentries lounged round a fire, swaddled in tags of clothing the best they could be. One who seemed to be a leader only leered with an evil eye solely visible among the wads which wrapped his head, and grinned, and made a gesture at waving them on. He croaked something about, We'll levy gainst you when you return.

Axle scorned to the rest when they were safely away from the fire and the little throng beating hands together, He doesn't sense it, but we won't come back past them rapscallions. We'll come another way.

There was persistent flutter of activity at the Schuylkill where throngs were toiling on the bridge.

145

No sense in going anywhere near that lot. They've already took everything worth handling.

They dragged past the house of Mrs. Hewes, and witnessed men at work carrying things out.

They say Zexcellency's going to move in there.

They watched idly but kept to their pace.

I come this far before, said Caffrey.

Devil you did.

I flinked out. Second night we was here.

Devil you did!

I come all this way, and seen some lights yonder.

How'd you pass the sentries?

'Twas simple. I just sneaked.

They regarded Caffrey with mildly ascending interest. What tuck you here?

Figgered I might find a rat.

Even rats are snowbound now, said Eben Armstrong, and there rose mild chuckle from the rest.

They might be snowbound in truth before they returned. The sky was toneless, dark as a leaden plate, but every now and then a large soft flake came wandering. Once in a while flakes seemed in actual flurry, but only for seconds.

They blew and wiped the fluttering stuff from their faces and kept peering keenly as they might on all sides.

Here. This was far as I come.

There seemed to be a road bearing to the left. They bent nearer the ground to hunt for marks. Footprints, perhaps? Snow had drifted in from an earlier fall that day. Cart or barrow paths, these were more apparent.

Did you see any lights down this way?

Can't recollect.

When they reached the first bend in the road, they saw no house. One wanted to turn back, the majority overruled and said they'd keep on to the second bend at least. They straggled on and round the second bend, truly enough they came upon a house. It was snug, compact, built partly of logs with a plank facing. A way had been cleared up to the door and the soldiers looked at each other in silence. They suffered certain smiting of consciences. They had participated in thievery of one sort or another theretofore; yet somehow the order which had come down from headquarters gave them a preliminary sense of guilt they had not felt in previous encounters with a ravaged public.

They heard fluttering commotion which might emanate from a chicken pen behind the house. The very sound warmed them and made them instantly more eager.

A trifling porch had been cleared, and there were marks discernible showing where people had recently come in or gone out.

Axle was the eldest of the lot and it seemed reasonable to delegate a certain authority to him. He tapped on the wooden porch with the butt of his musket.

Hello the house.

There came no answer. He waited a moment, then tapped again.

There was scraping sound inside, and a woman's voice called, Who be ye?

Soldiers. Axle rapped a third time in more peremptory fashion.

Be ye Hessians?

They responded with laughter. No, lady, we're Continentals from the camp yonder.

She said, Praise be, and there ensued a fumbling inside.

You guarantee you're Continentals?

Open up and take a look at us. You'll see.

I got a hole, she said. A wafer of wood was locked on from the inside, and there came a kind of smear in vision as a face peered out at them.

Oh yep. So you be.

Bolts were drawn and the door drew ajar a few inches and they saw her, wispy and brown and old.

Praise be you ain't Hessians.

Was they here before?

They was.

When abouts?

Must be over a week agone.

They take much?

They was loaded already, she said. Took never a morsel, I praise to relate. I think they was seeking a cow, but we ain't got none now. Our cow, she died about time of the first frost. She was old and couldn't calve no more, so we weren't too hard put.

We're from the Sixteenth Pennsylvania Reserves. Who be ye, lady?

I'm Madam Yuchlan.

Husband to home?

No, sir. He's to the village up yonder. She pointed westerly.

Queer the Hessians didn't take your hens. We heard 'em back yonder.

Reckon they already had all the chickens they could carry.

She offered such gentle reception that they felt even more awkward than before.

Regret to tell you, Mistress Yuchlan. We're instructed to levy on the countryside. We'll take what we can, and give you a notation. You can collect money from the quartermaster's department.

It's as you say, she told them softly. Just please to recall we lost a son, my spouse and me. He was Pennsylvania Reserves as well.

Whereabouts? Webster Wolcott asked so weakly that it was a wonder she heard him.

More'n a year agone. He fell in the attack on Trenton.

The soldiers shuffled their feet. Wolcott whispered, Can't we leave her be?

No, we can't leave her be, said Axle strongly. Wouldn't be fair or right. These folks ain't suffered much, and orders is orders. We got to get food for our mess and she'll be recompensed. So can we enter, Mistress Yuchlan?

Please not to stick bagonets amidst our bed. Be'n't no one hiding there. She laughed bitterly and flung the door wide.

They entered, still remiss. Now in no casual thievery but responding to orders of the day, they felt themselves intruders in a manner they'd never felt before. They stood, filling up the small plain room with its fire burning modestly low. They endured a strange sense of peace and warmth and good smells that brought them close to fainting as they drank the odors in.

Mistress Yuchlan lifted a pothook and took the cover off a simmering kettle. Fresh strong odors came up to enthrall.

I could offer you a bit, she said. If you're an-hungered.

An-hungered? We're fair to fainting, Ma'am!

It's got dumplings in it, she said bashfully.

But what of your spouse? He'll come back from the village and—

It don't matter, she said. To tell the honest truth, we've got most of a flitch of bacon left. I hope you fellers won't take that.

No, Ma'am. But what be this? Pork?

Kind of. Pricklehog. Some call it prickleback. 'Twas up in a tree and my husband, he took his shovel and belted it down.

Caffrey made declaration. Some calls them porcupines too. I never et any, but I'm fain to try if truly you can spare a bite.

She said, I got four bowls.

She offered spoons—three of pewter, one of horn —and ladled out the broth with bits of meat and dumplings.

There was a bench handy, three sat upon it. One made as if to squat on the floor, but Mrs. Yuchlan told him, We got a stool in by the bed, if you'd be so good as to fetch it. It's kind of weighty and I don't dast.

The four ate mainly in silence. The stuff was fabled, had been poured down from Almighty Clouds.

You can wrench the bowls in the snow out yonder, said Mrs. Yuchlan.

There was some belching as if bodies resisted the very fare which offered sustenance.

There's a speck left, gentlemen.

Axle said, Then save it for the Mister. We ain't set to gobble your whole. He wiped his mouth with his hand. I been musing, Ma'am. We dislike to take your all, but we daren't go back empty-handed.

She said, Please to give me that there note and I'll try to collect later. If I can.

Oh yes, you can. We got our orders, and this is fair and square. It ain't just thievery. But I been musing. What can you spare the easiest?

She considered. Reckon 'twould be hens. Please not to take the rooster, though. I always think a rooster kind of spurs the hens on. Makes 'em lay better.

Wolcott and Armstrong, said the self-appointed commander, you go get the hens. Get two. Wring their necks. We can't have 'em squawking round, and the blood's got to drip.

He dared not look at Mrs. Yuchlan as he said this. It seemed somehow as if he were commanding a destruction of the woman's own children. They were dainty hens, pet hens. Now they would be devoured.

Hang 'em outside to drip a minute. They'll quick be half-froze anyway.

He took from his pocket a small orderly book. Would you be so good, Ma'am. Reckon you got a pen?

She found pen and ink and he bent above the bench and inscribed faithfully.

Twenty-ninth day of December, 1777. Received by foraging detail from Mrs. Yuchlan. Two hens. Att. Continental Army Quartermaster, Valley Forge.

He signed his own name and tried to do it with a flourish but the pen trailed limply and spattered.

Just glad you ain't Hessians, said the woman. They was fair burdened down.

Behind the house had arisen a flurry of terrified squawking, the chickens cried havoc. You would have thought the whole flock was being pillaged, not merely two. Then the noise calmed and the boys came round to the door.

Axle and Caffrey looked at the face of their hostess. It was a pinched countenance dried and weathered by more vicissitude than the years themselves had offered. She might have been forty in age; in appearance she might have been her own mother. They thought of Trenton and snow there, and the firing. Vaguely they recalled a story of the Hessian commander Rahl being held up by his own men, standing dying when he offered his sword to the Continentals. They wondered how this woman's son had fared in the encounter, and hoped that the ball which claimed him came quickly before he knew it.

Sorry we had to do this, Ma'am.

It don't matter.

And we do thank you for the fine fare.

It don't matter, she said again. Oh yes, I reckon it does. I wish the best for you, young soldiers. The very best.

There were no more big flakes drifting and the clouds seemed lighter.

Could've left these chickens behint, and picked 'em up as we come back.

Nay. Someone else might come along and pinch 'em.

The hens, recently so vigorous with life, were cooling rapidly. Still blood splashed, but it was thickening and beginning to congeal on sundered necks.

When they turned off on the rude way which led up to the next house, Axle took out his knife, sliced a strip of bark from a nearby sapling, and bound the legs of the two dead hens together. He hung the burden over a cleft of a nearby stub and then the

soldiers approached the house warily with fresh curiosity.

Smoke oozed from a rock chimney. There was a
platform or porch at the front made carefully of
dressed stones. It had been there a long time, and the
men could see that it was brushed readily, for the only
snow upon it lay in a residue of large flakes which
had skittered down this day.

They stepped aloft on the stones and there rose
shriek and fumbling and what seemed to be a rush of
feet inside the dwelling. A woman was wailing, *Der
Feind, der Feind!* An older mildewed masculine voice
cried the same words.

Eben grinned at the others. That's German talk.
We had Germans next door to us in Philadelphia, and
I learnt a lot of words. They say, The enemy, the
enemy!

The front door was cut into two sections, upper and
lower, of the type commonly called a Dutch door,
though this cleavage was present in many houses of
Germans as well as Netherlanders.

Bolts rasped and the upper section of the door
swung slowly out. The muzzle of a weapon appeared,
slid across the frame in wary fashion. Two figures huddled within. A woman and a baldish man, both of
elder years, and the woman looked like a witch because she had her scant gray locks tied into knots
with bits of ribbon, and they pointed every which way.
Der Feind! she said again, and breathed out the two
syllables as if making invocation to rise and resist.

Devil take them, said Axle. His hand shot forward
and grabbed the weapon by its muzzle. Then he
grasped with his other hand as well. There was a short
struggle while the boys scattered, expecting the gun
to be fired, but not Axle. He jerked back and forth,
twisted, and the gun came loose. He lifted it across
the sill in triumph.

What in time is that thing?

Couldn't shoot nothing!

They used to call them a fusil or fuzee or some-

what of that nature. Look here: it hain't even got a
flint in the lock, and if he had a flint, I don't reckon
he's got the powder to go long with it.

The boys came back laughing, and they all
crowded around the half window and pulled it open
wider.

Desire to risk and defy to their last breath shone in
the faces of the pair inside.

Come on, said Eben Armstrong. You two speak
English. Don't give us any more of that *Feind* talk.

Caffrey said, We're not Hessians, old pair. We're
Continentals.

Hessians was here, yelled the witch. They take all.
All! Nothing have we got!

Not one thing, repeated her husband emphatically.
We got nothing, nothing. Go away!

What's your name, Granpa? Not that it matters—

Our name? It is Graupen.

Hessians they come, the woman wailed. They take
all. Everything. We got nothing for you!

When was they here?

The old pair inside looked at each other and then
at the boys once more.

Maybe two weeks. Three weeks maybe. They was
here. They take everything.

Your cow, Master Graupen, sir. I suppose they took
your cow?

Ja. They take the cow.

Ducks? Geese? Chickens?

Ja. They take all. Go away.

The woman cried, We got nothing!

Sheep? They kept baiting the pair. Sheep? They
took your sheep?

Ja, said the old man, but in a manner of doubt this
time, *Ja.* And then he brightened. The sheep, they
took two sheep.

Horses? You had horses?

Again the couple regarded each other before they
turned to speak once more. *Nein.* We got no horse.
They could take no horses because we got none.

Axle said, This is a long low house with a lot of trees around it. Caffrey and Wolcott, you take a look out behint. We other two are coming inside, folks. We don't aim to linger out here in the chill.

He pulled open the lower portion of the door, and he and Armstrong entered eagerly while the others went round to the rear.

The Graupens inched away, still insisting that they had nothing. They were poor, they had been stripped. The soldiers should go away and annoy them no longer! But already the invaders were at the fireplace, luxuriating in small glow and feeling comfort of the room around them.

It was a neat establishment, well brushed, with bright home-woven rag rugs upon the floor. Presently, even over sound of the couple's fretting, they heard a shout raised from behind the establishment, and laughter of the two explorers.

Look to the rear and see what's up.

Can't look. Hain't no back window.

They waited idly but still with speculation for a few minutes more, and then came the trample and approach of their mates. The door was flung open and the men came in, still frosty, eager to achieve their own warmth in turn, but still mirthful.

Well, what's the rub?

These folks spoke the whole truth! There hain't been a cow on this property since Hec was sucking, and we don't find no trace of poultry.

What in tunket did you find?

Apple trees! Reckon there's a thousand. Whole blame forest of apple trees.

Well, did you fetch some apples?

There hain't many left. Just bad ones—winter-killed and froze, not worth a gnaw. But they was something else!

What was there?

What would you say to a cider mill? It's kind of roofed over now, and frosted in with icicles and such, but it's a mill all right. And want to guess what's drug clean up against the house?

What's drug?

Wheelbarrow!

The Graupens broke into torrent of explanation, much of it in German and not easily to be understood.

Oh pray be quiet, you silly old pair, Axle snapped at them. So you're hawking cider, are you?

Praise be, they are! You can see a path: cuts through them apple trees all the way out to the road. Short cut. Easier than the way we come. They're in the cider business all right!

Well, where's the stuff at?

The old couple let loose a bedlam of outburst which was quelled when Axle shook his rifle at them.

Don't want to hear any more out of you two cider-makers and cider-sellers. Gentlemen, let's search about.

There was a room on either side of this main room and already the others had gone exploring.

Hain't nothing in here, came from the south. Just a bedroom.

Did you look under the bed?

Yup. Ain't nothing but a piss jar.

The word came back less rapidly from the room on the right. It was used more or less as a storage place, with hanging articles of clothing, old chests and kegs, but none seeming to contain cider.

Back to the main we come. Sounds kind of hollow under my feet.

Leave us move this scanty rug, said Axle.

They hauled away the rug and a wide trap door was revealed with a ring to raise it beveled into the wood.

Here we be.

They raised the trap door and a smother of pleasant odors issued up.

Look below. Here's a kind of ladder, nigh on to a stair, and Caffrey and Wolcott went down. They gave forth a mutual crow.

What you discovering?

Just about everything in the world! Their voices came up hollowly but with grace and fervor. Got enough potatoes down here to feed an army, and can you smell them onions? Turnips, too, nigh onto a cart-load. And oh, just see this cider! Barrels and barrels!

The old couple had fallen silent, but there was venom in their gaze. They were made to sit upon a bench.

Pass us down a cannikin!

Search was made among fireplace tools, and a stone jar and a small pewter mug were handed down. Oh, it's rare indeed, came the verdict.

Don't swill it all!

Couldn't be did, there's too much. We'd do better with a torch but we don't want to set the place ablaze.

Never. Don't burn it over this old pair's heads, though truly they deserve to have it so. When you going to offer us a touch?

The jar came up, and the mug, and eager hands reached to retrieve them.

Be it stout and hard?

Hard as any rock in the meadow!

They tasted and swallowed, they hooted with glee.

Armstrong had been silent, considering, but now he spoke. I mind when I got tagged for sentry-go tother night, there was talk about a cider-seller down the road. They wouldn't allow him in the camp, and I never seed him, but they said it was an old coot shoving a barrow, and he had it plumb full of cider. The price laid down is one shilling per quart, but he was asking one shilling tuppence which was mighty dear, but he found folks to buy it amongst those who had money. Them in my passel of sentries didn't have none neither; not a sixpence among us, I guess; maybe a few coppers. So we wasn't interested in going down to see. They swore how a lot of officers was out a-buying.

Axle ordered, Don't you fellers swill too much of this here and now. We can take it along.

Oh that we will!

But we got duties to perform. Start passing up them other things. Potatoes and onions and turnips and such.

Prettier load by far than them two hens!

Here's some cabbages, said a voice below.

Hand up a couple.

And parsnips too.

Make do!

How we going to fetch all this truck? And we got to fetch at least a keg of the good stuff, too.

A keg? Take two!

We'll tote 'em in his own barrow, said Caffrey with delight.

It made a mighty burden after they had wheeled the vehicle round to the front on a way which showed, even with the residue come down from the sky, scores of wheel tracks underneath. They balanced two kegs of cider with mounds of vegetables filling up the space between, and put their chickens atop.

The woman sat and wailed, and wailed and gestured, and wailed again. You take everything! she bawled. You take it all! Now we will starve!

You old addlebrain, Armstrong cried angrily. You got enough truck below that ladder to last you through two more winters. Lord knows how much hard cider you got left, too. Enough to blow up your whole blame shack, if somebody put a match to it in proper fashion.

Oh leave her lone, said Axle. She hasn't got all her buttons.

I'll leave her lone if she'll quit making them blame war cries!

After their long starvation, and dwelling as compelled in emaciated bodies, the boys felt a bit tipsy already and talked of broaching cider from another keg still below stairs, and having a final guzzle for the road. But Axle declared with authority, Nobody drinks more till we get home to our shed! We don't want to approach them sentries in any wild manner, and have them call the provost, and mayhap we all get flogged. We'll travel back with this load, and we'll travel straight as a troop of parsons going to a hanging.

Graupen had gone to the bedroom a time before and now reappeared. He was wearing a short thick homespun cape. His cap was wide enough to swaddle his bald dome and ears alike; pulled down it gave protection from the cold. His faded eyes, still canny in their glance, peeked knowingly out from under the brim. The cap, nigh to a hood, was of green felt, faded to the gray of old moss but still with a string tied round it beneath which depended a nondescript rag which once had been a feather.

The boys chuckled at seeing the man arrayed thus.

I'll wager you fetched that along from Germany or wherever you come from.

I go with you, *nein?* I wheel the barrow for you, *nein?*

Armstrong said, Nine is right. Ten too. You don't go nowhere.

We'll let him come long, said Axle.

He couldn't trundle that load ten poles' length. Fact is we'll be sore put between us all.

Graupen quavered, My barrow!

Course it's his barrow. How's he going to hawk more cider thout his barrow? We've levied on his stuff, now let's not take away the barrow too. He's got to have some means of support.

Never get that barrow past the sentries. They'll levy it!

No they won't. We got our foraging pass and we was ordered what to do. We're going to wheel this right to our shanty, and then I'll bring it back to the sentry line. If nobody else volunteers.

They trooped out, closing the lower half of the door, and there rose a scream from inside.

My poor Heinrich! Now I never see him more! I die here alone!

Not if you can beller like that. Come a quiet day you'd fetch everyone halfway to Valley Forge. What about that recipe? Or what's it's name, Axle?

Axle reopened the door and went back inside, tearing off another slip from the orderly book. Blossoming with sobs and protestations, Frau Graupen fetched pen and ink but the ink was dried to dust in the bottle.

I have here, the woman said, and opening a table drawer produced a ragged length of something that seemed like a sliver of brown wood.

What's that there? Caffrey looked over the door-jamb.

It's new-fangled, Axle said. They call 'em pencils.

Pencils?

New invention.

Corporal Winsted was to Zexcellency's headquarters where we lingered at Gulph Springs and he seen some people writing with pencils big as life. No ink, see? Just makes a mark.

Ain't no end to these queer inventions. Wonder what they'll think of next!

The two kegs of rum were apparent, but the boys looked hopelessly at the mound of vegetables.

Nobody could count it all. Say it was miscellaneous. How much we say?

Oh, ten dollars.

Mrs. Graupen was blurting talk about gold.

You can stow that and bury it, lady. Ain't no gold available to the commissary. Lucky we're saying ten dollars and not five. Why, one day that paper money will be wuth ten times what's printed on the face!

They went away with farewell plaint of the woman racking behind them. She cried out in German dialect. Her husband replied in the same until the soldiers hushed him up.

What was they saying, Eben?

Couldn't make out much, but it seems like she was telling him—no, he was telling her—he'd be back before long, and we'd promised him the barrow, and she was saying, Alas she'd never see him again.

That true and righteous? they asked the old man. But now he would say nothing. He grunted and trudged while younger bodies pushed the burden.

A breeze had come up and there was nigh to warmth in it. The sky was no longer blank and pressing. There were clouds. They seemed to have shape, and the boys saw sun on the tips of some, though no sunlight came through in their direction. They felt vigor and purpose never sustained by them during any early pilferings when they sneaked off slyly. All had torn down sections of fences to use the rails as firewood; most had assisted in the slaughter and consumption of stray pigs which came too close to the march or even might have been dragged out of their own pens. Yea, they had helped to slaughter a beef or two; verily they had taken lambs and geese; but this manner of permitted requisition was something they had never known. In finality it made them feel official as administrators of a certain justice.

Spose you was to home, in natural life, not in the Army, but home with your folks, and some soldiers came a-snagging. What would you do?

I'd run 'em off. Me and my brother Saul. We'd chase the daylights out of 'em.

Wouldn't give 'em nothing?

Nary a grain, to be frank.

But then what would you do if the soldiers come as we come now, with orders and a writ?

If 'twas the law, the Continental Army law, then we'd have to give in. Couldn't make no resistance.

But if 'twas like that, you'd be gone to the Army anyway, wouldn't you?

Aye, that we would.

Then you can't compare.

Can't.

They'd found a way in which two could manage the barrow together and they tried to pare their strides to proper length and pace. Even so, they upset the load one time: much of the goods were spilled out, they had to reassort and repack, nothing had been damaged too severely. They cut up two turnips and munched on slices as they went. They felt cocky and newly heartened and carried their rifles slung over their shoulders.

They encountered three more foraging details, two going out from Valley Forge, one group returning. This

batch had a ham which anyone might envy, but not
much else except some drab and moldy small pumpkins.

> *Soldier, soldier, how do ye fair?*
> *Soldier, soldier, will ye trade?*
> *Hain't no fair to call this fare.*
> *Soldier, soldier, I won't trade.*

They were approaching the sentry post and were
greeted as always with the drifting from the Army and
the community itself . . . two waggoners with their
vehicle drawn by four drooping horses . . . the vehicle
was empty. They'd delivered their load at camp. . . .
An officer, then two or three, mounted, going somewhere, God knew where. A tagging riffraff of children
from the few occupied houses near to hand, the children were wadded in scraps of blanket or cloaking,
some were insufficiently clad, they stood runny-nosed
and shivering and looked at everything with large
hunted eyes.

The party heard exclamations of envy, approval,
and whistles to go along with them as they approached
the nearest sentry station. They reckoned that no one
else had come with a barrow. First off Graupen with
his distinctive headgear was being recognized by several, and exclamation burst, Welcome, Old Kraut!
What's come with your cider? Here it be! when the
burden was pushed closer.

You men got two kegs in here. One keg to take inside, and one for the sentries. 'Tis a fresh regulation.

You dare to tetch that keg and you'll have my bayonet up your ass, said Armstrong boldly. We're duly
detailed as a foraging party, and we got it in writing.

The hubbub drew men from other points, some
came strolling indifferently, some trotting, but none
truly lackadaisical. An officer came. He rode his nag
from well beyond and seemed more than a little
amused by what he witnessed, although he did not
laugh openly.

What's ado?

Captain Baddeley, sir. Fortunate you was close to hand! These rapscallions are aiming to take our cider, and they hain't got no license. We was told off by the corporal and we own our paper fair and square. Do you give it to him, Axle, and Axle handed over the magic order.

The captain glanced at the paper and nodded his head. Leave them be, sentries. This is quite in order. You'll need to grow accustomed to these foragers. A new edict is in effect. Leave them to pass, barrow and all.

No, *sir,* came the anguished reply. That barrow is a vehicle. No vehicles to pass here less by special permit signed at headquarters.

Baddeley instructed them calmly, I'll go bail for it, and you may register your protest, or anyone else may do so as he pleases. You men wheel the barrow up to your hut and empty it there.

Master Graupen, sir. Apparently he recognized the German. You may wait here outside the sentry line, and your barrow will be fetched back to you.

A triumphant journey was made up the slope, across the open area which was even now called a parade ground (although there had been no parades held there) and on through freshly desolate woods past other cabins until they came to their own. Cries from neighbors—mixed admiration, approval, and rallying —brought their hut-mates forth and the delivery was effected amid a racketing which made the very non-commissioned officers cry out in disapproval, and made two generals riding near halt and look in some alarm and then ride on again. The solid vehicle came in for admiration from all, the moment it was emptied. Hurtz was tussling with Wolcott and managed to fling him therein. There was further riot and scuffling and again people rushed inside to feast their eyes and clamor for cider above protestations of Corporal Winsted.

He said, We'll all go now. There's time enough, and

light, and the weather's better'n you started in. Seems
like close to spring and breezy aloft.

Ain't no spring in January!

We all know that, but come along with you. We'll
wheel the barrow down when we go.

They told him that the old man was waiting for it.
You can't go again to his house, though. They got a
receipt, duly signed. They can't get scavenged twice.
That's the law. You got to go elsewheres.

We'll go, said the corporal, and I trust we come
back as filled with pride as you folks come. 'Member
what I said, too. You fellers wait on that cider till we
get back, till it's night and we have our other rations;
then everybody gets a noggin. If I find any man's been
at it, I'll report him and ask that he be crucified. Ain't
no joke being tied up to a post or tree in this kind of
weather. Your balls will freeze and drop off, and then
where'll you be? Come along, scuds. Let's march.

Away they went, trundling and banging the barrow
across ruts and over small logs.

Captain Baddeley had ridden off on more important
errand. Master Graupen still waited stubbornly and
had found a stump to sit upon. He hunched there, biding, unprovoked by any unwelcome attention of the
sentries who had figuratively other fish to fry. More
details were coming in with what other loot they had
managed to scrape up. Some were nigh to empty-
handed. Here was another ham, here more squash
and pumpkins, here a big bag of dried corn kernels.
Good eating, once they got it ground, 'twas hard to
grind it. They'd use stones as in an Indian mill when
they could find such a mill.

Master Graupen sprang forward to seize his barrow.
He did not even thank the men who offered it to him.
He said merely, *Ja,* it is mine. My barrow, and turned
and trundled it away. A yell of disgust followed him.

Well, you mought leastways give us the time of day!

But he was too busy pushing the empty rumbling
thing. Perhaps he hoped his wife had not fallen dead
in a fit of rage as witches were alleged to do some-

times. Perhaps he did not think of his wife at all. Perhaps he did not even consider himself fortunate, as indeed he was fortunate. Some people might have tortured him to force him to yield up his hoard of coins, wherever they were hidden. He was lucky. He did not know it as often the fortunate do not. He went banging away, bent and hurrying.

22

SOMETIMES he was attended by those gay bright images which fill the fancies of folk who are so far descended into ailment that they own no life or fire.

As if in their swollen toes and fingertips only a disordered memory goes perking.

This was partly recollection and partly lunacy. He saw two children at games, they played at battledore or term it shuttlecock. Or term it both?

What is thy fancy, Deborah? asked one.

Battledore and shuttlecock, she gave her answer.

For awhile he heard the sound of little paddles tapping at birds, saw the birds belabored handily.

Then it became the battledore and shuttlecock of infancy. These were cards come handed down from grandsires. But still the children studied them, they hoped to learn their letters thus.

A is for apple all shining and red. B is for boy as he goes to his bed, and small tight illustrations portraying both apple and boy. *C is for curds as they mix with their whey,* and it showed a bowl with a fine spoon sticking out. *D is for dog as it romps in its play.*

These peculiar relics began to yield to the current pastime.

But why did they call them so? What a device to be employed for young instruction!

Tunk . . . whir . . . tunk . . . went the game.

Each time a paddle struck the bird 'twas an explosion of a firefly.

So little . . . bitty . . . bright. . . .

Mistress Ellen, did this one take the broth?

He is very weak. He could not even turn his head away.

Did it run down?

I fear so. Yes, there upon his chest. And tatters of his shirt.

Mistress, let me wipe it clean.

There.

So.

My lad. Young sir. What is thy name?

He attempted with all the force of life left in him, tried to speak of the game of battledore and shuttlecock which he'd been watching, striving in, hoping to learn his letters in. So that they should term the sport . . . figures from a primer slate. . . .

Heard his own voice lengthened in distance.

Mum.

I fear he's very weary. Her tone fell soft. Much weaker.

I fear he's failing.

Aye. He knows not his own name.

Mum.

23

KARL HURTZ had worked in a tavern from the time he was eight and a half; first sopping up with mop and hand-whittled broom in kitchen, scullery, taproom, bedrooms; then as a room steward of sorts; then (a demotion when the proprietor fell ill) as hostler in paddock and stableyard; then in the kitchen, finally in the taproom itself. He was not a bound boy; Karl won a salary, but it was paid strictly to his widowed mother, every penny of it. He felt the delightful chink of coins in his own pocket only when some generous or bibulous traveler thought to endow him, and but stingily on most occasions. Nevertheless a tavern was the only life he knew intimately and his enthralling ambition was to possess one. He had learned to read and cipher, he retained only dim recollection of the long vanished period when he tried to spell out various jargons scratched upon a slate, and won a shaking or a slap when he failed to master the intricacies. He was not stupid, but only limited in imagination. (He began to learn that many people are so.)

He was seventeen when, according to an old saying, the Army broke out.

Amid vilest weeks of privation at Valley Forge he kept his Tavern Dream handily close to heart, and took it out and fondled it in secret moments, and learned that there could be a strength in bare ambition itself.

MY TAVERN.
WHAT SHALL BEE ITS NAME?
NAMES I HAV THO'T OF

Royal Georg Washington (for truly he is Royal).
General Georg Washington.
The Keg and Kettel.
The Kettle and Keg.
Liberty Korner (if on a korner).
Liberty Hill (if on a hill).
Valley Forg Arms (No. crossed out).
The Cherry Tree (one can be planted nearby).
The Apple Tree (Or Peech, Pare, Wall nut, and
*   such).*
The Spredding Oak (Would have to be an oak.)
The Liberty Bell. (Have pictur of a pretty bell.
*   Say a pretty girl on sign)?*

The Liberty Bell (or Belle? He was a little doubtful
about this) became a favorite toy, and he continued
with his Bell and Belle hanging prettily in the background.

These fancies were bound to hold limitation, so Karl
Hurtz turned with relief to a Table of Rates.

A hot meal of roast or boil with small beer or
*   cider. 1 shilling.*
A cold ditto, with Ditto. 1 Shilling.
Good lodging with cleen sheets. Per night. Six-
*   pence.*

This last was challenge and pother. How many
sheets would he need to provide, to begin with? Suppose not merely a lone lodger but indeed all his lodgers
were mired in mud on the roadway, and suppose all
became drunk before retiring, and crawled into bed
still wearing boots or moccasins? If he had a wife, she
could build a fire under the caldron at dawn. But suppose he had not yet got him a wife? He would need
to plunge deeply into debt to acquire the tavern in the
first place. He thought he knew a man or two, well
provided for, who would lend him the wherewithal in
manner of mortgage. But how much extra stipend
might possession of a wife require? Would she be will-

ing to eat what was left on the plates? (He had often done so, and greedily at that.)

Port wine per quart. 4 shillings.

This was fiendishly expensive, but a straying Congressman or Philadelphia merchant might hammer the table and demand the best.

*Wired Beer from London or Bristoll, per quart.
    1 shilling.*

Common Drink for Common Man. More sensible —and more common.

Cyder per quart. Fourpence.

Plain drink for plain customers.

He proceeded with his list of such enticing moistures. Punch, Country Brandy, French ditto, Rum. Madeery Wine (as he termed it), 4 shillings per quart. Claret at that same heady 4 shillings.

In gaunt relief he turned to other practical considerations, feeling that he was brought nigh to a potted state himself by the mere reviewing of the liquors involved in his reckoning.

*Corn or Oats. Per peck. 1 shilling.
Pasturage for a horse for a night or a day or 24
    hours. Sixpence.
Stablidge with good Clover or Timothy Hay, per
    night or a day or 24 hours. 1 shilling.
Ditto with Corn Fother or Marsh Hay. Per Night
    or Day or 24 hours. Sixpence.*

He saw them roosting on the bounty he provided, saw them appearing on horseback, stained with travel but delighted at the prospect of comfort within, saw them alert and able, a whole party arriving by coach, saw trains of waggoners pleased to come in and sleep upon the floor if the house were full. He smelled fine odors arising from his kitchen, saw an elegant cheese arrayed upon its board, with knife to hand and black bread to go along with it. He saw a scullery boy running to do something, saw a woman in snowy cap and snowy gown going to do something else (might she be his wife, known ordinarily as Goodwife Hurtz, and quite the toast of the journeying public?). His imagination soared like one of his own fancied and postured steeds leaping a fence. He saw children, big-eyed and maybe learning in the background, and polishing something or other.

No, no children. He wiped them out; yet somehow they lingered as spry ghosts might do.

He came back to the icy starving camp again, but he had been aided.

24

WITH the rest of the contingent who were already speaking of themselves as Wayne's Drovers, Malachi lay on his arms that famous night and at three o'clock in the morning, as typified by officers who possessed watches, they received orders to mount and be off.

No longer were companions twitting the boy about his horse. They had worn that joke to a frazzle, and soldierlike were looking for other jests to occupy them.

Few felt like posturing with cap and bells at such an hour in such a season.

Horses' hoofs played their tunk-a-tunk melody on cold planks and then, as they receded into dark regions beyond the Schuylkill, they made less noise and flurry.

An order came down to walk their horses. No trotting till daylight, and that was long away as yet. Daylight came officially only when clear vision was available to a distance of two hundred yards. Malachi knew not how the others felt nor did he care. He was occupied with his own exuberance, he was embarked on blissful sortie. He supposed correctly that their ardent commander was far gone yonder. Every now and then he put forth a hand to pat John's neck and often bent forward to whisper adjurations to the steed. He knew not exactly what he said, nor again did he care. It was a mingling of fantasy and dream and affection.

They halted several times for conference by the troop commanders and one could hear the easy drawling voice of Colonel Roedvig rising along with the rest. They passed a few farms but did not tarry. This in-between country had been raked dry by lobsters, Hessians, and previous parties of Continentals.

Malachi recalled the first farm they came to in rising daylight. The householder stood by the road, his gestures were mocking but informative. He held out his hands with palms up, made a slow motion of lifting his hands, then dropped them again to signal emptiness. He'd been picked, he was miming to them sardonically, picked clean. There came however a remote lowing from woodland beyond his house: a cow was out there, or maybe more than one, and a pair of riders were told off immediately to go in search. They came back as empty-handed as the farmer had been. They could find nothing. The beast or beasts had been hidden too well.

I trow they're not his anyway.

From a neighbor, no doubt. Let's be off. 'Twas wise to head for less-plucked countryside to the north.

At a crossroad there was a brief conference; then two troops bore ahead and to the right, and Malachi's own commander waved and pointed to the left fork.

They gestured in good-bye to departing companions but kept their voices down. The horses were bound to make enough noise as it was, puffing and blowing. Some of the horses were feeling hungry and they spoke about that in their own language, but there was no fodder to give them. The men themselves were hungry. Some had fetched along a small variety of rations, others had nothing. Malachi's hand sought out his own meager portion of beef. He chewed seriously for awhile, and again felt that pervading sense of adventure and official larceny. It was stimulating to be emancipated from the routine of hut-dwelling and dull wood-and-water detail. This was a boon which most soldiers might crave but never realize. The sense of private good fortune was a mystic shimmering thing which lingered like a light fairly between John's ears. . . . Weary? Had he ever been weary? He could not believe so. This was an escapade. He knew the word vaguely; he tried to say it but got only as far as *escape* and the rest was blemished. He rode exuberant as the few remote cocks they heard crowing from time to time.

Sun streaked at them. There came a comparative sense of warmth and peace to all. Their vedettes, riding well in advance, came back at the appointed ten o'clock to offer the watch which Colonel Roedvig had lent to them. He told off two more sentries to replace those who had come in. Including outriders and including the commander there were seventeen soldiers in this party. It was reckoned to be the smallest which had been assembled.

Two of the men looked knowing. Their names were Furman and Heath. They said that they had been there before—seeing folks, as they said—but ones who had left their abodes with the outbreak of Revolutionary activity. These men said that they were getting out of Quaker country. They'd encounter more Welsh now with a good sprinkling of Scots to go with them. The Scots were a wary crew.

Wouldn't give you the crumb off their porridge if they had any, I'll be bound.

This retinue of Wayne's Drovers made their first killing briefly before noon. One of the outriders loped back to report that he had glimpsed a man, perhaps a farmer, hastening down a road, dodging into bushes (apparently when he spotted the outrider) and then hastening across an open field and into brush beyond. So it might mean something? said the commander in his customary questioning manner. Suppose we look and see? The scout led the whole pack on a side lane until they could observe a house. Colonel Roedvig waved the picket back to outriding, and led his party to the front of the house, a substantial one built partly of logs, partly of hewn lumber. There was a cart standing in the yard but the tongue was held up by a stilt and there was nothing in the cart. If there were women within doors they kept out of sight, even when thunderous knocks resounded on their door.

Smoke from the chimney, men said. Someone's to home. Better keep knocking.

Which they did resoundingly until the whole house seemed trembling with violence of their aggression, though the door itself was barred.

They heard faint feminine squeals somewhere inside and they winked and nudged at this.

A voice broke upon their hearing, What you want?

The voice was crying from a distance. What you want? I got not a thing for you. You hear me? Nothing. But the voice was coming closer.

The householder arrived, breathing heavily and seeming to perspire in spite of chilly air. He was not a Scot, but obviously of Welsh ancestry, and he declared that his name was Gwenyth and that he was a loyal servant of the king. He slipped and scurried and flurried on that statement, made with too much haste, and when he was still out of breath and after his cagy glance had gone over their attire.

I mean the Congress, he said, still gasping. A loyal Loyalist. I mean a loyalist to the Congress.

So you're mingled in your belief? the colonel asked. I suppose we better take a look around? He signaled to three of the men and Malachi's heart bounded because he was one of those chosen.

Go look at woods and waters, they were ordered, and pushed away to the task. Desperately the householder cried after them, and then appealed to their commander again. He was a dark little man of middle years with a sparse scraggly beard and eyes that shifted and snapped with pretense even when he tried to force a bold and supposedly honest stare.

I got nothing for you at all! His plaint pursued the riders as they hastened in exploration.

They pressed through a skirt of woodland; there were numerous paths and trails there and it was easy to go. They came out into an open field where stood a large hayrick roofed against weather, and a more tightly roofed log building beyond. The soldiers piled from their horses and went to explore, and cried out when they saw the contents. There were two cribs in the structure, one crowded with a store of corn in the ear. The other— They went closer and peeked and felt. Bonanza!—a bin stocked with oats. The other two desired to return post-haste and tell the colonel what they had found. At least the horses would eat well, they were saying. Malachi favored looking further afield. He pushed through the next break of timber. He found two horses grazing in a meadow beyond. They were in only fair condition, and they wore bells which had been stuffed with leaves to make them toneless. There was no sign of any cattle and no dung was apparent anywhere upon the ground. He rode back and found that the other two had already rejoined the colonel with news of their discovery. Now he went to offer his own report.

The colonel nodded sagely. I thought he must have horses because he has a cart. How can you haul a cart without horses?

They're a sorry pair, said Malachi.

Sorry as yours? There rose general laughter from the group.

Farmer Gwenyth had opened his house and there were four of his family with him. A shrunken old woman who might have been his mother or his wife's mother; his wife, quite as surly as he himself; and two nondescript little girls. They were offering oatcake and the men perked with satisfaction at this. And more? the man was wheedling. We got some pickled pork. We'll feed the lot if you promise not to take a thing. I'm a good patriot, I tell you. I love the Congress. Are you from Valley Forge? I love Valley Forge.

By the Eternal, we don't! was the general response.

Young soldier, I think I ride with you to see those horses for my own self? the colonel said. And see that corn and oats?

During this errand the colonel found a receptive ear, or two of them, in Malachi Lennan. The colonel liked to talk and Malachi was an affectionate and profound listener. Colonel Roedvig dropped the bridle reins from his mouth into his hand in such occasion and made reminiscence in a solid stream. Each sentence ended in implied question of the Scandinavian mood. Malachi and the other soldiers wondered why the colonel had insisted that the Welshman eat of the same food which had been prepared for them in generous gesture. Did he perhaps think that it was because the food might be poisoned? Surely: that was a fact. The colonel had savored one experience with poisoned food in a campaign abroad—not in Holland, never, but in regions adjacent—but still they were Low Countries. Malachi could not quite understand where they might lie, and roiled his brain in trying to think of maps he had seen but rarely.

Yes, some people had sought to poison his men and they had eaten only a few bites. Their lives were despaired of, but a clever surgeon managed to save them. One should never ask what befell the peasants who had tried to wreak such mischief; no, it would not be fit to tell! But that was the reason he had mistrusted the Welshman: because of his eagerness to feed them. That was why he saw to it that the unwilling host should sample the fare, and before his very eyes. Yes, indeed, the man was indignant to the point of madness, but little good could it do him, though he had eaten and the food was all right, it had not been touched with any diabolical intent. Well, it was best to be on the safe side?

Thus peculiar kinship sprang between them, because the colonel liked to talk and Malachi found joy in listening. Nor did the colonel ever twit him about John the horse; not one word was said.

Rigid custom intended that the three officers should eat and sleep apart from the men. Malachi felt that the two captains might indeed work some savagery against him but as long as the colonel approved and summoned him, there was nothing that they could do. That very first night Colonel Roedvig saw the boy drifting about in the low firelight. Yes, they could have fires. They had sentries posted, and in due time it would be Malachi's burden to take up the same sort of duty. But the colonel summoned him first with a wave of his left hand (that very busy hand which did so much so constantly).

I was considering, the colonel said, about a raid like this we made one time in the Low Countries. Oh it was better weather than we have here at this time but there was rain and mud and the peasants had nothing to give us. That country had been swept by war and all the food was gone. The people walked along the roads going to seek food, and it was sad to hear the little children cry because they were hungry. Perhaps they could find food in some town? I do not know. They would have a cart sometimes and put the mothers with babies in the carts, or very old people, and they were crying and what do you say, sniffling, or do you say snuffling as with a cold? Yes, had we food ourselves we would have given it to them because we felt so sorry to see them in, how do you say it, such condition? Yes, I have seen many wars, many campaigns. I have been a soldier since I was young. It is my way of life and perhaps it is sad. You ask how did I lose my arm? Or did you ask? It does not matter. Now I will tell you about how I lose the arm? I have one carbine and I am careless with it, and I shoot myself in the hand. Then it all turns black. It hurts so badly and swells up and I have what you call a misery. And finally they say that I will die lest they take off the arm, so I say take it off, and so they do. That is how I lose my arm because I was a fool with a gun. No cannonball, no bravery, no riding out ahead. I ride many times later, and out ahead sometimes, but the time I lose my arm there is no hero and if there is, I am not he. I am but a fool to lose my arm in a foolish way? I even know that sometimes men shoot themselves so maybe they can lose their arm; then go home safely and not die in battle. This was not true of me. I have been in many battles, in many campaigns in the Low Countries, but when I lost my arm it is because I am a fool?

A householder said, I been raided twice before and now you come to raid me again. I moved, lock, stock, and barrel. We was down by the Raritan and we had a nice place and then the British come. They crossed the Delaware and come up there and took everything I had, and what they didn't take they burnt. All I've asked is to be let alone. I told them I was a good king's man, but that didn't make no difference. So we took what we could scrape together, and come here to this crick and got a new place, and I started farming again, and then last year you bloody Continentals come down from Morristown or somewheres and cleaned me out again. I got cleaned by the king's men and cleaned by the Continentals, so where's a man to say his faith belongs? I guess his faith don't belong nowhere. I don't trust nobody. Don't trust you, or your precious General Washington, or that precious crew of lazy hirelings or whatever they are that call

themselves: the Continental Congress. Continental
Congress, shit. What was they put on earth for? Just
to raid poor innocent people, same as the king's men?
I've hearn tell of Gypsies. They got some in the
New York country and over in Jersey where my
wife hailed from. They travel round and sleep in tents.
Guess that's what I'll be compelled to do. No, I don't
want any dang slip of paper. You say 'twill be re-
deemable. When and how? You can plaster rebel cur-
rency that ain't worth the ink that's stamped on its
face. Now, if you paid me in *gold,* paid a fair price
for all the dunnage is worth, it might be another matter. But just to rob a feller time out of mind and take
the food out of his wife's mouth and his too! I got
some other relations to look after too—when I can.
Take 'em baskets and kegs of rubbage when I can afford to, and lots of times when I can't. It smarts, I
tell you, like I was in a patch of scratch weed. You
come around with an armed troop of thieves and claim
you're saving us all. I didn't need to be saved from
nothing till this cussed war started, and 'twas a gang
of your kind of patriots started it. Robbed the ships,
and fired on the king's men, and I-don't-know-what-
all tempestuous deeds was done. Oh no, oh no, don't
pull out your weepons! You don't have to shoot me.
I don't want to be no martyr. 'Twouldn't do us any
good, now, would it? If you was to shoot me and I'd
have to lie here dead, then you'd just take my property the same way anyhow. All right, very well, I'll
give in. I ain't got no other choice. I'll take your blame.
paper, and try to collect on it like you tell me to do.
But it's hard lines, that's what I insist, hard lines!
You're grabbing everything I put away to get us
through the winter. Hoist it off in your waggon—I
should say, *my wagon* that you pre-empted—ain't
that the word for it? Very well, very well; don't shoot
me, don't hit me! Just give a man the right to run off
at the mouth a bit. I don't know who to trust, can't
trust no one. Found I couldn't trust that dratted king.
Oh he ain't here in person, I know that, he ain't in

the Colonies. I mean you don't call 'em Colonies any more, but leastways he isn't squatting in *my* privvy, is he? Reckon you'd burn *that* too, if he was, now wouldn't you? You say you're leaving me one horse so I can plow. Thank you, kind sirs, for that; and leaving us one cow that's fresh so we can have some milk. Well, ain't that sweet. You say you could take 'em all. Well, that's what that first batch of Continentals did with our pigs. They did take 'em all. And I heard they was just living it up in Morristown, high and merry, and old Washington was living in a tavern, living high, and so was all the officers. You say you was there too—some of you was—and you had a hard time gettin' fed? Spose I got to believe you're tellin the God's own truth, but it's hard lines, I tell you, hard lines. Like it says in the Scriptures, be a good husbandman, like it says, and look what I got for my pains! Enough to make a heathen out of any Christian. I'll try *being* a heathen, from now on.

Nay, we have not been combed before. They did come nigh, both redcoats and Continentals and more —I know not who. I fear there have been strangers about, feathering their own nests as it were, not answering to any rule or command. But we have been spared until this day. What would you now? As you are the Army of the American Colonies—States, if you will—I wish to offer all you need insofar as our small hoarding can satisfy you. Yes, there be this stack, left side of the house, and half a one out yonder. I have a waggon; yes, it is there; and pray take it if need be. I do trust that you will not see fit to take my plow. It is the only one I have, and the horse has grown a bit lame but he can still haul me through a furrow and that be what is needed. We have not much food surviving this winter. There is still hanging yonder one entire ham and half of another and those two barrels containing a store of pork. It was pickled in the autumn but is still fit fare. Be any of you soldiers among those who did fight at Germantown? That was where our son fell. No, no, he was not a youth. Somewhat elderly to go as a soldier, but he felt the need and the call, and we were proud that he obeyed the summons of his heart. His own son also went for a soldier. He is still among the living, we pray and trust. Be any of you hungry now, Gram and I can give you some fit fare, much as we can manage, but it will take a bit of time. Mayhap if we fetch out some pickled pork and serve you, that would do you well. This is but a Monday and Gram did bake on Saturday. She can still manage deftly with the oven and my grandson's wife was here to help her, so we still have oatcake in some quantity, and would be proud to ration you with it. In our root cellar there is not much remainder except for onions under the straw and a store of turnips. Aye, we do have vinegar in some small store, only enough to last us till the apples come again, but we should be happy to share with you, or indeed you may fetch away all, if there is that necessity. Please to survey our small premises as you will and bear away that which you desire. Nay, it is not that we are giddy with any wish to impoverish ourselves. We are humankind and such a course would prove absurd. But if the aged can aid, that is what we most wish to do. I have said enough now and will harangue you no more. Yet we do believe that your cause is our cause as well, and we seek for proof in the Scriptures, each morning and each eventide. We believe that we have it in the word of our dear God that this cause must prosper. We find in the Scriptures both promise and pride, and feel it ordained that we all shall prosper. Ah, true: one other matter. I did neglect to say that in the storage pit we still have a pumpkin. Pray take it if you have need.

It was at another larger farm, but two days after this visit, when the pickets rode in, shouting that they all should only see the mass of horses coming down the road. So they were: a throng, a pile of horseflesh, and the ground was a drum beneath their beating.

General Wayne and several of his officers rode in the rear, a bit bedraggled but triumphant.

The soldiers shouted back and forth. They reined close to the newcomers, heard gossip. General Wayne had swept through eastern Pennsylvania adjacent to the Delaware; across to Jersey; squirreled through the countryside there; recrossed as Coryell's Ferry and ranged now on homeward course. The horses were in splendid condition. A ton of forage might have been fetched for each, had they possessed the waggons. Nay, they had no waggons to fetch it away with, they'd burned the stacks instead. Aye, they'd brushed against a few stray parties of lobsters. They'd sent them packing. Aye, they'd come across some deserters as well. And pray what happened to them? Ah, pray don't ask. Grimaces and gestures told the story.

Mad Anthony Wayne yelled loudly himself, then he whistled. You there! Soldier! What be your name— Esau? Nay, nay! *Thy* horse! *Thy* steed! He whooped again, pointed and beckoned. The truth dawned upon Malachi: he was the one sought and importuned.

General Wayne's mighty finger was a hook lifting him out of the ruck and dragging him forward, he and John and all.

Lad, Pennsylvanian, militiaman in truth. I know you. What be your name, again?

Malachi Lennan, sir.

Gad, yes. Malachi to be sure! And the horse? Pray now, the horse? Be it Esau? Or— Nay, nay. The honey, the locusts—

John, sir.

And I indited you a pass, and you went through the lines. Oh save the day, save the night! John indeed! Locusts and—what be it, now?

Wild honey, sir, said Malachi faintly. The general heard, and all those nearby were laughing along with him.

Wayne's big bay reared slightly and swung to the left and the general brought him back into position with a flick of the bridle rein. For the barest instant his dark face showed the tightness of pain with compression of the lips. His old shoulder wound had affected him, would always affect him. Another mount had gone down under him, killed in an ugly combat which no one liked to recall. The general was never allowed to be free from this recollection, although Heaven knew he desired to be.

And I scrawled out for you a pass, and let you go by night to bring in this beast, and did I ask you his age? Never! What might it be, lad? Is he upwards of thirty years?

Malachi was choking. It was difficult for him to get words out. Knowledge came swarming over him all of a sudden. His knees tightened convulsively as he sat in the familiar saddle and he had to employ main force in order to wrest them back.

John is twelve, sir, said Malachi.

And swaybacked into the bargain! How long has he been in such condition, lad? Wayne spoke the last word with deliberate kindness, for he could see the white workings in Malachi's face close before him.

For some time, sir.

And yet you fetched him on this gruelly journey. Oh my soul and body! 'Tis no fault of yours, but he's long since broke asunder.

They were ringing close, staring faces, all those people giving heed to the general's remarks, and primary outcry in Malachi's own attempt at explanation. It was as if they heard the weeping within him before it began, before it had come wrenching to the surface of his being. How might he ever declaim the horrid truth, the rancor which came of utter deprivation? How might he say, We called him The Colt when we journeyed west?

John owned no other name until he was two and I found the honey for him, and that was ten years agone. Why I was seven then, and now I am seventeen. I've aged as well as he. I am a soldier. 'Tis an awful prank that makes a mount grow old with speed which his rider cannot grasp or equal. Might I tell the general—? I can never do so. I can talk with no one, no one. Our house burnt down and my parents and the baby sister were gone within it, and here I was with John, ridden in effort to neighbors' many miles away, gone to seek the aid which might help them, for all were lying sick abed. And then the storm, the lightning and the fury, the neighbors keeping me throughout the night, and my return to find some other neighbors in the course ahead, and telling that I must not venture forward, must not see the ruin of our house and the burned objects which lay within, and had then been dragged from ashes. Oh, we did not know! Could it have been the lightning, the stroke of God Himself, for why would He have struck them so when all did fear and acknowledge Him? Some said the Indians . . . had prowled about. There was talk of killings not too far away. And yet, and yet— The house burnt down, and those within it gone, and John was all I had, oh all I had, and I might love him long. No one could even understand the love I've given unto him, and I trow he gave unto me as well and still is giving. This wild knowledge—how it pesters and offends, and all in an instant embarrassed flick of time! The general's big steed shies and then he winces, and that is wrong. It is a jest to him. It is the darkest recollection that I own, that anyone might own, and yet is over in a second.

(Not over, but entertained and passed until it comes again.)

A staff officer, sitting his saddle next to Wayne, thought he heard the general whisper to himself, He should be shot. I've never got the heart to order it.

In louder voice Wayne said, Young Lennan soldier, you'd best be rid of him at once. 'Twould be a kindness.

Malachi could not speak.

This farmer here, hard by. You stripped him? he asked of the detail.

Voice replied, All that he had, sir.

A horse? Had he a horse?

No sir. Tories took it two weeks since. So he says.

Then take a mount from this stud, my boy. Over yonder, that chestnut. Cut him loose, one of you, and give him to the boy. Take thy saddle and bridle, lad, and give—

He looked again at the face of Malachi Lennan. He thought, And many say I am a brute. If God be not damned, I am a fair Disciple. He thought this, he did not say the words.

He said, Yonder stands the householder. Do you give your own steed to him.

The general—the general said that I was to give you John.

So worthy of the general! Very well. So this be John?

Aye, that is his name. (Now you might find a chuckle— No, sir. I'll find none.) I—I don't like to give up John.

Still he might be handier than no steed at all. But is he only saddle-broke?

Oh no, Mister. He's broke to haul and plow.

Now that be well. I've got a halter rope, I trust. Pray but allow me . . . here. 'Tain't much, but 'twill serve. . . . And John, you say his name is?

The vast disordered stud had gone pressing down the road with Malachi's own detail at the rear, but some were looking back, and seemed deliberately slowing in their pace.

Your name, sir? Please, I wish to know I might return someday.

Someday's too late, I fear. He won't last long. My name is Gunderson.

Gunderson? Ah yes, sir. And—my thanks to you—

The name was riveted against his recollection with all the metal bolts that men had ever forged along the Valley Forge stream.

I'm glad to have him, lad, I shall treat him kindly.

Oh yes, sir, I am sure you will. I—I must be off.

The farmer said, Come, John, and made as if to lead the horse away. John turned and lifted his head, tried to raise his ears in query. He made his nicker, he said, Why Malachi, and will you leave me thus? Ah well; you left me once before and I was treated kindly. But do come back, good Malachi, dear one, he said amid his strange horse question as he nickered once more.

Malachi headed down the road to join his detail. He thought he heard John whinny faintly once again as he was riding. He did not dare turn round, did not dare look back. The soldiers and other horses swam before his gaze. Dear God, he tried to say. Immortal God.

25

THE cabin in which Jem Baddeley was quartered had been partially destroyed by fire two nights after it was built and remained briefly a hulking little ruin in the officer's line of huts. Then, once enough men could be arranged for the purpose, and with officers themselves bending to the task, they rebuilt the thing in a style large enough to house four persons. 'Twas a crazy structure resembling an exaggerated outhouse and with the roof too low: tall denizens might stoop perpetually when they were sheltered here. Nevertheless Baddeley and another Captain named Erving and two lieutenants were pleased to dwell therein and feel comparatively uncrowded. They had one bunk apiece in the four corners; thus no one must need to dwell on high, nor gag there when smoke oppressed the cobbled-together ceiling. Men they commanded had heard about the place and called it for Lord knew what reason The Buttery. Then the lieutenants fell ill and were hospitalized. No one else came to take their place, and Baddeley and Erving had the structure to themselves.

It appeared initially that the two had little in common except sum of brief but violent military experience. In notion and attitude they were far apart. Each awarded the other polite respect, but there could be little common jesting between them.

Most of the nights these officers had to themselves, unless they were tapped for some special detail; and then there was Baddeley's own distraction with Mistress Gracie below the long hill, down the road, off on the by-pass, across the stream. The darknesses he could share with her were both winsome and jolly—a profit now which he was charging in imagination against a most uncertain future.

From peculiar source Captain Erving obtained a sleek fragment of board, and cobbled the thing up next to his bunk to employ as a table. It was of varnished hardwood smoother than any ribbon, and apparently had been broken off some item of smashed furniture.

I saw a soldier with it and bought it from him. I offered him sixpence, he was hesitant. I made it a shilling and he beamed and handed the board over.

Baddeley observed with puzzlement and a little awe, You wished a table. But why?

I am not pleased unless I own a table to write upon.

Erving was slim and had the jauntiness of one of athletic proportions. When he walked he glided springingly, resting weight upon the forward parts of his feet. His hair was black, he kept it short. He had a pair of shears among his small possessions and a fragment of mirror as well; and Baddeley witnessed him pruning his hair, clipping it close as he might (this in an age when most wore queues, or periwigs among the more able and important). His battered tricorn he wore tipped jauntily to one side. In worst weather he coddled his head and figure with a huge tight-knit muffler. He sported dancing eyes, you could never tell what color they were, they glinted as if exuding private jest but also intense determination. Commonly he was near to being frisky in manner. He wore a big pistol which he was constantly cleaning, rubbing, deflinting, and making what he called dry aims: cocking after the charge was drawn and there was no flint in the lock, aiming at imaginary target, clicking the trigger steadily, slowly, connivingly, until the hammer fell and the imagined round fired. His sword had a noticeable curve to it, 'twas almost more of a saber. He said that he had taken it from the British.

You captured the one you took it from? asked Baddeley with caution.

Erving smiled. Nay. I killed him.

The pair began to achieve an intimacy which came in more or less with the advent of the writing table. Next time Baddeley appeared, wending through darkness of an eve when neither of them had external duty, he found Erving seated on his bunk, a dripping light of candle beside him, and inkwell and pen handy.

I must needs keep my fingers in.

Your fingers?

Aye. My writing thumb, if you will.

You have such duty to perform?

Shan't call it that, but 'tis from the colonel. He gave to me notations, and asked that I incorporate them in a letter. So here away!

Later he lifted the inscribed results with an air of easy triumph and Baddeley gaped and gawked at the penmanship.

Copperplate!

Erving looked at him genially. Didst ever see any?

I'm not exactly certain, said the honest Jem. But I've hearn tell.

I use a very fine pen. Fine as to point.

Fine pen or no, 'tis— He hunted for a peculiar word and found it. Calligraphy, he said.

'Twas the doing of my parent. He's long been a schoolmaster, you see, and when I was very small and first able to make marks, my father did lay down an order. He said to me, Christian Erving—

Baddeley interrupted in surprise. Be that your

name? I heard someone—one of the officers, I can't recollect—heard him call you Chris, so I supposed your name was Christopher.

Nay. Christian.

Because you profess to be one?

Nay, with no more purpose than yourself, I fancy! My father is of Danish extraction, and he named me after the kings of Denmark. Christians by the drove, they had them in sufficiency and more. Some were wicked, some noble, so thus they did represent the core of Humanity. That's neither here nor there, but my father did teach me to inscribe. I'm not truly happy unless inscribing.

So you bought the board, that shiny table you use now.

Christian Erving touched it proudly. Truth.

In fact the proclaimed admiration of Erving's skill grew to be a common bond which had not knit them together before. Strain and silence were departed. They grew to speak eagerly and intimately.

When in proper mood (some might have termed it improper mood) Erving would circulate through their limited quarters, dancing like a boxer on his toes. He was a sophisticate such as Jem Baddeley had never encountered previously and might never meet again.

Christian the Second was a bloody tyrant! He cost Denmark the nation of Sweden for all time. But Christian the Fourth was noble and wise, although an embattled Protestant. As for dear Christian the Seventh, here in our own time, he began the abolition of serfdom some years since. What indeed shall I abolish, friend Baddeley, since I must earn my right to the name?

Such antic caused Jem to feel doubly enriched. Whatever the paucity of Valley Forge, he felt that he had been awarded two great gifts: on one hand, the shapely widow, whatever her facial condition and resulting eccentricity; and for a cabin-mate he now owned the acme of stimulation.

Sadly enough this was not long to be.

One night regimental duties claimed Jem till a late hour. He guessed that Erving might be gone on similar encounter but when he returned to the cabin, kicked the fire together, put on fresh wood and warmed the place a bit, it was tenantless otherwise. Christian Erving did not return until long after Baddeley was sleeping, and he still slept when Jem arose and went on duty, and was departed again when Jem returned. Thus they dodged for several days without even exchanging words. There seemed no ready explanation for such dislocated routine. It was not until four or five nights afterward when Erving appeared and sat himself down at his table.

Is it for this I have toiled? I am but a rag, worn to desperation, and all a-tremble. Would that I could tip a noggin!

Baddeley looked at him soberly. Why not tip one, and he dug out a flask from his supplies.

What be it?

Plum brandy. 'Tis claimed.

Heavens above, said Erving. You have saved me from I know not what! and his hand shook as he extended it.

Later he rested awhile with eyes closed and cheek against his open hand. Then his elbow slid off the improvised desk and he looked up and smiled. You know not where I have been, this day and night?

I've no enlightenment.

I have been at headquarters. And shall be there, Lord knows how long.

At His Excellency's? The Hewes' house?

Have we more than one headquarters?

Only one, I trow. Unless you be damned enough to be compelled to journey to York.

They both laughed. Erving demanded fervently that they share the additional modest portion of plum brandy between them.

This all came about through the doings of their colonel. He had marveled at the fine script Christian Erving offered, and declared that it was true offense if such art should not be more profitably employed. The colonel sent samples of what might be called Erving's wares to the Hewes' house. Soon an order came down for this calligrapher to appear in person.

Promptly the colonel advanced a lieutenant to take the captaincy which in effect Christian Erving was now abandoning in the regiment.

'Tis grim duty in its way, Jem, let us have no doubt upon the subject. The other secretaries greeted me stiffly, as if I were an intruder come perhaps from Philadelphia itself and bearing the pungent breath of General Howe along with me! But now we have had grain coffee together on several occasions and other fare as well, though I warn you that the tables in the Hewes' house are burdened but little better than our own. His Excellency is not one to dine and thrive while the rest of the Army goes hungry. Oh, what a man, friend Jem, what a man! Hast ever had word with him?

Baddeley explained, But to salute, be recognized, and pass on. He has seen fit to ask me a question or two on military matters. But no other exchange.

Erving closed his eyes again and lay back once more as if resting beneath a heavy burden.

God Almighty, Jem. They seek him out with wolves. They are liars, cheats, connivers of the vilest stripe!

Who do you mean? Or dare you tell?

Those damnable generals! Mayhap I should say no more.

Say more if you desire.

Erving said, You are aware that Madam Washington has come to dwell with His Excellency in the Hewes' house?

I heard as much a while back. Some said they had seen her.

Ah yes, she is there, bless her heart. She comes in occasionally, to speak to General Washington, briefly, when we are at work. I have an essential curiosity. I love to watch men in attitude toward their adored. Would that I might watch you in attitude toward yours, if I but knew her name.

Nor am I about to inform you! They had amusement together.

Indeed Madam Washington is here, and let me say that his eyes follow her when she leaves the room. But a moment. But they do follow.

Erving marched in his regular three-step, four-step circle for a time. Then, swearing loudly with such a stark oath as Baddeley had not heard him employ before, he brought from his tattered jacket several folded sheets of paper and sat down behind his desk.

Nor am I tipsy, he said, but am talebearer in truth. These matters burn within my knowledge, and I would turn lunatic if I did not explode them to someone. You are the victim.

The first bears the date of November ninth, soon after we had gone into our camp at Whitemarsh. It is addressed to Brigadier General Conway. It reads as follows:

> Sir,
>
> A letter which I received last night contained the following paragraph. "In a letter from General Conway to General Gates he says, 'Heaven has been determined to save your country, or a weak general and bad counsellors would have ruined it.'"
>
> I am, sir, your humble servant,
> George Washington

Christian Erving continued more fully, It seems that General Conway did not show his note from George Washington widely about, except to the Marquis de Lafayette. That, we may assume, was because Conway is wholly adept at French, which was the one and only reason for Lafayette's ever clinging to his company. Not once has Lafayette wavered in his devotion to our commander. He even wrote to Washington a subsequent letter—I mean the Marquis de Lafayette did—saying that he was convinced that Conway exuded ambition and danger. He said that he was bound to Washington's own fate, and would follow and sustain it as well by his sword as by all the means in his power.

But this is ancient history and we should refer to it no longer.

I fetch you up to the present. General Gates, for all his years in the Army and for all his knowing Washington far back in the Braddock days, is plainly stupid. He and Mifflin have gabbled about Conway until ear and mind grow weary of their effort. Conway now declares that the defamation attributed to him months ago was a forgery, and General Gates has confirmed this idea in correspondence to His Excellency. In fact he sent two missives in January, pronouncing the whole in word, as well as in substance, a wicked perpetration.

I render to you now a copy of our Commander's reply.

It is not my intention to contradict this assertion, but only to intimate some considerations which tend to induce a supposition, that, though none of General Conway's letters to you contained the offensive passage mentioned, there might have been something in them too nearly related to it, that could give such an extraordinary alarm. If this were not the case, how easy in the first instance to have declared there was nothing exceptionable in them, and to have produced the letters themselves in support of it? The propriety of the objection suggested against submitting them to inspection may very well be questioned. "The various reports circulated concerning their contents," were perhaps so many arguments for making them speak for themselves, to place the matter upon the footing of certainty. Concealment in an affair which had made so much noise, though not by my means, will naturally lead men to conjecture the worst, and will be a subject of speculation even to candor itself. The anxiety and jealousy you apprehend from revealing the letter, will be very apt to be increased by suppressing it.

Notwithstanding the hopeful presages, you are pleased to figure to yourself of General Conway's firm and constant friendship to America, I cannot persuade myself to retract the prediction concerning him, which you so emphatically wish had not been inserted in my last. A better acquaintance with him, than I have reason to think you have had, from what you say, and a concurrence of circumstances, oblige me to give him but little credit for the qualifications of his heart, of which, at least, I beg leave to assume the privilege of being a tolerable judge. Were it necessary, more instances than one might be adduced, from his behavior and conversation, to manifest that he is capable of all the malignity of detraction, and all the meanness of intrigue, to gratify the absurd resentment of disappointed vanity, or to answer the purposes of personal aggrandizement, and promote the interest of faction.

Erving sighed as one does on glimpsing initially a brave and masterly monument. Good God, he said, what verbiage!

Baddeley held to silence.

Think ye not so?

And that which you've read is His Excellency's letter to General Gates?

One of several.

But what's the good of it?

Good of it? 'Tis summing the matter up in a nutshell—

Large nutshell. I mind seeing a great nut fetched from the Black Islands. 'Twas called a coconut.

Christian Erving arose in anger and began tramping about once more. When he could speak his voice was unsteady.

I thought to make you my confidant because I believed you to be, along with myself, enraptured of our great Commander! 'Twould seem, however, that I misjudged—

You misjudged me not! Baddeley cried. I've gained the opinion that General Gates is stewing in his own juice. Why should not General Washington disregard the whole matter?

Erving was silent for a time, and finally sat down at his table once more.

He said, rather limply, His Excellency expresses the same opinion.

Pray read it to me.

'Tis of today.

Pray read.

> *Valley Forge, 24th Feb. 1778*
>
> *Sir,—I yesterday received your favor of the 19th instant. I am as averse to controversy as any man; and had I not been forced into it, you never would have had occasion to impute to me even the shadow of a disposition towards it. Your repeatedly and solemnly disclaiming any offensive views in those matters which have been the subject of our past correspondence, makes me willing to close with the desire you express of burying them hereafter in silence, and, as far as future events will permit, oblivion. My temper leads me to peace and harmony with all men; and it is peculiarly my wish to avoid any personal feuds or dissensions with those who are embarked in the same great national interest with myself, as every difference of this kind must, in its consequences, be very injurious.*
>
> *I am, Sir—*

With a noisy blowing out of his breath Christian Erving arose. I must quote emphatically again. *Makes me willing to close with the desire you express of burying them hereafter in silence . . . oblivion.* Stand you satisfied, good friend?

I trust His Excellency holds true to his intent.

Oh triple damn you to the uttermost cinders! Erving exploded. He has been wrought by every discord and uncertainty! That pack of cheats in York—our fucking Continental Congress—they've lied to us and to Washington until Hell won't hold it. He's been compelled by their orneriness—and the sluggard stupidity of Mifflin and a dozen like him—compelled to watch his army freeze and starve and go to a perdition unwanted, undesired, undeserved. A man comes into his presence and fairly finds our Lord Jesus hanging on the Cross. You should be on your knees to him!

Captain Baddeley dropped to the rough-cobbled flooring, and grinned up at Erving. I'm on my knees, he said.

26

THURLOW had reckoned the imminence of combat as all soldiers of all times and wars and places have assayed it.

First he feared that he would be killed.

Second, he wondered how he would behave, and dreaded that he would show panic.

Might he not tremble and dissolve when faced with the enemy . . . moving ranks of soldiery, the smoke of their firing, the smack of bullets? Might not he fling down his weapon, burst from the ranks, run screaming—or at best, irresolute—to the rear?

How was it in earlier centuries, before gunpowder was first exploded—when men brandished metal in their hands? And, before that, clubs?

How was it in an age of arrows and spears with hiss and flourishing and clatter?

How was it when the factions had only stones to throw at each other? And in even earlier millenniums they fought with their bare hands, choking and gagging. Would only the brawniest survive?

The entire matter of warfare was alarm and puzzle.

An earnest person lectured himself: cowardice was the worst demonstration he could project. Whatever the cost, he must remain in the ranks and do as the ranks were doing.

A warrior dared not become confused—should not assault his friends: only his foes.

He thought before the first shot was fired or the first projectile hurled: I must keep my limbs in enhanced position. Not go fleeing asunder.

He thought, I wish that it was spring with sun shining mildly, and I were a child again, concerned only with buttercups.

Yet that could not be. He was a soldier through some process of selection or election.

The ranks advanced steadily to meet him.

Think not of weeping mothers, grim-faced fathers. Think not of an idle forge, a basket remaining empty and becoming slowly cobwebbed; a dog untended, unpetted; a kitten desiring to lie near you cozily and yet finding no nest. Think not of the horse unfed and whinnying about it . . . the cow bawling for you to come and attend her. Yet hands other than yours must squeeze down those teats and extract the juices.

Delude not yourself—oh, never never delude with vision of a girl which came upon you in the night. You were close to waking and yet not waking at all, and the thing grew bigger and bigger and harder and harder, you were with her in welcoming grass, her petticoats were up, her drawers were down— God save the mark! She wore no drawers! You thrust it into her, and your face and hers were blurred together, so hot and moist and melting—hot and moist and melting— moist, moist, melting, melting—and you emitted a fair scream.

Then you were awake, and the act had been performed while you slept. You were sticky and fair swimming in the stuff, and you wiped it with your shirt and considered in vague justice that you must be damned because of the evil befallen you. It had happened to all boys in all times, but you didn't know that. Where there had been glee in illusion, now there was grievance in fact. . . . Eventually you would sleep again.

Concern yourself not with claptrap of your own vanishment or your own rude love.

You are a soldier. You are at war. The enemy comes tramping.

The enemy consists of Irishmen nerved by cider or rum and all the more quarrelsome on account. The enemy consists of British troops. Consists of Englishmen, solid and dependable. Consists of Scots who advance with weird music whining alongside like the haunting fury of witches unseen. Consists of Hessians grunting *Ja* and *Nein*. All the solemn legends of their raping little girls, and they will rape your sweetheart if you don't kill them first.

Consider General Washington. He is around somewhere, watching over you, ready to advise, counsel, command. Ah yes, there was that tale of General Braddock's army out in the wilderness and Zexcellency urging Braddock's men and Braddock himself to take shelter behind the trees and fight as the Indians fought—

Never lined like crimson-coated porkers to be chipped down by the foe at his will.

Echo of words bandied so often. Who said them? Israel Putnam . . . Old Put.

'Twas at Bunker Hill.

Don't fire till you see the whites of their eyes.

They're coming closer. Their muskets are ready, they will raise them soon.

Great Heaven and Earth and all the Prophets in between!

I've a Pennsylvania rifle and I could bring down a squirrel merely by barking him, at twice that distance shown. I don't need to wait until I see the whites of their eyes.

I can see them pressing toward us, and what a target they make. I'll select that one to the left. 'Twould be a pretty shot and I could make it, but what would Zexcellency think about it?

He wasn't at Bunker Hill anyway.

There begins sporadic firing over on the right, and it washes along the line in a pulpy breeze, and you have your rifle up, and you squeeze the gentle trigger now, and the man you were aiming at goes staggering, oh giddy dancer at a ball.

27

The camp fever generally gives some days notice of its approach, by a languor and listlessness of the whole body, and a peculiar sensation of the head, as if it were tightened or compressed by a hook. It is not very uncommon for the symptoms to run very high in the beginning, so as to warrant blood letting and an antiphlogistic course. But after some days, more or less, in different patients, the pulse begins to sink, a dry tongue, delirium, and the whole train of nervous and putrid symptoms supervene.

Brother, I got a black tongue. Too black. I can see it myself when I stick my tongue way out. I can see the tip. 'Tis all black. I been eating coal. No, I been savoring charcoal. I cooked that charcoal o'er a fire in the glade and then I et it, and it left my tongue all black.

My misery is caused by that there thudding noise. What is it? You say the Sisters are smoothing sheets with wood? Big blocks of wood they use to flat the sheets? But why don't they use irons?

Oh, irons are forbid: they got to use the wood.

That's how my tongue become so black. 'Cause I was trying to use it to smooth the sheets, but all the sheets was black and so it rubbed off on my tongue. I tried to smooth this sheet at Valley Forge with my black tongue but still we didn't have no sheets, and what was I to do? So I went out and rubbed my tongue acrost the snow, and everywhere I rubbed it all the snow turned black as well.

I'm sinking lower and I ain't got skin upon my hips, nor on my back. They're all so raw, but if I could but reach 'em with my tongue, I think 'twould cure. Mayhap there was some other soldier used his tongue upon my back and on my hips and made 'em all so oozing with the skin all off; and I would like to weep but I can't weep no more.

I'm just a little thing, and oh so small and still.

I need to get this hard black crust from off my tongue and ah and ah I'll stick it out and maybe some kind spirit will come and take the blackness clean away.

Oh, take it off, please do.

Brother, I tried to cry to him when he bent low above to see my tongue. You take it off.

Not I, said Brother. 'Cause I got to go and pray. I got to sing religious songs.

Then go and pray, if so you got to do, but pray that all this blackness shrinks from off my tongue.

Now I got notions. You could reach up with your fingernails and scrape it off. Oh, that'd be the chore to do. I tried to grate it off myself. I need to grate that charcoal tongue, but I can't do it. Can't even lick my hand.

I'll keep sticking out my tongue and maybe some kind soul will come and scrape it. I heard 'em say I got camp fever, heard 'em say that I got typhus.

I don't know . . . a million other men got typhus maybe. How many is a million? No, couldn't be. I see 'em marching off a dozen at a time from out the huts. I see our hut a-marching out. Why, where did they get all the clothes? They're parading forth, and each is sticking out his tongue, and someone's going to wipe that black away.

I can't put in my tongue—can't get it back inside, and my eyes hurt, but I keep 'em open and they feel so swoll and I'll just keep looking up, a-wondering.

28

HE was to General Howe's.

He couldn't never be!

Indeed I was! 'Twas when we was at White Marsh. Zooks! How did it come about?

I was there with a flag of truce. Zexcellency sent us himself, he did.

And Howe, he give 'em cider.

No, 'twasnt.

I mind his telling. 'Twas wine.

Tell again, Caffrey.

Well, 'twas all simple enough, count of a dog. He was at Mistress Spiver's place, and she's a long-time friend of my mother and wedded to a cousin, and all, and I was tolt to visit her house any time we landed nearby, for she'd fix me up with a good bowl of food, and so she did. I went by there, kind of to make my manners and call, when I got leave of duty, and e'er I got to the house, there was something going wrong. I didn't know quite what. I could hear some barking and carryings-on, when I drew nigher. There was Mistress Spiver out in her own yard, and withes had been placed atop her guard fence to build it higher, you see. And her own dog, Bonny, was inside but outside was a stranger. I hadn't never seen one quite like him before. He was so big and burly and looked so blame ferocious in his face and mouth. His teeth stuck out a long way. He looked like he'd be ready to gobble anyone if given half the chance. Whyn't you keep her in the house, good Mistress Spiver? was the first thing that I asked her. She says, Oh Caffrey Boy, I'm hard driven to cope with this. I says, I do think you'd best put your Bonny within doors. She says, I thought as much myself. Didn't take into count how she'd rip and rave. She's mainly hound, you know, and how she howls! I can't endure such carryings-on within doors, so she's got to be out here. Well, who's her friend, I asked to know, why I've never seen the like before, not knowing what that kind of bull was really all about. He just looked up at me and snuffled in good nature and then he turned once more and vowed again that he could climb that fence. And Bonny bawls out her lamentation. You might put 'em together, I says slyly to the mistress. At least 'twould bring an end to jinks like this.

Easy enough for you to give advice, young soldier, she fairly snapped at me. The care of the pups would not be yourn. 'Twould all be mine, and we're distraught with war, and winter's a-coming on and how do I know that I'll be able to get enough fare to feed Bonny and me myself, ourselves, without a whole slather of pups demanding the best?

So then I take a deep breath and decide I got to risk my hands, and so I does. He's just as calm, good-natured as you please. All he does is huff and puff and let me hold him by the collar. There was a plate upon that collar and I swear on glimpsing it at first, it had the sheen of silver. Meanwhile good Mistress Spiver keeps chanting her troubles abroad. She talks about the old saying about the heat in bitches. A week going in, say, and a week in, say, and a week coming out; but it was guessed that they'd be able to carry pups perhaps at any time in those three weeks; 'twould all depend. I told her 'twould be a very special batch of puppies. Almost royalty, I says. Why what you mean, Child Caffrey? Because, I says, there's this here plate upon the collar, and if I read it right, it says this big dog's name is Nimrod, and he belongs to Sir William Howe. And that did leave her gaping. But it was true, for there was the plate for any and all to see. Nor was there any way to prove how Nimrod come to be out past the British sentry boxes. I guess, I says, he just wanted to go a-wandering. And by this time he's slathering o'er my hand, and licking it, and looking like he wanted to eat my fingers, though he didn't even nibble: he was just a-slobbering.

And a lobsterback at that, she screams. You haul him out of here and stone him down the road and tell him to be gone!

That ain't no way to treat a kindly dog, I says, but give me a strap and I'll remove him from your premises.

So she relents and goes within, and pretty soon she's found somewhere an old strap—from a piece of harness maybe, hanging in her woodshed like as not—and she was kind enough to fetch a right big hunk of gingerbread as well. So I made my manners nice enough, and said that I'd return anon and you can just bet how I glutted on that gingerbread, though I did give a bit to Nimrod which he seemed to fancy. So we marched but not in my own direction: I set sail straight off for headquarters and you should have seen them sentries stare when they held me up, and wanted to know what I was doing there, and did I have a pass, and all that crap. So I says that this is a weighty matter, and here I've got old Nimrod or maybe young Nimrod that he was, belonging to our worthy foe. So everyone is coming round to see the English dog with all his teeth a-sticking out and looking just as fierce as Cain or maybe even Satan. And then there comes a captain and he looks at me real sharp and says, All right, Soldier, step this way. He takes me square inside, dog and all, and by this time I'm shaking scairt to death. I look past the opening and I can see Zexcellency a-seated there with all sorts of papers spread about him and aides a-writing letters at his behest. The captain goes in and talks a minute and Zexcellency kind of smiles, but sober-like, and says, Indeed. Let us greet the beast, and next thing that I know, I'm marching in and trying to duck and nod and throw a fair salute and scrape my foot in proper fashion all at once. But Zexcellency don't pay no attention to my antics; he just looks at the dog and smiles and puts his hand on him, and old Nimrod licks and sweats and grunts. A small note would be in order, think you not, Captain Colling? he say. So do take down the following.

And I would have learnt it to the bone before I even held the note in my hand, as it was fated for me to do.

General Washington's compliments to General Howe—does himself the pleasure to return to him a dog, which accidentally fell into his hands, and, by the inscription on the collar, appears to belong to General Howe.

Next thing I know I'm getting my sense back and here we go, a-marching on the enemy, square on towards Philadelphia itself. We are two privates strong, then the dog and me, and one lieutenant holding up a mighty flag of truce that once was a part of some young bride's finery, like as not. Anyhow it was good white linen and we hoped the sentries wouldn't shoot, though God knows what them hirelings would do if the British sentinels turned out to be Hessians. God only knows, we said. And then we're square a-passing Mistress Spiver's place, and there's old Bonny hound still out in the yard and she sees Nimrod, or more likely smells him, and so she starts to bay and carry on, and Nimrod, he goes grup-grup-grup-and-snuffle, and I have to hold his harness leash so tightly, and the soldiers give a cheer, and the lieutenant does he laugh. But on we go. There is no halt for romance now. You can bet that I was all eyes, for I'd never walked longside a flag of truce before and perchance never will again, Almighty only knows.

It's not too far to reach the redcoat sentinels: maybe a mile and a half at best. Then the outer sentries pass us in. The inner sentries, they do summon an officer, and he reads that note of General Washington's which our lieutenant gives to him, and then there's laughter once again. They pass us on, and e'er we know it we're walking right down the street with all the people looking curious to see us go, and we have an armed escort in the shape of lobsterbacks and they are laughing too. When we reach Howe's headquarters, the yard and steps are full of soldiers, and they know Nimrod, and he is greeted and petted by all. Slowly our lieutenant is sent within and then a minute or two passes and it seems that General Howe says that we're to have some kind of courtesy. Next thing we know, we're all stepping on those beauteous carpets, fair there inside, and witnessing gaudy things around, and portraits and the shiny furniture and richness of the hangings, and all that wonderment that I know my mother and my sisters would die to hear me half describe if I could recollect just how it looked; but it's all too confused and rich and awesome. Next thing that we know, Sir William Howe himself is standing there amongst us. Pray see that these men take some good refreshment, he says to someone, and in the same breath he's dictating something about General Howe's compliments and gratitude to General Washington, and he acknowledges receipt of one straying dog, and thanks the donor thusly, or words to that effect. Only thing was, the aide when he walked from the room, he dropped the first note that Zexcellency had sent along with Nimrod to be delivered; and there it lay a-flapping a little in a draught, and no one paying much attention, and finally you know who moved sidewise and picked it up. 'Twas me myself, and still no one was paying any heed. I jammed it in my breast pocket and there it felt so warm and cozy. Next thing, they're bringing us a tray of little cakes and bottles of wine and those we downed, and our lieutenant bows. Course Howe was gone. He'd vanished long before, nor did we see that fancy Mrs. Loring of whom so many jokes are told, but they do say that she is a pretty one, and somewheres above stairs I heard a woman laugh. I heard her laugh so happily but maybe it was just a servant girl, I'll never know.

Then our lieutenant says, Gentlemen— We liked the way he said that to us in front of all those British. He said, Gentlemen, we'd best not wear out our welcome. Sirs, we do thank you for your hospitality.

And then he bowed, and someone else was bowing and we were going out and march-march-march right down the street, and it felt strange not to have Nimrod there on leash a-marching staunch beside, behind, once more beside again, and then ahead of me. For in that short experience it seemed like I had signed a kind of pact with Nimrod and we was friends, companions, and life should be so sweet with nothing but exchange of compliments, and bottles of sweet wine poured out, and trays of cakes, and people bowing and joking still about Nimrod's antics with the Colonial dog, and all.

Well, back we went, the way I say, and when we passed the house of Mistress Spiver, Bonny was well inside by that time and not bothering round so much, nor howling neither. First off I didn't see Mistress Spiver 'cause as I say, she was indoors, but out she come as we were passing. I called to her, They kept the strap, I says. And— It don't matter, was what she cried to me, but I do hope they keep him tied!

And that was all it meant to her. She wasn't a soldier—couldn't be.

Not ever.

Nor would she know the wild strange feeling that you had when you stood by each other, and you were being kind to them—at least in fetching Nimrod home —and they were being kind to you in neat response.

Another day, another hour, and you'd be hoping to kill them, and they'd be trying to kill you. The bayonets would be ready. The powder in their cartridges and ourn, the bullets rammed on top. 'Twould be a case of shoot and kill and dodge once more. But meanwhile, that small paper on the inside of my shirt was warm against my chest.

29

I mind as how they desired for volunteers down in Virginia a couple seasons agone and we got a big chunk of volunteers. They come by the dozen and score, and finally by the hundred.

Odd thing about Virginia regiments; many of them is Pennsylvanians. You take the Fifteenth Virginia: nigh every man come from Pennsylvania. They'd moved down to us by the pack and passel. They was many of 'em Pennsylvania Germans who didn't want to be interfered with anytime.

So when they asked for these volunteers, they was standing round in droves, and the captain or colonel, if you will, said he'd only take the best shots. They needed but five hundred and there was many more than that come present. So he sets up a board 'bout one foot square and he takes a piece of chalk and on that board he makes a face with a great big nose on it.

He says to the men who are wanting to be recruits, Now harken well, hark ye. See that there nose? I put it up on that tree. Close to ten rods away, I hazard 'tis. Call it a hundred and fifty yards, if you want to go by yards; and if you go by city standards, 'twould be close to a block long or maybe more. Now, hark ye. I want each man to come up to this here mark I dig in the ground. Watch well. I dig it now with my heel, and one by one you come stand here. You got your rifles? You got your powder and your balls? Now mark ye, each is to fire in turn one single bullet from his rifle. That's all ye get to shoot: one round. And I'm going to select for my company of five hundred volunteers, or regiment if you want to call it that— I'll select the five hundred men who come nearest the mark with their single bullet.

He says, Watch ye. That nose on the face I made, that big nose is the mark. Now who will be the first to shoot? You stand in line. One bullet only. That's all you are awarded.

Trouble is, he had to set up a new mark and then another one, and then another.

Why did he do this?

Listen well. That nose was gone. It was cut clean out of the board when the first forty or fifty men had fired their rounds. You heard me. Forty or fifty men had fired one bullet apiece, nigh on to ten poles' lengths away, and they cut the nose clean out of the board. So they had to set up another board with another nose, and the next two or three score men who fired, they shot that nose out, and then the next batch did the same. If they'd owned enough noses drawed on boards, they could have filled up the whole army, I reckon, by enlisting only nose-shooters.

I know. I was there.

My rifle misfired and I missed the nose entire.

30

IN illusion he saw himself being attended by two Philadelphia physicians but neither of them was Doctor Rush: these both were Tories. He might have in sense seen himself attended by Doctor Mercer, the bold Scotsman and friend of His Excellency, even though Mercer had been dead for a year. Nay, these were Tories; one was Doctor Kearsley and the other Doctor Abraham Chovet. Kearsley had already been hustled by patriots more than two years previously. He had fired his pistol at a mob which stormed in front of his dwelling and he was dragged out and tormented through the streets while others in the throng pillaged his house. What a man to imagine in ministration! But he was there, and prescribing rum.

Doctor Chovet bent beside with long white hair hanging round his face, drifting from under the cocked hat which he insisted on wearing even when he went about his ministrations. Long since he had lost all his teeth, and his jaws moved perpetually as if he had a wad of tobacco between them, but no juice of the tobacco ever came forth.

He said between the mincing, I need to have you for an exhibit in my anatomical museum. Please to appear there.

Where is it, sir?

In Videl's Alley off Second Street, and it is a waxworks. I choose to demonstrate the activities of several portions of your body.

But, Doctor, can I thus be cured of my ailment?

That you can.

What shall you feed me?

Rum, my boy. Rum!

So in identical chimera the doctor offered him rum dipped out of a noggin with a large spoon, and it went into his mouth and down his gullet. 'Twas warm and comforting. He felt fit to rise and go back to the Army again. Later he wakened in more sense and he found a Moravian woman bathing his face and asking him if he desired broth. He thought it kind of her to attend him. There were so many soldiers lying miserable on all sides and some had groaned their last groan.

Do heal the others first, he kept trying to tell her, but the words sounded only in remote recesses of his brain and he could not shake them forth.

A man luxuriating in the name of John Jones had published a work on the treatment of wounds a scant two years before and this was a veritable Bible for those who possessed copies.

Slight puncture wounds require no therapy. Deep and tortuous ones should be incised and enlarged. Inflamation is best counteracted by gentle laxatives, soft cataplasms, sudorific anodynes, bleeding and warm baths. Opium is prescribed— if available. The appearance of gangrene signifies the need of a more nourishing diet, spiritous fomentations and a more intensive use of the bark. Abscesses need immediate incision and drainage.

I heard thee speaking. Thee seems stronger now.

Aye, that I am.

But thee speaks faintly.

I can't see thy face. Is thee—are thee—a Sister?

We are Spiritual Virgins here at Ephrata.

Where be Ephrata? Be it near Valley Forge?

We are a long journey to the west. Forty miles.

How come I here?

In a waggon with other ill and wounded. You—she hesitated, seemed hunting for words—wounded and sick alike, you were all packed close. Too close indeed, and she sighed.

Please to let me see your face.

We go veiled, she said gently. All of us must wear our hoods and veils. But this is too much palaver. Do open thy mouth now. Take it. It is barely warmed. It is cooled but 'twill do thee good. Now swallow.

Ah.

'Tis stout lamb broth. Possibly mutton, but 'tis stout.

Winter-killed mutton, he tried to say gaily in response and they both laughed.

All transverse wounds are in need of interrupted suturing with a needle dipped in oil. Following this a plaster is applied over the area for two or three days.

In gunshot wounds, one should first remove the ball and secondly control hemorrhage. A light dressing should then be applied with a retension dressing on top.

All major compound fractures require immediate amputation.

My limb is a-hurting.

Thee should take more broth.

Guess I had enough. My limb—

Which—limb?

'Tis my right. My right limb. I feel it throb.

Oh, she said weakly. Thee must rest quietly now. I'll leave thee. Do not speak more and try to sleep.

Sister.

I must leave thee now.

But Sister. I put down my hand! Just now! I'm feeling it all around. It ain't there! It's gone! My right leg. I can feel it—feel it attached to me. Feel it a-throb. But it ain't there.

Thee must trust in God.

But how can I still feel my limb when it ain't there? Sister, did they take it off? Oh, did they?

'Twas badly used, my son. 'Twas necessity.
Necessity! That they take my limb?

> *Dry, soft lint placed upon recent wounds
> is generally the best application through the
> whole course of the cure. At first it restrains the
> hemorrhage, with less injury than any styptic
> medicines; and afterwards, by absorbing the mat-
> ter, which is at first thin and acrimonious, it be-
> comes, in effect, the best digestive.*

But I'm a cobbler! I mean I'm fixing to be a cobbler.
Pa is a cobbler and we go about pushing our cart. We
go from door to door and fit the people with shoes
when they need shoes. We make em. I'm learning. I
mean I'm being taught.

Please, my son, you must rest. We must be at peace
and fall quiet here. I place my finger on your lips and
do not move—

Dash thy finger! I tell thee as I must! How can I
get about, how can I walk behind the cart? I'll have a
stump!

True. You will need a peg.

> *During incarnation (granulation) it is the soft-
> est medicine that can be applied between the
> rolled and tender granulations; and at the same
> time an easy compress on the sprouting fungus.*

A long time later she came back to him and strange
to say he felt stronger and hungrier too. She fetched
him more broth and gave him swallows of milk as well
but he claimed the milk was a little sour and she
laughed about this.

He said, Sister, I been a-pondering. We could get a
cart. I mean not the kind you push like we pushed
ours. I could be hauled in it. We could have an ox
though they come mighty dear. Perhaps an old ox?
Broke-down a bit but still able to haul a light weight?

I could ride, and keep learning 'bout the cobbling business.

Indeed yes, dear son. Course thee could. Now I must to prayers.

Everybody must to prayers. Everybody was praying all the time or if they were not voicing supplication by word of mouth they let it linger in their minds and hearts; all but the dead or dying. 'Twas difficult to tell which were dead and which were dying and sometimes lips were fallen still a long time before the spark was found to have left.

Sister (or an appeal to Brother when there were Brothers about as well, bearded and supplicant and many helping out in surgery) oh Sister, oh Brother, this feller next to me, he don't say nothing no more.

Be it so?

And then came the examination and often a hastening away of feet and a returning of more feet and then a lifting and carrying, a bearing off, and then someone would bring a new patient and put him there before the bed was changed, but surely they had nothing to change it with. The bed was a mere scrap of rag upon the floor and often there was not time for the patient's sweat to dry if he had been sweating before someone else was lugged in and deposited.

Oh Sister, oh Brother, oh Sister again. I can't speak because my lips are too frail and so is the impulse prompting my desire. But oh, I am grown smaller, to be a baby again, and want Mamma, and I am bred with desire to have her soothing me. Where did they put him? This one they just carried off?

Into the ground.

Into the ground, when it is congealed and hard? And how did they pry enough space? I heard tell that sometimes they dug the graves, and there was strife about it. At Valley Forge many died who could not be toted here, and I mind some New Jerseymen were dead and the graves were dug and meanwhile before they fetched the corpses some Pennsylvania men had dead of their own and they put them in the graves already dug and there was great rush when the Jerseymen come back and they dug up the loose earth and rocks and tumbled out the bodies and put their own dead into the holes they'd already fathomed, and soon the fists were flying and people were yelling, Fight, fight! and all were hurrying to see.

. . . Brother, must you also go to prayers? If so, please say a plea for me.

What shall I utter, poor one?

Say, *A Mighty Fortress Is Our God.*

For what? That hain't no prayer fit for the dying or for the dead!

Then say Isaac Watts. Say, *Are There No Foes For Me To Face.*

Poor one. That ain't the kind of prayer. I shall speak softly as one does for those who are sleeping with God.

Then say it soft, oh Brother, say it soft. But I still think *Are There No Foes* would be well to sing or say.

> *Thy saints, in all this glorious war*
> *Shall conquer, tho' they die;*
> *They view the triumph from afar*
> *And seize it with their eye.*

Observe you not? You have sweetness like a comfit in the mouth to take away the bitterness of dying, of falling apart, of rotting even while you know that you go down. Thus you might fancy that you see the worms ahead as golden things. They are bright. They are more gossamer and daintier than sunlight as they crawl and quaver. Whoever thought a man still living would welcome worms in fancy? Yet I desire all the hours and days and years ahead to be so bright. Though this be Heaven, in truth, and will the worms allow me to proceed?

Ho! Who glimmers there? God himself, and as He strides closer there are others along with Him and the radiance of His face is all a joy.

Oh look who's there! Little Leona. I scarce can member her. She died so long ago when still I was so small. Who would I desire most to see? Zexcellency, of course. But no, that can never be, for he ain't dead yet, like the rest, nor will be for a long time. I know that in the sum of knowledge that now comes to me. Why there's Uncle Moses—we always called him Uncle Moze—and right behind him is neighbor Fraunheim who was so kind to me when I was little. Hi, Neighbor Fraunheim, and what a light is on your face, on all the faces! And Uncle Moze is fair a-beam and oh it's all so purty, it dazzles fair my gaze. Why, all the flowers of the meadow and the vale, and they smell like clover but purtier still, and be those angels a-dancing in the clover, or is it right and permitted for angels to do a dance? But these are dancing and I'm seeking to run to them with uplift in my being. Oh God, oh little child Leona, oh kindly neighbor, oh Uncle Moze, and more, and more. Who be that a-squinting happily alongside? Why, 'tis my grandsire. And now he's never blind no more. He can see, he's looking out and laughing.

The hands of Brothers come seeking and a-dabbing at my face and wondering, but now they know, and they're both looking at each other and nodding as they bend above. I stand aloof and see them dimly so, see them still and they lift up the wan damp thing I used to be, but I am it no longer so let me turn and beam and seek the glories that await.

> *The little dogs and all*
> *Tray, Blanch and Sweet-heart,*
> *See they bark at me.*

Ah, there's Naomi. We always spoke of her as Nome, and see her dancing! And she danced when she was puppy-wise. And Blowser, good dog Blowser. We had him for so many years: thirteen in all. He only died two years agone, and here he is a-welcoming. Good dog Blowser, I've no bone for thee at the moment, but I'll find one. I will, I will! For where there are these Godly dogs, there must be Godly bones as well. Please let me scamper closer, closer, and touch the hands a-reaching out to welcome me.

One look back again, that's all I'll take. The Brothers, they are lifting up the shred. Why, was that me, myself? That thing? I care not, I am gone, all gone. Here to rejoin mine own. I hear them laughing now, they are reaching out their hands. I have no wish to turn and stare. Why this is fragrant, and the clover, it is all a-bloom and scenting round.

31

A platform had been erected on which any man might stand somewhat dangerously and the Reverend Mr. Jed Chattum was sculptured there with drums of the musicians piled across in front of him and below him, and he preached using a text from Samuel. Second Samuel that was, Third Chapter, Eighteenth Verse: *By the hand of my servant David I will save my people Israel out of the hand of the Philistines, and out of the hand of all their enemies.* Perhaps it was coincidence, perhaps not, but Thomas Paine had quoted liberally from Samuel as well, although not applying the identical text in his essay on *Common Sense.* Nevertheless he noted firmly that Samuel employed advice, cajolery and heart-felt denial of private purpose.

It was a fashion prevailing to quote Thomas Paine and Paine expected it—undoubtedly hoped that he would be quoted—and the mere fact that he declined to receive financial profit from the distribution of his tracts made—in the opinion of the Reverend Jed Chattum—made it essential that brave men who supported this belief might necessarily decline to live longer lives or to share any hours left to them in bowing before a king. As some men learn moral dignity only from the way in which it is described by means of church service, in the same manner did young fry find themselves achieving words like *bastard* and *banditti*. They cared not whether Thomas Paine had uttered the lines originally or whether God had done so.

They held—in submerged form perhaps, but it was persistent—a belief that the entire set of Scriptures was the work of God himself.

A French bastard landing with an armed banditti and establishing himself king of England against the consent of the natives, is in plain terms a very paltry rascally original. It certainly hath no divinity in it. However, it is needless to spend much time in exposing the folly of hereditary right, if there are any so weak as to believe it, let them promiscuously worship the ass and the lion, and welcome. I shall neither copy their humility, nor disturb their devotion.

They held responsibility to wife, child, parents, minister at home. It would be assumed that as soldiers they gave themselves unto religious rites with stark devotion whenever such rites could be offered. There was no other reason for the musicians to march and blat upon their fifes, or beat or pile their drums.

Turn out, everyone within reach of the preacher's voice! All must lend ears to hear it!

In England, a king hath little more to do than to make war and give away places; which, in plain terms, is to impoverish the nation and set it together by the ears. A pretty business indeed for a man to be allowed eight hundred thousand sterling a year for, and worshipped into the bargain! Of more worth is one honest man to society, and

*in the sight of God, than all the crowned ruffians
that ever lived.*

So his listeners felt themselves to be honest men and
in the sight of God at that. They enjoyed the term
crowned ruffians. They thought of lobsterbacks and
British generally occupying Philadelphia as such, to
say nothing about what had been done to Boston or
Long Island or— Each held to his own faith and region
in this notion. If queried extensively by parents, wives,
or homebound clergy in general, they would have insisted that they attended divine services with an en-
thusiasm amounting to glee. They accepted the shrewd
toughness of Paine along with the toughness of Samuel
as of Biblical and even Heavenly origin.

> *Every thing that is right or natural pleads for
> separation. The blood of the slain, the weeping
> voice of nature cries, 'tis time to part.*

Did the Reverend Mr. Chattum speak of Godliness?
Ah yes.
What was his text?
Why, indeed, he quoted the Scriptures to prove that
it was right and just for us to be rebelling gainst the
king and England and the lobsterbacks and all such.
He quoted?
Aye. From—I think it was Judges or Kings, and
Genesis I guess. And maybe Deuteronomy.

> *But let our imaginations transport us a few mo-
> ments to Boston. . . . The inhabitants of that un-
> fortunate city, who but a few months ago were in
> ease and affluence, have now no other alternative
> than to stay and starve, or turn out to beg.*

With which every determined yet passably ignorant
soldier might gain the rewarding impression that his
own personal troubles had been signalized not only

by Deuteronomy, but also by Matthew, Mark, Luke, and John as well.

There were other parsons besides the Reverend Mr. Jed Chattum, one of whom was the Reverend Mr. John Gano. He considered that many of the men at Valley Forge were in such severe straits as to clothing that he could not feel comfortable standing before and above them and preaching to them when they stood shivering in thin rags, insufficiently clad to accept even a morsel of sustenance, let alone of the Spiritual variety.

He went away on leave forthwith, but on his return was told by a soldier that the men had fared badly indeed (any soldier might feel flattered to have his opinion asked, and by a chaplain of God at that).

The soldier put on a long face and said that he had suffered gravely and so had all the men, during the Reverend Mr. Gano's absence, because they did not hear the Word of God. Ahh, said the soldier, It would have given us such comfort to have heard religion extolled by you!

I was thinking only of your comfort, the Reverend Mr. Gano stammered. I could not preach while you poor men were quivering half-naked before my eyes!

True, true, agreed the soldier in saintly fashion. But it would have been consolation to have had such a good man near us!

The Reverend was richly affected by this statement, and told the man's commanding officer about it.

Point him out, said the commander, and Gano did.

Lord 'a mercy! said the officer. That man is the worst reprobate in the regiment. He is liar, cheat, coward, swindler, dunce, and clown in one! And if he were to receive the hiding merited him, would not have an inch of skin left upon his back! (Which might have given the Reverend Mr. John Gano pause to plan a sermon on oafish soldiers in general terms.)

And, Willie, what was done for thy spiritual benefaction in such time of stress as when you shivered there?

We shivered long. We took turns—

You did not all attend religious benefit?

We had to club together. Know this, please: One man had moccasins. Another had pants. Another offered shirt or coat. Mittens come from one more. A hat of sorts from another. Might be the sum trappings of a whole hutful, and all on one man, to stand religioning.

But so you stood at last. What of the preaching itself. What text took he?

Well, he held forth quite a smear about Samuel and David, too. And they was always a-quoting Psalms.

Thee knowest some Psalms. Thee put them to heart long ago when small. But did he preach solely from the Old Testament?

Gad, no.

Willie! How dare—

Just a soldier word, Ma.

But to say *Gad* is masking an attempt to use the word God in vain!

No, 'tain't. Gad? Why that's just like—just a common thing to be said.

Very well, then. So answer my query. Of what New Testament?

Oh, Matthew, Mark, Luke, John, Thomas—

Thomas! There is no Book of Thomas, I'll have thee know!

Sure there be. He was always a-reading from it, or saying Thomas Paine says this or that. Thee just doesn't realize it, Ma. Thee hasn't been to camp nor to the Army.

32

In strict privacy Washington had despaired about his headquarters guard. He was annoyed almost to the point of intellectual disturbance by the backbiting, recrimination, jealousy, and slackness of assorted New Englanders, New Yorkers, bounty men, foreigners, and dissolute loungers who had been assigned primarily to such detail. He tried fervently to counsel himself that this was not a fair sample of the Army. Very nearly without exception militiamen were jealous of soldiers regularly enlisted in the Line. Those of the regular establishment in turn held the militiamen to be a troop of johnnys-come-lately, inexperienced, disorganized. The mutual acrimony persisted, words flew, and sometimes, when the men felt stout enough, fists flew as well. His Excellency tried to counsel himself stubbornly that once the burden of want was lifted—once a plenitude of food and decent clothing was available—the rabble would in turn become cohesive and prideful. In the meantime however, with troops of British cavalry whisking repeatedly up to the very limits of the encampment, he dared not risk being bundled off to Philadelphia. Without his presence half of his generals would quickly be at the throats of the other half. The indication of rivalry was too keen to be ignored. Were he himself slain in resistance or dragged away as a prisoner, the last core of stout Continental emergency would vanish as well.

He chose Virginians and gave word that they should be picked with care: the stoutest, strongest, the kind of men with whom he had ranged mountain woods countless times in years gone by. Now that Martha was come to dwell with him in the Hewes house, the responsibility for her protection became an added inducement.

He cared naught for the sneering comments of men like Gates and Conway, who had already identified themselves to be covert enemies.

The Virginians reacted as he had been confident they would. They stood seemly to their attention when circumstance required, were affable but always keen-eyed when lounging.

Such a party, ganged in front of the big stone house now, had their attention claimed by the slow arrival of a tiny figure whom any of them might have held with her standing on his hand for a platform. She was neatly garbed in a piece of print stitched from one of her mistress's old gowns. She shuffled in a pair of ancient beaver-lined boots much too large for her, and was shrouded in a russet cape and bonnet, obviously a hand-me-down from some other jauntier and elder female. She had her apron caught up in her hands and a bulky burden lay therein.

What in time you doing here, you limb? cried one of the men as the others came closer a-smiling. But when he called her a limb he spoke the word kindly.

Under the bonnet's shrouding, alert negroid eyes danced and rolled in the deep brown face.

I'ze come, she said, and then as if stricken she could say no more.

You sure has come. What fer? Who you belong to, you little half-pint?

'Long to Mister Mac. I'ze Mary. I 'long to him.

Where's this Mister Mac live?

The infant pointed vaguely in a general direction somewhere between the village and the Schuylkill.

One of the sentries said, There's a fellow named MacDonald got a place down there. Reckon she belongs to him.

What you want here at the Valley Forge camp?

I come see the General.

We got a scad of generals. You mean General Washington?

The child nodded violently.

They called to the lone sentry planted just outside the door. Here's one for you, Pacey, and the man Pacewell came grinning to join them.

She wants to see Zexcellency, but I reckon she hain't got no pass.

Pacewell said, Well, if she ain't even got a pass, I might give her one of my own. I can write a very good pass. Know how to write and cipher and everything. You write and cipher, young 'un?

Mary grinned and shook her head decisively. I got something for General Washington, she said, speaking in barely a whisper; but all the men heard because they were bending close.

I hear he short of food. I fetch him some, and she hugged the burdened apron against her body.

Grief and good day, said Pacewell. Well, you better come long with me. If you got food it's just as good as a pass. Come long, and he guided her up to the door and, putting his rifle aside, knocked heartily.

He expected to see an aide or perhaps Billy Lee, Washington's body servant, but instead it was Lady Washington herself who opened the door. She looked down at the child and her brisk eyes opened wider and gleamed in her bright face. Why, how do you do, young 'un, she said in her keen sharp voice.

She wants to see Zexcellency, the soldier explained. Ma'am, you reckon she's a spy?

Mrs. Washington said, We have been advised, soldier, that they come in all shapes and sizes. Heaven knows; but let us welcome her in, spy or no. She guided the child into the room and closed the door and could hear the Virginians making sport of the occurrence outside.

It had not been within the experience of this child to encounter anyone like the wife of His Excellency, nor was similar meeting common in the annals of many others. Martha was long past her young years, she was in her twentieth year of marriage to General Washington at this time, and had been married before that and had borne children to her first husband; yet she was still trim and dainty if plump of figure. Her hazel eyes had bright small lights in them. Her chuckling was not a mannerism put on for the moment; it came from imps within her spirit who were glad to be at home there, but were incapable of pretense or falsehood.

In common Virginia fashion of the time, she applied the word *limb* to the child, yet did not suggest that truly the girl was a limb of Satan as the term might have originated . . . only that she was readily qualified for dancing and capering.

Pray let me see, little limb. What are you cuddling in your apron?

The black child took a deep breath. Tis for General Washington, she said explosively. I wants to jine.

Jine? Join? What would you join, child?

Wants to be a sojer.

When Mistress Washington laughed, it seemed to the child that little pink bells were ringing far above. She shivered, partly at the sound and partly at what she considered in a kind of rapture to be her own effrontery. Yet it was as if she had been counseled by her creator to perform this errand and assume military obligation therein.

Indeed thee is a bit slight for campaigning, but a tiny gun might be made for thee. Come, let us see what the General has to say. And guiding the child along with her, she crossed the room, tapped at a door, then flung it open in response to direction within.

General Washington was seated in a large armchair, and before him at a table one military secretary scribbled rapidly with pen and ink while the other sat with his pen poised above a sheet of foolscap.

Pray, Your Excellency, said his wife, I beg leave

to interrupt you at your task. 'Tis not often that a recruit comes personally to headquarters to apply.

His Excellency arose. And you have such a recruit, Madam?

Here she be.

His Excellency came round from behind the table and bent down to put his hand upon the child's hood, and tipped her head so that her eyes might meet his gaze.

'Tis not often that a recruit applies in person at the Army's headquarters. There might be complications insofar as her master is concerned. Pray tell, who may he be?

According to the gossip of your sentries, sir, he is one Mr. MacDonald who lives nearby.

Both secretaries were chuckling. I know of him, Your Excellency, said one. 'Tis up the road a piece. A rather far piece indeed.

Madam Washington said, She says that she has some gifts for you.

Pray let us see them, little one.

Soon her gifts were arrayed upon the table.

Ah, now, said Washington. Some potatoes? Two apples? And what be these? Chestnuts, indeed!

The small voice below him said, Hain't roastet yit. I can roast 'em for ye.

His Excellency said, I am indeed honored at your presentation of such gifts, but a certain doubt assails me. Does your master know that you are fetching these delicacies here?

His wife spoke to him in half a whisper, Nonsense, sir. The child doesn't understand.

The guilty voice of the donor came up to him feebly, I jus takes 'em.

Then my dear Martha, we have a forager at hand. Ah well, he added as if dispensing of arguments with himself. Such are the demands of war.

Mrs. Washington said, Also, she is offering herself as a recruit. She wishes to be a soldier.

What age have you, little one?

I'ze seven, said the child.

We do have many young ones here, some far too young, I fear. Neither at present do we enlist the fair sex, of which, all jesting aside, you happen to be a member.

Martha Washington said, I suggested that an extremely small rifle might be fashioned for her.

True enough, but in the future only. Our gunsmiths are overworked and overwrought at present. Now I must haste back to my letter-writing. But do I not recall accurately, my dear Martha, that a generous lady of the countryside fetched us a gift lately? Was it not a jar of currant wine? Might not this little lass enjoy a swig, before she returns to her master and resumes the task of growing taller so that she may be a fit recruit one future day?

Martha Washington said decisively, We shall both broach it without further delay, Your Excellency. Also I have within my purse a very bright shilling which is fairly hankering for a new owner, and might be used to purchase sweets at a shop, at least in some happier future time. Let us make our adieus, my dear. Say good-bye to the General.

Good-bye, General Washington, the child whispered.

When she was gone on the homeward route, long after being cuddled and patted by the mighty Virginia sentries, she felt in recollection the touch of Washington's fingers upon her head and hood, thought again of that vast gaze coming down at her from his godly height, and was glad that she had pushed upon this errand; though she was a bit uncomfortable when she thought of certain consequences which might be waiting her once she was safely home. She reeled a little at this, but was sure no one would be aware of the missing potatoes, the apples, and chestnuts which accompanied them. She had a vague sense of being still mortal, but having strayed momentarily past the limits of mortality and among the few who dominated above, and were majestic and all-knowing in their rule. She would remember her visit to General Washington very long indeed. She would live to be a hundred years old, and would tell of it then, and say how kindly he treated her and so did his laughing wife.

33

I could not keep my eyes from that imposing countenance; grave, yet not severe; affable, without familiarity. Its predominant expression was calm dignity, through which you could trace the strong feelings of the patriot, and discern the father, as well as the commander of his soldiers. I have never seen a picture that represents him to me, as I saw him at Valley Forge, and during the campaigns in which I had the honor to follow him.

Pierre-Etienne Duponceau was but seventeen when first he observed Washington. Many other youngers of the same age observed Washington under other circumstances and their impressions were much the same . . . and some even more flattering.

Duponceau was secretary to the Baron von Steuben and may have been pardoned for wondering sometimes if he were not also secretary to von Steuben's fine greyhound Azor.

Do you inform the American Congress in this letter, my secretary, that I bring them letters from Benjamin Franklin, who will inform these patriots that I served as a lieutenant-general under Friedrich the Great. My own name is Friedrich Wilhelm Ludolf Gerhard Augustin, the Baron von Steuben. I am now, I believe, two years the senior in age of General Washington. I served Friedrich the Great throughout the Seven Years' War wherein I was wounded at both the battles of Kunersdorf and Prague. I had the honor to be distinguished before our Commander to the point where he made me a lieutenant-quartermaster-general. If I know much of soldiering from instruction and experience, this is due entrely to both of these knowledges achieved under Friedrich the Great himself.

To symbolize these honors, I am proud that I am permitted to wear the star of the Baden-Durlach Order of Fidelity upon my breast. Thus, in the past, I have served under the king of Prussia. In the present and what future may remain to me, I am here in America for the purpose of serving under nobody but General Washington.

I have visited the Congress at York and they were kind enough to offer me quarters there. Such hospitality I cannot accept. I come to Valley Forge. When I come to Valley Forge, I come to Washington. I have no desire or intention to serve elsewhere.

I come as a volunteer. I care not about the monument of rank or any other honor or compensation which might be offered me. I have not much English as yet, but on the voyage across the Atlantic I did read *Robinson Crusoe*. I did not read it to perfection. I do not contend likewise that any tasks which I now hope to undertake will be achieved with perfection at the start. This cannot be in soldierly experience. What I do say is that I shall try so hard, and shall expect all others to do the same.

I believe the officer must enter deeply into the life and meaning of his men.

I work hard and long. I am proud of this, for it is good for a good soldier to work hard and long. It is not good that men should be sent on duty—what, with no breakfast? The soldiers go on duty and they have no breakfast? This I do not like. This—how should I say it—I deplore! I will have no more of this! The soldiers will have their breakfast before they go on duty. They will rise early in order to do so, as I my own self rise early to check on them. I do not want much breakfast. I have a cup of coffee, so. And Azor is fed while my hair is being done. I have my coffee, my pipe of tobacco, and then I ride out at once and must seek far, through all the cold and still some darkness and still the frost. In this way only will I learn what it is that happens.

Officers must not live far from their men. They must not let the sergeants do the work of officers. The work of officers is most important. I have no intent that I shall permit some others to do the task to which I am sworn. And I must make each soldier feel the same way, that his task is most important in the world, now that he is a soldier. Every strength and every attention, the impact of his mind and his true self, must be devoted to his duty.

Let us have courage! Let us have skill. Let us have attention to duty. Without these, nothing else is good.

We take now the guns themselves and show how they must be managed. That is important. It is very hard to do this, when they are not all the same kind of guns. There are guns for shooting squirrels. Some tell me that they only bark the squirrels, and that is hard to understand. And I find it means that they can shoot so very well they do not shoot the small squirrel and let the bullet tear his body; but they shoot the tree tunk beside where he is seen, and *bang* goes the gun, and the bullet strikes the bark but not the squirrel. Just the same, he is killed dead by impact of the bullet so close to him. This great skill they have, so well they are feared by the British.

But some have not these rifles. Some have the muskets. Some have the Brown Bess which the English call their muskets. Some have even shotguns only. But I must drill with what I have, and I must drill my men and not leave this to some lazy sergeant who perhaps will not be there. By the great God, I am there, and they have had their breakfast, and now we are ready to work!

I show them how to poise their firelocks. There are two motions to this. Poise firelocks! I give the order, and I yell it out in proper way to do so, to give the order short and sharp so everyone will know. I take my gun. I have too a musket, and I show them how to hold it. First with the lock outward, the musket straight up and down. Second, I put my left hand above the lock right opposite my own eyes. That is it. Poise firelocks! Or maybe some say, Poise your firelocks, and *bang, bang!* Snap, snap! Like this we go!

Now that is well. I have them lined up. Twelve in the squad. Six in front rank, six in rear rank alternate behind them, for that is the way to handle musketry. It is the only way. One rank can shoot and then, while they are loading, the others stand so ready also to shoot and put effective fire down upon the enemy as he advances.

Now I say, Cock your firelocks! And there are two motions for that as well. Present! I call to them. With one motion, up they come. The right foot goes six inches to the rear, the butt end of the piece goes to the shoulder.

Next order is Fire! One motion to that. Next order, Half-cock your firelock! And that too is one motion. Next, Handle your cartridge!—and that is to take your cartridge from your pouch. There is no time for toying with a powder horn in this. There must be cartridges. What, they say? How can cartridges be rolled? They have no paper.

Then take it from whoever has the paper! There must be paper. The cartridges must be poured and ready, the powder assembled. Suppose a storm should come: the cartridges are dry. In ordinary case, and in their own closed cases. Unless there is a hurricane!

Are there hymnbooks in the churches? Then take the hymnbooks and make cartridges. There must be cartridges! I say, and when you bite the cartridge, bite the top well off, as shown, *hein!* Then comes the

order, Prime! Two motions only. Then charge with
cartridge! Into the muzzle is poured the cartridge with
the powder going down the barrel. And then the hand
upon the rammer. Draw your rammers! That is two
motions also. Ram down your cartridge! One motion
for that. Return your rammer! One motion. And so
the ramrod slides into place below the musket barrel.
Shoulder your firelocks! Two motions for that. Left
hand under butt of musket, right hand thrown at
side!

I see I must make the orders shorter, sharper. And
it is so hard to learn the English for this. Might I not
say *guns* instead of firelocks? We will try that, *ja.*
Guns! Instead of ordering perhaps to cock your firelocks, we should say, Cock guns! It is shorter, sharper.

Handle your cartridge! There must be a better way
for this, but without the good wide knowledge of the
English and American it is hard to do. Suppose I say
instead of, Ram down your cartridge, suppose I order, Ram? That only. Ram! Would it be a mistake,
now? Would people do wrong things? I do not know.

I am a man. I have a temper. Sometimes I get so
lost; so balked, especially because I know not well
the language. I swear! I swear in German, swear in
French. I try to swear in English, too. I do not know
the words to say and it is bad. I want to yell like any
woman, tear my hair. *Hein,* it is difficult! I find my
task so hard. Even standing so out in the cold, my
blood grows warm. I feel the perspiration round my
throat and on the back of my head. I feel it in my
fists when I do clench them. It is because I am grown
so intense.

This cannot be helped if one is to try so well the
job he needs to do.

I have this man, Walker, a captain, whom they
give to me to be interpreter. I shout a hundred times
to him. I say, My God, Walker. What bandits are
these with whom I must deal?

I feel like the Great Friedrich, whom I served so

long. A school inspector named Sulzer once said to him that he felt most people felt inclined to do right rather than to make wrongs. *Ach,* my dear Sulzer, says the Great Friedrich, you don't know this damn race! His saying, it became famous. *Ach, mein lieber Sulzer, er kennt nicht diese verdammte Rasse!* So often I think Americans are a *verdammte Rasse;* yet here I stand among them, and by my own choice.

Now we must to the bayonet again. They know not how to use the bayonet, and so important is this weapon. With an empty musket, what are you? You are nothing. You are not a soldier. You can only club your musket and hope to hit someone on the head. But what if you have a bayonet, and you know the way in which it must be employed? That is something else again. There are many battles which have been won and lost through proper or improper or unschooled use of the bayonet. It is the soldier's child, his dependent, his servant. His only hope at times. Now then, in this task we must instruct them.

The hour grows long and tiresome and late.

We must not fail.

There is so much to do.

. . . And of the manner of the march as well. This we must change. They must drag around no longer. That march by files: I study now of what they tell me of the Brandywine. *Ach,* it took too long to move. That was the reason. I teach them now to march so fast and firm. They will be proud to do so, and they cover ground. Zip-zip-zip! We now march away! A quick, fast step Americans should have. Not drag around the way so often the English do.

I rise early. I do not know how long I sleep. Some nights it seems that I have only naps. I lie awake, I think, I smoke, then I am weary, and I sleep once more, and then I am awake, and thus it goes.

Watches are important. Everything must go by the watch! All the officers around me, I make them set their watches all together. We go on strict and common time. If it is a matter of seconds, so shall it be a matter of seconds; but no one must be tardy. A common effort it must be, and all at the same time.

I light my candle, see my watch again. *Ach,* it is time I am up and about. I clap my hands to have my coffee brought to me. I have my pipe. I smoke again, and is there food for Azor? Food he must have, even if we are to go hungry ourselves. So some food is brought for Azor. It may be old fish. It may be meat too elderly for us to eat; but he too has learned to be a good soldier in this starving place. He eats in gratitude all that we will give him. But still it is enough.

Sometimes Azor goes with me when I ride throughout the camp and even on roads nearby. Sometimes he goes. More often he curls up to sleep where I have slept.

So out I go. The weather it is cold so often. Freezing. And it freezes on my horse. Sometimes it is warmer; still so dark and muddy when the rain comes down; but we have a task to do, and so we go.

So much that meets the eye is bad. Some sentinels I find have made a fire of logs and they are standing there or some are sitting, sleeping. They draw close to the fire; the sentries from three posts; so all the sentries from three posts are gathered now at this one post and no one guarding in between. I order them so sharp! I spread them out. They must resume the old position to which they were ordered in the first place. They do not like this: but who is there to care? Well now, I tell them, I will care! I take down the numbers of their company, their regiments. Some regiments have only three or four persons, some have a hundred. It is so awkward, so very mixed, and this we must straighten out. I find that they have had no breakfast and that is sad as well. No man should go on sentry duty when he has not had a single bite. Breakfast, *ja!* Shaving, *ja!* They must make themselves into good appearance. They must be proud to be the soldiers that they are, and they must show it in the manner they stand to duty.

I ride on. I reach the limit of the camp, and now what have we here? I see well as I look now, for it is growing light. I see two children. A small boy and a girl. They have a barrow and they wheel it there.

Where come you from? What do you in this place? I am in haste to know, so I ask in German. And now I am surprised because these children speak the German, but it is low. I speak it all: I speak low German, speak Alsace.

They say their name is Mueller and they live nearby. They wheel the barrow to the house of their good grandmother not far away; and it is filled with pine cones as kindling for her fire, and so they take it to her. I tell them who I am, but they are young, they do not understand. They are polite, but they stand and stare. His name—the boy's—is Barnabas, called Barney. Like Madam Washington, her name is Marta.

I say, You two should learn the English. Do you speak the English, *nein?* Have you read *Robinson Crusoe?* I myself read *Robinson Crusoe.* I read it on the ship when I came here. It is a wonderful story and you must know it is about a man who goes to an island all alone, and what does he find upon the shore? A human footprint, and he knows that someone else is there! Now you should read it, *nein?*

They are somewhat frightened by this time and so they stand and gape. But still they are eating something, and I would know what they are eating. They show me shyly. They have nuts. They show me how the nuts do grow. They have some in their barrow. First there are great husks and these must be broken loose and then the nut, it is inside. The boy, he shows me. He cracks it with a stone. But this is not like any nut I know. We do not have the hickory nuts in Germany. *Ja,* when I was young we went to gather chestnuts, but not these. He shows me and I taste the meat inside the nut and it is good. *Ja, das ist gut,* I tell them. You have more?

I tell them, Bring them here. They can bring many,
Oh, *ja.*

for the trees grow near their house and there are many
nuts that they have saved; and I say, Tomorrow do
you come, right here at this same time, and I will
give you silver money for the nuts. The children are
pleased, they say that they will be there.

I ride on. I watch the lines such as they are. *Ach,
ungeschickt!* I ride my route, as Frenchmen say; then
I go back, for time is coming for the drill.

We work so hard. We toil at drill. I say, Here at
Valley Forge, it is so strange. The food is better now,
they tell me, with the waggons coming in, but all were
starving weeks before. *Attendez,* I say to them. For
you all are soldiers now, and proud to be, so you'll
have food, and you must shave, and trim your hair,
and you must eat before you come on duty, *nein?*

I line them up: my squad. In front rank there are
six men, so. In rear rank, there are six as well. Again
I put them through the manner of their arms. I cut it
down to six positions, teach them of the bayonet. I
take the musket in my hands and show them—so.
The English do not do this. They say it is for a sergeant; he will show them how. *Ach, nein.* They must
learn it fast and well. Learn from an officer! So I am
their officer—their teacher—and my heart grows
warm within me when I see how they respond.

Quickstep—quickstep—quickstep, I say, and show
them how to march. An easy step, but fast. Not as
they have been taught. Not as they dragged about
when they were at the Brandywine. I tell them how I
learned when I was but a boy, and much of my talk
they do not understand. I tell about the *Frei Corps,*
and how we made all raids; and how King Friedrich
himself approved our tactics, and set them out for us
and showed us how to work in raids, and how to step,
and how to poise our arms and how to use the bayonet and make the enemy to fear us much. They do
not understand all my words. There is laughter sometimes when I say bad words; but any soldier, he will

swear, and this they know. I say, God damn. I say
son-bitch! I damn them all to hell sometimes. My temper grows short. Sometimes it seems they are too stupid, oh so very stupid, all on purpose. They do it to
annoy me, *nein?*

But it is not so long before they display the pride
and manner that I wish to teach them. And I bless
them, even while I swear, and this is right. These men
have now been trained. Oh, in so short a time, but
they are better than they were. I say, Now each of
you will take a squad. Each man in this now squad
shall have a squad to teach, himself! And I come
round. I watch you while you work. Then, when each
of you has trained his squad, they will go out and
teach, and more and more, all through the Army here
at Valley Forge. If each man teaches twelve just like
himself, then there will be another twelve, and yet another, and all those twelves go forth to teach. We have
an army, a new army, and we are alert! We march
like this—zip-zip-zip! We cut the handling of the arms
down to not ten positions, but to six.

You wish to sing as you do march? Now that is
good when you are training. You shall sing, and even
sometimes when you go to war, when you go to battle,
and so you will be singing as you go.

> *Der alt'— böse Feind,*
> *Mit Ernst er's jetzt meint:*
> *Gross Macht und viel*
> *List, Ein' grausam Rüstung ist,*
> *Auf Erd' ist nicht sein gleichen.*

The officers come to see, they watch, they talk
among themselves. I hear their talk and some are
scornful, but never to my face. They dare not show
themselves in scorn, they are afraid of me. They know
His Excellency approves what I attempt to do.

I say, Now you proceed with what I am teaching to
the men. Would you be taught as well? Take up a
musket and be taught! I show you how to hold it. I

show you how to load and fire in a proper way. I show you how to march, I teach the bayonet, you must teach it too! These squads whom I have trained, they can go out and train the others, and we must have an Army like the English never met before. This we can do because of the soldiers' own youth and eagerness. They hold a willingness to serve, no matter how they dragged about before.

Barney and Marta, *ja,* they bring the load of hickory nuts, they bring another load. They wheel them to my quarters and I give them both a pass. The sentries laugh at this, but only when my back is turned. So I have many hickory nuts. I set an orderly to cracking them, the nuts, and so fine nutmeats are prepared for our dessert. But what else do we eat when I am to give my dinner party? Whom do I invite? I invite young officers: the officers to whom I will instruct the work that I have set for them. So many are in rags that I say, No one can come whose breeches are not patched! All must be patched! I call them *Sansculottes.* They all must be in patches, or they cannot come to my fine dinner.

So what shall this fine dinner contain? I send a detail out upon the road. They look, they find a waggon stuck in frozen mud as waggons they are often stuck. The beef or pork, it comes in barrels and those barrels they are heavy and so the waggoners watch to see that no one shall observe them, and then they pour the liquid out upon the ground to make a lighter load. So often this poor meat will spoil because the liquid, it is gone. We find a waggonload of shad, strange fish that they have. We find the beef, sometimes the pork. Not often do we find mutton, but so we dine. We have the meat, sometimes we have the bread, more often not. Sometimes we have potatoes, but often they are very bad as well.

A soldier he must learn to do with what he can, and this I hammer into them as good philosophy.

Huzzah! The guests are now assembled in my quarters. Welcome, I tell them all. Welcome, you pretty

Sansculottes. And here is meat and these potatoes too, and then we have the salamanders.

The salamanders? What are those?

I tell you now. It is rum. And so we light it with a firebrand and here is flaming rum, all hot. Huzzah! We drink a health to all. Sometimes they even drink a health to me, and I am proud and bow my head, and thank them.

Azor is at the dinner party too. He is at all my dinner parties which he really helps to give, and they make much of him. They tell me how some dogs were eaten earlier when first they went starving into camp at this strange lonely place where there was nothing. No huts then, no tents, no way to live. The soldiers froze amid the snow and starved. And this was bad, for sometimes too when I was younger I was cold, and I remember, and sometimes too we had no food. But is starvation not a part of soldiering? *Ach,* yes. Unfortunate, but it is true.

Often, when the guests are gone, my mind is still a-flashing keenly. I lie upon my bed, I think of all the drills. What could I do to make them better? What could I do to make the Army step a prouder step and lift a prouder weapon and be a keen and able Army when the spring comes round?

Azor comes beside my bed. He wants to lie upon it. It is natural that he would do this: he is whelped from fine greyhounds of the line beloved by His Royal Majesty Friedrich the Great, and those dogs did love to lie upon the royal couch where the Great Friedrich was sleeping, and so I have seen him many times with greyhounds snoring close. All was not and is not war with him. The eminent Voltaire was once his admired friend, and later, sad to say, an enemy. But music of the flute was a beauty in the palace, and once upon a time, long before the Seven Years' War in which I was honored to serve, the worthy Master Bach himself came to be a guest. Men still prated of this, even when I was aide to the Great One. In memory I hear his performance of the Fugato from his own Sonata in

C Major. Even such delicate music may come down the years like magic of the bugles.

Say you not so, Azor?

He sniffs as if to say, It is the truth.

I say, Get up, and so he gets upon my bed, and together we are lying there a-thinking. I know not what he thinks about. Perhaps a race sometimes when he is absent from duties of the camp, and he may run so free and chase a rabbit once again—go coursing *ein Kaninchen? Ja,* says Azor, that would be good.

But I still lie and stare at darkness. How many soldiers, now I think, have been lying and looking into darkness thus? Oh many, many. From the dawn of time.

But this is not a period for dreams. It is time for action. If I do not get some sleep, then how can I act? How can I perform as well I should perform?

We must dress up this camp, I think. We will make it stronger, bolder, as His Excellency doth wish.

But go to sleep now for at least a while so you will be alert and able.

The face of Azor comes near my hand. He puts out his tongue, gives me a kiss. I pat him, so, and so we go to sleep, the two of us.

I have forty-seven years. I have learned much. How much more is there for me to learn? How long will I be permitted to learn? Is it not wise that I now give to others, to younger men, whatever I have packed into my head and into my heart?

The very breath of life one draws is uncertain. So too uncertain is the warmth and strength of the body, of the flesh and bone. Any man falls prey to little things which bite upon his strength and feed as mice might feed within a crib of grain; and so at last the man falls down, consumed by mice throughout his whole insides. So too is the life of a soldier, compounded many times of dangers. The musket ball may find him any moment. The solid shot may send the arms and legs a-flying, and I too have seen this done. But I am devoted to the cause of our good General. I am devoted to these rebellious Colonies.

But it is fruitless to merely sum up the perils of a soldier's life, or of any life; or to value one's devotion to a person, a kingdom, an ideal. It is enough merely to practice it as well as you can, to stay upon the strict path of duty; not to step aside from that path across the moor of life itself and be caught up in the *Treibsand,* and sink down and vanish forever.

I am fortunate because I am here. I am lucky that the flying metal of the enemy had not laid me low when I was younger, and the emperor himself could order that I wear upon my breast the bright star of importance. But the whole skein of human activity and—worse still—of military activity, it is so tangled.

Sometimes a keen eye can seek it out, can assess the danger or the charm.

The keenness of that mind, that Herr Doktor Franklin, *ja!* I remember when first I came into the very room where he was talking with some others, and I felt the power of his wisdom. The spice of his shrewdness came out, greeted me, and greeted all the world—the bitter humor. They were laughing with him. All the French were laughing, and it was good that they could laugh.

Here some of the young French officers deplore my presence. I can feel hostility behind me as I move so fast about my work and try to be as direct and honest as I can, and still to have a laugh with all the young, if they will laugh along with me. Many are jealous; but my own military secretary is a Frenchman too, and devoted to this cause. They laughed in Paris about the chubby old Herr Doktor Franklin, but they laughed with respect. They quoted much the things he said, the wisdom all along the line. They told what was said when the United States Declaration of Independence was signed, so very few miles from this very spot, in Philadelphia itself. They told of how one of the others said that these who took the risk of signing this great paper—they must all work together in concert. They must—and he employed the idiom of America—they must hang together.

Ja, said the old Franklin. If we do not hang to-gether, we will hang separately!

To ears of French and Germans this required some explaining, but still it was a thing to laugh about and often quoted; for lesser minds are apt to follow those who run ahead of them, as my Azor would follow his rabbit, his *Kaninchen.* So was I privileged to speak with the great Doktor Franklin and to tell him of my admiration for the Americans, for Washington him-self; and speak of my wish to come and serve. And more than that: I am convinced that it will not be long before the works of the great Franklin will be ac-counted of even higher importance than many now dream. His Excellency knows of this. We speak of it. We know! We do believe, and that is another reason for making our soldiers as able as possible. So that when spring comes, we will be able to drive out the British from the nation's capitol, as soon as a French fleet comes sailing.

Why lie I here awake, good dog? You sigh and snore beside me, sometimes you give a yelp. You think in dream that you are coursing. *Ach,* so also am I coursing in a dream.

I must not do so.

Sleep now, and arise early to have my coffee and my pipe, to be stout and keen. To go out, as I must, to the challenge of the winter and the camp, and the men themselves, and make them into good soldiers, the best I can. That is my assigned task and I am committed to it.

NOISE rose first from the direction of Sullivan's Bridge and the sun was shining blandly over the Schuylkill, saying I have promised you something for some days, now we shall fulfill as a rare treat beneath the water's surface. That surface was already being churned and torn as sentries gave up their posts and thronged from both banks, splashing into shallows or trooping on the bridge itself, getting their feet caught as waggon wheels had been caught so often between the strips of rough-barked planking, but all dipping and floundering at the surface of the river itself and emitting yelps of joy at what they were finding. Roger and his friend Thurlow, off-duty at this moment and without a care in the world except the eternal search for food, had hoped to elude the sentries and go into the stream itself hunting for clams. They were good eating if you could tread them out of the mud and some small quantities had been taken so.

Whatever are they seeking?

I can hear 'em yelling. Shad, shad.

What in tunket are shad?

Know ye not? 'Tis a kind of fish—

Fish worth eating?

Let's get onto 'em! See: even the troops have left the star redoubt and gone!

But we've naught to net 'em in.

Hands, man, hands!

By this time they both were running.

In the Hewes house Madam Washington heard the clamor and went down to be informed. This is the migration, she agreed. Mayhap it came early because of warming weather. Do you, she said to two of Washington's guard, pray inform the quartermaster that there are nets in that shed, the last one out behind this house. Mistress Hewes baled them there. I recollect she told that they would come in handy in the spring. Then something else ensued and we discussed it no further. Do you tell the quartermaster to fetch out the nets.

A native on the quartermaster's staff cried that Pawling's Ford would be best, and thither men hastened, dragging nets as they ran. Tribes tore, Valley Forge was in riot. People called and crowed, they tried to unfurl nets even as they bore them. From every quarter people were swarming with cans, baskets, buckets, and howls going up for cavalry, cavalry. Many were aware that horsemen churning the water with poles and tree limbs and lengths of brush would force the migrant fish more rapidly upstream where nets were being readied to receive them. But never biding for such onslaught, troops splashed wildly into the shallows even now, flailing and grabbing. Those ahead who still had jackets ripped them off and stuffed them with the trove, flopping and a-squirming. Just like salmon! cried out some few who held experience in waters to the far north. They're all full of roe and going upstream to spawn! 'Twas a fair shuttle now, men rushing to the stream as fast as they could pelt, others emerging dripping and happy, cuddling the flopping treasure in contrived bags of clothing. Sergeants and corporals found it impossible to hold their men to other duties which had been prescribed: the bawling and racing swept up the slopes to the foot of Mount Joy on the west, to the very cabins of Wayne the Drover to the south. Noncommissioned officers melted away from their chore of disciplining, they thronged down to the river with the rest, bound each to secure a single fish at least for himself. A single fish indeed? the scads could not be counted. Wet slopes began to be legioned by flopping little bodies, a man would drop one, stoop to pick him up, lose two more from his burden. Other hands would grab and snatch. *No shad, no soldier!* bright-minded boys were hooting, and the tiresome jest won maudlin repetition on every side.

Still within that first hour, an order of experience began to prevail, and a new rattle and bang rose above the hoarse whimsy. Coopers were at work, they were building barrels by the cartload. Dead and fallen trees were dragged up, fresh trees were chopped, the saws ripped. An odor of pungent sawdust ruled amid the prime delicacy of the fish themselves. Cavalry prevailed in their threshing and thrashing, they plowed the Schuylkill by twos, fours, and busy troops. The harvest flung itself up out of the water, broke constantly ahead of the riot, went down to the bottom, crushed against each other, burst in frenzy again and ahead and under the horses' legs and bellies.

Upstream at Pawling's Ford nets began to sag under the crushing weight of flipping silver. One net tore beneath its burden, fish were running loose again, going on to the freedom their impulse demanded, and eager netters floundered under contradictory outcry. They were laughed at, hallooed at, blamed, extolled. Carts and sledges were assembled to bear the new-made barrels up to the ford as fast as they were hooped. At first they waited in line but the coopers held stubbornly to their task and before another two hours had passed there were more barrels than bearers. This plump fresh burden must needs be parceled to various sections of the camp's square miles.

It seemed to many that the population of the stream had begun to thin appreciably when night came down, although there was dissension of opinion. Some swore that shad ran only in daylight hours, others insisted that they would keep coming through darkness as well. But a tired soldiery could not hold to such task through night as well. Activity thinned and where the scent of wood smoke had ruled before, now the sweet odor of cooking fish rose from every hut chimney. Everyone from His Excellency down dined on the plump provender. Boiled shad, nothing better in this world! Fried shad, a dish, a dish! Hear me now: we've got onions still in our Hut Seven. What say you to roasted shad stuffed with onions? As fancy fare as a tavern cook could serve up if you sat with that damnable Congress in York!

It was a wonder so great as to be beset with fear. Was this illusion? Was it but a dream? Could this be the very stream which they'd crossed staggering in single file when they plowed through the freeze to Valley Forge, when first they came? Might they not awaken from this fancy to find themselves as empty and shad-less as they were before?

'Twas but an ill fancy at best. With morning, fish were still churning the river, and barrels were packed by the hundred.

35

THE colonel of the regiment was named Melanchthon Parris, and he was a truly reserved individual given to tender imaginings although he had fought against the French and Canadians long before, and he had no wife, not chick nor child, no pet at home, no true home, but he had a niece named Hannah, he thought of her often, he thought of her tenderly because he had loved his sister immensely and this girl was the child of that sister, and he wondered how she did, and was confident that she would do well.

Her name was Hannah Hartley and her demon energies went spouting so far and determined that she could scarce control them. She was a demon with her diary as well when she set down her performance of one short day.

> Fix'd gown for Prude,—Mend Mother's Rid-
> inghood,—Spun short thread,—Fix'd two gowns
> for Welsh's girls,—Carded tow,—Spun linen,—
> Worked on Cheese-basket,—Hatchel'd flax with
> Sade, we did 51 lbs. apiece,—Pleated and
> ironed,—Read a Sermon of Dodridge's,—
> Spooled a piece,—Milked the cows,—Spun linen,
> did 50 knots,—Made a Broom of Guinea Wheat
> straw,—Spun thread to whiten,—Set a Red dye,
> —Had two Scholars from Mrs. Taylor's,—I
> carded two pounds of whole wool and felt Na-
> tionly,—Spun harness twine,—Scoured the pew-
> ter.

She was both mouse and eagle, building nests. She became a wild Mediterranean female upon a flouncing horse . . . she felt Nationly indeed!

A scant thirty months before when her fingers were smaller, slimmer, not yet so trained or able, they had whipped themselves into the orgy of coat-making which was shared by other females at their wheels and looms. The Congress said that soldiers needed thirteen thousand warm thick coats for winter campaigning; promptly the coats were made. Hannah had put her name sewn into the coat as many other girls were doing, but no husband had come to her as a result as yet.

Sometimes she dreamed she saw him appearing on the family doorstep and she went to curtsy to him when he said, Good young miss, be you Hannah Hartley? You made my coat for me.

Bounty Coats, they called them, and the king's men sneered at homespuns; but the women only smiled, so proud to be spinning at home, and doing all the rest that needed to be done.

She washed, she knitted, she weeded out the garden, she plucked feathers from the geese and saw them running, squawking in indignation. She prepared the pillows and the spread, she put the feathers in the mattresses that thus kept out the cold.

She dipped her candles in the spring and made soap in autumn.

She knew she was a female and fated to be smitten with The Curse. Her older sisters whispered of it when she was a tot. The elder women dropped their voices low and whispered too. They talked as if this bleeding were a horrid thing . . . and yet, and yet . . . there was a new shine in the eyes of girls, and once they had attained it they began to sleek their hair and not run hoydenish. Soon they looked at males with different eyes, their voices held a lower gentler tinge.

Why, Grandsire's lost his little flyaway and what's he got here now? Why, quite a lady!

Wanted at a Seat about half a day's journey from Philadelphia, on which are good improvements and domestics, A single Woman of unsullied Reputation, an affable, cheerful, active and amiable Disposition; cleanly, industrious, perfectly qualified to direct and manage the female Concerns of country business, as raising small stock, dairying, marketing, combing, carding, spinning, knitting, sewing, pickling, preserving, etc., and occasionally to instruct two young Ladies in those Branches of Oeconomy who, with their father, compose the Family. Such a person will be treated with respect and esteem, and meet with every encouragement due to such a character.

Can you hatchel and card, young woman?
Aye, sir, that I can.
He has a dark, sad face.
Can you spin and reel?
Aye, indeed.
His eyes are gentle but his chin is stout.
And cook?

Very well indeed, sir, if I do say it.

He is neat, but not too overly concerned with neatness.

Are you fit to do candle and cheese-making? And butter, too, when we have need?

I am adept, good sir.

He has a brawny body but is well-trained in courtesy.

Who was she, to whom he was once wedded?

He has the two young ladies and they are good to see, so quiet and so amiable the way they smile. Who was his wife? How did she die, and why, and why? He could get some other kind of homemaker, housekeeper, or what's-its-name.

He might find a tyrant! No, I'll not let her come. No tyrants wanted here.

Why should he not advertise and say, Good people of this land or neighborhood, I need a wife.

But that would be unthinkable. The gossips rear their heads, their eyes are glinting, tongues are clacking. Who is that woman gone to dwell and keep a house for Mr. What's-his-name? I fear she is no better than she should be: to go and live alone with any man like that, and keep his family. What is her church? He's not a Friend, and might she be a Friend, and is she regular in Congregation, and does she know her texts, and will she teach them to the young, and will she honor God as we all do?

Is she a paragon? She needs to be.

> *You'll mend your life to-morrow still you cry.*
> *In what far Country does To-morrow lie?*
> *It stays so long, it's fetch'd so far, I fear*
> *'Twill prove both very old, and very dear.*

She coddled ailing children, gaffers, ducks; she even tried to nurse an injured raccoon which children fetched to her door and she was bitten not too badly by it. She listened to the infants' jingles, gave them old jingles of her own, even made up new jingles to enlighten their fancy. She cried *shoo-lie-shoo-fly-roos* as she was churning, she sang from an imagined hymnal to greet the sun or when she witnessed sun's departure. She worshipped (she dared not call it praying to them) insects which chittered in the trees when the clime was warm; and glowing lights would seem to hang in northern skies in cooler session when the seasons changed. Children wanted to know what those shafting wands might be . . . she said, Mayhap the candle-glow from angels' tenements? One boy opined that these might be the fires of the Devil's own chambers reflected thus. . . . Ah, Nay, she swore, too filled with daintiness.

She toiled in field and at a furnace, plucked the gentle blooms of certain flowers to make a perfume for her petticoats and those of growing girls. Heed this, she said, they'll smell so sweet.

She pickled every kind of pickle you could think of or anyone could grow. She pickled fennel, samphire (but only if she lived near the shore of salt water), purple cabbage, nasturtium buds, she pickled green walnuts when the little things were still soft. She would have pickled lemons had she owned some lemons. She pickled radish roots and barberries and elderbuds. She pickled parsley when she grew it, mushrooms when the children found the proper kind, asparagus, and little fishes, too. . . . The goodman wanted baccy for his pipe: she grew the stalks, and dried and baked the leaves till they were rich and dusty-like.

She made a jelly, tended a hurt finger, hung above the dying, coddled up some chicken for the weeping who were thus forsaken.

If left alone to do it (seldom could this be) she'd walk her sixteen miles a day beside the flax wheel, and be proud of her six skeins.

The cobbler came a-marching on his rounds or wheeling his small cart. She traded for his shoes when they were needed, and drove her bargain tight but right.

The quivering wayfarer who came a-starving to her gate, she gave him mush and milk and more.

She saw God's face in blossoms, knew she heard Him in the cheeriness of birds.

She knelt imploring when kneeling seemed demanded, for all her busyness.

She lay beside her husband when the day was through.

36

IT must have been past midnight when the guard came to examine his irons. What seek you? Billy asked. Seeking to find if you are tight, was the dry answer. Billy said nothing in reply. The guard's hands went over his manacles and down to his ankles to discover whether the fetters there were in order, then stole up to see that the belt which held him to his chair was still fast. Billy sought to know whether the court had yet met and adjudicated, and what the sentence was to be, but some woeful pride kept him from questioning the guard any further. The guard was humming some wretched tune, a Scottish tune, Billy recognized that. When in Philadelphia he had been quartered near elements of the Forty-Second Highlanders and that was the thing they called "The Banks of Allan Water." The guard was still humming it as he went away and Billy closed his eyes and saw the Highland troops as they marched out to change guard, or on the one occasion he'd seen them warming for fancied encounter with the Americans. He reviewed his fortune and found it damnable. When he was captured by the Continentals he was one of but twelve. There had been two or three killed. Should he have been one of those killed? No, never. It was woeful but still better this way. He supposed he would be striped within an inch of his life; but might there not be some way to avoid it? Bribery? No good now, because they'd taken what gold he had with him in its small limp purse. 'Twould have been heavier, that purse, had he not spent so much on women, but the women were available, there were droves of them. Many were English or Irish from a shipload which had been sent; some had been abandoned because of the state of their disease or drunkenness; and of course there were the Philadelphia women themselves. He had his clap like most of the rest and (he made a face) felt his lips draw away from his teeth, felt the rest of his face scrolling, felt his eyes hot and nasty as he remembered the surgeon who'd said gunpowder was best, and had sprinkled a dose upon his lesion and then touched it off with a lighted candle. He could still hear his own howl go echoing, and wanted briefly to scream for his mother. She might do something to ease the hurt. She had eased his hurts so many times, never held a hurt against him. His father was a shopkeeper dealing in regular commodities of the edible line: salt, sugar, pickled meats, vinegar, treacle, soaps, all such. His father was usually stewed in rum by noon or early afternoon, and then it fell to Billy to tend shop. He appropriated what funds he could and when his father, waking sober, accused him of this as he did so often, Billy had only to appeal to his mother and then she howled in his defense. Mrs. Flarnay was forever eager to champion her one and only child. He had not been treated fairly, had been picked upon by others, had been made a butt. A notion flashed into his mind about the slide they had constructed, he and several other boys. True, the youths did not fancy him. Even as a tiny lad he had never been welcomed by mates, but he was endured because he was a child and they were children; and there was the proximity of village life. He had not thought of the slide in years and again the awful grimace must have misshapen his face: he felt his face hardening in whatever muscles lived within the skin, and wanted to put up his hand to feel the physical ignominy portrayed there, but his hand was held fast by metal.

'Twas a fine steep slide and they'd made it long and toughly slanting with a pilfered rope that ran from a high tree down to a low one and was suspended from a branch at its termination by other shorter ropes. A small board formed the sliding factor and they had nailed slats against a tree trunk going up and up, in order to reach the high beginning. Two-thirds of the way down, the rope had broken. They dragged it longer and knotted it, and great laughter ensued when the slider struck that knot and remained suspended for a moment, and kicking. Sometimes the board had not even halted at the knot. It bumped slightly, went over the knot because of the force already involved in descent, and then the slider went on to the termination of his journey. So Billy essayed the slide, his first after the knot had been formed. The board went whistling down the slope with his two hands gripping it on either side. It hit the knot with a thud, it wrenched, his hands flew loose, he was in the air and came down in a tumbling pile. The other boys ripped off their laughter at seeing him thus, but he felt only ignominy and shame. These dominations he was feeling forever. He was ignominious, and knew it, but pretended to be made of worthy stuff which he did most pompously. Now there could be nothing pompous about him. He had fallen in disgrace. He was not savagely misused by the tumble, but pretended that he was. He leaped up, staggered, roaring with his deep hoarse natural tone. He bellowed across that neighbor's yard, and his mother had come out on the stoop across the way long before he reached the center of the road. My back, oh my back, was all he could whoop. Mocking yells had gone down to silence behind him when his mother appeared, and the boys went springing away to hide and not be pinned to any responsibility. Oh my back, my back!

His mother was shouting louder than he. Oh you poor pet! Poor child! What's befallen? What ails you?

His hoarse hollow echoing voice would break forth again about his back. She dragged him within doors, sought to placate him, to make him lie down.

Oh where on your back, my child, where? Oh those wicked boys! Those wicked, wicked boys!

And he deemed them wicked too and bawled the louder. In the end she gave him a large fresh roll of bread halved and spread with syrup, and his father wakened in his chair nearby where he was lolling collapsed and not making any sense with his mumbles, and then his father went back into doze again.

Oh my back, my back!

This misadventure recurred to give him fresh torment now, although he had not thought of it in so long. After the death of his father, the store was his own responsibility but he idled with petulant remissions in his handling and care of the store, did whatever evil tricks he could contrive to eke out the provender. He found whitish sand, put it in the sugar, stirred cheaper lard into the butter, and all and all and all. Customers soon found that his arts were never artful enough and they fell away. Only strangers came in. His mother mortgaged the place and then she became ill and lay a-fret. He had not thought to join the Army until that time. There was a militia company with some of those same boys of the slide days participating in its drill, but Billy greeted this enterprise with scorn. With the termination of his mother's life, and foreclosure of the mortgage held by a local shyster, he was fairly turned out into the world, and thus hunted for the best enlistment bounty which he might find. It was for seventy dollars. He accepted the money and joined with a surly look of contempt for all. He tried to hold his head on high in pretense of being a smart soldier. He could fool the women perhaps (girls in crowds who assembled to see them march by) but his own mates and those who commanded them could not endure his pretense for long. He was punished by extra duties of all sorts and soon endured a flogging, then another. In sore dreams while recovering from such brutalities he had illusion of his mother, and once woke up cell-mates by yelling for her. On the long march to join the Army of General Washington, Billy had deserted, hid out in cow barns, told horrendous lies to kindly farm-folk who might feed him, and made his way to the king's Army which was not far off. Here he represented himself as a die-hard Tory who had been abused savagely by those of Continental persuasion, and wished only to serve as a redcoat. He was rewarded with a small amount of gold coin and he went into the loan business for a while, profiting with an enormous rate of interest which he demanded from his less-monied new mates. Had he believed in ghosts, he might have tried to invoke the spirit of his mother to help sustain him, but he was neither sensitive nor imaginative enough to do this. He went his small arrogant way, perforce alone, but with that same swagger of pomposity into which he had grown when small. He kept strictly to task however where immediate soldierly duties were concerned, because of memory of those floggings and the small amount of scars he still bore from them. He told other soldiers that these marks came from being whipped by the Continentals when he refused to join up with them and fight against His Majesty the king, but no one was especially impressed. Then came that puny fruitless raid near the Schuylkill River and the encounter with Continentals, the rapid shooting in which there were deaths on both sides and in which he was captured. A Maryland officer recognized him the first day he was fetched to Valley Forge and put the finger upon him figuratively and in fact.

This man is a deserter, he told the provost guard. He deserted from our Maryland regiment last year. And he gave name and data. Billy denied everything but it was useless. The officer merely fetched two more officers and a couple of privates to harden the opinion, and Billy was promptly put into irons and the court was at present judging his case.

It was dawn, a bright fair day for a change, when his guard came back to him, and the guard was not alone. There were two soldiers with him with fixed bayonets, and another officer who jangled keys and said that now the fetters should be removed.

Well, said Billy, still arrogant and holding his puffy head on high. What is the verdict? God have mercy . . . he thought of those beatings again and realized that probably he must endure the ordeal once more.

They're going to hang you, my boy, said the provost commander.

Hang me? roared Billy. They can't hang me! I've done nothing! Nothing!

A chaplain is on his way, said the officer. Best to commune with him, my boy, and make yourself presentable to Those On High before you go to meet Them.

You can't hang me, howled Billy again. No, no, no! You can't! And then the desire to call upon his mother overwhelmed him, and he screamed for her loudly at first, and then more extravagantly as he was dragged away.

They pulled him outside, he blinked at the light. Yes, there was a rope hanging down from a high limb, and a cart stood underneath with horse attached, and on that cart he was to stand and the rope would be put upon him, and then the horse would be started and Billy would swing in space. There were soldiers all around. Vaguely he might have heard the assembling but had been too busy with his own hysterical recollection to pay heed.

I don't want to die, don't want to die! Mother, mother!

The officer said in some disgust, Well, don't make such a noise about it, friend. Try to die like a man even though you can't be one.

Don't hang me, Billy was braying. Don't hang me! Don't hang me!

Two of the soldiers fainted dead away and dropped in their tracks and others bent down to succor them, but this he did not even witness and could not have pitied them had he seen it.

Don't hang me! Don't hang me! I don't want you to hang me! and it was all a mess in pattern and jumble as he was hauled forward by his fresh-bound arms. Don't hang me! Don't hang me! He looked up and saw that rope towering above, and thought of another rope and the slide and the little board coming down and striking the knot, thought of his striking the ground and then bounding up in pretended agony, saying My back, my back! Now he said it again and no one knew why he was saying it.

Don't hang me! Oh, please! And he called them dear ones. Dear ones, don't hang me! I don't want to die! Don't want to die! Don't want to—

They had lifted him into the cart and the soldier that stood at the horse's head was soothing the horse because it was affrighted at all this commotion, and the face of the chaplain swam before Billy's eyes. The chaplain said something more about preparing himself for death and dying like a man, but Billy did not want to die like a man, he did not want to die at all.

Don't hang me! Don't hang me! and this last yelp was cut short as the noose and knot jerked around his neck. I don't want to die! Don't hang me! Mother! Mother! He tried to call her name a third time but by that moment the horse had gone, and the cart wrenched from underneath him and he could say no more, and he dangled.

37

You people clack of tea, said Roger. Tea is not drunk the whole world over. Sometimes it's coffee. My Gram, she come from the Old Country; she come from the kingdom of Austria, and with her 'twas coffee. 'Twas coffee with all them Austrians. Big pot set or hanging by the fire so when people passed by the house she could give 'em a nice fresh cup. I 'member her coffee. Even here in Pennsylvania. It smelt good when you was clean down the road a spell. You'd wrinkle your nose when you come to her house if the door was standing wide and 'twas on nice days. When Grandsire went to do some trading in town she'd make sure that the sugar wasn't out. He bought it in them fine cones, great big solid cones of sugar, and he'd break it off with a hatchet and then she'd break it down littler with a great spoon, and put in several lumps, and so they seasoned coffee in the pots and 'twas fine to scent.

Grandsire, he needed new burrs to his mill, and there was much talk about this cause the millwright had to come and not only dicker, but had to set the wheel in place, and all and all. 'Twas mighty profit to the millwright and maybe he talked my Grandsire down to the grit, or could be his conscience hurt him one way or other. So he fetched Gram a present when he come, and guess what 'twas. A whole chest of tea. Small chest, too, but was solid tea, all fresh come and landed say at Philadelpheeay.

Gram had never drunk tea. Didn't know what it might be, for ours was a quiet place, with only folks that lived there coming through commonly, or coming all the way to mill with their grists from around about. But 'twasn't like a city, and I don't think my Grandma can be blamed so hard for what she went and done.

For he says, Here 'tis, Ma'am, a fine chest of tea, and fresh off ship from the Old Country. Or something like that, wherever the tea come from. So my Grandma, she 'preciated it like. And whilst the men were busy at the mill she fixed them up a dinner. 'Twas good, her dinners always was, and many's the time I've stood a-quivering waiting for the old folks to get up and go, so's I could set with brothers and sisters and get some of that fare our own selves.

She had a home-cured ham and 'twas mighty tasty. Our hogs fed fat on nuts and acorns in the autumn, and snow hadn't come as yet. She had cold ducks too and they was good. I ought to know: they was wild ones partly smoked, and I had shot 'em down myself, and was arching myself according. And stewed apples too, and all sorts of fine fare.

Now, thinks Grandma, 'twas so pleasant of that millwright to fetch us down the tea. Better I give them tea as well, and so she did.

She thought 'twas kind of like some greens—all dried of course—but doubtless welcome to the millwright since he seemed to set such store by it. The whole chest! She cooked it well, and course we young didn't know no difference. Tea weren't in our cupboard, and we knowed it. But that millwright, Mr. Lester was his name—I can still listen to the howl that he let out. Oh Lady, this ain't greens a-tall, but this is *tea*. I tell you, *tea!* And then my Grandsire, he speared himself a spoonful and he says, Kind of tasty, but it's tough.

Great times we had up there to Grandma's house and Grandsire's. That tea thing— It befell some months before my sisters found the puppies. The girls they went picking whortle-berries and they found the cutest pups. My sister Liz, the eldest, says, What darling puppies, and think how cruel some neighbor was to put 'em out to starve and die this way! Let's fetch 'em home. And so they did, a-carrying the puppies, there was four or five, in their berry baskets and in their aprons. They took 'em in, all prideful, and such darlings as they thought the puppies was. And Grandsire, he says to me, Son—he always called me Son—Son, get your gun, I'll do the same. So I took the shotgun of which I was so proud. 'Twas the one I used to get the ducks, and Gramp, he had his rifle. So he says, Little girls, come long with you, and bring the puppies. So we bore 'em back the whole long way, and he made those girls dump down the puppies in the woods where they was found, and then we streaked for home.

Good thing for us that that old mother wolf she wasn't round.

Oh yes, we could have killed 'em. The hired man there at the mill, he says to knock 'em on the head cause they'd be so bad in winter, and take the sheep and all.

But not with them girls' faces looking at you.

We never knocked 'em. Just left 'em laying there, a-squeaking for their ma, and so I reckon that she come in time.

38

PADDY was sprung to his lofty perch during midnight hours. Morgan's troops were quartered in a series of huts well down the slope, but they did not observe preliminary activity which proceeded under cover of darkness, even though there was a moon to inform them. All they knew was that the image swayed lightly in the breeze when they first poked their heads out in the morning. The earliest to rise went closer and looked, and a mutter began before any others joined them. An oak tree stood with a single branch protruding toward the east. The malefactors had shinnied up poles, for no ladders would have been available to reach such a height. With sunrise there shifted an amiable breeze, enough to sway the image slightly and make it seem to hang jeering. He was a madcap dummy, life-size, constructed of breeches and torn shirts cobbled together. There were even shoes of a sort, swinging from the end of the trousers. Worst of all was the stuffed round head with a face painted upon the fabric which formed his countenance. He wore an old tricorn hat as well and seemed leering at any multitudes assembled or to assemble, and the placard which hung from his stuffed chest left no doubt as to the identity. It read in huge letters PADDY. Morgan's men were Irish in core and extremity. No one could blame them for observing this mute as an indignity deliberately foisted.

'Tis on St. Patrick's Day that they do this!

So it is.

They bear no love for the good St. Patrick!

So they don't! They choose to make mockery to his faithful memory instead.

We should get our hands on them and pull them apart.

And who could it be that was doing it?

'Tis them Pennsylvania Germans yonder, I'll be bound!

Fresh breeze increased as the sun came a bit higher and Paddy swung affably in it and there was enough wind to make his very broken boots clack together at intervals. 'Twas as if he capered in mockery of himself and the lore that he represented.

I mind the telling of me Grandmother. He drove all the snakes out of Ireland.

And where did he drive them to?

To Pennsylvania! And the snakes fathered those very Germans!

Couldn't be the Germans, I tell you. They haven't

the wit. Stupid as they are, they know nought of St. Patrick.

Might it not be the New Yorkers on the other side?

There's good Irish blood in many of the New Yorkers, but not this lot. Prattisons they be, and there's many of Holland blood among 'em.

They hold no faith in good St. Patrick, nor love for his memory. They do it but to twit us.

We should be after twisting their bloody heads for the insult.

For so it's meant to be!

We'll take every word you utter as the truth, and in right good faith.

Up the good Paidragh? They mean down with him!

By training, example and experience the soldiers were polished to keen sense of necessity for combat and this was bound, as in all armies, to compel a habit of personal if not joint affray. Officers joined with the men in wrath inclining toward rebellion. They felt that they, of their creed and blood, had been singled out to be lampooned as monsters. Were they challenged to run a rugged race? They would run it, and quickly.

They witnessed their men checking flints in their guns, whether they bore the Brown Bess or Pennsylvania rifles. Grimly officers began checking the flints in their own pistols. Imagined spectacle of subservience to the English was a panic to haunt them forever, which might be the reason a lone Irishman often felt himself obliged to re-enact his status in the Battle of the Boyne when he grew hotheaded in a taproom.

> *'Twas the rising of the moon,*
> *The rising of the moon!*
> *Ten thousand blades were flashing*
> *In the rising of the moon.*
> *Oh Paddy dear, and did you hear*
> *The song we had to sing?*
> *Ten thousand blades were flashing*
> *At the falling of the King.*

In emotion engendered by ancient conflict they prayed to their Paddy and would not tolerate the spectacle of his being vilified. Rumors tore among them. 'Twas the Pennsylvania Germans. Nay, 'twas the Virginia Germans, who had long left their original confines and formed whole companies, and nigh on to regiments in the forces of a sister state. Nay, 'twas the New Yorkers. But look over yonder. See them, and are they not jeering at us? And what of the Massachusetts Prattisons beyond? Never did the British come through our lines to tussle with us here at the Forge. There be no British now, but there be these others who sneer, so let us wipe a blade or a muzzle or a fist in their blood.

Already some nimble youths had made their way up the oak, enduring more scratches than a few, but they reached the image and whacked it down. It fell a-tousle and the nearer men trooped round to have a closer look at ordained infamy.

So they would make a sport upon St. Patrick's Day. Is anyone here bound to make them salute Paddy, and kiss his holy corpse?

That I will!

And I!

And I!

Erin go Bragh!

The roaring of the mobs had carried even to the ears of His Excellency in the Hewes house, as a bright green bird of earliest spring might have flown and borne the tidings in his beak.

Why, what have we here? (Sentinel, secretary, aide, whoever you may be.)

'Tis a message for yourself, Your Excellency. 'Twas fetched by a bird.

Bird or no, his horse was always ready-saddled, and the roaring stopped suddenly as Washington pushed, mounted, between the two factions. He sat there, calmly regarding one mob, then swung to examine the other.

Need I remind you, he said, that there exists a strict

edict against the miscellaneous firing of weapons in camp. You will immediately remove all flints or caps from your pieces.

Rustle and light metallic clanking of this activity started slowly but gained force and speed as laggards turned their surly gaze upon His Excellency, and then somehow felt less surly than before, and their fingers moved to execute his order. He swung his mount in a slow circle, and the horse seemed to know that he was a part of a vision, and seemed to bow his head as if to accept with grace a plaudit.

Should a voice be able to tower, the voice of His Excellency was towering.

I have long been an admirer of the Great St. Patrick. We should celebrate his birthday more fittingly than by confronting his memory with glowering and arms. It may not be commonly known, but I learned a fact when young. There were DeWessyngtons in my ancestry, and some of them, I am happy to tell you, wore the brown cloth of the Benedictine Order.

He waited wisely for his speech to be applauded, and so it was. A vociferous yell came first from the Irish faction and already some of them were flinging up their hats.

I shall make herewith a proclamation, said His Excellency. All regular military activity in this camp shall cease as of this moment, and a holiday in honor of St. Patrick will ensue. We are privileged and proud to have a quantity of cider available. One can of cider shall be issued promptly to every officer and man.

It was not alone the Irish who were raising rumpus now. Everyone joined in, and more caps were going in the air, and the factions were intermingled. They were pushing forward mutually, and all over the landscape you could see men and boys rushing from distant quarters to see what was up, to join in whatever battle or demonstration now afforded.

The Commander-in-Chief spoke his final line of public utterance on this day. As for myself, he said, I look forward to the draught of cider with pleasure;

and there is naught that I enjoy more when holidaying than a good game of bowls.

Men trod upon the toes of others. They fell back quickly, still hurrahing, and some were pushed to the ground, perhaps some were walked upon.

Washington swung down from his horse. Close at hand stood a battery of small cannon, replete with their pyramids of solid shot ready to be fired in necessity. While the crowds tightened further away, Washington strolled deliberately to the nearest pyramid of balls. His great hand picked an eight-pound solid shot from the summit of the peak. He gazed ahead, smiling slightly and gesturing, and the throng stood apart and gave him space. He thought, Now, but others tumbled back as his arm swung with its burden. The ball leaped from his grasp, it sailed low and heavy. There were men who would later tell their offspring and their offspring's offspring of how that ball sizzled as it went through the air and then on the ground. It sang a small song of better days, and victories to come. It ceased motion at last in a swale of turf soon to be showing earliest green above trodden clay and darker earth mingled together. It rested in challenge but still in warning. The roar which went aloft was louder than before, and folks beyond the Schuylkill River spoke of it, and wondered what could be up.

Washington remounted. His horse was growing more and more nervous at all this petting, and was glad to be off. It reared and the men scattered, laughing to see his steed do this, and Washington waved them aside until he could ride free of the press. Behind him a brawny ex-smith who had not fallen to ruin in the starvation period just ended was calling to all to see how he would better His Excellency's bowl of the cannonball, and so he did, and Washington could tell this by howling which ensued behind him.

He reached his quarters, swung off while a groom held the bridle. He went within doors and Martha came to meet him.

Well, my old man. She spoke to him thus in fondness when they were solely alone, and sometimes even when there were others present or when she was speaking of him to womankind.

Well, my old man, what's ado?

I have them playing at bowls in the camp, he said. We are making holiday today in honor of the good St. Patrick. I cast out the first cannonball, but fear my skill has already been exceeded.

39

CONGER told the boys, Conestogas. Those was the names of the waggons. *Are* the names. They've still got 'em. Building new ones all the time. Or will, soon as the king's men get drove out and back across the water where they belong. You may have speculated, Why did they call 'em Conestogas? Indian name. They was a kind of Iroquois. Some folks called 'em Andastes. Some called 'em Susquehannas, like the name of the river. Funny name? Some say it means People of the Forked Roof Poles. That's count of they lived in houses like a lot of the Indians up north. Their town is up there a ways near Lancaster. You young'uns are too infant to remember, but they had a lot of trouble over there, years back. The Paxton Boys raised a mob and killed 'em all off, neutral though they be. Think that was in sixty-three. Hain't nothing left of 'em but the name and there ain't no people to bear the name any more. Just the waggons. I ought to know: I was a waggoner. Fore that I was a packhorseman. If you hain't seen that you hain't seen nothing. We had bright colors on all the collars, and the bells was stuffed during day times, but they rang like holy hell at night when the horses was out grazing. What did we carry? Everything. To them villages to the west. Tea, salt, all the ware they needed like wires and nails and brads and pewter. All the things they couldn't get in tiny western towns. Every horse carried 'bout two hundred pounds. Course, part of that was grain to eat, specially on the way back. We'd leave it here and there—hide it away—then pick it up on the return journey. We'd tote back all the things that the traders had to sell out west. Furs, principally, for sending over to the Old Country. Bundles of medicine weed. Things like such. We lugged lots of sang. You don't know what sang is? You're a smart one. It's ginsang. I guess some people call it gin*seng*. Great medicine. You never see anything if you didn't see those files of horses. I mind one time I counted four hundred and twenty-seven in one day. That's a lot of horses. Way an Army should travel: horsey-back. But we ain't got sufficient horses. All the farms are picked dry of 'em. Then, when the Indian trails was cut wider, we started to use Conestoga waggons. They begun to come in, maybe fifteen years back, somewhere around that mark. Shaped like a great big boat. Low in the middle, high at both ends. You know the why of it? 'Cause when you go up hill or down dale, all the burden of the waggons won't shift to the ends. Stays in the middle where it belongs. Oh, they was gay. We painted 'em blue. We painted the sideboards red, and put great big hoops on top. Took half a dozen horses to pull one. Some of those teams was beautiful matched. I had some dapple-grays. The harness cost a fortune. 'Twas all of buckskin and bearskin and they'd put fringe on it, the harness-makers would; red usually; and they'd tie ribbons on the headstalls and ribbons on the bells and make a wonderful sight and sound. That's what they called our horses, too. Conestogas. Waggons were Conestogas, teams were Conestogas, and pretty soon they started calling us drivers Conestogas. I wasn't a regular. I was militia. I knew my teams and my feed and how to keep the horses spick-and-span. I was new-wedded at the time, most belatedly, and the woman didn't want me to be a regular and be gone so long. That was the first militia I ever served in. We kind of envied the regulars but we was too busy most of the time to soak ourselves in envy. I've seen a thousand waggons in two days. Hard to believe, but that was not so long ago, when the roads got wider and we could get through. 'Twould break my heart to consider it if I'd choose to do so, but I don't choose. The sight is there in memory and that's the way it should be. Haunts the mind at night, however, and is busy in our private notions. Many's the time I doze, and then it all comes back to me. I see that procession like a ceremony. Blue painted bodies, scarlet sideboards, and all them waggon covers rising on the bows, and all them horses decked with ribbons. I hear 'em as well as see 'em. And when I truly smell 'em and see those hoofs squashing the horse apples that teams ahead have dropped, it scents like tonic and I want to suck it in with all my breath. Imagine power of those droves a-pressing on together in their long line . . . imagine six score, try and imagine more. Think of them ridges: Chestnut Ridge, Laurel Hills, Allegheny, Ray's Hill, Tuscarora. Did the girls troop out to see us pass when they was girls in any homes nearby? Oh yes: they assembled in droves. And did the little kids speed out, the smaller boys and girls, and run alongside, and behind and amongst? We'd lift our whips and pop the lashes and threaten. Make pretense we was going to offer them a good whipping if they didn't flee and not get squashed by teams and all the crush and grinding of our wheels. We drove thunderous, high and bragging, and 'tis no wonder that an old waggoner sees and hears and smells it in his dreams.

40

It having pleased the Almighty Ruler of the Universe propitiously to defend the cause of the United States of America and finally by raising us up a powerful friend, among the Princes of the Earth, to Establish our Liberty and Independence upon lasting foundations; It becomes us to Set apart a day, for fully acknowledging the Divine Goodness, and celebrating the important event, which we owe to his Benign interposition.

Indeed, 'tis well said. How do you term it?

General After Orders.

Did thee set down the time?

Not yet, Martha. Thinkest thee I should?

My watch tells me that it is now fifteen minutes over the hour of six; then suppose you say six P.M. How shall it be employed?

To be read to all troops on the morrow. Say at nine. To be published aloud by the chaplains.

Ah, those chaplains again! Old man, they're tedious in discourse—

I shall lay down an order for the chaplains to read it to all brigades, then let a cannon shot be fired after one scant half hour. That will signify the termination.

'Twould be well. Any chaplain who cannot thank the Power on High for the sanctification of our new alliance in one half hour is scarcely worth his salt. You will permit the troops to parade?

Think you they could be restrained?

Who might wish to restrain them, indeed? Not I.

And there shall be blank firing. Lord Stirling and Lafayette and the Baron de Kalb have already received
instructions to facilitate this.

Oh, my old man! Was it not a scant two or three
months agone that any man was punished for clearing his piece by firing a charge? How the world of
Valley Forge doth change! But will this not call for a
collation?

Washington smiled at her tenderly. Such a collation,
my dear, as has never yet been witnessed here; and
you're to have naught to do with it. Neither you nor
the other ladies. Instructions have been issued already,
and food will be in preparation during the night. Pork
and beans, that divine pair. And what beef we can
scare up, and bread as well; and rum and cider shall
flow not only for us who partake of the collation, itself,
but for the entire mass of troops.

Martha Washington huffed and puffed without
words, a mannerism common to her inclination. Well
indeed! It is taken well out of my hands—

General Washington bowed. I pray only that you
ladies will see fit to honor us with your presence.

She donned shawl and bonnet and went away with
a single servant to attend her. She must call upon Lady
Stirling and Mrs. Greene and whomever else might
be about, so that they could chatter over these strange
and beautiful tidings. When excited to this limit,
Martha was forever a-bubble. She delivered comment
and opinion without ceasing, she was as a girl in
gaiety, her hazel eyes snapping, her prattle going on
and on. In listening you would have thought her to be
eighteen instead of elder years.

That night Washington considered his own elder
years through lengthy vigilance, long after his woman
lay asleep and breathing soundly. In delight and reverence he measured once more the person of Benjamin Franklin, and the ideal he represented, and the
competence with which he strove.

Franklin is seventy-two in this year, thought His
Excellency. He was grown to a man's estate and had

already performed much when my first nurse fetched me to my mother. Mayhap I will see seventy-two? I fear not. I have bartered both body and spirit for too long . . . there have been so many illnesses . . . some known to those about me and some which I have managed to keep concealed, I do believe, with such skill as I was capable of manifesting. A seventh decade would put me into the nineteenth century, and what a weary way that seems ahead! There are my teeth: those wretched snags are going fast and something must be done about them—those left to me— in another year or two. I mind the staring of some nearby soldiers when they witnessed my pulling one of those fangs from my jaw by using my bare fingers. 'Tweren't much of a tooth, to yield so willingly, but they were awed nevertheless, and I too felt at fault in my own desolation and drive.

So what profits it to hazard about the future, a full generation hence? Deane and Lee are naught beside Franklin. I feel that Lee has acted the fool more than the sage and Deane has been fussed and battled, but Franklin remains serene forever. In his very serenity lies that mighty power which has fetched this thing about. I deal not in necromancy, even do I try to deny its existence, and yet the power of the future overwhelms me on this night.

There lies a strange certainty ahead.

Of this I am confident—Congress or no Congress —detractors and enemies, the fawning, the envious, those who would trick, those who would elevate themselves by sly and dishonorable means were it only possible. They've sought constantly to make me a wounded bird that they might drag down and revel in the picking and the stuffing and the cooking, as I were a very partridge. Devil take these swarms of avaricious Europeans who have sought their own elevation, at the expenditure of the Army and the expenditure of my sanity, who have heckled and sneaked, exuded their pomposity, tried to sell for fortunes their petty blades which in the end were but made of tin.

Still, one Lafayette has been worth a score of them, and I should not complain, nor will for long.

Ofttimes the reports have been meager, oft they have been lacking, sometimes it turned out that they were in error, yet the vast homely fact was bound to filter through. I do not voice this thought to anyone, least of all to my own fair plump little Beauty who lies here so trustingly. But I wished too that I might have gone abroad even as I yearned for sea when young, and was made to desist by my own mother. I recall Ben Franklin's telling of when he was a youth abroad, and working with the English printers, and they drank copiously of beer and twitted him about being, as they said, a water American, and gloomed that the water diet would make him weak.

They desisted, said our good Ben, only when they found that I could lay any of them upon his back!

So he was a wrestler early, as now at seventy-two it has been essential for him to wrestle with spies, tyrants, and the gaming royal court of France.

Word has come through letters in which the young Lafayette rejoices. He tells me much which I could not witness in imagination were it not for his accurate knowledge of the scene. The serene Franklin, wigless, with his gray locks hanging, his spectacles upon his nose, his fur cap in his hand, and carrying his stick. What use would he have for a rapier?

Lafayette tells me that they have paintings and drawings of the man in childish gaudy manner on rings, on lockets for ladies, even on lids of snuffboxes brandished by the gallants. He walks boldly and bravely each day, for that is good for him. When at last he dies, will he be ninety? His spirit will walk, I trow. He walks in his garden when it be fair, and through the house he has taken in the suburbs of Paris when weather is inclement. Does he keep no carriage? I asked my faithful marquis. Ah, *mais oui,* he says, but seldom uses it. He takes pride in marching so calmly!

I pray that we might have him here, I wish that he

were to be here upon the morrow. He will be, in time, but we shall toast him, every man shall toast him, every weary hero and sneaking poltroon who has been put about his military business so stubbornly by the valiant von Steuben. I can speak of this treaty at the moment only to the great Jehovah as described by our bold Ethan Allen, and the Continental Congress, if I should bend to deal with those so confused and laggardly. This treaty (and I shall say the words) is conceived in terms of irony and derision, more degrading to the pride and dignity of Britain than anything she has experienced since she became a nation.

Without Franklin what might have befallen? I dare not conjecture, and my young marquis may but shrug. The British have had access to Franklin's very house while swarming in our capital, but now we may recall only with joy his remark to the prattler who addressed him in Paris—I believe 'twas in last November—with saying that General Howe had taken Philadelphia. Franklin only bowed and smiled and said, I beg your pardon, sir. Philadelphia has taken General Howe! And doubtless they were thieving his own books from his library all the while, as they pilfered and caroused while we lay foodless and ungarmented so close at hand.

Now they will need soon to be gone and we must plan our campaign accordingly. Is ever there a coziness waiting the weary brain of the military? I know not. Nor do I crave it now. I long only to see and hear our fresh soldiery making merry on the morrow, as they shall be bound to do.

FROM THE JOURNAL OF ELIJAH FISHER:
May 6th. We had rejoicing on the account of the French declaring for us Independent and the howle of the Continental Army was ordered to three larm posts in the senter and the Army was all around us at there several stations (and there was a grand harbor bilt and all the Commissioners were Envited to dine with His Excelency) our

*guard gave the first fire then thirteen Cannons
then the fire began at the rite of the army and
went through the howl line and fired three rooms
apeace the Artillery Discharged forty-four Cannon and it was followed by three chears for the
King of France and three for the Friendly Powers
of Europe and three Cheers for the Thirteen
United States of America and His Excelency
gave orders that every Prisoner should have his
Freedom that belonged to the Continental army,
that they might taste the Pleasur of the Day. Can-
vas sprid over tables against the hot sun. An
excellent band played. And the feast was made
still more animated by the magnanimous bearing of His Excellency and by the discourse and
behavior of the Officers. Mrs. Washington, the
Countess of Stirling and Lady Kitty her daughter,
Mrs. Greene and other ladies favored the feast
with their presence. Wines and liquors circulated
most genially. To the King of France! To the
Friendly European Powers! To the American
States! To Mister Franklin!*

Lady Washington said to her husband, I think of
Morristown.

Aye, Morristown?

I swear, old man, you know not even whom you
have upon your arm. It is I, your wife in truth. And
all this while you thought it to be Lady Stirling?

He said, Let us halt to acknowledge.

They halted again for a moment, as they had done
several times before, and they turned and bowed
before the roar of ten thousand voices crying *ahhh-
ohhh-wah* and *whee* around them in a howling storm.
Then they began to pace slowly again, as on parade.

I swear, old man. Think you that you have the
fair Marie Antoinette upon your arm?

Nay, 'tis you, my pet.

General Greene just spoke in praise of you.

Ah so, wife? I am happy that he did not utter cavil.

He said that he had never seen you so radiant as on this good day.

'Tis good to be radiant. Think you not?

Aye. I too am radiant, but weary as well.

They paused again, turned and bowed, and a fresh-surged howl broke behind and around them from heights and valleys. There must have been many mountains unseen on which those men were cheering and the commander witnessed now that the very trees were full of them: men up in trees, waving violently as they roared. Ground between the trees was packed. His Excellency was weeping again for he had wept before. There was no one near enough to see him do this except his good lady. He thought the very dead had risen from their unwieldy couches into which they had necessarily been shoveled. What was it Wayne had said about the masses of humanity that *they had thought it wise to leave beneath the soil,* left unknowing or in misery; but now they too seemed exalted and exuberant and the ranks of them mingled with their living brothers as they hooted in triumph.

Now we walk again, old man. I did speak of Morristown. Does thee recall what I said of it?

He whispered, Nay.

I said that in Morristown as elsewhere, it seemed that I had heard the last guns of a closing campaign, and first guns of a new one.

Washington dreamed aloud. Von Steuben's rifle salute was masterly. The roar from right to left along the line, the following volleys from left back to right. He is a benign prince, and I commend him accordingly.

Old man, I do recall a penalty cited in the orderly book less than one month agone. A soldier would receive thirty-nine lashes on his bare back for discharging his piece, or otherwise wasting ammunition.

'Twas essential at the time.

They're still a-cheer. We needs must pause again?

They halted once more to bow and accept a plaudit but they were come close to their quarters now.

Martha said, 'Twill not be long before I take the road again. I feel it in my flesh . . . oh too much flesh, I fear! And in my bones.

Her husband told her, Suddenly too I have grown weary and wish that we may seek our bed. But—you will be traveling.

She said tartly, Old man, you shall have bed in a trice. I will be seeking Virginia quickly e'er you embark on your new campaign.

He thought, Ah yes, campaign. I must give it more thought.

He said, I have summoned a conference for—is it tomorrow? Nay, the following day.

His Excellency indeed suffered many wearinesses and fevers which meticulously he tried to keep secret from aides and staff officers, from generals and his entire military family; and from Martha herself. Sometimes he was successful in these endeavors, not always. She feared that such an attack was on him now and talked in her sprightly fashion, no longer of the ceremonies which they had just witnessed and of which they had been a part, but of trivia commonly gossiped throughout the command. That Pennsylvania major, what was his name. 'Twas a prank worthy of Wayne himself. A newly arrived contingent of Jerseymen come quaking to their fresh assignment because of rumors of smallpox at Valley Forge. They had heard of the enforced scratching of the arms, no one escaped that, yet seizures and resulting deaths were so small in number that they could scarcely gossip about it. And that major, what was his name? Forrest: was that correct? He had set to work gleefully under cover of darkness with willing minions, and placarded all the huts opposite the trembling Jerseymen. *Small Pox Here,* read their mighty signs. *Beware! Small Pox,* and every hut opposite the affrighted newcomers bore such a symbol. One look was enough for the Jersey troops when they rose with the dawn and witnessed the grim placards. They fled, to a man. They decamped, ran—deserted, if you would. Not for them the postules, fevers, and scars. Telltale little pits were on so many countenances there, not even excepting that of His Excellency himself; but had they known this, the knowledge would only have given wings to speeding feet of the newcomers.

Provost marshals waited grimly upon the sinning Major Forrest, and sentenced him to speed on track of the appalled contingent and fetch them back to Valley Forge. Then the marshals had their own gaiety on the subject which was soon shared by the rest of the camp.

All this twit Lady Washington poured out to her husband's hearing if not to his awareness. She feared that he was in affliction, as so often occurred, and made pretext to touch his wrists, his forehead, and seek the fever which might be burning in him. But when she finally slept he lay beside her, cool and thinking.

He was pondering in advance on a hundred problems soon to be champed on by the generals who were his subordinates, even though several of them longed to replace him and made few bones about it.

He entertained a hasty and affectionate vision of his Martha (with the British abandoning Philadelphia) setting out in her small chariot with uniformed grooms and post riders . . . going home to Virginia to, as he would have put it, look after the horses. Always he inquired tenderly after the health of each horse when she joined him on military sorties. But these speculations, idle as they might have been, were but a dust of sugar on the rich cake of his own joy at this moment.

Away with adulation! Banish the rich echoing litany of ten thousand veterans' voices raised in his behalf.

Let this cat not purr too handsomely, was his reflection.

A course, a course! They must gallop a course, but in which direction? There had been preliminary discussions on a date somewhat earlier, before the news came that Howe had been relieved of his command and that Clinton would be the new redcoat to contend with. A council had already been decided upon and the participants summoned for—was it tomorrow, the seventh? No, next day, the eighth. Doubtless many of the generals would repeat the attitudes which they had expressed in earlier conference. Thank that same Great Jehovah that the Conway thing was over and done.

Take the foreigners in whom he had faith and confidence: Lafayette, Duportail, and above all the good von Steuben. They would advise attack against no one. Despite all manner of rejoicing, they felt that the Valley Forge Army was too limited in scope and power. Let weeks elapse, grub for more supplies. Grub for more grub, as the soldiers themselves might put it. Let von Steuben go on with his training. Let Lafayette feint and harass as he so desired. What of Wayne? Philadelphia, to be sure, that would still be his objective. Nothing might curb the ardor of this reckless Pennsylvanian as long as Philadelphia lay in British hands. But what of Clinton? Would he stay and defend the American capital, the seat of all Howe's pomp and revelry during the winter when the Americans lay emaciated at Valley Forge; or would he decline to engage, and retreat across the Delaware, or go elsewhere by fleet? Knox, naturally enough, favored an attack upon New York. You could not blame him for his earnest desire to seize his own city, freed at last from sway of the enemy. Greene sided with him to some extent, but he wished to split the Army in two. He would that the militia of New York and the northern Yankee states be augmented by force of Continentals, and Washington himself should take command in a campaign against New York, while part of the Army was still held in reserve at Valley Forge. Lord Stirling too would split the command.

And now also there would be present both Mifflin and Gates. Thank Congress for that!

With miraculous speed a medley of review and

prophecy was spirited over him. The sense of it left him nigh to breathless and this was no boundary of momentary illness beyond which he had stepped.

He held in that twinkling the fierce awareness of his own historical importance.

He would not have spoken this knowledge to his Martha were she now awake and clamoring to listen. It was a staunch secret between him and whatever Almighty Power prevailed over the events of destiny. The nation with its sacred thirteen states (and whatever others came to range with them as wilderness yielded to man's track and as Frenchmen and Spaniards were compelled to give up their various offices) would cry for a leader duly elected.

He would be that leader.

His own statements and opinions and the regard held for him by other men came in a hurricane of remembrance. Stinging up through all weather of the past, hidden by years and labors, these verities were instantaneously become alert, clamoring to possess him. In no manner detracting from current efficiency, they would offer sap and vigor, as he were a tree about to be leaved once more.

His mother, save her memory, in the very month after Braddock's invasion was wiped to shreds, had demanded that he engage himself in no more frontier wars.

His reply, indited by his own powerful speeding pen:

> . . . If the command is pressed upon me by the general voice of the country, and offered upon such terms as cannot be objected against, it would reflect dishonor upon me to refuse it; and that, I am sure, must, and ought, to give you greater uneasiness than my going in an honorable command.

What of the Reverend Mr. Samuel Davis? Preaching in a sermon during that same year's August of 1755 . . .

*That heroic youth, Colonel Washington, whom
I cannot but hope Providence has hitherto pre-
served in so signal a manner for some important
service to his country.*

What of Gist with whom he had walked the wilderness alone, the two of them, except for the treacherous
Indian who fired at them, so very long before.

*Your name is more talked of in Philadelphia
than that of any other person in the Army, and
everybody seems willing to venture under your
command.*

Had he trained for Valley Forge and the shocking
mismanagement of the Congress back in 1756 when
he was responsible only to the Virginia governor?

*So much I am kept in the dark that I do not
know whether to prepare for the offensive or the
defensive. What would be absolutely necessary
for the one would be quite useless for the
other. . . . The orders I receive are full of ambi-
guity. I am left like a wanderer in wilderness, to
proceed at hazard. I am answerable for consequences, and blamed, without the privilege of defense.*

It was as if he heard the utterance of a capable
biographer ringing through years ahead.

*It is worthy of note that the early popularity of
Washington was not the result of brilliant achieve-
ments nor signal success; on the contrary, it rose
among trials and reverses, and may almost be
said to have been the fruits of defeats. It remains
an honorable testimony of Virginian intelligence
that the sterling, enduring, but undazzling quali-
ties of Washington were thus early discerned and
appreciated, though only heralded by misfortune.*

The admirable manner in which he had con-
ducted himself under these misfortunes, and the
sagacity and practical wisdom he had displayed
on all occasions, were universally acknowledged.

Acknowledged, by the tumult rising from ten thousand throats and mouths, resounding within his ears
hours after it had flared.

He sat up, rolled quietly out of bed, and in his long
night rail went to the nearest window. It stood partly
ajar and he pushed it wider as softly as possible. He
did not want to waken the woman. Most people still
slept with their windows closed at night, sometimes
even shuttered beyond the glass. There was that persistent dread of night air which he had sought to eradi-
cate. For so many years he had slept only in night air
with no walls or roof to keep it away, and Martha had
come to share this need in manner along with him. He
smiled as he recalled being privied to recent agonies
here in the camp when weather was finally warming.
They pushed the chinks out from between the logs of
their huts so that smoke might find egress and fresh
delicious air come in; and were in turn upbraided by
others who believed that the night breeze would fetch
all manner of disfavor and disease.

He stood, grim and patient in startling awareness of
the foreordained.

Intimate progressive sounds were bound to steal up
. . . distant routine change of sentries, the rattle of
weapons being adjusted, the squeaking of carts which
came even at this late hour and fetching food no
doubt, thanks to all that was great. And the sound of
other wheels on Sullivan's Bridge. Sometimes even
now and after all agonies and reversals he could be a
youth. He thought of various Caesars, Georges, and
Fredericks who had gone their way before. He wondered in impish curiosity, Indeed, and will they put my
picture on their money?

41

THE waggon could be heard coming a long time before
it could be seen. Ungreased wheels uttered a ritual of
agony as if seeking to voice combined plaint of the
heckled human freight who rode. We have been ill-
used, oh hear our wail. Two drivers sat upon a board
fastened at the front. They might have been soldiers,
might not. They wore some scraps of Continental uni-
form pieced out with fragments of civilian attire. Many
soldiers appeared thus and many people also who had
never shouldered a weapon or taken an oath to support their officers in this catastrophe. Some spoke of it
as Revolution, some called it Rebellion still. It was all
one to the cargo of this conveyance. They were male
but pieced out in clothing of men and women alike:
the citizenry had been benevolent when they came to
the hospital and saw the inmates' poor condition and
garbing. They offered as kindly people will in stress the
very clothing from off their own backs and heads:
hoods, shawls, bonnets, capes, tricorns, and pocked fur
caps. The men wore them as if to the manor and manner born. Some were still soldiers, some no longer soldiers but had been soldiers, and they chattered toughly
as if they had the wounds and powder and ashes of all
wars rubbed into their hides.

One stood somewhat removed, hunched with his
crutches and clinging to the hindboards of the waggon
box.

Whyn't you try to set, Lamey?

He answered, Too mean a-getting up and down.

Shove over agin me, you Peter. Come on, Lamey, set, we can make room.

I got to see my way, said the one called Lamey. I know it's long about here somewheres.

Don't you actually know where you're bound?

I got fair notion.

So you ain't going to the Forge?

No reason to. They give me my discharge fore I left Yellow Springs.

Me too, and I wish I had mine, and I trust to get mine at Valley Forge, and there was more such babble.

What are them crutches of yours, Lamey? They got such a shine to 'em.

Don't know. Some kind of wood. It is shiny, ain't it?

Did you whittle 'em out yourself?

Nope. See, 'twas like this. There was a fellow there at Yellow Springs, oh early when they first built the hospital and got folks in it. I guess none of you was there then. And this fellow, they took off his leg, and he had an uncle or grandsire or something like that, that come there to see him. He dwelt nearby and he says, Boy, I'm going to fix you some crutches, and so he did. He whittled 'em out himself. Must've been a regular cabinetmaker for they was fine. You can still see how fine they are.

Let me see one.

Laboriously the boy called Lamey altered his position and clung to the side of the cart and passed back one crutch and the others turned it over and over and rubbed it with their hands. Some said maple, some said oak, one said locust, and an authoritative voice declared, I say black walnut, as if that settled it, and finally the crutch was passed back to Lamey.

Anyways, he sought to manage 'em on the stairs and shouldn't never have tried. They slipped or something, else he was too wasted to handle 'em, and down he went. Reckon 'twas halfway down the flight before he hit, and being tangled up somehow he went headfirst. He didn't know a thing after that. Not one thing. Just

lay and kind of wasted away. His skull was cracked,
I see some of the fluid that come out of it when I was
trying to hobble around. Didn't look like regular blood
—looked much paler, like 'twas pink, then I heard a
doctor said that they called it cranial fluid. It's the natural ooze all around the brain.

I see some orderlies and such that had cranial fluid
on the brain! and the laughter went up in appreciation.

Lamey explained patiently, So 'twas sad enough I
guess. That's how he come to the end of his days. Then
one of the nursing Sisters, she took the crutches and
carried 'em off. Don't know where or why, but one day
she looked at me and she says, You're trying to creep
about, or what she says was Thee, being Quaker,
Thee's trying to creep about. I said Yes, I was, and
hoping to go faster. She says, I know what you need,
or I guess she said I know what thee is in need of, or
something like that, and she goes away and then comes
back and there I am, bold as brass, with new crutches.

A voice more sober than the rest said, Then I hope
thee said a prayer for him for whom they were made,
and there was some nudging on the heels of this.

Lamey looked down steadily at the speaker. I said
my prayers for him when he went kiting down those
steps in the first place. Reckon we all did.

Then in a new tone he cried, Whoa-hoa! 'Tis right
along here. But maybe 'tis burnt. Mayhap the British
burnt it, I don't know.

One of the drivers said, You'd better be certain
where you're headed, lad. If you don't know where
you're bound, we can't help you 'tis sure.

If I'm troubling you truly, I'll get out and crutch
my way along, Lamey cried angrily.

Don't get on no high horse. But tell us when you
want down. It ain't your own home you're seeking?

Nay. Belongs to someone else.

He caught his breath and made a strangling sound.
There 'tis. I believe so.

Place here on the left? The horses were pulled in.
He said, I feared 'twould be burnt.

Burnt?

Just feared. Here. This is well enough.

And No 'twas not burnt. How did that happen? The harrowing raiders, they must have been Tarleton's own, they had come clamoring and ripping, they pounded him down, he was a living example of one who is pounded down by steeds, but he was living yet, might that not be understood? Might not he in turn be aware of it, he and all others? The tears were in his eyes. He lifted one hand free from its crutch and brushed the moisture loose. Now he could see better.

Here, I'll aid.

Let us help you down.

At last the horses were standing still, the journey was done, he was getting out, a tedious process. Oh task of weariness and desolation. All the kind were aiding, one stronger than the rest was already on the ground. The ones in the waggon supported Lamey as he let his nervous legs hang from the tailboard. The crutches figured and shone, they were shining blissful crutches polished now with the varnish of warm bodies, oh this was a warm day, the crutches felt warm when they were so moist and polished. The man on the ground helped him support himself while the things were slid beneath his shoulders.

A weight, old, his bag of plunder.

He's got his loot.

So it was, made for him by some other noble soul who brought bags to men in the hospitals to keep their plunder and their loot within. 'Twas of blue woven cloth and only dirtied where it had been slid and someone was bleeding once upon a time, because the blood had dried but it was turned to purplish brown upon the bottom of the bag. That was not his blood, not Lamey's. He was bleeding no longer.

Both men upon the driver's board had turned to see him alight and one now spoke for both though none of his active cargo could hear. He said, Shit.

The other waggoner said, Aye.

Lamey's head was turned to one side and seemed

rigid there and permanently affixed in that position.
The scar started up at the crown of his head; thus half
his hair was gone. It had grown out wild and scraggly
and pointing this way and that where the scalp had not
been disturbed, but the scalp had been torn loose on
the other side and part of it was stitched into place
but no hair had come back upon it, and that portion
was merely a mass of pink scars. One eye peered
straight ahead—a lively eye and tough and knowing
—the other eye would have been as tough but it
pointed slightly to one side and the scarred lid drooped
above it. The side of the face below the scars was
seamed in its own manner. But the shoulders were
still stout and Lamey had developed them well by his
management of canes and crutches and whatever cum-
bersome lifting of himself he might effect. It was as if
his lower legs had been broken into fragments and
then nailed back together again. The long trousers
concealed some of the ruin which had been wrought,
and yet the feet turned this way and that way as he
moved. His right foot hung aloft, he made a grimace as
he forced it down and strode upon it. He was working
to walk, he was toiling to walk, by God he would walk
in time. He did not wish to be bothered with these
gleaming crutches through infinity. He would make
his limbs travel in the way he wished them to go, ah
he would, he would, and the concern of his intention
shone out in flame from his best eye.

Before him stood a house, the ruins of a hedge,
some tumbled fence rails, why there were two or three,
and how had those survived, why hadn't they been
carried off to build fires with? Or maybe the old ones
had been carried away and these were new ones
fetched from Lord knew where.

Good day, Lamey, said the waggonload.

Good day to ye all and thank ye kindly, but he did
not turn his head even then. His attention was cen-
tered on the house and more than that, upon the pigsty at one side and in the rear.

I feared 'twas burnt, oh I did fear.

The waggon went away toward Valley Forge making its high-pitched alternating shriek and scream. The riders watched while Lamey traveled.

What in time was it?

One of them bombshells burst upon him?

I ast him when first he come aboard. He said something 'bout a horse.

He couldn't of just got throwed.

Tried to ketch a cannonball and spit on it for luck!

All these too had been mauled, each in his own way, they had license to laugh if they so desired, and desire they did. All had witnessed so many burstings and tearings, all had felt their own bodies twitched and torn, but none so wickedly as the shape they saw going away with determination, grimly behind them. Two or three felt impelled to wave again but still he did not turn, he took no further heed.

A man and a girl came from the rear, walking slowly. The man still had some tool of endeavor in his hand, the girl merely stood and stared. They were drawn by the rune of the departing vehicle. It would have hauled up relatives from their graves if they had lain near.

The newcomer said to the girl in a high strong inquiring voice, Candy?

Yes, she answered, but in doubt.

I'm Mum, he said.

You was quite far gone that day. I thought you gone clean beyond them. I heard the horses and saw them pass going in the same direction you'd gone, but I wasn't much wherreted 'cause I knew you'd hear them too; you could hide. 'Twas the Terrys' house they burnt. We saw all the smoke, or I did first, and then Mother came to look too. The Terrys lost 'bout everything. They come down here later and spent the night and then went on to her sister's place next day. The British cavalry said someone had took a shot at them from the Terry house, time they was riding past before and it might have been true. They've got a son way too young, always running off to join the soldiery, then being sent home or fetched home, and he might have loaded up something and fired at them, but it was just the women folks that day and they were hysterical and couldn't scarcely talk straight. The enemy never did try to burn us out 'cept just once. Some kind of vagabonds, there were only four or five. They beat on the door and I guess they were drunk 'cause they cursed a lot and then they pulled over some straw and set it ablaze fore they went on their course. Father and I run out right quickly and pulled it loose fore it caught the boards. You can see: 'tis over there, kind of scorched-like.

But that day when you were tromped we had no knowledge whatsoever. We didn't hear the shot, or maybe we did and paid no heed cause there are always shots around . . . or were. 'Tis different now, and what blessing. Reckon you know the news as well as we do. The British are gone from Philadelphia and our cavalry went in when the last boatload was pulling out, and fired on it. Scads of Americans gone down from Valley Forge by this time and we heard His Excellency himself had gone. But I don't understand. You say you don't have to go back no way?

I got a discharge in my pouch, all signed by the provost officers who came to Yellow Springs. They said they had authority to do so. I even told 'em I had flinked and wouldn't I have to serve or be whipped or something, but they said, Son, you're a fire-eater for sartin, and went ahead and signed me out. They signed lots of others out as well. You never did hear bout my being tromped by the cavalry?

Not a word. But you did get that one you shot at. I never saw them but another neighbor told how they rode past, I reckon bound for Philadelphia one of those roundabout ways they always traveled, and they said there was one man tied on his horse like he was dead. Must've been the one you shot. But how did you get all the way to Yellow Springs?

I got no knowledge. I can't recollect anything 'cept

standing there and taking aim and that horse coming at me, and that's all. Up to Yellow Springs they told me I was fetched in a cart. So the lobsters must've thought I was dead.

But who would've had a cart? I don't—

I can't reason it. I guess they thought I was nigh to dead when I was fetched and they told me later that they was sure I was marked for death as well. Them Quaker women are wonderful. I recollect when they thought I was passing out they asked me my name and I tolt 'em, but they couldn't understand.

Throughout this conversation Candy's father, Lewellyn Pembroke, had lingered with them on the same long bench but at a little distance away. His Germantown wound had been through the neck and it left him with some insufficiency of breathing and speech. It was as if he said *ahh* time and again at intervals, and this defect became so natural that when people were with him very soon they paid no attention at all. The sound grew to have a personal merit about it. It was as if Pembroke listened to what was being said and thoroughly approved, or, if the conversation did not merit approval, he was telling you that he understood why; otherwise he was still a powerful man physically, with wide shoulders and long strong arms. He might have stayed at soldiering with the permission of his officers had he so desired; but calmly he desired no longer. With his son now dead, he felt that his wife and daughter needed him. He had gone out, fought, risked himself, 'twas a duty discharged, and he seemed to reason that this one family, his own, could not sustain the entire burden of the Revolution.

He had given Candy his eyes in inheritance, but his own manner was even more drawn apart and naturally blissful than hers. Beneath his high forehead great blue eyes looked out meditatively and trustingly. Not all persons with Welsh names were squat and dark. This man's pale gaze dreamed on and on. In his teens he had demonstrated that what he considered the rigidity of Meeting was not for him; and his charm had been such that his wife bore her expulsion cheerfully. He might have been a musing later disciple drawing serenity from Watts.

Dissolve my heart in thankfulness,
And melt my eyes to tears.

But when one looked at him and witnessed the calm withdrawn strength of his nature, one did not desire that his eyes be melted. People rejoiced that he was able, still strong and tolerant. The sighs awarded him by his wound appeared merely as a natural bestowal, they gave no call for derision or imitation. They were become as native to him as the flutter of breath in other humans.

He said to the two of them, I must get to my plowing.

Mum looked at him quizzically, then at Candy, then back at the father. Plowing? You got a horse, good sir? You didn't have none before.

Candy said, We got one now. Oh you must see him.

I can ride a horse to plow, said Mum. I already done it.

You, Mum? Ride a horse?

Course I can. It's only getting on and off that bothers me. I did it for those lovely Sisters up there, the ones that was a-nursing of me, nursing of us all. They said they wanted to put in some spring garden, so I helped. It's just getting on and off that bothers. Someone has to help me on and off, but maybe twon't be forever. The elderly surgeon, Doctor Otto, he said 'twas well for me to do things like that. He had a word for it but I can't recollect. He's a wonderful man. Real old too, but a regular caution when it comes to healing. He helped me to get healed.

Lewellyn Pembroke said dreamily, He and Almighty God.

Yes sir, he and—and the Almighty. But please to let me see your horse.

Mum fumbled for his crutches. Candy gave some

short exclamation. No one knew quite what she said, she didn't know herself. And then her hands were on the crutches, her hands were helping Mum to stand erect.

Man named Gunderson, said Pembroke. He stopped by quite a while back. 'Twas strange. He said this horse was the property of one soldier at Valley Forge and somehow or other had been give to him. He was a worthy man, so gentle and old. He said his wife had died, and she was took quickly, and then he decided he couldn't go it alone, he'd go over near Northport and live with his daughter, but that horse he wanted to get him back to his owner, so he went to Valley Forge, horse and all, and the sentries laughed at him and turnt him away. They said the horse was no fit fare for anything. I trust this elderly man did plead, but to no avail, so he made a heading for Northport and then he seen our place here and come in and said didn't we need a horse, and first off we kind of made sport of it, but then he was so serious that we couldn't sport for long.

They all went round the garden behind the house. The horse was there, attached to the plow, just as Pembroke had left him when Mum first appeared.

Mum said, He is kind of stretched out, ain't he.

He's sober as a judge, said Pembroke. Or like a judge ought to be at least.

Mum said, You see how 'twas. Those Sisters couldn't mount him very well, but one could hold the plow, she didn't have to pull it, so the horse could draw the plow but he needed a rider to keep the plow in the rows in proper fashion. Then the friendly Sister just holds the plow and the horse would do the pulling. I can plow a right straight furrow that way, and I did so many, and now they got their crop a-growing even fore I left.

Mum looked about. The high stump of a tree stood handy, beaten down on the surface from usage of many feet and many weights through years.

Now if you can aid me aloft, I won't need these crutches after I'm up there.

They both helped him worm his way to the top and Candy put the crutches to the side when the horse was brought close and Mum grasped the harness. He wormed himself up upon the wide deep-set back of the animal, and tugging at the reins, hauled himself to a firmer position and then managed to drag his right leg across and be seated properly.

Here I be, he said. Now if you'll be so good, sir, as to take that there plow by the handles, I'll show you how straight a furrow we can make. Then you won't need to put no power into it. We'll do the pulling, this horse and I.

His name is John, said Pembroke. There was something told about honey, but I can't recollect.

Candy had said that her mother was vastly improved in health and spirits but still Mum was unprepared for the woman's calmness and seeming gentility. She wore a cap over her graying hair. Perhaps it was a relic of her days among the Friends, but still many women who never neared a Meeting wore caps. Many would not appear in public or even privately without being thus coiffed. Her body seemed tiny and dainty under the masking of heavy gown and shawl. She seemed like a doll. She was even smaller than her daughter, she was nigh to being a tiny human plaything when viewed beside the comparatively massive shape of her husband. Yet when her face was at rest and she was not speaking so gently to them all, a wild haunted expression shone in her glance as if she were inclined even then to give way to some manner of frenzied outcry, a storm of tears and wailing.

They sat on benches drawn up to a square table which Candy explained that a grandfather had fashioned long before. He fancied himself a true cabinetmaker and rightly so when one saw how the portions were beveled together. Oatcake again, but the mother had baked it in a tin oven hanging over the fire, and it was rich and thick. A big pot held its portions of fresh greens and boiled bacon. The bowls were not served, nor was the oatcake broken until grace was said. Pembroke uttered it, seated with his wife on his right and Candy on his left and Mum opposite. There ensued a preliminary pause and hands came out beneath the table on both sides of the crippled soldier to grasp his own. Candy's hand squeezed tightly.

> *For all Thy blessings sent to us*
> *We thank Thee God again,*
> *And pray this food will make us strong*
> *To do Thy Will.*
> *A-men.*

Pa always utters the same grace, said Candy as she broke the cake and her mother dipped greens and bacon into the bowls.

Pembroke smiled wistfully and said, All my life. We were given it as children when very young, and were happy to have it. Some graces are tiresome long, with all the young fry and mayhap old fry too, hungry and wishing to feed. We've always had it thus, clipped neat.

His wife burst into a spasm of crying. Mum jumped nervously on his seat, then realized that neither the husband nor the daughter was even turning to look at the woman. Candy's hand came under the table again and patted his stiff twisted knee in manner of reassurance. 'Twas a paroxysm only, 'twould pass, did pass quickly. The woman lifted her apron to dry her eyes and soon was eating and even smiling along with the rest.

She bent toward Mum politely. Does thee fare well, Mum? How was the fare yonder?

'Twas good, he mumbled in somewhat embarrassed fashion with his mouth still full. Got much better as warm weather come on and the raiders wasn't about. Carts begun to fetch stuff to the Forge again and

they often stopped by Yellow Springs first. Us invalids
were nigh glad that we were there. Just like—

He twisted around to smile boldly at Candy in the
best fashion he could— Just like I'm glad to be here.

Scent and taste of the fare were overwhelming and
he was close to weeping in thankfulness now and
again.

You like my greens? the girl was eager to know.
Dug 'em myself.

Not truly?

Truly.

What be they?

Oh several sorts. There's dandelions coming long
and I got a lot of wild mustard, the small tasty kind fit
to eat, not the tough and bitter.

I could just fill up on it, said Mum when he passed
his bowl in response to the mother's gesture.

Don't fill too solid, Candy warned him. There's
more to come. Might you fancy gooseberry fool?

Never et any. Why they call it fool?

I don't rightly know, said Candy. 'Tis just the name.

By that time there was an explosion of weeping
from the mother again. He questioned to ask me, she
cried. Paul did! Have you forgot? Paul always wanted
to know why 'twas fool, and I couldn't tell him!

In this occasion more attention was paid to her.
Now, Purity, said the father gently, and Candace
spoke a placating word or two. Promptly the mother
was drying her tears again.

Candace said, Then I've got another surprise if
you'd like for it. How'd you fancy strawberries?

Strawberries! exclaimed Mum. We didn't have none
yonder. Wild ones?

Right out of our own meadow. I picked 'em with
pride, 'cause they're so small and dainty.

Mum wished to say, Like unto yourself, but thought
better.

And some strained honey to go along with 'em if
you crave more sweets.

Lewellyn Pembroke said, I'll fancy some berries

too, daughter, if you wish to fetch em, and a morsel
of honey maybe along with. Strange thing, he said,
looking across at Mum. That old horse John out there.
I fixed up a paddock for him out of rails and saplings
when he first was brung here. He was standing inside
that fence when I come back from the woods with a
parcel of honey in a bucket. Just watched some bees
going to a tree as usual, and got a speck for us. That
old swaybacked horse, he whinnied and whinnied and
had his ears up. And I did recall that when the man
fetched him he said something about honey and the
wilderness—something about locusts too, but I never
did get it quite exact. I'd swear he smelt that honey.

And you give him some, sir?

Then and since. He takes pride in it.

Matthew Three-Four, said Candy with authority.

*And the same John had his raiment of camel's
hair, and a leathern girdle about his loins and
his meat was locusts and wild honey.*

Could be the reason for naming him John, she
said.

Could be, her father agreed.

After the meal was done they returned thanks in
silence. Mum was glad of this. He was afraid something might be said which would cause the mother to
wail once more. But her hand came into his, and
Candy's hand sought his own on the right side and
thus they sat with lowered heads till he heard the
father say A-men.

Candy told him in explanation, We always read a
chapter. And to her father, May I read this one? I
know what it will be.

She turned to the 150th Psalm and read it aloud
with such feeling that Mum wondered what was steal-
ing over him. Could there be such a thing as a warm
chill? He did not feel at all cold . . . he felt contented
and grateful and graceful . . . yet there was that profound trembling.

Praise ye the Lord. Praise God in His sanctuary: praise Him in the firmament of His power.

She knew that *firmament* was another name for heaven. She was not sure about the word *psaltery,* nor had she ever known what a *timbrel* was and no one might explain to her because none of them knew and forever she had felt shyness in the thought of making inquiries. As for *cymbals,* she thought they must be something which made a loud clang and not to be confused with *symbols. High sounding cymbals,* it said and there must be a perfect glory in their ringing and she felt that glory in voice and soul. She knew what she would do now with the life ahead of her and this sublime energy of assurance ruled her utterance, gave it the power and beauty of the sun and all nature warmed by it.

Let every thing that hath breath praise the Lord. Praise ye the Lord.

They roosted on the bench outside the door and beyond the young elm tree overhead a portion of moon was kindly.

Hain't I taking you away, Candy? I'm such a scrap to do so.

Don't say that, 'bout being a scrap. No, Mum, Father is helping Mother ret up and she fancies it so. But you well know— She giggled lightly. You can't sleep in the pigsty tonight as you done before, cause the new pigs have got it instead.

I know. I heard 'em when I come. 'Member? We laughed about it.

I'll rest with Mother, Mum, and you can sleep with my Pa. 'Tis always so if men folks come. Old Mister Lovejoy come with his son a couple weeks ago. Three in a bed. Must've been crowded for Pa 'cause both the Lovejoys are mighty hefty. I judge that bed hain't been the same since, though I did make it true and neat.

They sat motionless and silent for a time and the earth kept moving and thus the moon found Candy's face and Mum peered at it with worship and wonder. Oh you're fair, he whispered finally. So very fair.

She laughed because she sought to be an imp because she was feminine. Ain't neither. I'm brown. You know that. You talk like I was yellow-haired, like so many of them German girls.

I don't mean that. I mean you're fair. Like beauty.

I'll wager you say that to all the girls, Mum.

I don't know no girls, 'cept you. Not no more.

Must have been some come to visit your hospital at Yellow Springs. Must have been some pretty ones.

They was kindly like, was all he said.

There fell another long silence with the moon, the breeze, distant sounds of the retting up in the house, voices of the parents falling gently, the insect noises, the beating of a moth which strove against a window pane, an angry argument momentarily between distant pigs, then more silence, if you could call it silence with all the business of humans and animals and nature and the insects again, combining gently in a chorus which was truly the soft speaking of God.

He was in their hearts now as the words of His prophets had been upon their lips or echoing in their minds before.

Mum, the girl said.

He made bold to squeeze her hand in reply.

You hain't wealthy?

No way, Candy, no way.

But if you was to go home, your folks could succor you? I mean take care, I mean take you in. Give you a place to dwell?

Oh, that they could.

You aim to cut for home now?

His great secret, his extensive ambition came up and tapped and cried and chatted and chattered and flaunted. Anew he was overwhelmed by its paramount excitement as he had been, before, when first struggling to be aware of his predicament and wondering how to cope with it. And later feeling the snap and fervor of true accomplishment.

Candy, I got a secret. You want to share it with me?

She drew closer to him on the bench. I'm all ears, she said. Ready to listen. I got ears like a bunny rabbit.

Well. You know what is battledore and shuttlecock?

Seems like I've hearn tell. But not that I really know. No, I don't know, truly. Battledore? Ain't it a kind of fight? And the shuttlecock. Has it got to do with roosters?

Let me tell. I learnt about it from Grandsire. Grandsire Davis, fore we left Philadelphia. I can just barely 'member being in Philadelphia for I was right young then. Then they moved to Abernathy, and that's where they live now. Grandsire told me 'bout this and I've always kept the notion. It come back to me when I was laying hurt up yonder, fore I could scarce see anything, even know for sure that I was still living, 'cause I was right poorly took. Well, 'twas two things. 'Twas a game to play. You had paddles and a tiny critter made out of feathers. 'Twas called a bird. And a net in between. You had to bat the bird back and forth. Sometimes they didn't use no net a-tall, said Grandsire. Just each side who was playing had the little paddles and they hit this tiny bird. 'Twasn't a real bird, naturally, just plain pretend. They'd bat it back and forth, back and forth. Then— Funny, they used the same name for little things. Little books to tell children how to spell, and they called them books battledore and shuttlecock too. I don't know why, but they did do it. I can even mind some of the rhymes he said they had for to teach the children their letters. *A is for apple, all shining and red. B is for boy as he goes to his bed.* And they'd have pictures showing how 'twas done; and that way they taught the alphabet.

He was silent for a moment, thinking about it.

Candy ventured, I don't quite see how it could be

both, I mean a game to play one time, and pictures
and letters another.

I don't quite reckon it neither, so forget about the
letters. Letters are printers' work. I hain't no printer,
nor desire to be. Leave that for great men like Dr.
Franklin. He's brought the French folks to help us,
with their fleet and all, and lots of soldiers and generals and such. We won't wherret ourselves about the
hornbooks nor nothing like that. I'm just thinking bout
the paddles and the bird. So that's what I set up, yonder
at Yellow Springs. 'Twas a wonderful game and anyone might play, even ones who could barely move
about. I couldn't play well myself, but I showed 'em
how.

You had birds and paddles and such?

I whittled out the first paddles myself. Done it
clean solitary and 'twas hard work, and everyone wondered what I was about. Then I showed 'em. I member well my first bird. 'Twas a bit of cork, like from
a medicine bottle, and all stuck full of chicken feathers. Them sick soldiers thought I was mad in the
head, though they did like to watch me work, and
wonder what it was about. You can't guess who 'twas
who saw it first, to recognize it for what it really was.
'Twas Dr. Otto himself. The elder Dr. Bodo Otto. He
was German too and come far from the other side,
and he's right elderly, but oh a mighty surgeon and I
tell you now, he made something out of me and out
of a lot of others. Well then. He seen what I was
a-doing and he begun to laugh. Ah, he says, What have
we here? I know what we have here, and he named it
correct, right off. Said he'd seen it played. He took one
of my two little paddles and got someone else who
could stand and get around real good. Shot through
the belly that feller had been, and they didn't think
he was worth shooting himself when they fetched him
in: but that German doctor, he pulled him through.
He says, Now we show you all, and they went to
batting that thing back and forth, just like Grandsire
had taught me long before. Well, you ought to seen

those people take to it, all who could stand or move. Even them wonderful Sisters. The Quaker women, they come out too, a-laughing, and tried their hand. And then later a net was put up and you had to bat the bird acrost the net. That made it hard to do. You know, Candy, I hain't storying at all: but last thing I seen when that waggon drove away from Yellow Springs I looked back and folks was a-playing, right then and there, with my battledore and shuttlecock. I was proud. You hear me? Proud as someone! Who was it, who was so proud?

Lucifer, she said.

True enough. Lucifer. Who was he?

Reckon he was an angel that fell out of Heaven.

Again they listened to the strain of vehicles and mounts in roads near at hand. The main Army was gone away, gone to the Delaware, other troops were in Philadelphia. Congress had come back to Philadelphia; yet a raff were still bound to haunt that sprawling town of huts and, freshly, of tents. The stragglers, the provost guards remaining on duty, such a flock could not be lifted all in an instant, it would take a while. The girl in her mind and Mum in his own thought considered the passage pigeons which came at peculiar seasons in masses, broke down the boughs of forest trees with their weight, talked in their seething until they could be heard for miles, and then lifted again—the main body—to darken more distant skies; but left their stragglers and squabs twittering about the old roost. That was when neighbors would assemble with high boards fastened around their carts, and drive out with torches and clubs to return with vast pitiful cargoes, many of them still cheeping forlornly, and squirming. It was long ordeal for the womenfolk; they had to pluck and clean them and put them down in barrels larded against the climate, a fat and pickled sample of the millions which had been there before. Only their residue remained.

Likewise this residue at Valley Forge operated in roadways, disordered woodland, scarred open fields.

Pa seen him, said Candy wistfully.

Seen him? Seen who?

The Markee de Lafayette.

I seen him too. I saluted him with my rifle and he give it right back to me, soldierly and prompt. But why you considering him?

He got struck down at the Brandywine Crick, same place Father did, but thank mercy he healed up again and went back to the Army, and they do say he sits at General Washington's right hand. But I keep thinking of something he said.

Mum asked doubtfully, Who on earth tolt you what he said, any time, anyhow?

'Twas a soldier. He came by here a-begging, same as many did. Course we took him in awhile and fed him prompt and then he went his tiresome way, but not so hungry as before. He told us 'bout when the soldiers come through Baltimore, way off in Maryland. I never been there, but it must be a right clean distance. The girls in the place, they was all prettied up and dancing and trying to make courtly manners, and Lafayette he was young and handsome. For all his honors they say he's but a boy still, and I guess the young ladies were all tricked out, wondering why he wouldn't join them in the ball, 'cause he wouldn't dance no way. So they asked him and the Markee de Lafayette said, Ladies, you dance so prettily, but the soldiers have no shirts. He bowed and 'scused himself and went back to his camp and that just broke up the ball complete. All those elegant young city ladies, they was home at once, sewing on shirts, and they give em all to the soldiers. So he told.

Well I never got none, said Mum. Course I wasn't to Baltimore.

Candy said, So many soldiers. Guess there wasn't any plenitude of shirts in the long run.

Mum thrashed around nervously on his portion of the bench. He knew that the hour was growing late, they both were aware of it, yet still clung to their positions. Candy, he said, It's so strange you should speak of the Markee.

Why so, Mum?

Because he comes from France and— They got a game there that they play. We don't have it here, but Dr. Otto tolt me. They call it tennis. They mark out lines on the grass on both sides of a net, and when you bat a ball over the net you get a point in your favor. If it lands in a certain place, before the person on the other side can bat it back to you. Don't you see, Candy? Don't you fairly see? Oh, maybe I never tolt it to you right!

See? she asked wonderingly.

It's like my game, Candy. That I was telling you of. The battledore and shuttlecock? You knock it cross the net and it makes a new kind of game out of it.

Yes, she said slowly, it might.

Might? he cried, almost in rage. It does, Candy, it does! That's what I been telling you about all along. Now what I aim to do is this. I'll make the little paddles. They don't have to be of wood neither; they can be wove out of willow or something. Something tough and strong. I could do that. I got good use of my hands for such and I could make the nets and the shuttlecocks to go with 'em, the little birds. Then I could take and peddle 'em from door to door. Just let people try 'em once. I tell you, Missy, I'd have a sale right off!

It was a long time before she spoke, and then it was only after drawing in her breath deeply in form of wonderment. Mum, I'm so stupid. I ain't got ary wit in my head. Mum, you hear me? 'Twould be a wonder! And with the war now moved away, why folks hereabouts would take to a game. So many ain't had no joy for so long. And you—like you told, those doctors and those sick and hurt folks up there and the good Sisters who were nursing them and all—you said they liked to play. They tuck to it like lightning, you said.

That's what I mean! he crowed. I go into business.

Peddle 'em from house to house and door to door. Bet you I could sell scores!

Hundreds, she breathed in admiration. And when he looked at her in the falling moonlight, he saw that she was crying.

He said slowly, I got a bag of plunder.

Yes, she said, but wondering. I tuck it inside when you come.

Candy, you want to fetch it?

She was gone gently but softly and now there existed only one candle agleam in the main room of the house. Then she came back lugging the little bag, and she put it down beside him, where he fumbled with the drawstring.

I don't own much, he said. Not no more. My rifle's gone, and all that goes with it. Figure that Tarleton took it or his men when they rid me down. I had only this one thing, and it was kind of round my shoulders and pretty bloodied up and muddied up, but the ladies at Yellow Springs did wash it for me. Oh, they couldn't get all the bad stains out, naturally enough. It's all colored funny and dark where the blood was, but it's still washed clean.

Mum, whatever are you describing to me? I don't—

Your tippet. The one you knitted yourself and carded the wool for, the yarn and everything. You give it to me and I carried it off when I went.

He brought the garment out and pressed it into her hands. Now you recall? he asked.

Yes, she said gently. She sat stroking the material.

You tolt me about it. You said the wool come off your own sheep and you even helped in the shearing, then you carded it, then you spun the yarn. You said you wanted it to help warm me.

Yes. And then what did I say to you?

I don't 'zactly know.

You asked me if you could come back. You said you wouldn't be fleeing. I know your words now. I can hear you say 'em. You said, I'll be as good a soldier as I can.

Guess I wasn't too good a one.

You said you'd be as good a soldier as you could be, and I said to you that of course you would. And what else did I say? One more thing.

He sobbed, I don't know. Can't recollect.

I said, When you come, I'll greet you with pride. I can hear my own voice a-saying it now. And then— Do you know the rest?

He whispered, We kissed good-bye.

Mum, let me kiss you with pride and welcome.

Their mouths met. They kissed, welcoming, with pride.

Bibliography

Wearily but affably, with the manuscript of *Valley Forge* already in the hands of its publisher, the author is struck by memory of conversations with Dr. Roy P. Basler, who has spent a determined lifetime at the Library of Congress when he wasn't writing Lincoln books on his own.

Recently, at an informal luncheon where a lot of writers gather each Friday, Roy was pursuing one of his and my favorite subjects. He was extolling the little-known book which strays here and there, like an amiable but constantly roving doggie— The privately cobbled-together book— The family annals assembled with zeal and reverence by ardent souls who make no solemn claim to membership in any clique of authors, but are moved by addiction to their own regions or their own families.

Such a book was and is *The Annals of the Families of Caspar, Henry Baltzer and George Spengler,* compiled by Edward W. Spengler, n.p., York, Pennsylvania, 1896. This came into my hands while I was writing *Valley Forge* and I leaned upon it devotedly.

There were a few others roving around and thus I profited wherever I might. Another such book, but more specific in subject matter, was *The Private Soldier Under Washington,* by Charles Knowles Bolton, done by the Kennikat Press, Port Washington, New York, 1902.

My first conscious reading on this subject occurred in early boyhood when I was endowed with *A First Book in American History* by Edward Eggleston, published by the American Book Company, New York, in 1899; and *Short Stories from American History,* put together by Albert F. Blaisdell and Francis K. Ball, and published by Ginn & Company, Boston, 1905. There was a kind of tough saintliness in these books, probably unavailable to most youthful scholars today. I wish that they might be tenderly revived.

In reverie one goes from the famed Pulitzer Prize biography, *Benjamin Franklin,* by Carl Van Doren, done by The Viking Press, New York, in 1938, up and down the list. I was privileged to become acquainted with Mr. Van Doren more than forty years ago, when I wrote *Long Remember,* and his words about Franklin return now in reverie. One recalls a final paragraph in the work in which he referred to his subject as not being "an individual, but instead a harmonious multitude."

One thinks that the same opinion might have been applied even unto Washington himself. My friend Richard E. Glendinning, Jr., first gave me temporary possession of his treasured three-volume biography of George Washington, done with a hail and salute by Washington Irving in 1857. Vaguely there rose an anecdote about this illustrious namesake being presented to the illustrious Dignitary himself, when Irving was a small boy in New York. I suppose George Washington patted Washington Irving on the head, or looked down from Godly height, much as described in the incident of the little black girl, Mary, in *Valley Forge*.

There are several staunch and true old-timers represented: the works of Edwin Tunis, for instance; and that sound volume by Seymour Dunbar, *The History of Travel in America,* before which every historical novelist should dutifully genuflect, no matter which century he happens to be dealing with.

The two-volume work by Sydney George Fisher, *Men, Women and Manners in Colonial Times,* is replete with various excitements and a good many puzzlements as well. Nevertheless it was of persistent value. An even more affectionate embrace goes out to Alice Morse Earl, *Home Life in Colonial Days,* published by Macmillan in 1913. This was and is truly a labor showing an ardent lifetime's devotion. It bristles with rewards for the fumbling researcher with every chapter, on practically every page.

Specifically, the true Valley Forge volumes done as histories of the encampment and region, which most claimed the attention of this researcher, were *Valley Forge* by Harry Emerson Wildes, Macmillan, New York, 1938; and *Valley Forge: The Making of an Army,* by Alfred Hoyt Bill, Harper & Brothers, New York, 1952.

Of these, the Alfred Hoyt Bill book was much the less cogent and productive for this author's purpose. Actually only one hundred and five pages of the entire volume are devoted to Valley Forge and Philadelphia; there is firm reliance on General Howe's Army in the Philadelphia scene itself.

(I keep forgetting that I am not reviewing these books, I should be listing them only.)

Mr. Harry Emerson Wildes went ahead with the history of Valley Forge for months and years following the departure of Washington's Army, and it is replete with the legends, ghost stories and gossip of the countryside.

These two volumes were valuable to this researcher; or rather, to this novelist, who had necessarily to be researcher to begin with.

A far greater share of the material was inspired by the other books mentioned above and which are herewith included in the general list.

1. ARMES, ETHEL, ed. *Nancy Shippen: Her Journal.* Philadelphia: J. B. Lippincott, 1935.
2. BILL, ALFRED HOYT. *Valley Forge: The Making of an Army.* New York: Harper and Brothers, 1952.

3. BLAISDELL, ALBERT F. and BALL, FRANCIS K. *Short Stories from American History*. Boston: Ginn and Company, 1905.

4. BOLTON, CHARLES KNOWLES. *The Private Soldier Under Washington*. Port Washington, New York: Kennikat Press, 1902.

5. BOYD, THOMAS. *Mad Anthony Wayne*. New York: Charles Scribner's Sons, 1929.

6. CHAPEL, CHARLES EDWARD. *Gun Collecting*. Coward-McCann, Inc.: New York, 1939.

7. DUNBAR, SEYMOUR. *The History of Travel in America*. New York: Tudor, 1937.

8. EARLE, ALICE MORSE. *Home Life in Colonial Days*. New York: Macmillan, 1913.

9. EGGLESTON, EDWARD. *A First Book in American History*. New York: American Book Company, 1899.

10. FISHER, SYDNEY GEORGE. *Men, Women and Manners in Colonial Times*. 2 vols. Philadelphia: J. B. Lippincott, 1898.

11. FORBES, ESTHER. *Paul Revere and the World He Lived In*. Boston: Houghton-Mifflin, 1942.

12. GORDON, MAURICE BEAR, M.D. *Aesculapius Comes to the Colonies*. New York: Argosy Antiquarian Limited, 1969.

13. IRVING, WASHINGTON. *The Life of Washington*, 3 vols. New York: n.p., 1857.

14. *The Military Journals of Two Private Soldiers*. Poughkeepsie, New York: Abraham Tomlinson, 1855.

15. ROBERTSON, JAMES A., ed. *New York in the Revolution*. Albany, New York: Press of Brandow Printing Company, 1898.

16. ROELKER, WILLIAM GREENE, ed. *Benjamin Franklin and Catharine Ray Greene: Their Correspondence*. Philadelphia: American Philosophical Society, 1949.

17. RUSSELL, CARL P. *Guns on the Early Frontiers*. Berkeley, California: University of California Press, 1957. (Verbatim account of Indian tor-

ture taken from Journal of Samuel des Cham-
plain.)

18. SPENGLER, EDWARD W., ed. *The Annals of the
Families of Caspar, Henry Baltzer and George
Spengler.* York, Pennsylvania: n.p., 1896.

19. TUNIS, EDWIN. *Colonial Living.* Cleveland: World
Publishing Company, 1957.

20. ———. *Frontier Living.* Cleveland: World Publishing Company, 1961.

21. VAN DOREN, CARL. *Benjamin Franklin.* New
York: The Viking Press, 1938.

22. WILDES, HARRY EMERSON. *Valley Forge.* New
York: Macmillan, 1938.

Besides Dr. Roy P. Basler, former Chief of the
Reference Department at the Library of Congress, the
author wishes to thank Dr. Ronald Wilkinson. Also
Mr. John Broderick, Acting Chief of the Reference
Department during Dr. Basler's absence.

I am indebted deeply to the *Quarterly Journal of
the Pennsylvania Historical Association* and to the
*Quarterly Journal of the Historical Society of Penn-
sylvania.*

We know you don't read just one kind of book.

That's why we've got all kinds of bestsellers.